Muerto Vallarta

Greg Coyle

D1736369

flooding peach press
Portland, Oregon

This is a work of fiction. The names, characters, and incidents portrayed in the story are the product of the author's imagination or are used fictitiously. Any resemblance to actual persons, living or dead, is entirely coincidental.

FLOODING PEACH PRESS
Portland, OR 97214

Copyright © 2022 by Greg Coyle

For my wife and coconspirator, Shawn, whose loving support and keen editor's eye animates every word.

In memory of my mother, Marcia, whose devotion to her kids and books inspires me still.

Chapter 1

The Dos Arcos Internet Café bore little resemblance to a café. It had computers. It had a random assortment of dining room chairs and tables. Decoration consisted of posters of soccer players and video games. Its café ambitions relied on a small refrigerator out of which Cokes, beer, and cans of cold coffee were sold. The computers made the poorly ventilated, low-ceilinged room hot and stuffy. A sputtering AC did little more than suck in dust from busy Calle Insurgentes.

Cesar Castillo sat hunched at his computer. Ownership had been the result of dumb luck and a generous uncle. Uncle Chuy, as he was known, had owned the building and favored Cesar since he was a little boy. Before his death the uncle had worked a provision into the building's sale that allowed for his nephew to carry on as a tenant paying the same rent in perpetuity. In recent years, the new owner, a retired dentist from Cuernavaca, had chafed at the limitation and begun a campaign to evict Cesar.

It really didn't matter. The business wasn't doing well anyway and hadn't been for some time. Most of the tourists who'd once been his bread and butter now traveled with their own laptop or tablet and had little need of the offerings of the Dos Arcos Internet Café. That left mostly Cesar's friends as patrons, and they rarely paid. The truth was, Cesar really only kept the place open because his apartment wasn't air conditioned, and of course to tweak the building's new owner.

Sundays tended to be even more dead than usual. Still, he would linger at the shop on those evenings, because his fiancée would be at her father's condo for what she generously called "family" dinner, generous because in the months they had been together, he'd never once been invited by her father to join them. She would apologize for her dad, and Cesar would pretend not to care.

Tonight, even his friends hadn't shown, except for Miguel, who was always there. Two other customers had also wandered in and sat at computers. Cesar actually looked forward to closing up early tonight. Today was actually Miguel's birthday, and a party had been scheduled for later down the beach. Cesar hated to miss any event sponsored by

1

Miguel's family, as the Peñaherreras owned the best bakery in town and would surely be bringing their signature pies.

Plus, Cesar was ready for a break. He was tired. He'd been working late the last couple of weeks on a project and had not been sleeping much. It had been long hours, often working until the early hours of the morning. He needed some rest and was glad to have a reason to wrap up early. At quarter to six, the brilliant oranges and reds from the sunset exploded in the shop windows across the street and cast a peach-colored glow through the tinted glass on the shop's front door.

"Five minutes," Cesar announced.

"You coming, right? Don't tell me you got to work," Miguel said. "And remember, no present, no pie."

"My presence is my present," Cesar said.

Miguel pushed the keyboard forward like an empty dinner plate and stretched. He rose with a sigh. "It's no Xbox, but whatever," he joked. "I got to go. Got to get my auntie."

At the door, Miguel said, "And I'll bring your book."

Cesar had months ago lent his friend a book about SQL, or structured query language, a programming language designed for managing data. Miguel had been telling him for weeks he was bringing it back the next day, but it never appeared.

Cesar closed his laptop. "Here, why don't you just take my laptop? If you put the software on it, you can keep the book."

"Good, because I don't know where it is." Miguel laughed. He put the laptop under his arm.

"Go. Fuera de aquí," Cesar said. Get out of here.

"I'm out," Miguel said, jingling the bell on the door as he left.

The one gringo customer was next to leave. Dressed in the standard-issue shorts and tank top, backwards baseball cap, round shoulders burned the color of pencil eraser, he finished his beer in a gulp, paid, and departed without a word. This left just Cesar and the one remaining customer, a Mexican man in his 20s, his hair slicked back, gold hoops in his ears. Cesar knew the type. On the street, he was all cojones and talk, but at home his mother ruled, and he shared a room with his little brother.

Cesar turned off the music.

The guy wasn't even looking at his computer, but instead concentrated on his phone. "I have three minutes," he said.

"Come on, man, I got to get out of here."

The man smiled and dropped his sunglasses from his forehead to his eyes. "I'm only fucking with you, bro," he said. He closed out of his computer, and stood, tugging at the short, pointed beard on his chin. He drew a few peso coins from his jeans and dropped them in front of Cesar.

"Nos vemos." See you. He waved without looking back and took himself out the door.

Usually at this point in the evening, Cesar would turn up the music, smoke a joint, and inspect the systems to ensure nothing had broken or walked away during the day. But tonight, he just wanted to get going. He quickly powered everything down and shut off the AC. He didn't even count the day's meager take, instead just dumping the handful of bills and coins into the safe to be dealt with tomorrow.

As he prepared to go, two thoughts struck him. Number one, sooner or later, the new landlord was going to prevail—landlords always did. And when he did, it was going to mean goodbye to the shop and his job. Cesar could barely cover costs as it was, but what would that mean for his and Molly's marriage when he lost the place? What in the hell would he do next?

Number two, and he hated to admit it, but Molly was really his only chance of saving and updating the shop. The problem was everyone else knew that too, which put Cesar in an uncomfortable spot, especially with her father. He clearly saw Cesar as an opportunist and had told him as much, and more, just a couple of nights before.

The meeting of father and fiancé had been Cesar's idea and it had not gone well. He hadn't even told Molly he was going to do it, as he was pretty sure she would have discouraged it. She always seemed scared to bring them together, but all Cesar knew was that had his own father still been alive, he would have told him to go talk to the man, face to face, man to man. It is a sign of strength and respect.

Mr. Brandt had not minced words. "Do you want me to be straight with you, son?" he'd asked. "I think we both know what I'm going to say, what has to be said."

But Cesar had not blinked. He had a thing or two he needed to say as well. "Yes, sir, that is why I am here. And to tell you, to promise you, that I love your daughter, I love Molly, and I will take good care of her."

To this her father had shaken his head. "Son, you and I both know that's not true. You can't. That's the plain fact of it. Nothing to feel ashamed about, it's just the way it is."

"Sir, I do love her."

3

"I'm sure you do," Mr. Brandt said. "But—and listen to me closely here—you are going to leave her alone. Let her go. Please don't force my hand. I don't want that, and you don't want that."

More had been said, and some of it had made the blood rise in him, but it didn't matter. He hadn't been asking for the man's permission. He had gone there as a courtesy. It was the proper thing to do. In the end, he and Molly would make their own decisions. And if that created a problem for her father, then that would be his problem.

He turned off the lights of the shop, and backed out of the place, locking the door.

"You open tomorrow?" a voice asked. Cesar jumped, surprised to find the Mexican guy with the earrings standing there.

"Yeah, yeah," Cesar said. "We open at 9 a.m."

"Cool," the man said.

"Hasta mañana."

"OK," the man said just as a van pulled up to the curb. Its side read Tres Hermanos Electricidad. The driver rolled down the window. "Compa, dónde está la Calle Aquiles Serdan?" Where is Aquiles Serdan street? Aquiles Serdan was a narrow street two blocks over, running along the river, that people had the hardest time locating.

Cesar approached the driver pointing directions just as the sliding door of the van opened and Cesar felt himself pushed violently from behind. Something was forced over his head, the door slammed shut, and they sped off down the cobbled street.

Sitting in an antique oak press-back rocking chair he'd borrowed from the warehouse downstairs, Joe Lily thought again about the situation in which he found himself. He'd been over it so many times by now, he knew its every crack and contour. And each time he found himself staring at the same undeniable conclusion: Unless they were the recipient of some unexpected windfall, some turn in their luck, the business had three months, six at the outside, before it would have to turn out the lights.

The problem was that this particular conclusion was just not an option, not for Joe. Too many other dominoes would fall if that one did. The first was his mother, Valerie. She'd already endured more than her fair share

4

in the past year. There'd been his father's unexpected death. Heart attack sitting in the chair at his barber's. Then there was Joe's own ignominious return to Portland. He'd explained what had happened, but the newspaper headlines didn't help. It had all taken a toll on his mother, dulled the glint and mischief in her eyes that were as much a part of her as her flinty laugh. And if the business were to crash too? He just couldn't let that happen.

Then there was the little matter of his own child, his own marriage. Triage for that particular disaster looked just as difficult. His first thought was of his daughter, Elinor. In just a couple of months she'd be two years old. What would his ex-wife say to her about him when she was old enough to understand? "Your father has a different definition of family." "Your father let us down." He could take the lies his father-in-law told about him. Even the one-sided, smear pieces in the paper he'd learned to deal with. But the possibility that his daughter would think them true, that he'd been so fixed on money that he'd hurt people, including his own family, that burned deep down where he couldn't quite get at it.

He'd first seen Allison Lansdowne on day two of their freshman orientation at Great Plains College. During the class's Q&A with the college president during orientation week, she'd raised her hand and asked who had the best pizza in town. Everyone had laughed and she had too, which seemed to Joe utterly lovable. Five feet five, she exuded this air of fearlessness that managed to make her even more feminine. She was natural, confident, and quick to smile. And she was funny, that was the thing. Sarcastic like no girl he'd ever met.

That fall, Joe had made an attempt, after a couple of beers at a tailgate, and gotten nowhere. Later, Allison would claim that she didn't trust the super-handsome guys. "They tend to be lazy," she'd said. Still, things change, and one October afternoon three years later, after Joe had scored a goal to beat her team in intramural soccer, she'd invited him to a party. That was all it took.

They cut quite the image walking on campus. Allison would virtually disappear when she wore one of his hoodies, nothing left visible but her pony-tailed head and her legs from the knee down. At a touch over six feet with wide, square shoulders, and a long, loping stride, Joe could seem less the boyfriend than the babysitter.

When in their senior year Allison was hired by Ward and Williams, a preeminent private equity firm in Manhattan, she persuaded Joe to apply as well. "My dad's a partner there," she'd said encouragingly. Wall Street had never been his interest. Money and the hustle for it didn't excite him the way it seemed to others. But he figured he and Allison would be together—and it was New York. It would be an adventure.

Whip smart, connected, and endowed with the looks and charm that immediately distinguished them from their peers, they both excelled at the firm. During those first years, they worked long hours, late nights. They made names for themselves when many of those who'd started with them were gone before their first year was out, still more before the second. By year five, a fraction remained, but those who did, like Allison and Joe, or Joseph as his business card said, thrived. The rewards were dazzling, and the promise of what was possible completely and totally blinding.

Joe had proposed in London to Allison during a visit to the firm's office there. He'd had an elaborate plan, but instead found himself, in a gush of eagerness after an evening of Indian food and a play at the Globe, doing it over gelato along the Thames. "I have a ring, I promise. But it's back at the hotel," he'd said. They'd been married at the Lansdownes' place in Montauk, the broad lawn a Renoir painting of 250 guests.

Joe enjoyed his work, enjoyed the competitiveness of it, but wasn't passionate about it and would from time to time float the idea of cashing it in, doing something else. Maybe opening their own business. But then life would intervene, nourished and propelled by promotions, bigger clients, loftier associations, still bigger clients, trips to the Lansdownes' villa in the Virgin Islands, Elinor's birth, and the hunt for a place on lower 2nd Ave. Too many distractions and demands. Most weekends were spent at the house in Montauk, boating, playing tennis. It was on just one of those weekends that things began to go sideways.

Joe's cell phone buzzed, pitching him out of his reverie.

"It's your mother," she said. She always opened her calls that way, even when she was calling, as she was now, from the shop's office downstairs.

"Hi, Mom," he said.

"Honey, Alan is here to see you."

Joe had been waiting for this. He had been putting off their accountant for days. "OK, I'll be right down."

Alan Pruitt was an old friend of his father's, and when his dad had started The Caravan, the import-export business that had been like another member of the family for as long as Joe could remember, Alan was the first person his father had brought on.

"I know, I know," Joe said as he reached the bottom of the stairs and saw the tall, stooping figure of the accountant.

"You haven't returned Alan's calls," his mother said.

"I know. Alan, I'm sorry. I've been buried."

The man ran his hand over his gray, frizzy hair, which he had pulled back into a haphazard ponytail, a relic from a bygone era of his life that he could not part with. "You can run, etc.," the man said.

"Do you mind if we walk and talk?" Joe asked. "I've got to go through and take pictures of everything down here. I told him years ago, 'Dad, you got to get this stuff online.'"

"Lead on, Macduff," Alan said. He kissed Joe's mother on the cheek. "Next week, dinner at our place, right? Linda will kill me if I don't bring back a yes."

Joe's mother smiled and nodded unconvincingly. "OK, I'll check."

As the two men made their way into the cluttered warehouse, the accountant said, "You've got to get your mom to start reengaging with the world. It's time."

"I've tried," Joe said. "I try. But she's a masterful architect of excuses."

"'Mom, we're going to Alan and Linda's. Bring your potatoes au gratin and a bottle of pinot noir.' I just wrote your script for you. You're welcome."

The two men moved into the Caravan's dark, dusty, cluttered interior. The nose was immediately greeted by the rich, earthen smells of aged pottery, the sourness of old leather worn smooth, the exhalation of old, forgotten furniture, handmade by unknown hands in far-off places. They stopped before an ornate oak vitrine. Joe snapped a picture with his phone. "One of the challenges is I have no idea what all is in here."

"I'm afraid you've got one or two other challenges," said Alan. He had a birdlike way of walking, face and chest pressed forward and hands sunk in his pockets, giving his long arms the unmistakable appearance of flattened wings.

Joe ignored the remark and paused at a set of tall wooden doors with a carved relief on the front. "Just look at these. Think of the people who made them. The forest that the trees came from. The hands of every person who opened or closed them in the last 150 years. It's incredible."

"Joe," Alan said. He laid one of his large hands on Joe's shoulder.

Joe nodded.

"You inherited a very tough situation. No lie. And you didn't have to take it on. I know that. But your dad, god love him, he was not a numbers guy. That's why he had me. Only I can't fix this."

"I'm working on it."

"Numbers guys and Wall Street guys, they're not the same, you know that, right?"

Joe let that pass. "Can you just buy me a little more time? Write another letter, ask to see another document. I swear I'm working on it."

"Do you think it's up to me? It's the bank, Joe. You should know that better than anyone." He took a deep breath and exhaled. "The bank always wins. I'll do what I can. But this is, it's not good. I don't know how much longer I can stall. And then that's it. Do you understand what I'm saying?"

Joe did understand. The events in his own life over the last year had taught him that sometimes there's nothing to be done but watch the house burn.

At the door, Joe said, "Thank you, Alan. Really. And Mom and I will be over for dinner, I promise."

"Alright, but we won't let you in without your mom's potatoes," Alan said. "And about the other stuff, you need to act soon. I'm serious, Joe."

The two men said goodbye. Joe returned to his apartment upstairs. He poured himself a cup of coffee.

"What about you? Any ideas?" Maximus, his three-year-old bulldog and resident confidante, lifted his head but elected to keep his thoughts to himself. Joe had barely been back a month when he'd made a trip to the industrial north of the city to drop off a U-Haul trailer. The depot sat right next to the Oregon Humane Society animal shelter. He'd taken little notice of the building until returning to his car from dropping off the U-Haul keys. It was then that he spotted him being led from the van toward the building. Something inside him had taken over and barely 30 minutes and some paperwork later, the hound sat quite happily in the seat beside him.

Cesar had lost track of time. His mind had been fractured. After beseeching his tormentors again and again to explain what he had done and receiving no answer, he had finally stopped asking. Now he relegated it all to the same delirious, inexplicable unreality of nightmares.

The van had driven for hours, climbing, turning. The men did not speak until they pulled onto what sounded like a dirt drive and stopped. His hood still on, Cesar had been walked from the van, into a building and down a long hall. Their shoes echoed on the tile. The men deposited him in a room, removed his hood, and chained him to a pipe. When he asked again who they were, one of the men slapped him hard across the face. "Cállate!" he said. Shut up.

It was a house, a hacienda; Cesar believed he could tell that much. But it was no place he recognized. His room was entirely empty. Dust on the windowsill, pale outlines where paintings had hung. He sat on a beautifully tiled floor. A wealthy person lived here or had lived here. Hours passed. The sky in the window went from light to dark, and the dark seemed to last forever. Maybe he slept, he wasn't sure. Finally, the glow in the window brought another day into the room.

At some point into the second day the two men returned and walked Cesar to a dining room, where he sat at a long table and was served a plate of huevos divorciados with cold tortillas and hot coffee. He tried to eat slowly, but found that he could not help but inhale it all like a ravenous street dog.

Outside the dining room's windows he heard horses, their hoof falls and chuffing. Also men's boots crunching on dirt. Someone demanded, "Are we finally fucking ready?" This was a new voice, one that cut easily through the others. It was clear that the voice was connected to an instrument tuned tightly at the pegs.

The men directed Cesar to stand. He was tired and ached from his night on the hard floor.

"Where am I going?" he managed.

They said nothing and dragged him through a grand foyer with a wide staircase and dramatic chandelier that hung from a broad-beamed ceiling some 20 feet above. When they passed through the pair of large double front doors, the glare from the sun was too much.

"Over there," the new voice commanded.

The men dragged Cesar to a spot in the middle of a dusty paddock. They then lifted and placed him inside the metal barrel standing there, one end of which had been sunk into the ground so that it didn't move. Still squinting at the glare, he could just make out a man sitting in a chair

9

in a patch of shade made by the roof of the house. He wore a suit and tie, his glossy shoes dusty at the tips.

"Why are you doing this?" Cesar implored.

"One day, when I was a boy, we were out in the field, working the coffee. Something happened, a snake maybe, and our burro he got scared. Stepped right on my foot. Broke it just like that. The fucking bone, it was sticking out. You know? Horrible. I fell to the ground, screaming, laying in the dirt, rolling there in pain. I cried, "Papá, Papá, my foot." My father, he came to me. He looked down at me there. My face wet with tears. 'Stop crying,' he said. 'Bones break.' He made me work the rest of the day." The man nodded at the memory.

One of the other men appeared carrying a large roll of what appeared to be fishing line. In his other hand, he carried a knife.

"There is no why, no who," the man said. "There is only the broken bone. Do you understand?"

Cesar shook his head, his voice choked from crying.

"And this." The man gestured generally toward the barrel in which Cesar had been placed. "I do this because I really don't want to see you shit yourself. They always shit themselves. I don't need to see that."

Through his tears, Cesar could see two men atop their horses. They wore their cowboy hats tipped to shield their eyes. From behind him came the sound of more horses. "Who are you?" Cesar implored.

"Does it really matter?" the man asked. "Unless I'm Jesus Christ—and I am not Jesus Christ—unless I'm Jesus Christ, I cannot be petitioned."

Cesar squeezed his eyes tight, hoping that by contracting everything, drawing everything in like a collapsing star, he might disappear and transport himself to Molly's arms.

"But I'll tell you anyway. Because no matter where you go from here, whoever greets you at the next place, they will know me. They will say, 'Ah, you met La Cabra.' That's what they call me. Because I take care of the garbage. That is what I do. And you, Cesar Castillo, you are the garbage. Maybe too smart for your own good. Maybe too arrogant. Sticking your nose into things that aren't your business."

"Please," Cesar pleaded. "I can fix whatever it is. Please."

The four horses took up positions equidistant from Cesar about 30 feet off in each cardinal direction. The man with the spool of line handed the loose end to the first rider.

Tears mixed with sweat ran down Cesar's face. "You have the wrong person. I swear!"

At this, the man stood, and walked toward Cesar, moving from the shade into the circle of horses and bright sun. "No," he said, "You are the right person. Cesar Castillo. Son of Vera Castillo Moreno and Francisco Jesús Castillo. Owner of Dos Arcos Café on Calle Insurgentes. Yes? You cannot know this, because you do not know me, but I do not make mistakes. Does the rain make mistakes? What about the river or the moon or the mountain lion?" He shook his head.

He stepped back to let the man with the line unspool it from the hand of the horseman. Moving to Cesar, he wrapped the line once about Cesar's neck and then with the same line continued in the opposite direction to a second rider. Here, he cut the line free from the roll with the knife and handed it up to the rider. The line tightened at Cesar's throat.

But Cesar knew. He knew what this was about. His work online had had an effect, and it had brought him here. As the horse moved, the line tightened at his neck. He tried to free his hands.

"Every man wonders what he'll do when his time comes," said the man calling himself La Cabra. Now in the full sun, he was fully visible. He wore a tan suit crisply tailored to his slim frame. Cufflinks blinked in the sun. Bright white shirt, red tie. The crease in his hair seemed carved by a blade.

The man with the spool started a second line, walking it to the third horseman and handing him the end and once again unrolling it back to Cesar, where it was similarly wrapped once around his neck and continued to the fourth rider. Each rider tied off the line on his saddle.

When the man with the line was done, La Cabra motioned for his knife.

"We have no control how we enter this world, so how we leave it, that is our only way to show the kind of man we are. ¿Cierto?"

Cesar tried to speak, he tried to say that he had stopped his campaign, that he was getting married, but the lines around his neck choked him into a garbled cough. Each time one of the horses moved slightly, the lines would cinch tighter around his throat.

La Cabra wiped the sweat from his brow with a handkerchief. He stepped close and grabbed Cesar at the side of his head. "Now you want to stay very quiet. You don't want to make a sound. It will spook the horses." And with that, the man cleaved Cesar's left ear free of his head in one smooth motion.

Cesar screamed, and the line cut into his neck. But the riders pulled tight on the reins to keep them steadied.

He moved to the other side of Cesar and repeated the same act. Standing before Cesar, the man called the Goat tidily wrapped both ears in his handkerchief and tucked them into his pocket. He threw the bloody knife into the dirt. Cesar heard a rushing sound like water or air passing over a microphone. La Cabra gave a small bow and then produced a pistol from his jacket that he pointed it at Cesar and then fired into the sky. The horses jumped, bolting in opposite directions.

Joe started most days by taking Maximus for a walk. They'd hit the park on the next block and then carry on to Ground Control for a coffee. He liked to get out before the street had fully woken up. It was a habit he'd picked up during his years in New York. In those days, he would venture out, see the shops opening, and bring Allison back her cappuccino and everything bagel.

At the coffee shop, Joe leashed Maximus to an outside table and gave him his favorite reward, one of the desiccated pig's ears Joe bought in bulk from the pet store. The dog immediately laid down and got to work. Inside the small, warm shop, things buzzed with the first wave of the day: students, people in their blue scrubs bound for the Oregon Health & Science University hospital.

Joe ordered his standard drip coffee, no room.

Ava shook her head. "You're so predictable. Why don't you try something different sometime? Mix it up. How about today you get a latte or a macchiato? I make an awesome macchiato."

"Why would someone do that to good coffee?" Joe said. "After all the work that went into planting it, cultivating it, shipping it, roasting it, you're going to adulterate it with milk and whatever? Seems criminal to me. Or maybe it's just a good way to hide an inferior product?"

"You know what, I'm going to make you a macchiato whether you like it or not," she said. "I don't care. You're going to try something new.

And you're going to get one of our fresh blueberry scones. Why? Because they're fucking delicious."

"OK, OK," he said. He watched her long fingers tap in the order, fixated on the tattoos decorating her hands just below the knuckles: on the right, "live," and on the left, "free."

A weathered paperback lay just to the side of the cash register, face down. "E.M. Forster?" Joe said.

"What's wrong with E.M. Forster?"

"Nothing, nothing." Joe smiled, admiring the tattoo of a deer head on her chest, the antlers following the line of her collar bones.

"Good," she said, letting a smile creep into the corners of her mouth.

Joe enjoyed their morning back and forth. Having made his order, Joe stepped aside and grabbed a discarded *New York Times*. He found a table in the window and tore off a piece of the scone. On the front page was a story about how the US government was hurtling toward a shutdown. Another detailed the disappointing jobs report. The world had his old industry to thank for the shithole the economy now sat in. Below the fold, a story about a US oil company getting hacked and another about a drug cartel killing in Mexico. Every day some new version of bad.

"Macchiato for Joe!"

He retrieved his coffee and peered down into the cup.

"Just try it and quit being a coffee robot," she said.

Joe took a sip and raised his eyebrows inconclusively.

Ava shook her head. She retrieved a dog treat from a jar on the counter. "Tell Max Ava loves him."

Joe and Max took their time getting home. Joe wasn't in a hurry, though he knew he probably should be. Alan had been crystal clear: things needed to happen and they needed to happen fast. But once back in his apartment above the office, rather than get to work, Joe scrolled through pictures of his daughter on his computer. It had been months since he'd seen her. His sister-in-law had secretly Facetimed him once when she'd been babysitting Elinor. But that had been it.

Looking at the pictures made it better and worse at the same time. He let the idea that she might forget him, that she might have already forgotten him, enter his mind and the thought felt like a punch in the gut. They had been happy; anyone who knew them would have agreed. In one picture Allison is holding Elinor in her parents' pool. Elinor's eyes are closed, maybe from the splashing, but she is laughing. Allison is laughing. It made Joe smile too. They *had* been happy, but it all seemed so long ago and far away. Just then Joe's phone buzzed.

"It's your Mom," she said too loudly.

"Hi there. Everything OK?"

"Well, I think so. We just received a phone call from Mr. Villaseñor." She pronounced the double ll's. "From Mexico."

"Porfirio Villaseñor? He's the only Villaseñor I know. You remember him. He was a supplier of Dad's forever."

"Oh, I know him. I didn't know if you remembered him," she said. "Such a nice man. Well, he wants to talk to you. He wasn't sure the business was, you know; he'd heard about everything. But I told him it was still going just fine. I explained that you were taking over for Dad."

"That *we* are taking over," Joe said.

The line was silent for a moment.

"Yes, yes," she said. "Anyway, so Mr. Villaseñor wants you to call him right away. He sounded very excited to speak with you."

Chapter 2

"Joe, I'm so sorry about your father. He was a good friend. We had good times when he came down here. I will miss him." Porfirio Villaseñor spoke slowly, deliberately, and with a sincerity that touched Joe.

"Thank you, Porfirio. I know he really enjoyed working with you too. And he loved it down there. One of his favorite places in the world. He always said that."

Porfirio and his wife Carmen owned the best antique shop in Puerto Vallarta. As Joe's father described it, the place carried the finest collection of Mexican and Spanish artifacts anywhere in the state of Jalisco.

"I was so happy to hear from Valerie that you are taking over things. I wish my son would take over here."

Joe laughed. "If it makes you feel any better, I don't think my dad would've predicted it either. Funny how life works. But he was the expert. I just hope I can learn enough fast enough to keep us going."

"Well that's why I called you, Joe! You're going to owe me a big lobster dinner for this, because I've got something for you. Not sure I ever saw anything like it before. Once-in-a-lifetime find. I'm telling you."

Porfirio went on to describe that just the day before he had come into possession of the furnishings, art, carpets—everything, floor to ceiling—of a large, extremely well-appointed hacienda in San Sebastián. The house had fallen into the hands of the state after its owner, a wealthy attorney, had died and no one had stepped forward to claim the place. Porfirio had only begun to unpack the boxes, but the value of the items was clear. The right person, selling to the right customers, stood to make a great deal. Taken to auction, it could be into the six figures.

"*I'm* the right person," Joe assured him, uncertain what exactly he had just promised to buy or how he was going to pay for it.

This sent Porfirio into peals of laughter. "Yes, yes," he said. "I think so. But that person, he needs to come down here to Vallarta, you know, right away. Fast!"

Without thinking, Joe said, "I'll be there tomorrow. Don't let anyone touch my stuff!"

This was followed by more laughing. "OK. Carmen will sleep with it."

They quickly talked logistics. A plan was made to meet as soon as Joe could get there.

"Porfirio, thank you. I owe you."

"Lobster!" Porfirio cheered.

Joe hustled down the stairs to the office.

"Some possible good news," he announced. "Porfirio just got this collection of pieces from some hacienda. Said it could be worth, well, a lot. And he wants to make it available to us first."

"That sounds promising," Valerie said.

"I'm going to head down there tomorrow, see what I can learn."

"I think that's a very good idea. I'll get you all booked."

"Great. But what do you think? I'm sure Porfirio will give us as good a deal as he can. But it's likely going to be a good-sized check we'll need to write. How do you feel about that?"

She turned from her computer and looked straight at her son. "Joseph, I trust you. This will work or it won't. I know you will do your best. You always have."

Joe couldn't say anything for a moment. "Thank you," he said. He didn't realize how much he needed to hear that.

His mother smiled. "And as for the money, your dad would love to know that the insurance money was going to items from Puerto Vallarta."

An American woman, blonde, late 20s, stepped purposefully through the doors into the lobby of Banderas Properties. A.J. Brandt stood at the elbow of one of the firm's two receptionists, pointing at something on a computer screen. Her brows pinched, her face glowering, she blew past the waiting clients and set upon A.J.

"What did you say to him?" she demanded.

A.J. stood straight, dumbstruck, eyes wide.

"What did you say?"

A.J. took in the room as everyone fixed their eyes on him. "Wow. Honey. Honey, you're clearly upset about something. Why don't we go upstairs?"

"I want to know what you said to him."

"I don't know what you're talking about, said to who? Honey, let's not do this here."

"Cut the shit, Dad! What you said to Cesar! He's not returning my calls or texts. I just stopped by his work and there's no one there. The door's locked. What did you do?"

A.J. stepped to her and tried to take her by the arm only to have her jerk away. "OK, OK, just relax," he tried. "Take a breath. Let's go upstairs."

"I'm not going to *relax*," she spat. "I want you to tell me what you said to him. You might have ruined everything!"

"Honey, you—"

"Tell me!" Her voice rose one hysterical octave.

"Christ, get a grip. We are not doing this here." A.J. exerted himself, pushing her out of the public area and toward the stairs leading to the offices.

"It's been three days!" she said. "He's never not returned my calls for three days. Not even one day. I even went to his mother's. She hasn't seen him."

"Let's go to my office."

"Did you talk to him? Tell me that."

A pause hung in the air for a long beat. "Honey, I was just trying to help."

"Help? How does telling him to leave me help?"

"You have to trust me. You're too young to see it, but this isn't right for you right now. You're just getting your life started, for crying out loud."

"Will you please stop using that as an excuse for Christ's sake! I know Cesar came to talk to you. And now he's not calling me back. Am I supposed to believe that's a coincidence?"

"You are disrupting the office. Look, do you not care about your future? And even if *you* don't, *I* do. And as your father, I'm going to do whatever I need to do to protect it."

Molly's cheeks were red, eyes wide and wet. She was breathing heavily. "Go to hell!" she said and stormed past the reception desks and waiting area and then punched her way out the door into the bright sun.

"Molly, come on ... ." Brandt stood there impotently, staff and guests quietly looking on.

He climbed the stairs back to his office, aware that everyone was watching him. He slumped into his chair just as his business partner appeared in his doorway. "Wow, she's pissed," said Darrell Haddock.

"Not now, Darrell."

The two men had met nearly 10 years earlier, barely a mile from where they now stood. A.J. had come to PV to go fishing, get away, a trip he in no way could afford. But hooking a marlin and marinating in a bottle of tequila seemed the perfect response to impending bankruptcy. He'd liked the Hemingway flavor of it.

As it turned out, the fish had eluded him, but he had met Darrell, and that had changed everything. A.J. had been drinking at Cuates y Cuetes, a beach bar where Calle Rodolfo Gómez runs into the ocean. Back then, the area was laid back. Cold beer, decent food. The fishing boats brought their catch right onto the beach just feet away. It had been the night before A.J.'s return flight home and he was working his way through a bucket of Pacificos, trying to forget what waited for him, when a guy had approached and said, "Best fucking fish and chips on the planet."

A.J. had looked up to find a squat man with a bushy mustache and a large block of a head that only barely fit into the baseball cap he wore. "Yeah? I've already eaten. I'll have to remember that for next time."

The man laughed. "No, your shirt, bud."

A.J. looked down and remembered his T-shirt was from Spud's Fish and Chips, a place near his home east of Seattle. The guy, who introduced himself as Darrell, had grown up in the next town over and explained that every summer he'd hung out at the lakeside beach next to where the small restaurant sat.

"I almost died on that goddamned lake," Darrell said. "Took a ski to the fucking cranium. Still have the scar." He pointed to a divot at his hairline. "And I'm proud to tell you that I also got my V card punched on that lake. In my friend Paul's boat. Judy fucking Burroughs. Old double-duty Judy. Tits till Tuesday."

One drink led to another and Darrell explained that he'd washed up in PV chasing a woman, at the same time he was escaping from another. The budding Mexican romance had withered before it really got started, and without much of a compass, Darrell had stayed in Vallarta and found himself selling timeshares. "I know it sounds crazy, but it was the best decision I ever made." By the end of the night, he'd convinced A.J. he should do the same.

18

Today, the two were now principals and partners in one of the most successful timeshare businesses in the state of Jalisco. You could not visit Puerto Vallarta without seeing billboards for Banderas Properties or without being hailed by their touts as you ambled down the street. The company owned properties up the Pacific Coast as far north as Rincón de Guayabitos and as far south as Boca de Tomatlán.

Molly had arrived about six months earlier, at loose ends. A.J. explained that because of certain things that had happened with his ex, he and Molly had been estranged for "a while." He wasn't proud of it, but life was a messy business.

Now, Darrell pointed in the direction in which Molly had just stormed off. "I'm sorry about that, bud. But that's precisely fucking why I never had children. That I know of."

A.J. exhaled slowly. "Yeah, that little exchange was more than I was expecting too. But thanks a lot for eavesdropping."

"Hey, how could I avoid it? You weren't exactly using your inside voices."

"A father has to do what a father has to do."

"And?"

"And what?"

"So, what *did* the father have to do?" Darrell leaned in as if sharing in confidence. "You have your goons whack him?"

"Christ, Darrell, don't say stupid shit like that. If I had goons, you would know it. You would be one sad, thumbless sonofabitch. Now quit bugging me, and go close half as many deals as me."

"I'd rather be thumbless than dickless," said Darrell pointing at A.J., quite satisfied with his comeback. "Hey, I think we need to go out and destroy a couple steaks and some tequila tonight. That'll fix you right up."

"Not tonight," A.J. said as he directed his partner into the hall and closed the door. He needed to make a call, and this time he didn't want his partner overhearing.

Joe's plane touched down at Puerto Vallarta International Airport around 4 p.m. Out the sliding glass doors of the air-conditioned arrivals area, Joe was assaulted by the gloriously hot, damp air of coastal Mexico. It lathered him in a tropical embrace, and if he had had any hesitation about the trip, it all evaporated as his cab took him south along the coast. The radio played a Mexican ballad, and Joe rolled the window down to smell the ocean, which peeked from between buildings and then opened up into a magnificent blue expanse as they reached the cobblestoned Malecón.

This whole gambit hinged on this El Dorado of a collection Porfirio had assured him he was holding for him. They had negotiated a little, made a show of it, but then had settled on a price pending Joe's inspection of the items. It was a figure that Alan, their accountant, would have surely lost his mind about had he known. Joe trusted Porfirio. He had to. Joe's father had worked with Porfirio for 20 years and Joe suspected that once he actually saw the cache he'd realize Porfirio's price was part condolence.

As the taxi rattled south toward the hotel, Joe flipped through an imagined catalog of the items he had been told were waiting for him in this cache of Porfirio's. The bounty supposedly included a large and varied assortment of colonial antiques dating from the eighteenth and nineteenth centuries, finely wrought hacienda pieces, incredible ironwork, masterfully sculpted hardwood furniture, superior ceramics, all clearly chosen by someone trained to separate the common from the collectible, the standard from the sublime. He would know for sure tomorrow at 9 a.m. when they met at the shop. In the meantime, he would have a drink, or two, a nice meal, and dig his feet in the sand.

The cab finally dropped Joe off at Hotel Mercurio. It had had a different name when his father used to stay there, but it still sat a couple blocks off the beach up quiet Calle Francisco Rodriguez in Viejo Vallarta, or Old Town, as the tourists liked to call it. The hotel sat nestled between a bakery and a private home that climbed up the steep hillside behind.

"Buenos días," Joe said as he entered the airy foyer and dropped his bag.

"Buenas tardes," corrected the clerk, a young Mexican man, his dark hair crisply parted on the side and oiled to a bluish sheen. "Checking in?

"Buenas tardes, right. Yes. Lily, Joseph Lily."

As the young man consulted his computer, Joe took in the place. It had been at least 15 years since they had last been there as a family. He was frankly surprised it was still here. It had received a facelift. Brightly colored paint, artwork, and flowering bougainvillea gave the hotel a festive air. Just past the check-in desk ran a short breezeway that led to the open-air pool area and patio. A small bar now sat on the opposite side. A few guys relaxed with drinks.

Joe handed over his passport and signed in. A couple of guests entered from the street, their flip-flops beating out a syncopated rhythm as they walked.

"Just one?" the man behind the counter asked.

"Sí," Joe said.

The man nodded and smiled. "OK, sir, you are in room 109. It is the last one this way," he said, pointing down the short breezeway and to the right. "Do you need help with your bags?"

"No, gracias," Joe said. "I got it."

"Have a good time."

Joe grabbed his bag and followed the man's directions. The three stories of rooms all faced the central brick courtyard and the pool, its water gone a rich blue in the shade of late afternoon. Two swimmers still floated about, drinks in hand.

Joe stepped into his room, glad to have finally arrived. He dumped his bag on the floor. The room was comfortable, if a little plain. A queen-sized bed, a pair of leafy plants, an engraved wooden headboard beside a painting of a colorful hacienda. It was a long way from his days with Allison. Back then, your hotel, like the brand of suit you wore or the school your child attended, was all part of a very keenly curated brand. You *were* these things. And if you didn't go along, it meant you didn't care to play the game, and no one likes that.

Joe showered and took himself out into what was fast becoming early evening, the first streaks of sunset beginning to appear in the sky. The cobbled street tumbled down to the beach a couple of blocks away. The neighborhood was abuzz with activity. Lights blinked from restaurant interiors. Small lanterns glowed from the sidewalk tables that began to fill with laughing tourists, their sunburned faces shiny with sweat and lotion.

The temperature had barely cooled from the heat of the day. The tropical air weighed you down in a pleasant, soporific sort of way. It made Joe's skin tingle.

At the corner of Francisco Rodriguez and Olas Altas a man stepped out from his small booth and said, "You are from ... Minnesota!" A sign read: Banderas Properties.

Joe was not in the mood, but still found himself answering. "Oregon."

"Oregon! I hear it is very beautiful. Welcome to Mexico!" He extended his hand.

"It *is* beautiful," Joe said, shaking the man's hand. The man's shirt was embroidered with a gold flag design that also said Banderas Properties. His pin read "Roberto."

He held onto Joe's hand. "So, what are your plans for tomorrow, Oregon? Fishing? Maybe you want to go parasailing?"

"I wish," he said. "I'm actually here on business. Too busy."

"Ah, what kind of business?"

"Thanks a lot," Joe said. "If I need some parasailing, I know where to find you."

"Oregon, come on, you can't work all day. It's Mexico!"

Joe waved goodbye over his shoulder and continued to the beach.

"OK, Oregon, I'll see you later!" he yelled.

Joe walked directly toward the sunset, which cast a blood-red glow across the Bay of Banderas. He passed souvenir stalls, the tired salespeople sitting on plastic chairs beneath hanging T-shirts. A coffee shop bustled with people on their laptops. A small boutique, a realtor's office, a restaurant offering "The Finast Italian food in Puerto Vallarta."

He joined the beach and checked his phone. "La Palapa. 4.5 stars." The place greeted him with neatly pressed wait staff who showed him to a table facing the water. Strips of umber and gold and orange were slipping toward the horizon. Joe ordered a margarita. The day's sunbathers were gathering their things on the beach in front of him.

La Palapa was busy, with most of the tables occupied. Just next to him sat a couple in their 60s, what was left of the man's still-wet hair hastily parted, her round shoulders showing the sunburned outline of where her swimsuit had been. On the other side dined a larger party of Mexican businessmen in suits and ties, and one woman, her dark hair pulled into a tight bun on her head. One of the men held court, the others smiling and nodding their assent while trying to eat their meal.

Joe had been to meetings like that, too many to count. You could have scooped up the sycophancy with a spoon and spread it over your $15 crostini. The thing he had come to realize, though too late to avoid being ensnared himself, was that everyone at tables like that is lying. It's angling, jockeying, selling. Laying the groundwork. Avoiding the tripwires.

Joe enjoyed a spectacular yellowfin tuna steak and watched the sea and sky change. A steady stream of tourists plied the beachfront, moving along the string of restaurants. Torches sunk into the sand showed the way as the sky went dark. Voices mixed with music. Next to him the large Mexican group was finishing up, everyone standing and shaking hands and speaking in a rapid-fire Spanish Joe could not follow. He was impressed that the one woman did not seem cowed. Being beautiful helped, he thought.

As the diners filed out, the waiters converged on the table, clearing and cleaning. Joe thought that when he was done with his meal, he might walk the beach, look at the stars, find a spot for a nightcap. He had a long day tomorrow. Just then he spotted a small purse sitting under what had been the woman's chair. Instinctively, he jumped up, grabbed it, and raced in the direction the group had gone. Turning the corner onto Olas Altas, he and the woman nearly collided.

"Oh, perdón!" she said, eyes wide.

Joe held up her purse.

Her face broke into a wide smile. "Thank you!" she said. "I got to my car and realized. So nice of you."

Getting a better look at her now, Joe could see that she was indeed stunning. High cheekbones, impossibly smooth chestnut-colored skin, full lips, and behind her dark-rimmed glasses, big, deliriously brown eyes.

"It seemed a larger tip than you wanted to leave," Joe said.

She laughed, fitting the purse strap over her bare shoulder. "Maybe I was too eager to escape my companions?" She smiled.

"I've been at those dinners. It's painful because you know you can't even rely on booze to get you through it."

"Yes!" She laughed. "I texted my sister that. Two more glasses of wine would make this so much better."

Joe put his hands in his pockets. "And now you have to submit to an after-dinner drink because the boss wants to?" he asked.

She shook her head. "No, my boss, well, let's just say he doesn't need another drink." She smiled again, and then clutched her purse. "But thank you so much for this!"

"My pleasure."

And before he could suggest that maybe they should find that after-dinner drink, she had turned and taken herself up the street, making altogether a stunning picture. He hadn't even thought to get her name.

Maybe it was better this way. He was tired. So he paid his bill and wandered out on to the dark beach in the brittle moonlight, walking barefoot at the surf's edge.

He decided against another drink and returned to the hotel. He was greeted by a different guy at the front desk. Passing into the central courtyard, Joe found the poolside bar busy. The pool glowed sapphire blue.

That night Joe dreamt that he was on an airplane, and his daughter, he knew it was his daughter, was the flight attendant, but she didn't know him. She said "Here you are, sir" when she handed him his drink. He desperately wanted to tell her, but he didn't know how.

One could easily walk right by Porfirio Villaseñor's shop. It sat on Calle Madero, on the east side of Calle Insurgentes, which splits Old Town in half. The business had a plain door and a small copper sign reading "Villaseñor Antigüedades." Once inside, visitors find a place chockablock with weathered equipale chairs, wrought iron candle sconces, old shoe forms. The counter was nearly swallowed by an assortment of old oxidizing rings of old keys and ornate crosses of hammered tin, bowls of milagros. It made altogether a rather slapdash-looking array.

A short, dark-skinned man appeared from the rear of the store, speaking in what seemed a fit of frustration to a teenaged boy who nodded dejectedly before disappearing again into the back of the store.

Somehow he recognized Joe instantly. "Joseph! ¡Bienvenido!"

Joe extended his hand. "Porfirio."

"Look at you!" Porfirio cried, peering at Joe over glasses perched on the edge of his nose.

24

They shook hands—Porfirio's grip was that of a man half his 70-plus years.

"It is great to see you," said Joe.

The man just stared at Joe and shook his head. "Incredible."

The last time Joe had been in Puerto Vallarta he had just graduated high school. His father had persuaded him to forgo a camping trip with friends to join him and Joe's mother on a buying junket cum family vacation. Porfirio had taken them fishing one day and on another afternoon had led them into the jungle to swim at a secluded spot on the river.

Shorter by a foot, Porfirio reached up and put his rough hands on Joe's shoulders and looked him in the eye, expression serious. They each knew what it meant.

"I am sorry."

"Thank you," Joe said.

Porfirio nodded. "And how is your mother?"

"She's doing OK. She's putting a good face on it, but I think things are harder than she lets on."

The two men stared at their feet a moment in a kind of silent benediction. From the rear of the store could be heard the sound of people opening and moving boxes and crates. Porfirio motioned for Joe to follow him behind the small counter. On a wooden beam, photographs had been stapled over the years, many of them now turned ghostly from age, curled at the corners. Porfirio gestured to an image of a younger Porfirio standing with Joe's father. The two men, along with Porfirio's wife, Carmen, were standing and smiling in almost the very same spot Joe now stood.

"Ha! That was before your father lost his hair!" Porfirio said. "And before I got so fat!" Porfirio laughed.

Joe was about to ask after Carmen when a piercing scream came from the rear of the store, followed by a crash. The two men raced in the direction of the noise. They darted down a short, cluttered hallway, throwing aside the curtain that led into a large room full floor to ceiling with crates and boxes. A sharp, sweet smell met them as they entered. The teenaged boy stood dumbstruck with fear as a young woman clung to him, crying.

Joe turned to the items that had apparently fallen. Stray stalks of packing hay decorated the ground. The two men slowly approached, hands covering their noses for the odor. The young woman clutched at the boy, driving her face into his shoulder. A carved wooden trunk lay on its side. When he got closer, Joe found, laying on the floor next to the trunk, cocked an at odd angle, a human head.

Porfirio immediately called his brother-in-law, an officer in the Puerto Vallarta police department, and closed the store. Joe's father had told stories about the things he'd found in purchases over the years: a loaded gun, a stuffed weasel, a real snake, cash, countless spiders, photographs of one particularly "comely" young woman. But Joe could not recall his father ever talking about something like this.

No one spoke. Joe felt sick. The horror of the discovery hung in the air like a vibration, moving through them, swirling around them in a dark eddy. The girl continued to cry inconsolably as they stared at the scene uncertain what to do next.

"Joseph, I'm sorry," Porfirio said.

"So, is the trunk part of the ... "

Porfirio nodded. "Everything here. All of it." He gestured to the enormous collection of antiques that filled an entire corner of the shop's storage space.

"Of course it is," Joe said.

Soon the brother-in-law arrived and was introduced to Joe as Paz. Peace. No one else seemed struck by the irony. He held the severed head lightly in his gloved hands as if inspecting one of Porfirio's silver candlesticks. Joe realized now that both ears had been removed and, it appeared, stuffed into the mouth.

"Narco," Paz said.

"The cartels. Every time, every time they have to do something more horrible than the time before," Porfirio added.

"How do you know it's the cartels?" Joe asked.

Paz said, "They do like this. They don't just kill. They want to be the worst killers in the world. Like the terrorists. Cutting off heads. Everywhere now they are cutting off heads. One is known for cutting the ears. They are called Los Primeros. The most violent. They say that the lion rules the jungle, but that Los Primeros rules everything else. No ears means you can't hear nothing anymore. And you put them in the mouth, and now you can't say nothing. It's an advertencia, a warning."

Where the ears should have been now gaped dark, encrusted holes. Rictus had pulled the skin tight across the face.

26

"Who's the message *to*?" asked Joe.

Paz shrugged as if it were not an important question.

Joe looked for answers on the face of the deceased. He looked to be a young man. Longish hair, a couple of days of beard growth. Handsome. The kind of man he could imagine turning the head of a visiting American coed. Now in death the skin was gray, the eyes sealed. The bottom lip had frozen open into a crude pout. And Joe noticed something odd. Looking more closely, Joe believed he spotted, were they *letters* on the inside of the lip? A "c," an "o," an "s" maybe, and was that a "B"? Joe couldn't make sense of it.

Paz removed his rubber gloves. "A couple of months ago they found six men, no heads. They were in the back of a truck on the highway," he said. "We're still looking for the heads."

Another officer placed the discovery in a cooler and closed it.

"Do you know who it is? The victim?" Joe asked.

Paz directed his colleague, speaking a clipped Spanish.

"No," Paz said, turning to Joe. "Tell me where this trunk is from?" He said this to Porfirio.

"Everything in this area right here, it's all from the same place, a hacienda in San Sebastián. Bermúdez is the name."

"I guess we need to speak to Señor Bermúdez," Paz said.

Porfirio shook his head.

"Muerto?" Dead?

"Sí."

"Well, we're going to have to look at all of the items here. There may be more … evidence."

Porfirio looked at Joe and nodded.

"No one should touch them," Paz added.

Porfirio offered a sympathetic hand on Joe's shoulder.

The other officer had begun to separate out the boxes.

"These yours?" Paz asked his brother-in-law.

"Actually, they're mine," Joe said.

"You will need to sign for them."

Joe knew the answer before he asked the question: "So, I'm guessing I can't ship them to the States today?"

Preoccupied, Paz was only barely paying attention.

"Mande?" What?

"I was going to ship them back to the States today," he said.

27

Paz shook his head. "No, no, these boxes, they all must be inspected, tagged. They are evidence."

"Any idea when it might be possible to get them back?"

"No sé," he said. "If we find the person who did this, but I don't expect that." He then turned abruptly and joined his colleague as they addressed the rest of the items, methodically dismantling Joe's last chance to save the business.

payaso: heard anything about C-dope?
elmago: what you hearing?
payaso: nothing he's gone dark
payaso: not been on for days
elmago: on vacation maybe
elmago: he works a lot
payaso: it don't make sense
payaso: things heating up
payaso: and he just stops?
payaso: don't make sense
elmago: I got it covered
payaso: u don't know where he is?
elmago: fuck no
elmago: why would I know?
payaso: u two been beefing lately
elmago: so what?
payaso: just saying
gorrión: C-dope still MIA
elmago: well fuck him then
elmago: we got shit to do
gorrión: u think they got to him?
payaso: shut the fuck up
gorrión: they were pisssssed about the hack
XXX99: hahahahaha
gorrión: maybe he's sick
elmago: we got to stick to the op
elmago: they don't know what we know
XXX99: surprise!

elmago: we're going to make it burn

gorrión: C-dope has the 0day local root exploit against openwebmail that their servers run

gorrión: If we get into that server we can root nameservers and control its entire internet space

elmago: can u figure it without C-dope?

payaso: we gotta wait

elmago: for what??

payaso: C-dope

elmago: no we go!

XXX99: :D

elmago: fucking light it up

gorrión: hive mind, motherfucker!!!!

Chapter 3

J oe woke with a wicked hangover. His phone showed that his mother had called numerous times. Alan had called numerous times. Instead, after the events at Porfirio's, he'd decided to do a few laps inside a tequila bottle. Now the proceedings of the day before came rushing back, banging into the sides of his head like the memories were trying to get out.

He stood under the shower until the hot water was gone. What now? He'd played his last chip on this longshot, and not only had it gone sideways, it had turned upside down. Even if he did somehow, by a miracle, gain possession of the items—and they *were* superior pieces, just as Porfirio had said—would he have to disclose that a man's head had been found knocking about in one? And who knows what other discoveries might have followed once the items had been removed to the police station and opened.

Before anymore could be done, Joe needed food. Something greasy and spicy, and a cup of coffee. Joe dressed and entered an altogether entirely too bright morning. On Olas Altas street, the tourists were overly eager, in clashing colors, and too-loud voices. He needed something quieter, darker. So he kept to the shady side of the street and after a few blocks settled on a simple cart sitting on a sleepy backstreet.

He knew menudo, a fiery soup of peppers and tripe, was the much relied–upon hangover cure among Mexicans. After serving Joe's food, the guy behind the counter opened his newspaper, and there, splashed across the front page, shouted a grim picture of an earless head. The headline read: Carteles suman otra baja en la guerra espeluznante. "Cartels add another casualty in grisly war." The story had made the papers, with him and Porfirio just visible in the background. And here he'd thought things couldn't get worse.

The bowl of menudo helped. Maybe not a miracle cure, but miracles seemed in short supply at present anyway. At a nearby newspaper seller, Joe picked up a copy and headed over to Porfirio's. At the shop, you would never have known that the day before a human head had come tumbling from an upturned trunk. It was quiet, the only real noise made by a bee repeatedly running itself again and again into an unrelenting window. Porfirio appeared from the back.

"Joe!" he exclaimed. "Buenos días."

Joe displayed the paper.

"Sí, yes, I saw it. People, they keep calling me!" He seemed to Joe rather too excited at the turn of events.

"What does the article say?" he asked.

Porfirio offered a shrug. "Not so much. Paz said these things happen all the time now. The cartels just kill. No reason. They're not saying who is the man."

"But they know who it is?"

"I think so."

"And the rest of the items," he asked, "they've all been taken?"

"Sí," Porfirio said, frowning. "They took everything."

Joe nodded.

Porfirio added, by way of good news, "But they didn't find anything else. No more ... bad things. That's good."

"Yes, no more body parts is good," Joe said.

They stood for a long moment, the bee buzzing vainly at the glass.

"I'm sorry, Joe. I cannot take them back," Porfirio said.

"I know. I wouldn't ask you to." Joe let out a long sigh. "And you were right—the pieces are special. When I get them home, I know they'll go quickly."

"You sound like your father. That man, he never give up. He could always figure something. I think you are a lot like him."

Joe put his arm around Porfirio's shoulder. "Thank you. I really appreciate that. I'm trying. I really am. One favor, if I can ask, do you think you could get the name of the victim? The former owner of the head?"

"I will talk to Paz."

"Perfect," Joe said. "And we're still going to have that lobster dinner, I promise."

"OK, OK. I can bring my girlfriend?"

"Girlfriend? What about Carmen?"

"No, too expensive to bring them both." And he collapsed into self-satisfied laughter.

The two men shook hands. Joe was just about out the door when he thought of something else.

"Hey, I wonder, could you also give me the name of the person those items came from?"

31

"Por supuesto, I have it here," Porfirio said. He returned to the counter, checked his ledger, and wrote the name down on a piece of paper and handed it to Joe. "But you know the man is dead?"

"Yeah, you mentioned that. Seems to be going around. Thanks, my friend. Talk to you later."

Back at the hotel, Joe found no shortage of information about Ruben Bermúdez. Son of a diplomat father and socialite mother in Mexico City. US educated: Princeton, Yale Law. Single, never married. A bit of a golden boy, and something of a fixture in the business and political arenas in Mexico, always representing key figures and influential interests. About 10 years ago, he ran afoul of the law in the Virgin Islands. Possession of cocaine, but he'd been released. And for a time, he made the papers for squiring around a young actress from a popular telenovela called "Caldero de Amor," the "Cauldron of Love." Men with money were the same everywhere, Joe thought.

But then, starting about three or four years ago, Joe noticed that the types of stories about Bermúdez had changed. He seemed to have revised his business plan. His name began to turn up less with the blue bloods, and more with a shadowy and dubious clientele. From the looks of it, he had become the go-to counsel for those traveling at the margins of the law. Suspected gun runners to the Middle East. Acquittal. Money-laundering banker. Acquittal. Hotelier cum drug lord. Not guilty. It was a who's who of the rich criminal class of Mexico.

And then Joe found the man's last story: Attorney Ruben Bermúdez found dead. According to the report, he'd died from a gunshot to the head by a high-caliber weapon. Though the reporter did note that the shot could have been delivered by his own hand, he also mentioned that such a demise was a common calling card of certain cartel killers who would often conduct executions in this fashion to illustrate what happens when you talk. The killers had never been found.

For reasons Joe could now sort of guess at, no one had come to claim Mr. Bermúdez's uncommonly fine collection of heirlooms. So the state had assumed possession and ultimately sold them to Porfirio (maybe he had his brother-in-law to thank for that). The only problem was that one of the items, an exquisitely crafted wooden trunk, lacquered and adorned with carved flowers and brass fittings, had ended up as the final resting place for a severed human head, and that had taken care of that.

32

But Joe had never been one to let things lie. If he had his mind fixed on something, there was little, even good sense as his mother would point out, that could divert him. On those occasions when Joe had locked on to something, his dad would say, "Uh oh, we've roused Juggernaut Joe." And Juggernaut Joe would put his head down and throw himself at whatever the thing was with all the power and unpredictability of a boulder rolling downhill.

The single-mindedness had mostly served him well: good grades, good athlete, a self-learner who as a teen had once built a shortwave radio from scavenged parts to connect with a friend away at his grandparents' for the summer. His doggedness got him a scholarship to Great Plains College. It got him hired at Ward and Williams. But it could have a dark side too. It could make him blind to unwanted consequences, for himself and for others. He'd come to know that about himself. What had happened in New York had just been the latest, if most devastating, example. The truth was, you could be committed to doing what's right and still blow things up along the way. You could ruin a marriage.

Joe had spent a lot of time thinking about Juggernaut Joe since then, and now he could feel the same undeniable instinct working in him again. He simply had to figure out who's head was in his trunk, who had put it there, and why. One step at a time, he'd just take one step at a time, he promised himself. And he'd start with a little trip out to Mr. Bermúdez's house.

It took a couple of hours to get out to San Sebastián del Oeste. He took his rental car north up the coast, past the airport toward Ixtapa, and then northeast. As he passed the little town of Las Palmas, Joe got a text from Porfirio. It turned out that the head in the trunk originally belonged to a man named César Castillo, 26 years old. He was the owner of an internet café located just three blocks from Porfirio's shop. Joe wondered what the man had done to the cartel to deserve such a fate.

Following the GPS, he began to climb, leaving the baking flatlands and swaying palms for cooler climes. After about an hour, he found himself in the mountains. Gold and silver mining country. Not far past the small coffee plantation of La Quinta, he turned off the asphalt onto a dirt road. After about a mile, he joined another smaller road, which wound him through beautiful tall trees adorned in climbing orchids and bromeliads, finally opening up to reveal a broad clearing. And then there it was, a stunning hacienda sitting alone on grounds offering an unobstructed view of fields of blue agave and the valley below. A place certainly worthy of the items Joe had purchased.

Joe left the road and parked in the shade of a stand of trees. The sprawling house was white-washed brick and beams. Joe imagined Bermúdez and his guests sitting beneath the arcade of arches and columns, taking a cigar and a cold drink out of the sun. Everywhere big bursts of colorful bougainvillea climbed. Birds darted from sun to shadow and back again. It was a tranquil place, and not one—from this perspective—that might be connected to two grisly deaths.

The grounds seemed abandoned. No cars. No signs of life. Fallen chayote dotted the yard, the waxy fruit looking altogether to Joe like shrunken heads. Joe listened to the breeze as it passed through the trees, whispering through the higher branches. It was truly a beautiful spot. The house, the grounds. He approached and peeked through the windows. The rooms stood empty with vaulted doorways and wide-plank hardwood floors. Through the large front window he could see a dramatic Talavera-tiled foyer and a second set of windows to an inner courtyard, where a fountain, also decorated in beautiful mosaic, sat dry.

On the other side of the property, past a set of empty stables, stood a broad expanse of open campo. In the middle sat a barrel Joe assumed must be for feed.

"¿Quién es usted?" a voice demanded. Who are you?

Startled, Joe jumped. He spun to find a Mexican man standing with a machete pointed at him.

"¿Qué estás haciendo aquí?" the man demanded. What are you doing here?

"Buenas tardes," Joe said.

The man waved the machete at Joe. "Why you here?"

"Just looking, just looking," Joe said. "I was driving. Saw the house. I only wanted to take a look. I'm sorry. It's just so beautiful."

"You can't be here." The man squared himself against Joe.

"I'm sorry. I didn't know. Was there a sign? I didn't mean to trespass."

The man appeared to be in his 60s. A beaten cowboy hat on his head, soiled blue chambray shirt on his back. The knuckles of his weathered hands shone like chestnuts.

"This is Señor Bermúdez's property!" the man declared.

"It doesn't look like anyone lives here."

The man gestured with his machete for Joe to vacate.

"OK, OK," he said. "I just wanted to take a look. Lo siento, señor," Joe said.

"Vete de aquí," the man said.

"I'm going," Joe said, slowly beginning to make his way back to the road. He felt the man's eyes on him as he moved toward the car. He had traveled 20 feet or so when the man, with the same angry voice, said, "He was a great man!"

Joe paused and turned.

The man still wore the same expression, but something in his demeanor had changed. "He did much for this community. He gave people jobs. He helped the school. That road, he fixed it when the government wouldn't do anything."

"Where did he go?" Joe asked, playing stupid.

The man didn't speak for a long moment. And then he said, "He is dead."

"Oh, I'm sorry."

The man's shoulders slumped slightly like someone had been holding him up and had just let go. He took a deep breath. "I come here," he said. "I cut the weeds. I water the flowers. Look after things."

"That's good of you," Joe said.

The man readjusted his hat on his head. He seemed at a loss for what to say next.

"My father, he just died also," Joe said. He hadn't intended to use this, but it just sort of came out.

The man fixed his eyes on Joe's.

"It was a surprise," Joe said. "His heart." He patted his chest.

The man removed his hat and bowed his head slightly. "Mi más sentido pésame," he said, expressing his condolences.

"Muchas gracias." He wanted to keep the man talking, see what he could learn. "How did Señor Bermúdez die?"

The Mexican's face changed again, this time closing up like a flower. His eyes went dark.

Joe knew that in some of these communities the cartel bosses were seen as heroes. Songs were written about them the way songs were penned about certain outlaw gunslingers.

The man shook his head. Baring his teeth, he said, "The government killed him."

The government? The newspapers had made no mention of government involvement. The government had been pursuing him on charges of money laundering and fraud.

"The government? Why would they do that to such a good man?" Joe asked.

An interior voice seemed to be working on the man, and after a moment's consideration, he shook his head again. "It is OK, you can look at the house." He waved his machete in the direction of the house, and then slid the blade into the sheath at his hip. He then, with no further preamble, started back into the trees from where Joe guessed he must have come. Joe decided on a different tack.

"Wait," Joe said. "Look. I have to apologize. I wasn't totally honest with you."

The man stopped and turned to Joe.

"I knew this was Señor Bermúdez's house."

The man stiffened and looked intently at Joe.

"My father, he owned an antiques business in the US. You know, furniture, art, old things. My mother can't work it on her own, so I am helping her. I bought some of Señor Bermúdez's beautiful antiques. From a dealer in Puerto Vallarta."

The man, not totally tracking, gestured toward the house. "All gone."

"Yes. I bought the things, the antiguedades."

"You have Señor Bermúdez's antiguedades?"

"Yes. Well no, not anymore. I bought them but the police took them."

"Did you buy from Señor Vega?"

Joe searched his memory. "Señor Vega?"

"He come here last week."

"Last week?"

"They stay two nights. He say they take care of the plants, but no."

Joe spoke slowly, as calmly as he could. He wanted to convey nothing but easy comfort. "What can you tell me about Señor Vega?" Joe asked. "Maybe he can help me."

A.J. got to the golf course early. He liked to get there early. In his mind, it gave him a certain advantage. The truth was, he would take a hot

36

shower and enjoy a leisurely breakfast, watching the mist slowly lift from the course. He loved the quiet, the slow resolving into morning.

A.J. took his time on the putting green, trying to put everything that was happening at work out of his mind. With projects as big as the one he found himself in the middle of, you had to accept a certain play in the steering wheel. There would be surprises, setbacks. The key remained to address each in its turn and keep the ball moving forward. Because the rewards, especially for this current undertaking, promised to be enormous.

He was thinking for the millionth time how he was going to tell his partner when he saw the man's bowlegged approach, hurrying as he always seemed to be doing, pulling his clubs behind him like they were resisting.

"I've been fucking trying to call you all morning!" Darrell started in. "Why don't you answer your goddamn phone?"

"Forgot it at home. Now I'm glad I did."

Darrell shook his head. "Man, in our business you got to always have your phone."

"Wait, *you're* giving me business advice? It's like you give me golfing advice."

"Hey, it doesn't take a goddamn genius to know if they can't get a hold of you, they can't buy from you," he said. "And it doesn't take fucking Tiger Woods to know your short game sucks ass."

"I don't know," A.J. said. "Feeling good this morning."

A.J. and Darrell were not friends in the conventional sense. They tended to keep their lives separate. Still, they were committed to each other in their way, each believing that he had saved the other. They also shared certain things in common, even if A.J. acknowledged it less and less: a messy romantic record, an impulse to escape when things got bad, a stubborn optimism that everything would work out.

As they climbed into the golf cart, Darrell said, "I was calling you *because* ... because I want to talk about something. I got an idea."

"Oh shit," A.J. said.

The cool morning air found them as they took the cart down the path toward the first tee. They passed two greenskeepers fixing a sprinkler. But otherwise the course remained quiet, perfect.

As they sighed to a stop near the tee box, Darrell said, "OK, just hear me out before you shit all over it."

"Do we have to do this now? Can't it wait till we're back at the office?"

"You're going to want to know about this idea as soon as possible. Plus, I never know who's listening at the office."

A.J. exhaled. He was not in the mood, but he knew Darrell well enough to know the man would not be dissuaded once fixed on a course. "OK," he said.

"OK. A question for you: Where do the wealthy like to go, travel to?"

"Can't you just tell me your idea without a goddamn quiz?"

"Just answer me: Where do the wealthy like to go?"

"You mean like a hotel? A city? I need more."

"Where *in the world* do they like to go? For the food, the wine."

"Rich people want to go wherever other rich people are," A.J. said.

"OK, so where is that?"

A.J. shrugged. "New York, Vegas, the fucking Cayman Islands—just what are you trying to say?"

"They want to go to Italy! Right? Everyone wants to go to Italy. Venice and whatever," Darrell said. "Come on, tell me that isn't true."

A.J. climbed out of the cart.

"Sure. I guess. I'm not sure it's just the rich, but yeah. People love Italy."

Darrell grinned. "OK, yes they do! They fucking love it. The food, the wine, you know. But it's too far away for a lot of people. Too tough to get there."

"Really?" A.J. asked. "Too tough to get there? Every major airline probably goes there."

Darrell ignored this and barreled forward. "So, I think *we* should make Italy *here.*"

A.J. retrieved his three wood from his bag. "Make Italy in Mexico."

"Exactly!" Darrell said. "We use that Mismaloya property. We've been trying to decide what to do with it. So, I think we take it, and we build our biggest resort ever down there. We make it feel like Italy from the second you walk on to the property. Cobblestone streets, little, you know, Italian restaurants, cafés, maybe even, like, a Roman stadium for shows or whatever. We can figure all that out. But it's all Italy. I've done a ton of research and there's nothing like it anywhere."

"Except Italy," A.J. said. He grabbed a tee and ball from the dash of the cart.

38

"Well, right, but they would get that *in Mexico*. So, you still get the great weather, the beautiful beach, the this, the that. And if they want to leave Italy for a bit, no problem. They can just hop a bus or taxi and in minutes they're back in Mexico! Like being in two places at once that people love! People would go crazy for it. It would be a one-of-a-kind destination. People would flock to it."

A.J. sunk his tee into the patchy piece of grass at the tee box. He straightened and surveyed the contours of the hole.

"Dogleg left?" he said to no one in particular. The green fairway sloped down the short rise on which they stood and spread out before him, some low trees scattered along the left margin. He took a few practice swings. A sprinkler could be heard stuttering somewhere nearby.

Darrell hadn't moved. He waited, his gloved hands wringing each other. A.J. took another practice swing, saying nothing.

"So?" Darrell asked.

A.J. positioned himself beside the ball. "What do you want me to say?"

"What do I want you to say? You *should* say that you think it's a fucking great idea and let's get started right now, that's what you *should* say. You should say that it would be huge, that it would bring people in from all over, that it would transform the coastline, *and* make us a boatload of money. That's what you should say!"

A.J. drew his club back, and then drove it through the ball, sending it out and up into the denim-blue sky. As it flew, it slowly began to bank right in a long, gradual arch until it left the fairway and found the leafy limbs of a small group of trees.

"Fuck," A.J. said. He walked back to the cart, thrust the club back into his bag. "The idea is a nonstarter. Sorry to have to tell you that. I love that you're thinking. But it's too much capital investment. The truth is, we really need to think about selling that property. We could do a lot with that money."

"Sell? What are you talking about?" Darrell said. "You've got it wrong, pard. Get rid of it? That's crazy. We need to make something great with it. My idea will work. It would put Banderas Properties on the map."

A.J. waved Darrell to the tee. "Go, for crying out loud."

Darrell took a ball and tee from his bag and set up. "I have a guy working up some plans. He did a big resort in Orlando."

"Will you please just hit the goddamn ball," A.J. said.

Darrell stood stiffly beside the tee and with an awkward inside-out swing struck the ball on the button, sending it 150 yards down the middle of the fairway.

Without missing a beat, Darrell said, "And he loved my idea. Said it would be, what did he say, 'monumental.' Monumental. It totally will be." His face was alive with the thought.

"Look, I'm sorry I have to be this guy again. But it's not going to happen. It would take decades to get our money back, if we ever did. We want a shorter, more certain path to profit. Lower risk. That's our business model."

"I don't care about any business model," Darrell said. "Fuck your business model. It's about doing cool shit, leaving our mark."

"Who the fuck do you think you are, Richard Branson? We operate timeshare properties. Timeshares. Go work for Donald fucking Trump if you want to build gaudy gold-plated bullshit that no one wants to stay in. It's not what we do."

"Because you say so?"

"You know what, yes—yes, because I say so, because I fucking say so!"

Darrell shook his head. He inserted his driver into his bag with the authority of a sword being returned to a sheath. He smiled. "Well, this time it doesn't matter what you say," he said.

Joe's phone rang. He knew he owed his mom a call, but he just couldn't bring himself to answer. He couldn't tell her that the business his father had built, the business that had sustained the family for the last 30 years, the business that he took over and staked his own life on, that it was slipping under the wheel.

After another ring, the phone stopped. He would call her later. He would have to see how everything played out, and then hope that the words came to him when the time was right. When the phone began to ring again a moment later Joe snatched it from the table, exasperated. "Yes, Mom, what?"

"You really talk to your mother that way? You *should* have gone to jail."

Leon. Fucking Leon. How did he always know the exact right/wrong time to call?

"Fuck you," Joe said, relieved.

"Yeah, that's what they all say. Speaking of fucking you, just imagine the magnificent beating your ass would've taken if you *had* gone to jail. Pretty thing like you?"

"I know some who think I deserve that."

"Not again with that self-flagellating bullshit. You were making money for your clients, doing what the brain trust told you to do. Subprime was going to change everything. You didn't know it was built on a mountain of shit. Everyone took it in the teeth. That's on management, not you."

Joe just wished he could go back. Maybe there was a different way, a better way to have played it.

"So, what you up to, Cubbie?" Leon asked.

"I think about three beers."

"Well, that's a good start."

"Yeah, I think I'm going to need a little more than that today."

"Well, it's a damn good thing I called then."

Everyone should have a Leon. A Leon can make the difference. A Leon can save a guy. He had certainly saved Joe Lily. Or at least he had contributed to a change in weather patterns that enabled Joe to trim his sails in a different direction.

Leon's background was hazy even to Joe. Leon managed very deftly to keep much of it a mystery. But over time Joe had studiously pieced together a few strands. When Joe had started at Ward and Williams, people would talk about Leon in reverent tones. By some accounts, he'd been among the smartest guys the place had ever seen. Cocky to a fault, but with an undeniable humor, he seemed able to turn just about any situation to his favor. Like fucking Gandalf, one of the guys had told Joe.

Still, no one seemed to know where Leon came from, what his origin story was. What was clear and widely acknowledged was that he'd made the firm a great deal of money, astonishing amounts. His fans said he had this uncanny command of the clock. Know when to strike, know when to hike, he would tell Joe. This dance seemed to come easily to him, and he'd taken an accelerated climb up the Wall Street pecking order, building a life of steadily escalating wealth and influence. One newspaper article about him had called him Wonderboy. From Malamud's *The Natural*. Because he was always hitting home runs.

41

The stories about what happened next differ, but the prevailing mythology went that during a vacation to Costa Rica (with the ex-wife of a rainmaker at a competing firm, the story goes), something happened, something happened, and he cracked. Blew everything up and disappeared. He'd supposedly reprised a moment from the movie *Apocalypse Now* and scrawled a note from the rainforest to Ward and Williams CEO Everett Williams that read: "Sell the house. Sell the car. Sell the kids. Find someone else to do your dirty work. I'm never coming back." And he never had.

This was roughly at the same time that Joe's own ascendancy was in full bloom. He was a superstar not just at Ward and Williams, but was fast becoming known across Wall Street. Clients came to him. Everyone wanted a piece. Profits dropped like April rain in Portland. He and Allison were wined and dined. They went sailing with the boss. And then one night he received an email from someone named "Noel."

"There is no inoculation from risk," the person wrote. "I don't care what anyone at W&W tells you. Because here's an undeniable truth: If 40 percent of the concrete in your foundation is shit the foundation is shit. And we know what happens to a house built on a shitty foundation. Those mortgages everyone wants? The ones that are delivering those unbelievable returns? Bad fucking concrete. I know this, and I think you know it too. So, you've got some tough choices to make, Cubbie. Here's some advice from someone who's been there: Without the chin, a beard is just a pile of hair. Be the chin."

Joe had tried to dismiss the email as the ravings of a madman: Be the chin? What in the hell did that mean? More likely it was the work of some jealous colleague or a gag being sprung on him by friends. This person did seem to know that Joe had been packaging B- and C-grade loans in with A-grade loans. He'd been told that Ward and Williams had cracked the code on risk. Bringing lower-grade loans in with higher-grade ones inoculated the bad ones against danger. Someone had cracked polio, human flight, the human genome. Now they'd found a way to solve investment risk. After all, his bosses surely wouldn't move forward with a strategy rigged to explode in their hands. That would be crazy.

Still, the idea and the strangeness of the email from this mysterious Noel stuck in Joe's mind. So he kept watch. But when the weeks went by and the sky didn't fall and then still didn't fall, Joe let the concern go and forgot about it. He had plenty else to occupy his attention. He was working 15-hour days to meet the growing demand for these products.

The returns were jaw dropping. His clients were happy and getting rich. His numbers were through the roof, and his bosses were very pleased. He got promoted. He got bonuses and invitations to speak at industry events. He and Allison found themselves something of a fixture in the society pages. And then Elinor was born and the happiness jumped to stratospheric levels. Maybe it was because he was so busy that he didn't see the cracks. Maybe he ignored them. It was a distinction he would torture himself about later.

Soon enough, there was no missing it. The elaborate architecture he'd been working inside had begun to buckle. You could see it. But even as the rotten loans began to wobble and threaten to detonate, his mentors, those he looked up to—George Lansdowne, Ben Bernanke, even the master himself, Alan Greenspan—they all assured the doubters that things were fine. Trust the market. Trust the market. Trust the fucking market.

More weeks passed and things only got worse. The looks of cocky jubilation over subprime that had become standard around the office were gone, replaced by a kind of creeping dread. A cloud was gathering. You could feel it. Once more he took his concerns to his father-in-law. This time, George Lansdowne told him to shut up about it. Did he want to freak investors? The market was suggestible. And then those same four words: Everything will be fine.

But then that very weekend, on the Lansdowne's deck in Montauk, George Lansdowne said, "I hope to god you don't have any personal exposure here, Joseph. Tell me you and Allison got your money out. Things are about to get medieval out there."

Joe was dumbstruck. "George, of course I have exposure. You told me everything was going to be fine. I came to you, more than once, and every time you said don't worry, trust the market. Party line has been we're good, keep selling. So I kept selling. I've convinced people to go all in on this, George. Many people. They're going to lose everything."

"Joseph," he said, "let's be crystal clear about this, it's got to be family first here. Family first, do you understand? And I never told you shit." He finished his drink, pitched the ice into the yard, and returned inside.

It was about this time that his clients began to call, only now it wasn't to celebrate and sing his praises. They called day and night. Left angry messages, desperate messages. They didn't like what they were seeing and wanted answers, assurances. Friends he'd convinced to invest. Risk-free investment. Double-digit returns. The thought of it twisted in his stomach. He couldn't sleep, couldn't eat.

One evening, after they'd put the baby down, Joe told Allison he had to do something. He didn't know what, but something. Since Elinor's birth, Allison had decided not to return to work. She asked what others at work were doing. "They're selling, they're fucking selling like nothing is happening," he said. "If Dad said everything is fine, then everything must be fine," she said. "He knows the market better than anyone."

Instead, the next day, after another sleepless night, Joe went into work early and started with the A's and began calling every Ward and Williams subprime client to tell them the situation, to encourage them to get out now. He'd barely reached the C's by the time management had gotten wind of his campaign. His computer access was immediately cut, his credentials and privileges revoked. And when two security personnel appeared at his desk, he collected his things and allowed himself to be led out to the sidewalk.

The move sent shockwaves through the agency and would in the days to follow impact the entire industry. Clients filled the phone lines, lined up in the firm's waiting area, all demanding answers. The Ward and Williams PR team worked fast, and by 5 p.m. that night Joe's face was splashed on every TV channel, on the front page of every paper: Ward and Williams' subprime superstar sabotages firm. Disgruntled poster boy for subprime seeks revenge on Wall Street. Disgraced Ward and Williams VP lied to clients.

What he didn't necessarily see coming was Allison's response. "You've bankrupted us," she screamed. "You've bankrupted my parents. Why? Why did you do it?" She cried for days, devastated. Joe tried to convince her that he'd had no choice. He'd tried talking to his boss, to her father, but no one would listen. And if they were bankrupt, so were scores of clients who'd trusted Ward and Williams, and invested everything on the firm's advice. "We are young. We'll rebound. We have each other." But she could not be persuaded that his act was anything other than the very worst kind of betrayal.

The market's fall continued for weeks. It seemed to have no floor. Ward and Williams, a respected, long-standing member of the Wall Street ecosystem, collapsed. And they weren't the only ones. The wreckage lay everywhere, and there was a real fear that the entire global economy would follow. As fingers were pointed, many tilted in Joe's direction. Hadn't he been subprime's biggest cheerleader? Hadn't he been among its most successful purveyors? And *now* he's calling foul? No one would take Joe's calls. And then one afternoon after another dustup, Allison packed her bags and left with Elinor. If being some kind of hero was so goddamn important to him, then he could go ahead and sleep with his fucking cape, she said.

At some point, Joe remembered the mysterious email he'd received weeks earlier. He dug it up and wrote back. "You were right. I should have listened. I didn't. And just as you predicted, everything has turned to shit. Any advice now? P.S. I don't know any Noels. Who you are and why write to me?"

The response shocked and shook him.

"We humans, we're not much for learning from our mistakes. Hold onto that email, and you can send it to the next generation of fools when they dream up their own version of stupid. The only ones who say the market is free are the ones who believe they've found a way to manipulate it. I know because I was one of them. As for Noel, that was just a fun little game I played for my own enjoyment. Read it in reverse and it might ring a bell. I used to be a rainmaker at your firm or now your ex-firm. I've been following your career there for a while because, well, it bore a certain resemblance to my own. And now you're at your own crossroads, Cubbie. Which way do you go?"

Leon. The famous Leon. And that email started a correspondence and friendship that Joe had come to rely on.

Now, more than 18 months later, Joe found himself in Puerto Vallarta, Mexico, once again facing long odds and not sure how to proceed.

"I don't know," Joe said.

"Come on, Cubbie," Leon said. "Have you learned nothing? Remember, the swimmer can be swallowed by the riptide, or he can use its energy to propel him out. Don't give me this hand-wringing bullshit. Position one is what?"

"I know," Joe said.

"So tell me."

"Action."

"Bingo," Leon said. "Make a list, order it, and then execute. Ask questions. Push on things that seem solid. Shine a light into rooms that seem dark. Who said you can't take these items out of the country? Have you tried? First thing I'd do is hit up customs. Work an arrangement. Maybe you take all but the trunk? Who knows? The point is you're wasting time counting grains of sand. Fuck that. And speaking of time,

I'm out of it. My lunch is here——." Joe heard Leon's muffled voice speaking a language he didn't recognize. "Wish you could smell this. It's glorious. It's so glorious it's giving me a hard-on."

"Thanks for that," Joe said. "Where are you?"

"Somewhere in Thailand. Beautiful country full of beautiful people. Here's the thing. Do you think as I dig into this sublime roasted duck that I'm going to be thinking about what I'm eating tomorrow? Or the next day? No. I'm 100 percent here. It's just me and the duck, right now, nothing else."

"You and the duck. And your hard-on."

"Yes! Exactly," Leon said. "Remember that. Now get to work. *Laéw-jer-gan.*"

Talk to customs. So absolutely obvious. But first Joe thought he might drop by Cesar Castillo's internet café. Porfirio had pointed it out. Joe wondered how he'd kept the place afloat in these days of ubiquitous laptops, tablets, and cell phones. And it wasn't exactly well located, sitting on Calle Insurgentes, a busy street traveled by buses and cars and taxis from Viejo Vallarta—Old Town—over the Rio Cuale into the center of the city.

The door of Dos Arcos was, of course, locked. Cesar no doubt left work that night thinking he'd be back the next day. Instead someone had grabbed him, drove him to who knows where, and cut his head off for him. But why? Why had a cartel singled him out? The lowly owner of a struggling internet café. What could he have done? And what had they done with the rest of his body? Inspection of the remaining antiques had apparently not turned up any answers.

Joe cupped his face to the glass of the door and peered inside. Clean spots on dusty desks identified where computers had been. Joe wondered what had happened to them. Here was another reason the business's survival perplexed Joe: There were only spots for maybe 10 terminals. How much revenue could that possibly generate? Still, it didn't seem like a bad life from where Joe was standing. Run a small shop in a tropical paradise. There was a lot to recommend it.

Joe was just about to head back to the hotel when he saw a light go on in a back room. A jolt of cold surprise shot through his body. After a line of clattering public buses passed on the road behind him, he could also hear noises coming from inside: rustling papers maybe, drawers being opened and closed, feet shuffling on the tile floor.

Joe knocked on the door. The noises inside stopped. Joe paused briefly, and when no one appeared, he knocked again.

"Hello?" he shouted through the glass. "Anyone there?"

Still nothing, the person presumably hoping Joe would go away. But he didn't go away. He kept knocking. "Excuse me. Hello? Permiso? I left my wallet." Knock, knock, knock. "Anyone there?" He would wear the person down. "Hello?"

Finally, exasperated, a rather disheveled-looking young woman appeared from the back, her face pinched into an unhappy grimace. "We're closed," she said.

Joe was dumbstruck to find that the someone in the shop was not Mexican at all but instead a blonde woman. Late 20s maybe, pretty, the slender frame of a runner with square shoulders holding up her tank top. She appeared harried and pale, with a messy head of hair. Her clothes were wrinkled, and she had generally about her the look of someone who had not slept.

"Sorry, I think I left my wallet!" Joe said. "Please. I'll only be a minute."

Finally, when Joe wouldn't leave, the woman relented, unlocking the front door.

"Thank you so much," Joe said. "I'm really sorry to bother you."

"I have been cleaning in here and I haven't seen a wallet."

"I was … " But before Joe could finish, the blood seemed to run from the woman's face and she began to sway. She would have fallen had Joe not reached out and steadied her.

"Are you OK?" he asked.

"A little lightheaded." She reached out and grabbed him at his elbow.

Joe eased her onto one of the chairs and looked for water. He stepped into the backroom. Files and papers littered the floor. Cabinet and cupboard doors hung open. Items that had been stuck to a corkboard dangled from tacks.

"You don't need—" she said.

Joe interrupted. "You need some water." Amid the mess, Joe found a few bottled waters and quickly returned to the woman. She remained pale and glassy-eyed.

He handed her the water and took up a chair. She drank deeply from the bottle and in a few minutes the color had begun to come back into her cheeks.

"Your wallet," she finally managed to say.

Joe had forgotten all about his ruse. "I guess it must be somewhere in the hotel," he said.

She looked at him closely.

"You're dehydrated," he offered.

At this, without warning, she put her hand over her mouth and began to cry.

Joe didn't know quite what to do.

"My fiancé," she managed through the tears. "He was … killed." She put her face in her hands.

"Cesar was your fiancé?" Joe asked.

She nodded. And then, after a beat, turned to Joe and said, "How do you know his name?"

Joe needed to get his story together. "I met him here," he said. "And then I saw the story in the paper. I'm so sorry."

All she could do was nod, wringing her hands in her lap.

"I didn't know he was engaged," he said.

"We were going to be married next spring," she said. She shook her head. "The cartels. They are not human."

"You think it was a cartel?" Joe asked.

"I know it was," she said.

"I'm so sorry."

"I should never have come to Mexico," she said.

"How long have you been down here?"

"Six months on Monday. I hadn't seen my dad in 10 years. My parents are divorced. If you met him, you'd know why. Over the last year we started communicating again. My mom tried to talk me out of it, but I didn't listen. He said come down. He had a job for me. He has this timeshare business. Banderas Properties? You've probably been hassled by one of their guys. It was great at first, but then he started pulling the same shit on me that he used to pull on my mom, the same exact shit: controlling, refusing to take responsibility. I would have left if I hadn't met Cesar."

"How'd you and Cesar meet?"

"I hate telling people. It sounds so bad," she said. "We met at a bar. We were both there to watch the World Cup. I actually spilled a beer on

48

him. He would tell you I did it on purpose. And maybe I did, I'm not saying. But I did notice him. I mean, what girl wouldn't? With that hair and his smile. He …" She covered her face in her hands.

Joe let her cry as traffic rattled by out front.

She moved loose strands of hair from her face and shook her head. "I don't know what I'm going to do. Maybe I'll just go home, back to the States. Crimes like this aren't ever solved in Mexico. Not that it matters now. I came down here this morning to get his stuff and I found nothing left." She waved at the empty room. "Gone, everything is gone."

"Stuff was here before?"

"Yeah. All the computers. The cartel must have taken them." She shook her head. "Or maybe someone read what had happened and took it as an opportunity to see what they could steal. He would be heartbroken. He loved this place."

"Where did Cesar sit?" he asked.

"That's his desk," the woman said.

The desk was also without a computer.

"Did he have a computer here?" Joe asked.

"Did he have a computer here? Cesar *always* had his computer. That was the only thing we fought about. He spent hours on it. I'd say, 'We're in Mexico, let's go to the beach, let's go out,' but he only wanted to work on the computer."

She stared into the empty room. "You know, we actually talked about turning the place into a self-serve yogurt shop. Isn't that ridiculous? Anyway, his landlord will be happy. He's wanted Cesar out of here for a long time."

"My name is Joe," Joe said, extending his hand.

"Molly," she said. "So, you met Cesar?"

"Yes," he lied. "But only really briefly."

She gave Joe a serious look and then it was gone, like a cloud passing in front of the sun. "I'm really sorry to dump all this on you."

"Not at all. I'm sorry to have barged in here. And I'm really sorry for your loss."

"Thank you, Joe."

Later, when Joe returned to his hotel, he realized with a chill that after telling Molly he'd been to the shop, and met Cesar, he'd asked where Cesar sat. Hopefully she hadn't noticed.

gorrión: we've got to do something!!!!

elmago: he did it to himself

payaso: what the fuck are you talking about? he cut his own fucking head off?

elmago: these people are vicious. You come at them, they'll come at you twice as hard.

gorrión: how did they know? that's what I want to know. someone talked.

elmago: what, you think this is some kind of spy shit? Come on.

payaso: why is that crazy?

elmago: these guys know people. they have resources. Think about it.

payaso: fuck you. You never liked C-dope.

elmago: what the hell are you talking about? enough of this bullshit.

elmago: if ur not committed then go back to your facebook.

payaso: you said C-dope was weak. That he thought small. That's what you said.

elmago: so what?

elmago: both of those are true. He was not a leader for what we want to accomplish.

payaso: we don't need a leader. We don't want a fucking leader. There are no leaders here.

payaso: you never understood that. There is no leader. There can't be. That's the point.

gorrión: hive mind!

elmago: fuck you. Do you want to actually achieve something?

elmago: that's the question

payaso: no, that's not the question.

payaso: the question is who killed C-dope?

payaso: Who fucking cut his head off?!!!!

elmago: you a detective now?

elmago: and who tried to protect him by telling him a cartel op was a bad idea? I did.

elmago: I said I'm from Culiacán , where they're from.

elmago: I know how they work. That's it.

unodostres: everybody chill

elmago: we need to focus on frak/op.

unodostres: does the cartel know what we have?

elmago: how the fuck should I know? I'm not cartel.

elmago: you know that right? You smart enough to get that?

payaso: yeah, and also I'm smart enough to see patterns.

gorrión: ok, let it go.

payaso: we got to hit them again, bigger. wreck them for what they did!

elmago: that's a fucking deathwish. we focus on frak/op.

payaso: not yet. this first.

gorrión: lets dedicate it to C-dope.

gorrión: agree?

unodostres: yes!!!

Chapter 4

"Amigo! Hey, Oregon!"

Joe turned to search out the voice. People moved every which way. An arm shot up from the timeshare booth on the far corner where Olas Altas meets Rodolfo Gómez. Joe had not slept well.

"Oregon, how's it going?"

It was the timeshare tout from earlier. He sat at a booth shaded by an awning that read: Banderas Properties. Joe walked over and shook the man's hand. His name tag read "Roberto."

"So, you still working? Or are you ready to go fishing today?" the man asked.

Joe smiled. "No, no fishing. Not feeling so great today."

"Ah, the tequila diet. You start it and you immediately lose two days!"

Joe laughed. "No, no tequila, but actually there is something you could help me with."

"OK, yes, what can I do for you, Oregon? You name it. And then maybe you take a sunset cruise. It's a beautiful way to see the city."

"I actually need to visit the Banderas Properties offices, the main office. Do you know where I would find it?"

"Sí, of course," Roberto said.

Joe found the Banderas Properties building on the far side of the bridge connecting Old Town with the Malecón. A touts' tent was positioned in front, giving the staff a strategic position from which to feed on the endless stream of tourists.

Maybe it was something about Joe's expression, but rather than intercept him, the guys just nodded and smiled and let him pass into the building without comment.

In the cool air-conditioned office two women sat at computers. Twenties maybe. Latina. They could have been sisters, and Joe could discern something about their boss in their hiring.

The women smiled. "Buenos días! Bienvenidos a Banderas Properties."

"Buenos días," he said. "Is Molly available?"

"OK, one minute please," said the one whose name tag read "Angela R."

"Joe!" Molly called from the second-floor landing.

"Good memory," Joe said.

She came down and extended her hand. "It was actually my first boyfriend's name."

"I hope that's good," he said.

She shook her head. "Not good. He cheated on me. With the mom of my best friend."

"I'm not sure whether to be aghast. Or impressed."

"Aghast is good," she said. "But luckily for you, my favorite cat was also named Joe."

"That *is* lucky."

"He was a stud."

"Parallels everywhere," he said.

When he saw he was breaking through, he said, "I'm sorry to barge into your day. But after meeting you yesterday, I'm afraid I have a confession to make."

The two girls at the desk had gone back to their computers.

Molly tilted her head. "Well you better come up here," she said. "I think confessions are supposed to be given in private."

At the top of the stairs, she waved him past a closed office door.

"Ignore that. A little partner strife," she said, gesturing toward the door. Through the half-glass of the wall Joe could see two men in serious conversation. One, presumably Molly's father, sat behind a desk and jabbed his finger at the other. "That's not how it fucking works!" was what Joe thought he heard him say.

She shook her head. "My dad, he doesn't know how to read people. He's not good at it. He never has been."

Molly led Joe into another office. "Please, have a seat," she said. "Can I get you some coffee?"

Joe sat. "No thanks, I'm good."

She was almost unrecognizable from the day before. Now she wore her hair pulled tightly back into a ponytail. Her face, dirty and flushed the last time he saw her, now looked fresh and clean with just the right amount of makeup, setting off the blue of her eyes and the white of her smile. Her outfit included a short, crisp skirt and a sleeveless top.

"Nice," Joe said, admiring the airy, bright space, aglow with the gold sunlight from its one large window.

"It's one of the ways my dad got me down here," she said. "'You'll have your own office, your own piece of the business.' He failed to remind me that he's still an asshole. And that it's still timeshare. That might have been good to mention."

Joe could hear her father's mumbled voice through the wall. "When we ran into each other at the shop, I got the impression that maybe you were planning on leaving PV?"

She didn't speak for a moment. "Every day I say that. I don't know why I'm still here to be honest. Especially now that Cesar is gone. But I really don't want to go until I know what happened."

"It must be incredibly difficult, dealing with all of this."

"What choice do I have?" She stared at her hands for a moment. "But you were going to tell me something? Make a *confession*? Who can say no to that?"

"Right, yes," Joe said. "It bugged me all night after meeting you. I should have told you at the shop. It's actually about Cesar."

"About Cesar?" She cocked her head slightly and a furrow appeared between her eyes.

"When we talked yesterday? I, well, I wasn't exactly honest about why I was there."

"OK," she said.

"The truth is, I run an import-export business. In Portland. Oregon. I came down here because I'd purchased a number of items from an antiques dealer, an old family friend who's actually located not too far from Cesar's shop. The items I bought had all come from one particular estate."

"OK, but what does that have to do with Cesar?" Molly asked, her eyes fixed on him.

"I bought the entire collection sight unseen. So, I'd just arrived at the store, to the antiques shop, to see all the stuff for the first time. I'd been told how great the items were and was eager to see everything, and—"

"It was your trunk."

Joe exhaled slowly. "Yes."

She covered her mouth with her hand. "Were you the one who, who found …?"

Joe shook his head. "No, it was one of the assistants in the store. But I was there."

Molly turned away.

"I'm sorry," Joe said. "I should have told you."

After a long moment, Molly nodded as if she had concluded something. She retrieved some tissues from the desk and wiped her eyes, cleared her throat. "I still just can't believe it," she said. "I have moments when I think about 'Oh, I have to go pick him up from work,' or 'We should go see a movie tonight,' and then I remember. It doesn't seem real."

She collected herself, drew a couple of paper cups from a dispenser near the door, and filled them with water from the garrafón, the large water jug. She put one in front of Joe.

Joe took a drink.

"OK, so if you weren't there for your wallet, why *were* you there, at the shop yesterday?"

"So that's a good question," he said. "I don't know exactly. Because of what happened, all of the items that I purchased have been confiscated by the police. I can't take it out of the country. I paid a lot for them and I can't afford to just leave them here. So, when I learned where the shop was, I don't know, something just brought me there. Maybe there'd be some clue about what happened. I'm told that the police—"

"Don't do a damn thing?" She shook her head. "To them, it's just another cartel killing."

"That's what people have been telling me," Joe said. "I guess I figured if I could learn something, maybe I could help."

"I wouldn't get involved," Molly said, shaking her head. "It will just frustrate you like it has me. They don't care. And you never know what danger it might put you in. These are despicable people."

"Do you mind if I ask you a question?"

"Joe," she said, "my fiancé, the love of my life, is dead. Nothing you ask can hurt me now."

Joe felt guilty for forgetting, for even a moment, that what he'd intersected represented the horrifying end of one person's life and the utter devastation of those he left behind. Joe's concerns about some antiques, even his concerns about the business, seemed paltry by comparison.

"Well, so did Cesar ever talk about the cartels? Did anything like that ever come up? Maybe he talked about a friend who was involved or got into trouble with them?"

Molly looked down at her long hands on the desk. "I mean, these days just about everyone seems to be touched by the cartels. But Cesar was

55

focused on his business, his mom, and, you know, us, the wedding. And soccer, of course. Always soccer." She managed a weak smile.

"I think you mentioned something about the landlord of the building wanting him out? Any chance that there could be something there?"

"Possibly," she said. "That had crossed my mind too. Seems like Cesar fought with him every month when the rent was due."

Joe thought for a moment. "I guess if the landlord was cartel, and knew that Cesar was getting married to the daughter of a timeshare titan like your father, he might think it was a good time to squeeze him."

"You know, there was one time Cesar mentioned the cartels. We were at my place one night and he was really angry. I guess he'd been arguing with one of his friends online."

"What were they arguing about, do you know?"

Molly shook her head. "He said I wouldn't understand. Damn. If we could just find his laptop. I don't know what happened to it."

"I noticed all the other computers were gone. That wasn't you?"

"Me? No. I have no idea what happened to them. By the time I got here everything was gone. Probably the people who took him took the computers too."

"What about friends of Cesar's? Anyone who might know anything?"

"I don't know," she said. "Maybe Miguel? His family owns a bakery pretty close to the shop. But I don't think he really liked me." She glanced at her cell phone.

"Well, I should let you get back to work," Joe said, getting to his feet.

Molly stood, absently playing with the engagement ring on her hand.

Just then, a loud noise came from her father's office, a thud like something heavy hitting the floor. Joe and Molly immediately moved to the hallway. They heard the two men bitterly arguing now.

"*I* got *you* hired in this business, you arrogant fuck!"

"You better wise up, Darrell, and listen to what I'm goddamn telling you. Or you're going to get yourself killed."

And then the office door flew open. A heavy chair lay on its side. A man stepped out of the office, medium height, compact in build, a blonde ring of hair encircling the bald patch on top of his head. Molly's father slammed his door shut.

"Your dad's a fucking liar—and an asshole!" he said to Molly before pushing past Joe and storming down the hall.

"Darrell Haddock," Molly said. "Dad's partner in crime."

Javier greeted Joe as Joe entered the hotel from Rodolfo Gómez.

"Buenos días, Señor Lily."

"Buenos días," Joe said.

"There is a package for you."

"A package?" The man pushed a small box across the counter to Joe. There was no postage, so Joe concluded it must have been delivered by courier. "Gracias."

It was not yet noon and the pool and bar area were already busy. Small groups sat and ate or milled in the pool and chatted.

On his way back to the hotel, Joe had managed to find the bakery Molly had mentioned. Panadería Esperanza on Calle Madero. He knew it was the right bakery, because when he asked the older woman at the counter about Miguel her face had gone very serious. At first, she said nothing and then offered only that Miguel was not there. When he looked down to retrieve a business card from his pocket, he saw the woman's reflection in the window as she glanced toward the back of the store. In his best broken Spanish, Joe said he needed to speak with Miguel. It was urgent. He wrote the name of his hotel on the back of his business card.

Back in his room, Joe stared at himself in the bathroom mirror. He looked tired. He felt tired. Sleep was coming in small parcels on an irregular delivery schedule these days. Upon waking, his mind would instantly begin to race, scouring the surface of his imagination for some path forward. One thing that he could say was that finding a human head in your trunk has a way of focusing one's attention. When he and Allison were in New York, it seemed they lived in a perpetual near future, a place not tomorrow but not 10 years from now either. These days, he didn't seem to think much beyond the current moment. Maybe that was good.

He remembered the box he'd been given at the front desk. He took it to the bed. Who knew he was there other than his mom and Alan, their irascible accountant? Opening the package revealed another box, and a note: "Cubbie, you need to be properly provisioned for this project you're embarking on. Lucky for you I'm a helper. Namaste, Leon. P.S. Go talk to customs. Ask for Señor Quiñones." Fucking Leon. Joe retrieved the smaller box and opened it to find a small bag populated by a dozen tightly rolled joints. He'd said it before, but everyone needs a Leon.

Joe laid down and promptly fell asleep. When he awoke, his phone told him it was after 2 p.m. He wanted to get to the customs office before it closed. He didn't know how Leon knew someone in the customs office in Puerto Vallarta, Mexico, but he didn't know a lot of things about Leon.

At Gustavo Díaz Ordaz International Airport, it took Joe a few minutes to get clear directions to Señor Quiñones. As he saw new streams of eager tourists pushing their luggage carts into the arrivals area, he realized that after just a few days in town, he felt a bit like a local.

After some searching, Joe found the customs office at the end of a long hallway. Señor Quiñones stood, came out from behind his desk, and extended his hand to Joe. "You must be Señor Lily," the man said. "Leon said you might come."

"He did, did he?" Joe said, shaking his head. "What doesn't Leon know?"

Señor Quiñones smiled. "So it is," he said. He looked to be in his late 50s, with a graying mustache, but retaining a head of thick black hair. He wore his glasses at the end of his nose, giving him altogether the appearance of an avuncular college counselor. Something about the man was familiar too, but Joe couldn't place it.

"I met Leon many years ago," Señor Quiñones said. "The memories are ... hazy."

"That sounds about right," Joe said.

"Leon is, what do I say? My family are farmers and I would say that he is full of fertilizer."

Joe laughed. "Yes, though he would tell you the most beautiful flowers come from it."

"Sí, sí," Señor Quiñones said. "But I am sorry to say that I am on my way out of town. I must go to Mexico City. I'm afraid I will not have time to discuss your situation. I hope you will accept my sincere apologies. I don't know what can be done about your predicament, but I know time is an issue. So I have asked my colleague to help. Let me ..." He raised a finger and then punched a few numbers into the phone.

"Buenas tardes. Sí," he said. "Esta aqui. Gracias." He hung up.

"Please," he said, pointing to a seat. "It will be just a moment."

Joe took a seat. He was trying to remain optimistic about the proceedings. When it became clear Leon had laid some groundwork for him, he had begun to get his hopes up that there might actually be a solution.

Señor Quiñones sighed heavily. "The times, they are tough in Mexico these days," he said. "So many killings. So many. Innocent people. And in the process, the cartels, they are also killing the country. It is very sad for Mexico." And he did seem genuinely upset. "Ah, yes," he said, standing.

Joe reflexively did the same, all of sudden turning to find himself face to face with the young woman whose purse he had returned a couple of days earlier.

"This is my colleague, Veronica Espinosa. She will help to see if there's anything we can do about your situation. If anyone can make it happen, it is Veronica."

And Joe believed it. Dressed in a fitted dark-blue skirt and cropped jacket with a black blouse decorated in small white flowers, she changed the weather in the room. The surprise made him dumb.

"We've actually met," Joe said.

At virtually the same instant they both said: "La Palapa." Joe realized that was why he recognized Señor Quiñones as well.

"A pleasure to see you again," she said.

"Igualmente," Joe said.

She turned to Señor Quiñones, who was understandably a bit perplexed. "When we had our team dinner," she said. "I forgot my purse and Mr.—" She turned to Joe.

"Lily. Joe Lily," Joe said.

"Señor Lily kindly returned it to me."

"¿Cómo se dice 'gallant'?" Joe said.

She smiled. "Sí, muy galante."

"Well, then it would seem that I'm leaving you both in good hands," said Señor Quiñones. "Now, I am sorry, but I really must go. At least I'm already at the airport. ¿Verdad? Veronica, do you need anything more from me?"

Veronica shook her head.

"OK. So very nice to meet you, Mr. Lily. Sorry I cannot stay. Good luck."

The two men shook hands and then Veronica led Joe down the hall to her small office. Joe stopped at a picture on the wall showing Veronica and a group of others standing with former Mexican president, Felipe Calderón.

"We had such hope for him," she said. "Finally, someone was going to do something about the corruption and the drugs."

"It didn't work out that way?"

59

"Not exactly. Some might say it made it worse. I think it showed that one man can't do much to fix a system that has been in place for so long and makes so many people rich."

"If the US would stop buying their product, that would help."

"Yes," she said. "But the cartels have diversified now. They are learning the lessons from corrupt business, from the mafia. It's not just drugs anymore. They're in construction, oil, banking. They have even taken over the tortilla business in some places."

"Tortillas?" he asked.

She smiled. "It's true. Tortillas. I'm afraid today it's hard to know where government, business, and the cartels separate. They are all mixed up like a bowl of pico de gallo."

"But don't you work for the government?"

"Por favor," she gestured to the chair facing her desk and then sat. "I do, yes. And so do my parents actually. Both of them. So maybe I can say there are two governments. There is the one made of people who see it as a way to serve others. And then one with people who see the job as a way to serve themselves."

The thought took Joe right back to Wall Street. He wondered if anyone could say there were two Wall Streets. He knew of just the one.

"Perhaps that sounds naive to you," she offered.

"Not at all," he said. "It sounds astute." He knew well enough how easily one could mistake selfish ends for magnanimous ones. That turned out to be his father-in-law through and through.

She gave him a long look, not exactly smiling but seeming to see him clearly for the first time.

"But the question is," he added, "can one of those governments help me get my stuff back?"

Veronica Espinosa smiled and laid her hands flat on the desk, her red nail polish popping on the dark wood. "Sí," she declared. "Sí. I've already—"

The desk phone interrupted them. "Excuse me," she said.

Picking up the receiver, she spoke in a different voice, this one a firm, clear, declarative Spanish. Joe liked the way she said her name when answering: V-row-neek-a. She turned her brown eyes on him as she spoke, suggesting to Joe that the call might have something to do with his sequestered items.

After a few moments of back and forth, conversation that Joe couldn't follow, she replaced the receiver. "That was actually the office of the

60

man who has your items. I contacted them this morning after Enrique asked me to look into the situation. Unfortunately, I'm afraid I don't have an answer for you yet. The good news is they haven't said no. As you know, your situation is … complicated. The police are involved and that is difficult. But he assured me that he understood your situation and would see what could be done."

Joe tried not to convey his disappointment. Against his better judgment, he had allowed himself to hope. But he didn't want Veronica to think that he held her in any way responsible.

"I understand. I know it's a long shot. They found a head in my trunk. I get that that is going to complicate things."

She shook her head at his incorrigibility. "Yes. But we'll keep working on it. In fact, if you will give me just one moment, I want to check something with my colleague."

"Of course," he said. He now doubted these efforts would amount to much, but anything that kept him in her company seemed to him worth exploring.

"OK, I'll be right back." She stood and smoothed the front of her skirt. "Sometimes," she said, "it can help to have these conversations in person." She smiled again, and they both understood.

Just as she left Joe's phone began to ring. It was Alan, his accountant. He couldn't put this conversation off any longer.

"Alan," Joe said.

"You avoid me at your own peril, Joe," Alan said.

"I haven't been avoiding you. I've just run into a little … complication down here. Sorry. What's up?"

"It's not what's up, it's what's down, and the answer is every fucking thing to do with this business. I've been calling to inform you that on top of the other shit, you are now being sued."

"Sued? By who?"

"One George Lansdowne. Your beloved father-in-law. I don't need to tell you that this is not what we need right now."

Joe closed his eyes, rubbed his temples. "OK. I guess I should have expected this. That's how they play. I just figured she … I'll figure something out."

"They're fucking parasites. Despicable, soulless, opportunistic assholes. They think that the greatest expression of one's skill and intellect is to use it to make money. Greed is good. It makes me want to vomit. And how in the hell you ever found yourself among them, it's, it's …"

"Yeah, OK, OK, I get it. I understand," Joe said, glancing up to find Veronica standing there, her eyes fixed on him now with a serious expression. He tried to smile but couldn't make it work and instead just looked away.

Alan continued. "It's a disgrace that you let yourself be duped by them. A fucking waste and a disgrace. And what's your reward? The assholes for whom you made all this money, they are suing you because you called them on their shit. You turned off the money spigot. But you can't *ever* turn off the money spigot."

"Yeah," Joe said. He held his hand over the phone. "Sorry, almost done," he assured Veronica.

"So the question is," Alan went on, "what are you going to do about it? Right? How are you going to respond?"

"I don't know," Joe said. "That's the thing. I'm working out some details, or trying to, and it's just, it's gotten complicated."

"Let this happen and it will destroy you and your mother. Do you understand what I'm saying?"

"I'm really sorry, Alan. I'm afraid I've got to run. I'll give you a call as soon as I know more from this end. Thank you for checking in. I really appreciate it. I'll be in touch very soon." Joe hung up.

At first, he couldn't quite bring himself to look at Veronica.

"Sorry about that," he said.

"It's fine," she said. "Is everything OK?"

Joe felt oddly disembodied, as if he were drifting in the room as a witness, his actual body sitting below, slightly hunched at the shoulders, hands limply collected in his lap.

"I should've taken that outside."

She gave him a stern look. "No," she said. "I should've given you some privacy."

Joe waved that off.

And then before he quite knew he was doing it, he found himself talking about his father.

"My dad died almost a year ago. He was getting his hair cut. Same place he'd gone every other week for 30 years. But this time his heart just decided to quit. Right in the chair. Can you believe that? He wasn't necessarily the healthiest guy in the world, but he'd always been strong as an ox. So much energy. Always doing something. It just, we just didn't see it coming. It was like an explosion. Like a bomb had gone off. And we were the survivors of the explosion. We shuffled around like robots. Hearing nothing, feeling nothing.

My dad, he was just one of those people who made stuff happen. You know what I mean? He had this, this gravitational pull that kept things in orbit in our world. The business, why I'm down here, it was his business. He built it. He loved it and took care of it. For as long as I can remember, it was the fourth member of our family. And now it looks like it's going to take me about a year to destroy this thing it took him a lifetime to build." Joe shook his head.

When he saw tears in Veronica's eyes, he concluded he'd said enough.

"Can I take you to dinner?" he asked impulsively. "Let me take you to dinner. What do you say?"

She smiled weakly, wiped the tears from her cheeks, and nodded.

Veronica grabbed her things and the two exited a rear door, avoiding the throngs in arrivals. Veronica said she knew the spot, if his back was up to it. Joe assured her he was ready to go wherever she wanted to take him. So she drove them south, around the downtown on the wide periférico, or peripheral road. They traveled through the first of Puerto Vallarta's two tunnels. Traffic was heavy. Before they reached the second tunnel that leads into Old Town, she turned off the highway onto a cobbled street and then some distance farther on she turned again, this time onto a dirt road.

"You know it's wrong to rob a guy with a failing antiques business, right?"

"Hold on, it gets a little bumpy here," she said.

They drove up a winding, rain-rutted track that bounced them around inside the car. They were both laughing. When they finally reached the top of the hill, Veronica pulled into a small dirt parking area next to a sign that read Las Carmelitas. Joe found himself on this beautiful eyrie removed from the bustle and heat below. The simple, open-air restaurant looked out over Banderas Bay, the coastline embroidered in a frill of crashing waves. They ordered margaritas and watched the sun spill itself in roses and umbers and brilliant oranges across the horizon.

As they sat, Joe asked her about her life and family, her work. Her divorce. They ate grilled prawns and spicy arrachera. When the stars appeared, and it got chilly, the waiter brought them heavy woven blankets that they wrapped around their shoulders and draped over their legs. Out in the distance the fishing boats looked like stars.

On the bumpy drive back down, they left the windows open so they could hear the cicadas and the frogs and smell the cooling earth. It seemed to Joe that they had traveled very far away, far enough to forget for a moment about heads in trunks and a business teetering on the brink.

As they pulled up in front of Hotel Mercurio, Veronica said, "This is your hotel?"

"Yes," Joe said. "My dad used to stay here when he came down. We stayed once on a family vacation too. A long time ago."

She leaned across him to peer into the foyer. At the check-in desk, Javier flipped idly through a magazine. Farther on in the pool area, beneath the strings of lights, people sat drinking in the small bar.

Veronica sat back and then looked at Joe. "Something you want to tell me?" she asked.

"No. I don't think so. I mean, I wanted to tell you to come in for a nightcap, but I hadn't gotten to that yet."

Her face broke into a wide, mischievous smile.

"What?" he asked.

"Well, this is a gay hotel," she asked. "You didn't notice?"

Joe's eyes shot back to the entry. Looking beyond the bricked arch and into the pool area, it was all suddenly clear in one embarrassing flash of understanding. The bar was, in fact, all men. He traced his memory and had to admit that since arriving he hadn't seen a single woman beyond those on the cleaning staff.

"I thought the wives were shopping."

Veronica descended into glorious peels of girlish laughter. "Well," she said, "How about we go to my place?"

By 10 a.m., the demonstration was already well under way at the Tianguis Central, the Saturday market. In the plaza, on a makeshift stage, a man shouted into a microphone and pointed down the coast. Over his dress shirt he wore a T-shirt that bore a drawing of an oil derrick with a slash through it. Wide sweat circles radiated out from his armpits. Through a tinny PA system, he inveighed against multinational rapaciousness, the US, what he called a new era of colonialism.

The audience cheered and whistled. They pumped their fists and jabbed their signs into the cloudless sky, chanting: "¡Sin fractura hidráulica en Jalisco!" No fracking in Jalisco!

Darrell stood to the side and took in the spectacle. He loved this about Mexico, that a walk back to the office after an errand could mean stumbling onto a demonstration, a parade, a religious rite. In the US, Darrell could not reframe the facts of his life to be anything other than a crater in the ground: failed businessman, failed husband, failed father. An utterly forgettable record. He knew that when he died, when the last breath had escaped his body, memory of him would disappear with it. But not so in Mexico.

The old Darrell Haddock had been relinquished at the border. Here the math was different, and when he calculated his measure, he added up to something. Co-owner of a very successful business. Country club member. Competitive fisherman. He counted the well heeled and the well connected as peers. He owned a goddamned speedboat for crying out loud. And now, now he'd set into motion the next phase, one that would push him still higher. No more deferring to his partner. No more following someone else's lead. A.J. didn't think big enough, that was his failing. He didn't have the courage, the heart, the fight. If Darrell had to leave him behind, well, that was life in the jungle.

Somewhere in the crowd, a young woman kept the chant going into a bullhorn: "¡Sin frac-tur-a! ¡Sin frac-tur-a!" It didn't take long before the crowd took up the chant. The man on the stage held the microphone in the pit of his arm while he clapped in unison. "¡Sin frac-tur-a!"

Joe and Veronica had finally fallen asleep in the luminous hours of very early morning. The night had been both a lifetime and the blink of an eye. That is the contradiction of such moments, when after having been alone for a time and perhaps wondering if you won't be alone forever, you lay together with another, limbs mixed up under the sheets, feet running deliciously over feet, and you wonder if the other reality, the one without that person, wasn't in fact just a passing fever.

Veronica lived east of downtown a few miles. Her brother, an architect, had designed the small but elegant townhouse. It was narrow and vertically nestled amongst the branches of a cluster of jacarandas like the most incredible tree house. Joe loved its large windows, its ceiling of rugged beams, and especially the broad cantilevered sliders that when opened turned the living room into a large patio.

They had drunk wine. They had huddled amidst the blankets and pillows on the couch, watching the dots of light from distant boats, and it made them feel even closer, even warmer and happier and luckier that they were not lost out in the black of the midnight Pacific. She introduced him to the Mexican composer Manuel Ponce, whose piano concerto floated in the evening air like songs brought in on the breeze.

It all had unfolded slowly. He sensed she needed it to be that way. She leaned into him and he used his own hands to record the smoothness of her bare shoulders, the shiver it gave her when his hands moved under her long hair to her neck, the beat of her heart as she drew his arms around her, wrapping her from behind.

"I don't do this," she said, her voice hushed.

"Lay on the couch and look at the stars?" he said. "You should. It's good for you."

She lay back against him, holding his arms holding her. Her hair touched his skin at the open neck of his shirt. It smelled like roses. He kissed her neck and she arched her head just as a cat might, letting go a slow, low exhalation. She turned to face him, supremely relaxed, her lips parted slightly. Then she stopped, and a cloud passed over her brown eyes.

"What is it?" he asked.

"I don't do this," she said again, this time a whisper. She leaned over him, her shoulders peaked, her neck gloriously long, her blouse hanging open.

"It's good to try new things," he said. And he pulled her down onto him and they tumbled over each other. Couch to floor to bedroom, where it smelled like her rose perfume. Everything tilted. Joe disappeared into her and left everything else behind.

Joe awoke to a fresh breeze from the open window. The curtains undulated like the surface of water. The room was all gossamer light. Mornings in Mexico. He realized he was alone. Veronica's clothes still lay over the arm of the chair in the corner. The evening came back to him in brilliant snapshots. He was about to get up when Veronica entered the sunny room. She stood before him smiling, parts of her naked body going from shadow to light with the movement of the curtains.

"Buenos días," she said. She carried two cups of coffee. "You're awake." She handed him a cup and climbed back into bed, apologizing that she had an appointment that morning. "I can take you to the hotel."

"It's not necessary."

"I like to drive all the men I sleep with home. It's the least I can do."

"I'll make sure to give you a good Yelp review," he said.

Out on the street, the rest of Puerto Vallarta was long awake. They joined the slow progress of the other cars and buses and motorcycles heading toward the city center. Joe stared out at the shops, the owners here and there out sweeping the sidewalk. Kids in their school uniforms walked in small groups.

The traffic was thick, and by the time they neared Viejo Vallarta, everything had slowed to a crawl. Cars barely inched forward. On the sidewalks, people with signs moved with purpose toward some destination that was still out of view.

"What's going on?" Joe asked.

Veronica shook her head. "I don't know. Looks like maybe some kind of demonstration?"

On Calle Insurgentes, they creeped forward. Cars honked. Busses shuddered in idle, spewing out acrid exhaust. She tried cutting down Aquiles Serdan only to find more traffic.

Veronica rolled down her window and yelled to a group moving briskly down the street toward the small plaza. They shouted back. She rolled the window back up. "It's against some mining company."

"Mining?"

She shrugged. "That's what he said. Down the coast."

Veronica turned down Calle Vallarta. With the window down, you could now hear the echo of a megaphone, its message bouncing around the buildings. As they got closer to the beach, the crowds grew thicker. One person carried a sign that read: ¡Sin fractura hidráulica en Jalisco!

By the time they reached Calle Carranza, traffic had all but stopped.

"I think this is as far as we're going," she said.

The noise from the demonstration had grown louder. A megaphone voice followed by the rumble of others shouting and chanting.

He put his hand on the door handle. "Thank you."

"It was my pleasure. The Mexican customs office, we're full service."

Joe laughed and exited the car.

She rolled the passenger window down. "We still must figure out about your antiques."

"I'd almost forgotten about them."

"Can you call me later?"

"Try and stop me," he said.

She smiled. He tapped the top of the car. She waved and turned onto Calle Carranza. The sun beat down, and after the AC inside the car, the heat made Joe shiver. Suddenly, he found himself among a buzzing crowd. Over in the plaza, on a small stage, a woman had taken over the microphone. It reminded Joe of the Occupy protests in Zuccotti Park just as his New York life was crashing and burning.

As Joe worked his way toward Olas Altas, traveling at the perimeter of the crowd, he spotted amongst the throngs a face he recognized. It took a minute to place it, but as he got closer he realized it was Darrell Haddock from Molly's office. He looked calm and relaxed like he was simply taking in some street musician. Yesterday at the Banderas office it had been a very different Darrell. He'd burst out of Molly's father's office, red faced, eyes flashing. What had he said to Molly? "Your father is a fucking liar and an asshole."?

Joe approached and Darrell nodded. "You got to love Mexico," he said, voice raised for the din.

Joe took in the spectacle. "Is this a regular sort of thing?"

Darrell shrugged. "Yeah, pretty regular. For being, I don't know, pretty quiet people, they do love to get out and make a racket sometimes." He checked his phone and returned it to his pocket.

The bullhorn drowned them out for a beat, and then Darrell extended his hand. "You were at Banderas yesterday. Darrell Haddock."

"I was," Joe said. "Joe Lily."

"Sorry we didn't get a chance to meet properly. A little bit of chaos yesterday."

"Really? I didn't notice," Joe said.

"Bullshit." Darrell exited the thick of the crowd and Joe followed. They found a patch of shade beneath a small tree at the perimeter of the plaza.

"It's a total cluster over there these days," Darrell said. "Sorry you had to step into it."

Joe waved it off, but wanted to keep Darrell talking. "Every office has its days," he said. "I'll bet it's no small thing running a successful business in Mexico, especially with a partner."

Darrell made a face. "It's not a partnership when one is fucking lying to the other one. That's not how being partners works."

Joe kept his eyes fixed on Darrell. "Damn. I'm sorry to hear that."

"I got him started in this goddamn business. He landed here and didn't know which way was up. He was just another fuck-up escaping to Mexico."

"You must have taught him well. Seems like the business is doing great."

"It is. But he's forgotten how we got here." He shook his head. Color had come into his face. He worked his teeth against each other. "And now he thinks he knows better. *He's* the dealmaker. But you can't treat people like that forever without it costing you. Ah, never mind. Why am I going on?"

"Man, I'm sorry. I can imagine having challenges with your partner would get pretty tiresome."

"Yeah. Well, just remember what they say, 'Vallarta is a sunny town full of shady people.' That's all I'll say about that."

A.J. turned his car off of the highway and drove up a rutted dirt track. The road veered left then right, which, by design or good luck, took him out of the sight line of passing cars on the main road.

Given recent developments, and the quickly approaching groundbreaking of his biggest project yet, he needed confirmation. He needed support. A.J. had done his part, but Garza had to do his. What was A.J. paying him for otherwise? It certainly wasn't his personality. The man had an annoyingly grandiose image of himself, perhaps ladling on one too many scoops of machismo. He borrowed the slow, deliberate gait of a movie gunslinger. In his boots, jeans, and signature white cowboy hat, he looked the part too. He even copied the broad handlebar mustache of Mexican renegade Francisco "Pancho" Villa. At his open shirt collar hung the cross of his faith, and he spoke with all the grumbled gravitas of a stock TV lawman.

After years of working in Mexico, A.J. had come to understand that everyone in law enforcement had connections, but Garza's had seemed limitless. When the deal and the ultimate plan for the property had begun, he'd been able to quickly get A.J. to the right people. Almost within days, doors that had been closed miraculously opened. Garza was quick to remind A.J. that it was no different in Los Estados Unidos. Politicians took their opportunities where they found them. Hell, recent Supreme

Court decisions brazenly conceded that elections were openly bought and sold anyway. Americans call it the free market, Garza said. But that meant free to take advantage. If others didn't exploit every loophole and opportunity, well, that was on them.

A.J. parked next to Garza's truck and got out.

"Buenos días," said A.J.

Garza nodded.

A.J. looked around and seeing only their two vehicles, asked, "So, when are they coming?"

"¿Quién?"

"Whoever. The person you set this meeting up with."

Garza adjusted his hat. "This is the meeting." It was always this way with Garza. Speaking in riddles. At first, A.J. thought the man simply lacked a command of English. But it became clear that he either preferred to or could not help but communicate in a way that always hid part of his meaning or its implications out of view. The more he spoke, the more elusive his message became.

"What are you talking about?" A.J. said. It was already hot. He felt the sweat tracing his spine to his beltline. He was not in the mood for this.

"I am here," Garza said.

"But your friend's also coming, right?"

"He would never meet us here," Garza said.

A.J. was already exasperated. "Then what the hell are we doing?"

Garza spat in the dirt. "Step into the shade, Antony. Mucho calor." From the first, the man had for some reason referred to A.J. by his first name. No one had called him that since he was a child.

"Look, sheriff, we're about ready to launch this. You said your friends are behind it, correct?"

"Sí," the sheriff said.

"And you said that we would seal that commitment today, correct?"

"Sí."

"But the person we are making the agreement with would never meet us here?"

"Sí."

"So what the fuck are we doing here? Be clear. Be as clear about this as you were about the money!"

Garza had been leaning against the hood of his truck. Now he stepped forward. He dropped his hand to his sidearm and pulled it from the

70

holster. A.J. knew that these men weren't his friends. Use them, but don't trust them. And unless you're tired of living, don't go straight at them.

Garza raised the pistol. "I will be clear."

"Hold on now," A.J. said, placing his hands before him.

The sheriff took aim at A.J.

"Whoa." A.J. raised his hands. "Come on. I was just…"

Garza fired twice. Pop! Pop! A tree branch behind A.J. exploded in a shower of splintered wood. The reports clapped off the nearby hills.

A.J. covered his head with hands.

"¿Claro?"

"OK, OK!"

Garza cracked a wry smile.

A.J. never wondered about the choices he made to build his business. He did not suffer as some do from a whispering conscience or nagging uncertainty. He believed sincerely that those who became great—great businessmen, great leaders, great whatever it was—at some point had to put themselves first to put themselves ahead. Plenty of smart, talented people found themselves suddenly at the rear of the train for having waited for someone else to invite them aboard.

Still, there were times, like now, when he wondered at the wisdom of certain alliances, certain choices. He would have to think about that. In the meantime, he would have to keep his eyes open and treat the sheriff with a greater reserve.

Garza holstered his gun, adjusted his hat. "Antony," he said, "these men? They are serious. Serious like death."

A.J. turned and walked back to the car. He snatched the map he'd brought and laid it out on the warm hood of the car. "Are we done with the lesson?" He smoothed the map with both hands as if trying to clear the murky water of a shallow pool enough to see the bottom.

Garza did not move, his hand resting on his holstered weapon. He gestured up the hill. "My grandparents, they used to live back there. Farmers. They had nothing. A hard life. So difficult. But they were happy. My brothers and sisters, we would go there. And my abuela, she always cooked for us. She made the best rollos de guayaba. Do you know rollos de guayaba? In the winter, we would get so cold at night, I remember. We all slept together next to the stove." He shook his head.

A.J. was only half listening. He was not one for looking back.

"Show me on the map," A.J. said.

Garza exited his momentary daydream and came to stand next to the timeshare developer who had promised to make him rich, who had already bought him this new truck. He tipped his hat back to review the map.

A.J. said, "Your grandparents didn't have many choices back then. But just think of the opportunities the people in this area will have now. Better jobs, better roads, better water and electricity, better schools. Better everything. It will improve their lives. Maybe their grandkids won't have to sleep on the floor."

Sheriff Garza straightened. He smoothed his mustache. "That's what you Americans don't understand," he said. "Progress is progress. But sleeping by the stove together, that is life."

A hot breeze blew the map off the hood and onto the ground.

The pool area at Hotel Mercurio was already abuzz. Men of every color and age. Joe wondered how in the world he could possibly unravel the situation he found himself in when he couldn't even see that there wasn't a single woman staying in his hotel. He was glad that his accountant, Alan, had not witnessed his obtuseness. He would never hear the end of it.

It was Friday. Joe had expected to be back in Portland by now. His mother had expected that too. And that same accountant. But his conversation with Darrell at the protest only confirmed that there might be some explanation for all that had happened, some knot he could untie that would free his stuff. He had to see it through. Joe sat at the pool bar with a Pacifico when he spotted Molly at the front desk and watched her move briskly through the short breezeway.

Molly exuded an air of physical confidence as she moved. She wore a pair of crisp shorts and a sleeveless top decorated in yellow flowers. On her head she sported a headband of a matching color that kept her hair pulled back and out of her face. She looked put together and pretty. He could imagine her on her college campus walking across the quad to class.

"I'm afraid I'm not interested in buying a timeshare," he said.

"Ha." She sat down across from him, glanced about, and then leaned in, "Why didn't you tell me you're gay? You didn't need to hide that."

"I only just realized that, if you can believe it. I guess I didn't read the website well enough. They've accepted me as one of their own."

"I'll bet they have," she said. Her high cheekbones and angular features made an attractive frame for her broad smile.

"I was in the neighborhood at a meeting," she said. "I hope you don't mind that I just dropped in. I learned something interesting today about my fiancé. I thought maybe it could help you get your stuff out of hock."

"Please." He gestured toward a chair. "Something to drink?"

She sat. "No thanks, I'm good. It's the least I can do after you helped me the other day at the shop. I was in quite a state. Plus, you know, in a weird way I feel responsible for your things getting commandeered."

"That's crazy talk," Joe said.

She exhaled and looked at her hands. "I forget sometimes and just can't believe it's real."

Joe let the silence sit. And then said, "Sure I can't get you something?"

"No, but thank you. I can't stay. I just wanted to tell you that I've learned that Cesar did have something of an online life I didn't really know about."

"An online life?"

"He was a part of some kind of, I don't know, internet club. I don't even do Facebook. But I guess they were sort of an anticartel group. I read some stuff Cesar wrote and it's all about the gangs. Especially this local one, Los Primeros. I don't know if you've heard of them. One of the girls in the office translated it for me. Pretty harsh stuff. He talked about how they were murderers and a cancer that's killing Mexico and that the people need to rise up and take back the country. Stuff I've never heard him talk about."

"You had no idea?"

She shook her head. "No, we never talked about anything like that. We talked about the shop. About his asshole landlord, my dad, you know, stupid stuff. He never mentioned the cartels or this group or anything like that."

"How did you find all this out?"

"Well, when I met you that first time at the shop? I was looking for anything I could find that might explain what happened. Why someone would do that to him. I found some papers. Most were just bills and receipts or whatever, but these seemed important maybe. I wish there were more, but it's only a few pages."

She retrieved a brown file folder from her purse and handed it to Joe.

73

"Cesar is gone. But there's nothing anyone can do to bring him back. If I can help your situation, that would make me happy."

"I really appreciate that," Joe said.

Tears had welled in Molly's eyes. "I'm sorry. And I'm so sorry you had to be involved in this."

Joe said, "The antiques business isn't for sissies."

Molly managed a weak smile.

"Oh, by the way, I ran into your colleague," Joe said.

"My colleague?"

"Darrell," Joe said.

"Darrell." She shook her head. "Poor Darrell. Sorry you had to endure that ridiculous scene at the office. He's, well, let's just say he's not the brightest bulb on the string."

"I saw him at the protest on the plaza in Old Town. Haven't they been partners for years?

"Those two," she said, shaking her head. "They're like an old married couple. I think Darrell knows my dad is why the company is doing well and he resents it. Anyway, I'm sorry, I've got to run. Thank you for letting me barge in on you."

"Thank you. It was nice of you to stop by. And thank you for this." He tapped the folder.

Molly grasped his hand as she stood. "Good luck with everything, Joe." And then took herself purposefully across the pool deck and out into the sunshine.

Joe took up the loose pages Molly had left. At first, he couldn't make heads or tails of them. And then he realized it was the transcript from what looked to be an online forum. The contributors all went by screen names: gorrión, elmago, C-dope, payaso. His phone told him that "gorrión" means "sparrow," "elmago" translates to "the magician," and "payaso" is "clown." And "c-dope." C for Cesar?

elmago: the way to change things is to fucking shout it.
c-dope: who gave you the right to do that?
c-dope: who said you could act on your own?
c-dope: we don't do that
elmago: who died and made you fucking king?
c-dope: you don't get it. we have no head, no face.
c-dope: our power is being shapeless. Orchestrate, coordinate, strike.
elmago: bullshit

c-dope: you betrayed everyone here
elmago: we need to focus on frak/op, we can do something there.
elmago: messing with the cartel is stupid
elmago: that'll just get you killed
c-dope: the cartels are a disease, a cancer and they must be stopped
c-dope: and if the police won't do it, we will
elmago: you're going to bring down los primeros? By doxxing them?
c-dope: that's just one part of the campaign
payaso: and it's not just us. it's growing!!
elmago: you're not going to hurt the cartels. not going to happen.
elmago: but companies, oil companies. yes. they have to play by the rules. Makes them vulnerable.
c-dope: we've got plans for them too
c-dope: but los fantasmas is a black box
c-dope: we strike and disappear
elmago: we have to use the media!
elmago: get our story out there, put pressure on
elmago: that's how it works
c-dope: not for us
c-dope: you can't fight us because you can't find us
payaso: ghosts of mayhem!
elmago: bullshit. we need to engage, not run and hide
elmago: like subcomandante marcos and the zapatistas
elmago: julian assange and wikileaks
c-dope: julian assange? really? the fucker is trapped in the Ecuadorian embassy.
payaso: look what happened to them
elmago: our campaigns need someone to take charge, to get out there
payaso: you talk publicly and you put a target on our heads
elmago: fucking right, that's why it's powerful
elmago: no pussying out
gorrión: seems risky. especially with los primeros.
c-dope: exactly
elmago: forget los primeros!
elmago: corporations! we hit the greedy corporations. like this fucking American oil company.
elmago: but you have to use the press, just like they do
gorrión: i thought it was a pretty good interview
gorrión: sorry, c-dope

elmago: gracias
c-dope: we're not the fucking zapatistas!
elmago: true enough, my brother
elmago: but we should be
elmago: and we will be
c-dope: not if you want me to participate

Chapter 5

Archivaldo Ríos waited. The man had said Archivaldo would receive a call when it was time. When this whole thing had started, they had given him a cell phone. The instructions were clear: never make any calls on the phone unless instructed. Its job—and his—was to *receive* calls. When it rang yesterday afternoon, it was only the third time he had had to answer it. The man on the other end had told him that a car would come for him the following morning. He was to be ready. He was not told the purpose or destination of the trip.

That night he'd been too anxious to sleep. He'd tossed and turned and had finally given up, spending most of the night online. Was something wrong? Had he failed in some way he couldn't see? His fretful mind lurched from one possibility to another.

In the morning, he showered and waited. The house was empty except for the cat, who would normally sit with Archivaldo, but this morning stayed away. Archivaldo worked to ignore the voice in his head that urged him to run. Go, it yelled. Get out of town. But where would he go? The truth was, these people were like death itself—they cannot be run from.

At 9 a.m. a dark SUV pulled up in front, its windows tinted. It idled there for a moment and then his phone rang. It was time. Archivaldo stood, took a deep breath, and walked outside. At the car, he was patted down and then directed to a spot in the empty middle row. A man in sunglasses sat in the very back. The first man jumped into the passenger seat next to the driver. Archivaldo didn't recognize the men and none spoke to introduce themselves. They slowly drove on, out of the neighborhood, through town, and into the surrounding countryside.

The man in the passenger seat turned on the radio. Softly, absently, he sang along with the music: Sonaron siete balazos, Camelia a Emilio mataba, la policía sólo halló una pistola tirada/Del dinero y de Camelia, nunca más se supo nada. Seven shots rang out, Camelia killed Emilio, the police only found a pistol cast aside/Of the money and Camelia, nothing more was ever known.

The vehicle climbed for a time, passing through a small village seemingly all but empty save for an old man leading a desolate-looking burro. They drove on into open country, which they traveled through for what felt to Archivaldo like a long time. At length, they turned off and came to a crude gate. One of two men sitting in the shade of a nearby tree rose and lifted the wooden arm, letting Archivaldo's vehicle pass and proceed up a long, winding dirt driveway to a small house. The house, a simple ranch with a shaded porch, sat on a handsome bluff by itself, overlooking a sea of sage and scrub and saguaro. A man appeared at Archivaldo's door and opened it. He patted Archivaldo down again and then directed him up the steps of the house to its covered patio.

Archivaldo didn't know this place. He wasn't sure he'd ever even seen the road that they had driven on to get there. What could this be about? Given what had happened, perhaps Archivaldo was no longer needed. The situation had changed. He wasn't exactly sure by whose hand, but it had changed after the murder. Wasn't that all they had wanted? But if he was no longer needed, couldn't they have told him that on the phone? Why bring him all the way out here? A warm breeze moved up the hill and found the porch, bringing with it the smell of dry, hot earth.

The two men at the gate had returned to the shade and Archivaldo could see that beside them lay two rifles. Just then another man appeared on the porch, the screen door slapping the jamb behind him. Archivaldo quickly spotted the gun in his belt. He motioned for Archivaldo to follow him. Again, he was patted down.

"Weapons?" the man said.

"No," he said.

The man led him inside where he found a rotund man dressed in a track outfit sitting before a television playing CNN on low volume.

His eyes not moving from the TV, the man said, "Mr. Ríos, you're on time. Time is the only currency that always holds its value. Did you know that? Have a seat."

Still without breaking his concentration on the TV he said, "B, where is my shake! How long does it take to make a fucking shake? Fruit. Ice. Blender!"

The man who had led Archivaldo into the house turned and left the room.

The boss finally turned from the TV. "Eat or be eaten," he said apropos of what Archivaldo didn't know. "You married, Señor Ríos?"

Archivaldo shook his head. "No."

"Well, marriage is a beautiful thing. Beautiful. Don't let anyone tell you different. I believe in it so much I've done it four fucking times. This one, she's gorgeous, and a big-hearted girl. She wants me to eat better. I told her she'll never meet anyone who is a better eater than me!" He grabbed his considerable stomach. "But she's got me on this shake diet. Shakes. When she first said it, I thought, 'Just shakes? Now that's a goddamned diet I can support.' But it's not *shakes*, is it? Not the kind we like, Señor Ríos. These have got shit in them like, I don't know, spinach and seeds and tree branches. But she thinks I need to try it, so I do it for her. It makes her happy. We want to make them happy, right? And what the fuck, I do feel better. I won't lie. More energy. Calmer. I'm calmer, wouldn't you say, A? What's he going to say? Let's get you a shake too, Archie. A, get one for Mr. Ríos. You'll thank me. Plus, here's the other thing. I don't know why, but it really fucking gets her going. Seriously. Those fucking shakes are like a goddamn aphrodisiac. She's on me like a fucking chupacabra. For that, I'll drink them every day. Every goddamn day. Isn't that right, A?"

The man smiled.

Archivaldo understood it was his turn to speak, but he didn't know what to say. He managed only, "What does the 'A' stand for?"

The lieutenant remained silent, letting his boss answer.

"A, it's the letter that comes before B. Don't tell me you've got the brain damage, Archie. We'll have to take you out and dump you with the pigs. Doesn't matter what it fucking stands for. The guy that let you in the door? He's B. C is down with the car. I treat my guys right, but I don't give a shit about their names. Who cares? They work for me because I treat them right. And I don't have to worry about learning a fucking new name every time. Life can be short in this business. Isn't that right, A?"

"Yes, sir," he said.

"There you go."

On the TV, garish graphics showed a falling NASDAQ. The man stared at it for a long moment before pinching up his round face like a baby who is about to cry. "Turn it off! Fucking turn it off!"

The one called A produced the remote and clicked the TV to black. His boss continued to gesture at the now dark screen. "I'm just bleeding money. Right now, as we sit here, money is just melting into thin fucking air. It's going to give me a goddamn heart attack."

A long silence followed. Archivaldo sat quietly, his hands on his knees.

"Alright," the man said finally. "So Archie, how was the drive? Everything good?"

79

"Yes, yes, very good. Thank you," Archivaldo said.

"Listen to that, you ungrateful cocksuckers. Nothing like a simple thank you. But just wait till you get that shake, then you'll thank me. A, find out what the fuck is going on with our shakes."

The man called A exited the room.

"OK, turn the goddamn TV back on! Turn it back on," the man said, waving at the screen as if forgiving the device its earlier transgression. He exhaled and leaned back on the couch.

"OK, let's talk," he said. "I find these things are better discussed face to face. Something I've learned. So let me ask you this: What was my one rule when we started? It was just one simple lesson to live by. What was it?"

Archivaldo cleared his throat. "Follow instructions."

The man pointed at Archivaldo. "Exactamente. Follow instructions. How has that gone, following instructions?"

"Sí, good," Archivaldo said. His mouth was dry. "I'm doing just what we talked about."

Archivaldo felt good about how things had gone. Everything had actually fallen into place better and faster than he'd expected. Those he was told to infiltrate were nothing to be afraid of. They weren't nearly as smart as they thought they were. It was their anonymity that gave them courage. Push hard and they would crumble.

So why, then, did it look like the man in the track suit was getting more agitated?

"Doing just what we talked about," the man said. "Doing just what we talked about. What did we talk about? Tell me what we talked about."

Archivaldo sat a bit straighter.

"No, no, no," the man interrupted himself. "Let's try it this way. What I want, what I want is for you to tell me the thing you don't want me to know. *That's* what I want to know." He scrubbed a hand on the stubble on his head.

"The thing I don't want you to know?"

"Right. That thing that you think 'Ah, the boss doesn't need to know that. It's not important.' Or 'I had to make a different decision than the one we planned, but it's not important.' So what is that decision?"

Archivaldo suddenly felt very out in the open. His stomach turned sour, just as it did as a boy when his father would return home after drinking raicilla with his friends.

"I don't—" Archivaldo started.

"No, no, I don't want you telling me you don't know. Because if I don't know about it and someone else asks me and I don't know, it can be embarrassing for me. If I'm not prepared, then I can get burned. I don't like getting burned. You don't want me to get burned."

Just then the lieutenant entered the room with a tray and two large glasses.

"Get the fuck out!" the boss shouted. The man immediately turned and left.

"Now listen, motherfucker," the man said, "I'm going to give you a couple of seconds, and if you don't tell me, things are not going to fucking go well. You understand?"

Sweat raced down from Archivaldo's armpits. His mind departed him. He could think of nothing, nothing that seemed important or consequential. He tried, "There is one of the guys who is resisting. He's fighting me, but—is that what you mean?"

The man stood, his tight tracksuit cutting into him. His mouth now puncturing his face like a poorly sewn seam that had popped open.

"What about the guy who had his fucking head cut off!" He spat the words out.

If Archivaldo was confused before, this completely undid him. "What?"

The man moved to the window behind Archivaldo and snapped the curtains closed.

"The fucking Mexican. The one whose head you cut off. That ring a fucking bell?"

In one deft move the man took up the length of the curtain cord and wrapped it around Archivaldo's neck and pulled it tight. Archivaldo gasped and grabbed at his throat.

"You know, the guy you decided to kill and then toss his head into a basket? The one that ended up on the front page of the fucking paper? No? Still not quite picturing it?"

He pulled the cord tighter.

"No!" Archivaldo managed. "I didn't! I don't (garbled), I swear! I only ... did ...."

"That doesn't make sense to me. I think you thought it was your decision to make. Take him out. Problem solved. But it's created problems for me, you fat fuck." He twisted the cord. Archivaldo scratched at the man's hands.

"I … swear!" Archivaldo choked. He shook his head. "I swear! No … Never …"

"I think you are lying. That's what I think. You thought this guy is not cooperating and you thought, 'I'll just take him out.' Like that. No? Not the way it went down?"

Tears ran down Archivaldo's face now.

"No," he gurgled. He shook his head. "No… " Crude sounds came from him. Desperate sounds. "… anything. I … I…"

"Sorry. Not convincing. So before I fucking collapse your windpipe and throw your fat ass in with the fucking pigs, I want you to tell me."

Archivaldo scratched at his neck. He shook his head as emphatically as he could. Tears ran down his face. "I … didn't …"

Consciousness was ebbing. Only a small window remained of his vision, a small circle filled by the TV, part of the table.

"Should I believe him?" the man said.

There was no answer.

Then the pressure relented and Archivaldo fell to the floor in a spasm of coughing and crying. The ring of pressure burned at his neck.

When he had composed himself, got himself to his knees, wiped his face, he saw the man sitting at a nearby table drinking a neon green–colored mixture from a large glass. He held the straw and pulled hard.

"Drink your shake," he said. "You'll feel great."

"I know, Mom. I'm sorry. Things have been crazy down here," Joe said. He had finally connected with his mother and he was getting his spanking for not checking in sooner.

"I didn't know what had happened to you. I'm old, Joseph. My heart can't take that kind of thing."

"I'm sorry. I thought about it, if that makes any difference. There was just always something that interrupted me. And you're not old."

"Your father, when he was traveling, he made a point to call me every evening before he went to bed. Just to say he was OK," she said. Joe could tell that just hearing his voice had already calmed her.

"I know. I'm sorry." A feeling of love and protective zeal washed over him as he thought of his mother, now without her husband, sitting in that empty office in Portland. What an asshole he was to have let her worry.

There were times when he believed he was putting the Joe of the past behind him, finding a better way to live in the world. But other times he realized he still had some distance to go, and in moments of weakness, like now, he wondered if there was only the one Joe and no other.

"I'm just glad to hear that you're OK," she said.

"I'm OK," he said. "But it does look like I'll be here a while longer, unfortunately. There's a customs issue I've got to iron out. I've got a contact and they're trying to help me unravel it."

He could hear the dog. "Maximus misses you," his mother said. And Joe knew what she meant.

"I miss him too. And you," he said.

"Well, now that I know you're fine, and that you'll stay in touch, I feel better. I should let you get back to things. I hope you can fix the customs problem soon. But we're fine here. I just got a call from Alan and we're going to have lunch tomorrow."

"Perfect. Tell him hello for me. I need to contact him too."

He had been prepared to tell her what was going on, but when the opportunity had passed he was glad he hadn't. Why did she need to know? Either the issue would get worked out and he would be able to bring the items home, or not.

"I will. Say bye-bye, Maxi," she said.

"Thanks, Mom. I'll talk to you soon. I promise."

"OK. Be safe down there."

He would try, but it seemed to be getting harder by the day.

When Joe got to the corner of Calle Basilio Badillo and Insurgentes, he turned left. He took himself two blocks down the street to Cesar's shop. A sign hung on its door: Se renta. For rent. He peered into the window. The place had been totally cleared out. Everything was gone, the room cleaned and repainted.

Joe didn't know what he'd expected to see or if he really had any expectations at all. But something kept bringing him back there.

"It's not for rent anymore," said a voice from behind him.

Joe turned to find a tall Mexican man holding a box in one hand, a drink with a straw in the other. He wore a mustache and glasses that he tried to hitch up his nose with his shoulder.

Joe didn't like being startled. His nerves were ragged already, and he felt just the slightest bit like he was slipping into a bad place. "The sign says it is," Joe said.

The man sipped from his drink. "Just rented. I need to take the sign down."

Joe didn't say anything.

"I have another place, if you are looking for a business space. This road is busy. You want more quiet."

"What was here before?" Joe asked.

"A tenant who didn't pay his rent," the man said. "It was an internet cafe. Who has internet cafes anymore? But now he's finally gone. A salon is going in. It will be very nice. Very modern."

"Did the previous tenant, did he move his shop somewhere else?" Joe asked.

The man looked squarely at Joe for a beat. "No. He's out of business."

"Oh," Joe said. "Too bad."

"Why too bad?"

"Because I need the internet, not a salon."

The man set his drink down on the sidewalk and retrieved his wallet. "Here's my card. If you want to look at the other place I have. It's very nice." He picked up his drink and took a sip. "I like renting to Americans," he said. "They understand what a contract means."

Joe deposited the card in his pocket. The man nodded to Joe as he pushed open the front door of the shop and disappeared inside.

Did Molly know the shop had been emptied and re-rented? He needed to talk to her. But right now all he wanted was to get to La Palapa and Veronica.

He found her sitting at a table overlooking the ocean, but she was staring at her phone. She wore a strappy summer dress, her naked shoulders brown and smooth.

"Are you looking at pictures of the ocean?" Joe said.

"Hola," she said. She got to her feet and on her tiptoes wrapped her arms around him. Joe felt that glorious pressure she made against his body.

"I like the new uniform of the Mexican Customs Officer," he said, taking her in.

She smiled conspiratorially. "I'm sick," she said, raising her eyebrows.

"I'm so sorry for your illness. But that's the best news I've heard all week," he said, and he meant it. Talking to his mother had taken the air of him and he feared that if Veronica were not here, if he were to be left on his own today, he didn't know what might happen.

84

"I have to travel for work tomorrow, so I thought why not?"

"Dos margaritas, por favor," Joe said to the waiter.

Veronica kicked off her flip flops and rested one beautiful brown foot atop the other, her rich vermilion nails catching the sun. She ordered their lunch, selecting the best things from the menu: ceviche fruta de la pasión, camarones adobados con enchiladas de jaiba, arrachera de res. They watched the parasailers above, legs dangling into oblivion. They joked about the parade of tourists that passed endlessly before them. They sighed indulgently when a breeze passed through the open-air restaurant. The dark cloud in Joe receded.

Once they'd finished lunch, they paid and wandered down to the beach. They carried their shoes and traced the water line, letting the ocean cool their feet. Veronica held her hair back from her face in the breeze. She talked about her family in Mexico City. Her father, who had just retired from the diplomatic corps. Her mother, who loved to be at their ranch with the horses.

"We will see how long that lasts now that my father is home full-time," she said, smiling.

A sister in LA and a brother in Miami. Joe talked too, but he didn't tell her everything. There was too much to explain. So he said only that he had been married and it hadn't worked. That he didn't see his daughter as often as he would like. He tried to keep the conversation on her.

"I know what we need," she said. She grabbed his hand and led him off the beach and up a shady side street. "Just come on. Trust me!"

He followed her into a small, poorly lit shop. It was of that breed of store you see everywhere in Mexico, the tiendita, with dusty shelves full of staples: cans of salsa, juice, cooking oil, soap, tortillas, bottled water.

Veronica led him to a small freezer, lifting it to release an exhalation of frozen cold and revealing a rainbow assortment of handmade paletas—popsicles.

"As a little girl I would eat 10 of these coconut ones in a day," she said.

They each picked one from the neat, colored stacks. Joe also grabbed some beer from the cooler.

"Now your turn to follow me," Joe said.

The two worked on their paletas and walked through a part of the neighborhood that Joe had not seen before. Quiet, residential feeling. Cobbled streets climbed and then disappeared around the corner. Houses staggered up the hill, jacaranda trees tipping overhead.

When they entered the breezeway of the Hotel Mercurio, they could see the pool area was busy.

"Buenas tardes, Joe," Javier at the desk said.

"Buenas tardes," Joe said.

As he unlocked the door to his room, Joe said, "You brought a bathing suit, I hope."

"I'm sick," she said. "Why would I have a bathing suit?"

From her bag she produced a colorful bikini. He kicked the door closed and took her in his arms. They fell onto the bed. She slipped her flip flops from her feet. "I never knew," she said, "that I could have so much fun in a gay hotel." She hid her face in his chest and laughed.

He grabbed her and she pressed into him.

Things happened in life. Things one could never predict. Crazy things, even unspeakably horrifying things. But also wondrous and beautiful things. You were recipient of them both and he today, right now, he would celebrate the good and the beautiful by being present in it, by making the very most of it. He felt her breath on his damp neck. In a moment, their lips met, they tangled their feet.

As they moved against each other, Veronica's dress moved up her legs, revealing slender legs of glossy supple brown. She rearranged herself, sat up, swinging her dark hair to one side. She shimmied the dress up to her hips, revealing delicate panties in the same color as her toenail polish. She swung a leg over Joe to sit atop him, and her hair framed her face and a mouth that still bore some hint of the smile, but that had now turned more serious.

"I have trapped you," she said.

"Now what?"

Veronica took his hands in hers and placed them on her breasts.

"I can feel your heart," he said.

She closed her eyes. He gently tugged the top of her dress down, presenting a stunning combination of sharp shoulder, brown arm, round breast, and red bra. She was small, but not fragile. For a long moment, he simply admired her there. And then Joe rose up the headboard until their hips met and they were facing each other. He grasped her, pressing his face against the divot at her throat, her heart ticking madly at his cheek.

Veronica removed her bra and held his lips to hers. Her skin was warm and smooth and smelled of the rosewater perfume she wore. He kissed her shoulder, the depression at her collar bone.

They moved over each other with a languid, unhurried grace that seemed almost like a dance. The fan whirred above them, moving the hot air around. Veronica lightly bit his ear, breathlessly whispering to him in Spanish. They took their time, explored and kissed and found their way into each other.

Together, they climbed higher and higher, swimming in the thin air of the moment until one final step sent them over the top, both finally relaxing in one satisfied exhalation and a mess of limbs.

"The Mexican customs office is really thorough," Joe said.

They laughed, and when they had, after some moments, returned to their regular bodies, back to the real world, they lay for a long while together, indulging in the closeness, listening to the mix of voices and music outside, the splashing of water.

Words came into Joe's head, but he didn't say them. Veronica smiled because perhaps she knew what those words were. Maybe they were the same as her words. So they said nothing and in time she kissed him lightly and took herself to the bathroom.

Joe lay amidst the tangled sheets and closed his eyes. He tried to hear the ocean a block away and though he couldn't entirely make it out, he liked knowing that it was so close. The shower came on.

The door to the bathroom cracked open. "Ven," she said. Come.

He joined her under the hot water. Once done, and Veronica readied herself, Joe smoked one of Leon's joints. They spent the rest of the afternoon lounging between the pool and their table, sharing toasts with a raucous reunion of guys from Omaha, Nebraska.

Later, after the stars had been up for a while, and the sun and drinks and the day's events had settled fully into them, Veronica said, "I should go."

"Go? Why?"

"Sí," she said. "I have to travel tomorrow, and I really need to get ready."

"Damn, right. I forgot about that. How long will you be gone?"

"Just two nights," she said.

She changed, collected her things, leaving her lingering fragrance. She climbed into the back of the taxi and they kissed through the open window.

"What a perfect day," she said. She put her hand on his. "I'll call when I get back."

And the taxi rattled its way up cobbled Calle Francisca Rodríguez.

The man they called the Goat entered the arrivals terminal at Puerto Vallarta International airport. He was not happy. The flight had been late, and he did not like being late. Plus, truth be told, he did not care for flying. The whole proposition of lifting hundreds of tons 30 thousand feet into the air seemed to him a conjurer's trick.

Aside from a suite of other skills, Rafa Vega's real genius was turning anger and fear into calm and quietude, even into a kind of elegance. This was the picture he cut as he strode from the plane. His suit could have come right off the hanger, showing no signs of having been mashed into an airline seat. His shoes gleamed in the fluorescent light. His hair was neat and crisply parted, his face cleanly shaved and his nails buffed and manicured. These things were important to him. He'd once removed the nails of a man because he said the man's failure to care for them invalidated his right to keep them. As he walked through the terminal, he took a moment to adjust his tie in the reflection of a sign for Banderas Properties. He liked the knot hard and tight at his neck.

With unhurried purpose he strode down the concourse and through the terminal. Around him tourists pushed carts overloaded with bags. Such people sickened him, the pale, slovenly mass of them in their T-shirts and flip flops. He could not understand what malign calculus had deemed the US the masters of his countrymen.

Once through the sliding doors into the blazing outdoors, a black SUV pulled to the curb and a young man quickly appeared and opened the door. Inside, his newspaper and cafe con leche waited. Happiness was the little things. This he had learned over the years. His line of work had revealed a great many submerged details about the human animal. Among them was the fact that when faced with extinction people invariably blathered on about the mundane, the everyday. When his own day came, he would be no different, he was sure. It would be his cafe con leche, his newspaper, and Sunday soccer on the TV that would occupy his thoughts.

The truth was, a man could not control what he was good at. The alignment of passion and skill and purpose could be cultivated, but it could not be planned or faked. There was a reason that he was sought after. He carried on a conversation with the universe through his work. He did not simply "take care of the garbage," though he did not mind the name that had been attached to him. In his mind, he was a storyteller, a musician. He conducted a symphony of pain. There was a brilliance in that. Some couldn't appreciate the soaring artistry of Mario Lanza. Some were not overwhelmed by the grace and power of Ramón Ramírez. But that didn't make either man any less than what he was, a genius.

The car took him north. The ocean raced alongside in brilliant blues and greens. Palm trees ticked by. He sipped his coffee. Maybe he would stick around for a few days after his work was done, he thought. Go fishing. The thought moved through him like the coffee, warming his blood.

They crossed the river and continued up the coast. In the distance, to the east, disfigured some by the haze, rose a string of low green mountains. Somewhere in those hills still lived his family. Or so he presumed. They hardly seemed like family anymore; it had been so long. Coffee growers. Again, at least they had been at one time. They were country people, from the rancho. It didn't make them bad, only small minded and vulnerable. He'd never felt a part of that world. And when he was old enough to express that, he'd begun to speak his mind, regularly clashing with his father. It could have only ended one way.

Even so, he liked when work brought him to Jalisco or neighboring Nayarit. It felt familiar. He had spent a lot of time on this coastline. As a young man, he'd dated a girl from the town they'd just pulled into, San Pancho. But her father had intervened. No daughter of his would date a farmer's son. He wondered if she was still around. Chances were good. Chances were also good that middle age would have transformed her so inexpertly as to make her unrecognizable. That was a kind of death too.

After traveling the littoral road, they turned west toward the water until they pulled into the palm tree–lined driveway of a large house facing the ocean. A striking, multilevel construction, the place boasted large exposed timbers, enormous windows, an open-air balcony covered by a palapa roof. His employer's representative greeted him, leading him into the airy, tiled foyer.

"You made it. Welcome to Casa Encantamiento. How was your flight?" The man seemed dressed rather too casually in linen shorts, a light shirt open at the collar, and loafers without socks.

The Goat smoothed his tie and took in the room. "Flying." He grimaced. "I don't trust another man with my life."

The man laughed. "I couldn't agree more. And the food, don't get me started on the food."

He said nothing.

"But," said the other, "when this is your destination, somehow it makes it all worth it. Let me show you to your room."

He did not move. "No. Tell me first that you secured the items that I asked for."

"Of course," he said. "All the items have been gathered just as you requested."

"Take me to them."

"Now? Yes, of course." The man produced a cell phone from his pocket into which he said a few words. A third man appeared from the rear of the house.

"Please show Señor Vega to the office," he said. "Ignacio will take you and then bring you to your room."

He followed the man through the entryway and down a hallway lit by shafts of light from high windows. He was led into a large room with a tall, timbered ceiling and lined with books and artwork. Three large black cases sat on the floor. He knelt and opened each one in turn. He ran over the list in his head and checked it against the contents of the cases. Everything seemed to be there. He would be ready. But then he was always ready.

Chapter 6

J oe lay in bed staring at the listless revolution of the fan. Things had only grown more complicated over the past couple of days. He retrieved his phone from the bedside table to text Veronica bon voyage, wishing selfishly that she weren't leaving town.

So far, Joe had only spoken with Molly about Cesar, and she admitted she knew little about his online life. He needed to speak to this Miguel, Cesar's friend. Perhaps he could shed some light on how and why the cartel would want this owner of a failing internet cafe killed. Joe had stopped by the family bakery and left his card, but nothing had come of it. It was time to try a different tack.

Panadería Esperanza sat between a small dressmaker and a shop selling what looked to Joe like textbooks and other academic supplies. An old man sat in a chair in front of the bookstore, asleep in the shade of a jacaranda tree. The smells emanating from the bakery hung deliciously over the sidewalk. Joe entered, joining a short line of customers. A young man operated the cash register.

When it was his turn, Joe stepped up.

"The pan dulce looks great," Joe said.

"Sí," the man said.

"Give me one of those, an empanada de pollo, and a coffee, negro. Por favor," Joe said.

The young man rang up the order.

"I stopped by to see you a couple of days ago," Joe said. "My name is Joe Lily. You're Miguel, right?"

The man looked up, connected eyes with Joe for a long beat, but said nothing.

"I was hoping I can talk to you about Cesar Castillo," Joe said.

The young man's face remained impassive. He turned his attention to the woman standing behind Joe, "Can I help you?"

"Excuse me, sorry," Joe said to the gringa behind him. "Miguel. Look, don't you want to help Cesar? All I ask is just five minutes. That's it. Then I'll get lost. Five minutes. For Cesar."

Miguel handed Joe his bag and coffee. "Have a good day," he said.

Joe paused a moment and then stepped out of the line. He took up a stool in the front window and ate and sipped his coffee and looked out on Calle Madero. It seemed peculiar to him that Miguel, who Molly said was Cesar's closest friend, clearly did not wish to speak to him. Why would that be? Then again, Joe was a stranger. What reason would he have *for* speaking to him? In a world in which people cut off other people's heads, it can be dangerous in the extreme to step outside of your lane.

Joe found himself thinking about his dad. Thinking about what he might do in this situation. Whatever resourcefulness Joe had he had learned from him. The man had managed to turn his passion for culture and travel and art into a life and livelihood that sustained the family. At least most of the time. Joe closed his eyes, wishing he could access his dad and his guidance right now.

In time, Joe finished his food and dispatched his coffee and had stood to leave when he spotted, just a half block up, and much to his surprise, Miguel hurrying across the street. Joe quickly deposited his trash in the can and exited the shop. He kept Miguel in his sights, staying a good distance back, keeping others between them. Miguel turned east. He had his phone to his ear. People walked on the street, but not so many that Joe didn't feel conspicuous. It was a block Joe couldn't remember having ever been on before. Small shops, windows cluttered with hardware items or leather goods or small darkened restaurants with just a handful of tables. Miguel crossed Calle Constitución.

At one point, Miguel stopped and turned around, sending Joe ducking into the nearest doorway. Then Miguel was on the move again. Joe tried to unravel Miguel's reasons for sneaking out of the bakery. Why not go out the front? They traveled up another long block, this one with leafy trees that provided some momentary relief from the sun. At the next corner, Miguel abruptly turned right. This put them on busy Calle Insurgentes. Blue buses clattered past on the cobbled street. And then a half block on Miguel stopped. He looked both ways as Joe sneaked in behind a group of Mexican women in hotel uniforms. Miguel stood before a door and retrieved keys from his pocket.

When Joe finally reached Miguel, he said, "They changed the locks. It's going to be a salon."

"Fuck," a startled Miguel said. He looked at Joe. "You followed me. Why won't you leave me alone?"

"Because I want to help you. And me. And maybe even Cesar."

"Cesar is dead." Miguel continued to try his key in the lock, but it was no good.

"The landlord said Cesar owed him money," Joe said.

Miguel half-heartedly kicked the door and then leaned his head against the glass.

The traffic roared past behind them. It occurred to Joe that this was the second person who had keys to Cesar's place. He wondered how many were out there.

Joe hung back and after a long moment Miguel wiped his eyes with his sleeve and Joe realized he'd been crying. He said, "That asshole hated Cesar. He was always hassling him."

"I got that sense. Why?" Joe asked.

"Cesar's uncle used to own the building. When he died, he put in the contract that Cesar could stay here as long as he wanted at the same rent. The guy always wanted him out."

"That's a nice uncle," Joe said.

"Cesar was a good person."

"I'm very sorry," Joe said. "I know what it's like to lose someone you care about."

Miguel exhaled slowly. "It's empty in there. Everything's gone."

"It's hot out here. Let me buy you a beer. What do you say? One beer. I'd love to hear more about Cesar. And maybe, if you're interested, I can explain why I keep bugging you."

"I don't drink," Miguel said.

"OK," Joe said. "Maybe something else. You name it."

Miguel stared down the street, ran a hand through his thick black hair. "OK."

Miguel took Joe to the other side of Calle Insurgentes and down the block to a place called Licuado Feliz.

"I haven't been here since … what happened," Miguel said. "Cesar and I would come here."

Behind the counter, a woman in a blue apron used a large press to turn halves of melon into juice. Behind her the walls were a riot of color made by a staggering variety of fruits. Reds, yellows, greens, and oranges, like some forgotten Frida Kahlo still life.

They ordered and Miguel said he didn't want to talk about it, that he just wanted to move on, but that not talking wasn't helping either.

"I would tell him that every country has corruption. Look at the fucking US. But he said *they* don't have the cartels. He called them a cancer that was killing Mexico. Maybe he was obsessed about it, I don't know."

"What do you mean obsessed?" Joe asked.

"He just talked about it all the time. Especially in the last year or so."

"Where did he talk about it? Like at the shop or when you guys were hanging out?"

Miguel shrugged. "Everywhere. But mostly online. He talked about it all the time online."

"You mean like on a blog or something?" Joe said.

"Sorta," he said. "He hated that everyone was so … scared to talk about it. He would say that silence is death. And then when those bodies were found in Culiacán, he just got, I don't know, he changed."

"What did he think one guy with a laptop was going to do to a violent gang?"

Miguel looked at his feet. He took a long sip from his drink. And then without preamble he pulled down his bottom lip to reveal the skin underneath. The tattoo proved much easier to read on Miguel than on Cesar.

"Los Fantasmas," Joe said. He shook his head. "Cesar had the same on his lip. What is it?"

"Cesar started it. He always said there was no leader. Except he was really the leader."

A silence passed between them.

"OK," Joe said. "Cesar started Los Fantasmas. But what the hell is it?"

The young man shook his head. "I shouldn't be telling you any of this. But fuck it. What does it matter now? Los Fantasmas is, I guess you'd call us a hacker group. We have certain skills. With computers."

"What sort of skills?"

"We can disrupt things, you know? Fuck stuff up. You would be surprised how little security most companies have for their systems. It's a joke. So we break in, mess shit up."

"Why?"

Miguel smiled and shrugged. "Because we can," he said. "At first, it was just for, I don't know, it was just for laughs. We would compete against each other to see how fast we could get in. We were just fucking around."

"But that changed?"

"Yeah," he said. "That was Cesar. He said we should use our powers to inflict pain on Los Primeros. When those bodies were found, everything changed for him. Some in the group disagreed. They thought it was too dangerous and they dropped out. But others joined. We started doing these campaigns against Los Primeros."

"Campaigns? What do you mean *campaigns*?" Joe asked.

"Look," Miguel said. "Cesar, man, he had cojones. Like I said, he was all the time talking shit about Los Primeros. He just hated injustice, you know, and corruption. He wanted to fight back. And then one day, we were at the shop and he just starts jumping around, running all over the shop, and yelling all crazy, you know? Like Chivas just scored or something. But he wouldn't tell me what it was."

"You asked him," Joe said.

"Yeah, I asked him, of course," Miguel said. "He said he found something, that's all he would say. Said it was too dangerous for me to know."

"About Los Primeros?"

Miguel shrugged and shook his head. "No sé. He never got a chance to tell me. But I always think maybe that's what got him killed."

After meeting with Miguel, Joe returned to the hotel and the *chuck chuck chuck* of the fan put him right to sleep. An hour later his cell phone rang.

"Where are you?"

"Porfirio? I'm at the hotel. Why?"

"Can you come over here? To the office?" Porfirio's voice was pulled tight, urgent.

Joe shook himself from the groggy grip of his nap. "Sure, of course. Is everything alright?"

"Just come over here as soon as you can, OK?"

"I'll be right there." He dressed quickly.

Joe stepped into the fierce brightness of the late afternoon, still feeling dulled from sleep. He hurried down Calle Rodolfo Gómez, through the sidewalk tables on Olas Altas, and then past the square, the final few beach restaurants. He turned up Basilio Badillo, past the restaurants and bars and shops that have earned the street the moniker Restaurant Row. He crossed busy Calle Insurgentes, not far from Cesar's shop.

Upon entering Villaseñor Antigüedades, one is immediately met by the smell of dry, weathered wood, aging iron and leather, dust. Porfirio stood at the register and urgently waved him in. "Ven, ven," he said.

"What's going on?" Joe said.

Porfirio only shook his head as he led Joe to his office and closed the door. "I'm not supposed to have this. But my brother-in-law, he called me and said I must see it." He looked Joe in the eyes but then only shook his head.

He produced a thumb drive from his pocket and then dropped his short, squat body into the chair at his computer. "Things are bad," he said as he plugged the drive into the computer.

At that moment, Joe's phone rang. He let it ring and then thought he better check. He made a promise to himself to be more available to his mom. It could also be his accountant, Alan, with news he wouldn't want to know but needed to know. It was Veronica.

"I'm sorry, I need to take this," Joe said.

"Joe!" Porfirio said, pointing at the computer.

Joe gestured that he would be right back and stepped out of the office and into the small warehouse where this whole horrible ordeal had begun.

"Buenos días," he said.

"Buenos días," she said. "¿Cómo estás?"

"Great. I spoke to Cesar's friend at the bakery."

"Was he helpful?"

"I think so. I'll tell you when you get back. Aren't you supposed to be traveling?"

"I am. But too many meetings. I actually have to run to another one now and just wanted to call and update you about your stuff before I go."

"Oh, excellent."

"I'm so sorry, Joe, can you hold a small moment?" Veronica covered the phone and spoke to someone in Spanish. "I'm sorry about that. Someone just asked me something. OK, so it's not much of an update, but I can say that customs is now really talking with the police department. The big bosses here are involved. I learned that today. So I will keep trying. But this is an unusual situation. ¿Verdad?"

"'An unusual situation.' I love that signature Mexican understatement."

She laughed. "It is true. I think we have the Catholic church to thank. I like to think it makes us very strong too. And patient. It is all part of God's plan."

"Well, all I know is I'm appreciative of your help."

"I'm trying, really," she said.

"I know. I know you are. And I can't thank you enough."

"Then you should take me to dinner when I get back," she said.

"Love to. Maybe breakfast too."

When Joe returned to Porfirio's office, he found his friend gone. His laptop was open, and when Joe approached what he saw on the screen froze him cold. The computer was paused on the image of a room, maybe a garage or workshop. Spare, unadorned walls, what looked to be a concrete floor. It was a little hard to tell; the lighting was not great. In the middle of the room sat a man, and the man was bound to a metal chair. A simple back that rose to the man's neck. The paused image was not crystal clear, but Joe recognized the man immediately. The stocky frame, the ring of hair encircling the bald spot. The toes of one foot were curled under. His hands were balled into fists. What in the hell was he looking at?

"Porfirio!" Joe looked about for an explanation. But Porfirio had stepped out. Joe waited a moment and then hit play.

"I told you," Darrell Haddock pleaded. "Please, what do you want?" The fear in Darrell's voice matched the animal terror on his face. It was a different version of the man than Joe had seen in the park during the demonstration only the day before.

A second voice, this one Mexican, responded off camera. "Señor Haddock. All of the time for talking, for promises, it is done. You break the contract, there are results. I cannot help that."

"I told you I'm going to pay," Darrell pleaded. "I am. You have my word. I run a very successful business. Please!"

A shadow climbed up the far wall and then dropped off again. "You accepted the money, but you miss one deadline and then a second. Every time, complicaciones. We don't care about complicaciones."

"It's my partner," Darrell asserted. "He's making it impossible!"

The man breathed in, exhaled slowly. He spoke to another person off camera. Darrel tried to free his arms, pulling hard, his face turning red beside the whites of his wide eyes.

"Bastante. You signed a contract. Do you break your contracts with the bank? With your customers? No. But you break it with Los Primeros? I do not understand your thinking. You have made the wrong choice."

"I just don't have it," Darrell cried. "Please, give me a day and I'll have it to you. One day. Please, God.'"

"God cannot save you here," the voice said. "In this world, Los Primeros is the creator and judge."

"My partner!" Darrell tried. "He has money! I can get it. I can tell you about the deal he is working on right now. Huge. Millions of dollars. We—you—could get in on that! I can make it happen!"

Sounds could be heard off camera. Clasps opening. Metal on metal.

"What are you doing?" Darrell said. "What is that? OK, yes, yes, I made choices. You're right. You're absolutely right. Dumb choices. I don't know what I was thinking. Señor, please. No. No. But I can fix them. Let me tell you about this plan my partner was secretly doing. He tried to keep it from me, but I figured it out. It's worth millions!"

The man off camera said something in Spanish.

There was a clicking sound followed by a loud hiss and a bright light off camera came into the scene. Darrell's eyes widened and he pulled hard against the restraints binding him to the chair. He cried loudly now, beseeching the man to listen, to stop.

"He was trying to cheat me!" Darrell declared. "I showed him this business! I taught him! He didn't know anything. And then he does that to me? I, I know what I did was stupid. But I will pay back every peso. I swear to you. Let me pay it back! Oh, fuck! Please, I—"

The man raised his voice for the first time, "¡Cállate! I don't care what you did or who you did it to. That is not my problem. I told you, the time for stories is done. Prepare your confession for God, but don't make it to me."

The bright light illuminated corners of the frame and then its source came into view. A hand appeared clutching a welder's torch. The flame shot from the tip of the tool in fierce red and gold.

Sitting frozen at Porfirio's desk, Joe had not been able to take his eyes from the screen.

Darrell yelled and tried to see what was happening, to pull away, his voice rising in volume and octave. "What are you doing? No! I'll pay it back. Today, today!"

He pulled hard at the binds, shaking the chair, which it became clear had been affixed to the floor for just this reason. "No, no, no!" he screamed, writhing as the flame got closer. "Let me talk to my partner. He'll help! I swear, one phone call." He strained to stand, his face contorted, his mouth wide. "No! AHH! Call A.J. Brandt! Call A.J.! I'll pay! HELP!"

And then just like that the video abruptly ended.

Joe sat and stared at the black screen. His mind reeled like a forest that a fire had just swept through. Everything charred and crumbling. All color gone. All life gone. Silent. What had become of the world? The question floated across the desolation of his mind looking for a place to land.

Joe had been about to leave when Porfirio reappeared in the office.

"You watched it," Porfirio said.

Joe nodded.

Their faces slack and drawn, they looked at each other for a long time without speaking.

Joe broke the silence. "I know him."

"You know him?"

"Sí. He's A.J. Brandt's partner, Darrell Haddock. I just saw him yesterday. I can't believe it."

"Who is A.J. Brandt?"

"He's the father of Molly Brandt, who is, or was, the fiancée of Cesar Castillo."

On his face Porfirio wore that inscrutable expression so common to the Mexican people in moments of tragedy: a mix of pain, reverence, and fatalism leavened by the stubborn knowledge that things go on despite it all.

For Joe, what he had seen had scored itself into his mind. This was not simply murder; it was a message from Los Primeros. But to whom?

"Someone delivered it to the station," Porfirio said. "No name, nothing. Horrible. So horrible. I do not know why there are such people. It makes me sad for my country."

Joe exhaled, and asked, "Do they know where the video was shot? Did they find … anything?"

Porfirio's face turned darker. "Paz did not say if they knew where." He wiped his face with a handkerchief.

"So where did they find Darrell's body?"

Porfirio lowered his eyes and said nothing.

"What?" Joe asked.

His friend cleared his throat. "Do you know el guiso?"

Joe shook his head. "I don't think so. Who is he?"

"No," Porfirio said. "It is not a he. In English I think it means like a stew."

"A stew? Like a carrots and potatoes in a pot kind of stew?" He was confused.

"Sí," Porfirio said. He looked hard at Joe.

And then Joe understood.

"It is a way they use," Porfirio said. "Los Primeros, they are known for it."

Joe's stomach turned over and he thought he might wretch just as his phone buzzed in his pocket.

"I've got to go," Joe said.

Porfirio nodded.

"I'll call you later."

"OK, my friend," Porfirio said.

Joe tried calling Veronica, but it kept going through to voicemail. He sat at Cuates y Cuetes looking out over Playa los Muertos, a name that had become sadly all too fitting.

A lot had come out of his conversation with Miguel. Cesar's shop was, as it turned out, more than a shabby little internet cafe. According to Miguel, the place served as the nerve center of an active hacker group with ambitious goals. Los Fantasmas, the Ghosts. At first, maybe it was just mischief, taking over a website to prove they could. But that had changed.

As Miguel told it, he'd arrived one morning to find that Cesar had clearly been at the shop all night. Food cartons everywhere. Beer bottles. And Cesar looked it. Disheveled, red-eyed. "I got in," he'd said cryptically. "Got in? Got into what?" Miguel asked. But all Cesar would say is "You'll see."

From that point forward Los Fantasmas took a different tack. It wasn't just about having a laugh anymore. They began to organize, strategize, and attack with a purpose, a goal. Cesar channeled this loose confederacy of bored and aggrieved activists into a coordinated political ops team. They launched a campaign against Los Primeros, a key cartel based up the coast. Cesar authored scores of anticartel posts. They hacked websites related to members of the cartel, posting messages about the end of cartel corruption. The notoriety of the group grew, though their identities remained a mystery, much to the frustration of those they attacked.

That was about the time El Mago joined. He called himself the Magician and made his presence felt right away, bringing a point of view that he shined into your face like a flashlight. He liked to mix it up. Take people on. And unlike most, who tended to defer to Cesar, or C-dope as he was called, El Mago didn't care who he challenged.

"Cesar was a screwdriver, but El Mago was a hammer," Miguel said.

Miguel explained that the two just didn't get on and battled almost from the start. They butted heads about what projects they should pursue and then how to pursue them.

"I don't know. Cesar was a proud guy. Smartest guy I ever met. He helped me out a lot. But he was competitive, I guess you could say. He had a very clear idea about what Los Fantasmas was. We had no leader. We were all one level. Remained in the shadows. That was Cesar."

"And this El Mago?"

"He wasn't like that. He said we should be out there, use social media, use the press. You know? He said Cesar needed to be like Subcommandante Marcos had been for the Zapatistas. If we really wanted to change things, that was how we would do it. And he was definitely against messing with the cartels. He said that would just get us killed. Who *allowed* the cartels to exist? The government. Business. That's where we should focus."

"Any idea where El Mago is, where he lives?" Joe asked.

"Culiacán," Miguel said.

Joe consulted his phone. "About eight hours north."

"No," Miguel said. "That's not a good idea."

"Come on. I just want to talk to him. Maybe we'll learn something."

Miguel insisted it was a bad idea that he wanted no part of. But Joe Lily had a talent for persuasion, and after numerous appeals, and Joe's promise to cover all costs, Miguel finally relented. He would join Joe to Culiacán to see if they could make the Magician appear.

The next morning, Joe waited at the bus stop. Miguel was late. Joe tried him half a dozen times with no answer. And then Joe watched as their bus closed its door and pulled away. Joe thought about going down to the bakery. Giving Miguel hell. But what good would that do? The truth was, he needed Miguel more than Miguel needed him. So when another bus arrived with Culiacán scrawled on its front, Joe decided to climb aboard alone. He would figure it out.

Joe liked being on the move. He always had. He and his father had shared that. The bus stood only about half full. Some dressed as if heading to work, others with old bags and boxes wrapped in twine they shoved under their seats. Even though Joe was the lone gringo, no one took notice. He leaned against the window and admired the flatlands over which they traveled, the ocean stretching alongside.

About an hour in Joe finally received a text from Miguel. He claimed that his mother had fallen ill and he'd had to work. It seemed a flimsy excuse to Joe's mind, but Miguel had also given Joe a phone number: "I think this is El Mago's number." This he followed with "Cuidado. Seriously." Be careful. Joe tried the number but got only an automated female voice in Spanish on the other end that he didn't understand.

In time, the bus left the coastal plains and began to climb, joining a windy road that finally dropped them once more down near the beach. They passed Sayulita, Rincón de Guayabitos. The ocean sparkled in the morning sun. People got on and off. After San Blas, the bus turned inland, making a stop in Tepic, the capital of the state of Nayarit and site some months earlier of a cartel gun battle in the central plaza that had left six dead. It had even made the papers in Portland.

Hour followed hour. They resumed their northward trajectory, roaring past mile after mile of open scrubland dotted by little towns that would appear and then just as quickly disappear. Some people stopped to watch the bus roar by, but most paid their passing no attention at all. Joe tried the phone number again but again with no luck.

By the time Joe arrived in Culiacán it was late afternoon. Still, the heat of the day found even the shade made by the trees in the city's plaza. Joe found a small taquería and had a quick bite to eat and a beer, wondering if every guy he saw might be El Mago. Miguel had never actually seen his Los Fantasmas cohort, and so could give Joe no description. It seemed to Joe a more fragile sort of alliance if those who claimed to have your back did so anonymously. Joe tried the number again. This time it rang through, but without an answer.

Joe tried Veronica again as well, also without luck. He left a message. Joe hadn't planned much beyond getting himself to Culiacán. Now there, he found himself at something of a loss. Travel eight hours by bus to a city he didn't know to visit a man he didn't know who likely didn't want to be visited. He bought a bag of peanuts from a man in the park and found a bench in the plaza to take in the late-afternoon scene.

Joe had read some about Culiacán and the killings that had become all too common in recent years with the birth of Los Primeros. The group had distinguished itself by its brutality. A lot of ex-military who brought a discipline and a grotesque precision to their rule of the area, which now spanned much of Sinaloa and Nayarit as well as a growing portion of the states of Sonora and Durango. But the home-base was Culiacán, and Joe half-expected to see military vehicles and soldiers stationed at street corners. But the reality differed little from any of the other Mexican cities Joe had visited.

This time, Joe tried texting the number that Miguel had given him.

Then Joe's phone beeped.

"¿Quién es?" the message read. "Who is this?"

Joe quickly texted back. "My name is Joe." He hadn't thought much about how he would explain who he was. "Miguel gave me your number."

There was a brief pause and then: "Wrong number. I don't know Miguel."

"How about Payaso?"

Joe waited. He was about to ask again when his phone beeped: "What do you want?"

"I want to talk to El Mago," he wrote. And then he added, "I want to talk to the spokesman for Los Fantasmas."

Again, Joe waited. A long few moments passed. And then, "Where are you?"

"I'm in Culiacán. In the plaza."

El Mago followed this with another question: "What is your last name?"

"Lily. Joseph Lily."

His phone beeped again. "There's a bar. Las Ranas. Meet in 30."

All of sudden the weariness of the long bus trip vanished. Joe thought quickly about his objectives for the meeting. It might be his only chance to speak to the man who went by the name El Mago and established himself as Cesar's adversary. Had it been a battle for leadership of Los Fantasmas that had led to Cesar's death? After asking a young woman in a shoe store about the bar, Joe found it down a cobbled side street hung with colorful papel picado banners.

There wasn't much to the place. A dozen tables, a wooden bar, concrete floor. Ranchera music played on the stereo. The eyes of the four or five men fixed on Joe as he entered. Broad shouldered, sure of foot, brown hair combed back off of his face, Joe moved with confidence to the bar. Wall Street taught you its own brand of ball-knocking bravado. Blink and the jungle would bury you. Survival meant speaking the language of men, the one articulated in gesture and swagger and bullshit gravitas. He had taken to it with more ease than he liked to admit.

The bartender pushed a bottle of beer across the bar to Joe and he shuffled to a table in the corner near the front, back to the wall. His analyst brain calculated the dimensions of the situation: He was in a strange city, one known for its bloody cartel and a spate of recent public killings. He was by himself, visiting someone he did not know and who very likely did not like being bothered about the murder of a person he may or may not have been locked in a power battle with over the management of an anonymous hacker group that had its hands in some very dangerous places. There was plenty of downside.

Joe texted El Mago, "I'm here." He sipped his beer and waited. He stretched his legs, crossing them at the ankles. A few fans turned idly as the music played. The beer went down easily. A woman entered holding a dirty baby, her hand extended. Joe gave her the change in his pocket. Joe could see the rear of the bar through the reflection in the front window. The men had barely acknowledged his arrival and were relaxed and chatting. Just end-of-the-workday beers. It was the same everywhere. Just then an older man entered, removed his hat, and assumed a stool at the bar. That couldn't be him, Joe concluded.

He waited. Ten minutes passed. Another 10. Nearly finished with his beer, Joe checked his phone. It had been almost an hour since El Mago's last text. Had the man, true to his moniker, disappeared? Joe took up his phone and began texting: "I'm waiting at Las Ranas. Are you—" Just then, a chair at his table screeched and Joe found one of the men from the back of the bar sitting across from him.

"So who the fuck are you and what do you want?" the man said in a competent English.

Up close, the man looked young, early 20s. Unlike his friends, he wore no facial hair. No cowboy boots. His hair was thick and coarse, and he was big, his girth spilling over the sides of the narrow chair.

"The magician hiding out in the open," Joe said.

The man leaned in, "Who are you?"

Joe took his time. He exhaled slowly. "Check your phone. I told you who I am," he said. "You keep me waiting, and now you're in my face? Why the bullshit? If you didn't want to talk, why did you come?"

The young man could not hide his surprise at Joe's response.

Joe continued. "I want to speak with El Mago, the leader of Los Fantasmas. If you're him, I just want to get your opinion on a few things.

104

If you're not him, or you want to pretend you're not, that's fine too. I'll get up and go, and you can go back and drink with your friends."

The man sat back, took a breath. He appeared to be thinking about the choices Joe had just given him. He glanced back at his friends who drank their beers and looked on impassively.

"OK," he said finally, "what opinions?"

Joe nodded. "I need another beer before I do anything. You need one too." Joe motioned to the bartender who brought over two more sweating Pacificos.

Joe raised his bottle to El Mago and took a drink.

"So how did you get the name El Mago?" he asked.

"None of your business," he said.

"The magician doesn't give away his secrets. OK."

"I've got about 10 minutes and then I need to go," El Mago said.

Joe set his beer down on the table. "I'm a friend of Molly Brandt."

El Mago shrugged. "Don't know her."

"You don't know Molly Brandt?"

"I just told you," he said.

"She's—she *was*—C-dope's fiancée."

Joe kept the table with the other men in view.

"I thought you said Payaso gave you my number."

"He did, but I'm really here because of Molly. I'm trying to help them both figure out what happened to C-dope, to Cesar."

El Mago sipped his beer. "How do you know about Los Fantasmas?"

"I put two and two together."

"And remind me why you're here. You came all the way from Vallarta. Why? What do you want?"

"Let's just say I have an interest in figuring out who killed Cesar. You two were friends, right, you and Cesar?"

El Mago took another drink. "I don't know anything about what happened. Fucking horrible. I liked him. He was a smart guy."

"What do you think happened? Police say it was the cartel. Maybe from up around here? I guess C-dope really hated them. Do I have that right?"

"The police. They don't know shit about anything. They probably did it. They are the real gangsters. They do whatever they want—lie, steal, kill—and then blame it on whoever."

"Are you saying that it wasn't the cartel?"

"I don't know who did it."

"You haven't heard anything?"

"I told him, I said that he better, you know, take it easy with that shit. The people he was targeting, they don't fuck around. I told him that going on about it, it's dangerous. I told him that."

"I heard that you guys didn't always agree. Was that something you argued about, about his campaign against Los Primeros?"

El Mago instantly stiffened. "Don't say the name."

"OK," Joe said. "But what about you and Cesar?"

"He was a smart guy. But he never really understood what Los Fantasmas could be. He could be the Zapata of the internet. I tried to tell him, but he didn't listen. All he could think about was, you know, battling those guys."

Joe understood he probably didn't have much more time with El Mago before the window came down, and he wanted to get something useful out of the visit.

"So you're from here, would the cartel, would they kill a guy for writing shit about them on some website? He talked too much and for too long and that was that? Help me understand."

El Mago started to say something and then stopped. He emptied his beer. "Look, man, C-dope, he got himself into some shit. The guy could fucking hack anything, a computer, a phone, a fucking can of Coke, whatever. But he couldn't back it up. That's what got him killed."

"Couldn't back it up? What do you mean?"

"We're done," El Mago said. "You better get on home before you get hurt out here."

Joe worked up a smile. "I appreciate your concern."

Just then two of the men sitting at the table behind them came to stand behind El Mago.

"¿Estás bien?" one asked.

Joe said, "The Zapata of the internet. Seems to me that's what Cesar was, or was becoming, if someone hadn't learned his identity. I wonder how that happened."

El Mago shook his head.

But Joe was done being careful. He had little to lose. "You weren't a little jealous of him? Didn't you want to be in charge?"

El Mago stood and pushed his chair back.

"Fuck you," El Mago said.

"How about Ruben Bermúdez? Do you know him?"

106

Just then, out of the corner of his eye, Joe saw a flash as one of the men swung for Joe's head. Joe caught the man's wrist midflight, stood, and deftly pivoted so he had the man's arm behind his back.

"No need for that. I came here with respect. I'm just trying and help a friend. That's all."

"You should not have done that," El Mago said, a shadow of fear having come into his eyes.

The second man produced a knife from his boot and said something in a low voice that Joe didn't catch. The bartender watched placidly from behind the bar.

Joe threw a handful of bills on the table and gestured to the bartender for another round for his new friends.

"¿Todo bien?" Joe asked.

After a tense moment, the second man sunk his knife into a nearby table top. Joe released the first man as he backed away to the door.

"Cesar may not have been your friend, I don't know. But he didn't deserve to die. I'm just trying to figure out why. Wouldn't you want that for your parents if it had been you? Think about it."

Joe exited the bar and moved quickly down the street. When finally at a safe distance, he took a deep breath, removed his phone, and stopped the recording. He also saw that his ex-wife had called. That could not be good.

Joe passed a largely sleepless night in the hotel. What had he learned about Cesar? "The guy could fucking hack anything. But he couldn't back it up." What the hell did that mean? And "He had gotten into some shit." Was this shit different shit than the obvious shit? Breaking into people's computers does tend to piss them off. Shouting about the cartels across the internet might have exercised them a bit as well. Was *that* this particular shit? And if it was, was it really enough to get a man's head removed from his body?

All night these and other questions tumbled about in his head like dirty sneakers in a dryer. Plus, part of him expected to receive visitors during the night. Visitors who hadn't taken well to having been disrespected in their own town. Visitors who came to have the last word. But no one came, and so Joe had just laid there staring at the ceiling as it turned from dark to light with the sunshine sneaking it through the blinds.

He wasn't entirely sure what he had expected from his trip to Culiacán , but as he headed back to the bus station in the morning, he consoled himself with the truth that there is always some wisdom in movement. He *had* met El Mago. Or at least someone that answered to that name. And he saw that the man had friends. Maybe they were just old friends who had agreed to accompany El Mago for this unexpected meeting with an American. Maybe they were Los Fantasmas too. Though that seemed unlikely. Or, maybe they were exactly what they seemed, while El Mago was not.

Joe caught the first bus south. He was tired, but something about the passing landscape, the plainness, the emptiness, transfixed him. How far he was from Portland. How far from his life. He let sleep sneak in via the hum of the bus tires the creeping feeling that he was no more real or lasting than the low clouds hanging over the fields to the east. Almost imperceptibly he was lifting into the ether, dissipating, disappearing.

At some point, Joe fell asleep. When he awoke, they were nearing Rincón. He saw a text from Porfirio. "They think they know who killed Cesar." Right then he wished he'd brought one of Leon's joints with him.

As soon as they pulled back into Puerto Vallarta, sighing to a stop in front of the Walmart and Sam's Club, Joe called Porfirio.

"Rafa Vega," Porfirio said.

"Rafa Vega." Why did that name sound familiar?

"I don't know exactly how they know, but that's what my brother-in-law said. He's a known guy. A very bad man."

"Yeah, I saw his work," Joe said.

Joe stood a short distance away from the buses and other travelers. A young girl and her baby brother, each dressed in rags, offered him the Chicklet gum they were selling. He gave them each a 50-peso bill which they took without fanfare or comment.

"Is he cartel?" Joe asked, watching the kids move through the crowded platform.

"No," Porfirio said. "Well, sí, he *was*. He was Los Primeros. But he left."

"Left? What do you mean?"

"I don't know. But I guess he left, quit. That's what they said. He's not with them anymore."

"I didn't realize you could do that. So who is he with now?"

"I don't know."

"Rafa Vega," Joe said again.

"They call him the Goat," Porfirio said.

"The Goat? Why the Goat?"

Porfirio paused. "Because he takes care of the garbage."

"Clever." Joe saw Cesar's head on the floor of Porfirio's shop. "Did your brother-in-law say if anyone knows where he is?"

"Vega? No, he didn't say."

"Or maybe where he lives?" Joe asked.

"He's from the mountains. Talpa. His family, they are coffee farmers."

"Talpa." The late-afternoon traffic made a mess of the broad intersection in front of Joe.

"Where are you?" Porfirio asked.

"We just pulled into Vallarta. I spent last night in Culiacán. A little research."

Porfirio's voice changed. "Joe, por favor. I don't want Paz telling me any bad news. Let the police do this."

Joe's eyes settled on the enormous cruise ship sitting in the marina across the street. "I'll be careful. I promise. Thanks for the call, my friend. I'll check in later."

Next, he texted Molly. She deserved to know. "Hey there. Some things to talk to you about. Just learned the identity of the man believed to have killed Cesar. Ex-cartel. From Talpa. You up for a trip into the mountains?"

elmago: you're a fucking snitch

unodostres: what R U talking about?

gorrión: ????

elmago: someone here gave out my fucking phone number

unodostres: why would someone do that?

gorrión: how do you know?

elmago: I know because that's what they said

gorrión: who said?

gorrión: what are we talking about?

elmago: why don't you ask payaso?

payaso: what do you mean?

elmago: you tried to fuck me

gorrión: what??

gorrión: no

gorrión: why would he do that?

unodostres: hold on what are we talking about?

elmago: why don't you tell them payaso

elmago: go ahead

elmago: I want to know too

payaso: I don't know what you're talking about

gorrión: maybe your phone got hacked

elmago: tell them payaso

payaso: I don't even have your number

payaso: fuck you

elmago: oh now you don't know my number?

elmago: that's the line you're going with?

elmago: pathetic

unodostres: who called you?

unodostres: how do you know where they got your number?

unodostres: and why payaso?

gorrión: we don't have each other's numbers

elmago: a few months ago i was going to go to PV

elmago: i was going to stay with payaso and C-dope

gorrión: when was that?

payaso: yeah but you never showed!

payaso: we waited for you for fucking three hours

gorrión: who got your number?

elmago: i had a family thing I had to do

elmago: emergency

gorrión: who got your number????

elmago: he gave my number to some American

elmago: and then the guy shows up

unodostres: what do you mean shows up?

elmago:in Culiacán

unodostres: WTF?

elmago: yeah

elmago: he kept calling and texting me

elmago: he said payaso gave him my number

elmago: speak up payaso!

110

unodostres: why???

unodostres: what did he want?

gorrión: why did he contact you?

elmago: he asked about us, wanted to know about us!

elmago: you just better hope that payaso didn't give out your numbers too

elmago: we could all end up like C-dope

payaso: fuck you

elmago: yeah you may have fucked us all

payaso: the guy wants to help figure out who killed C-dope

payaso: that's it

payaso: he can help

payaso: you have something to hide?

Joe's phone pinged. A text.

"What the fuck?!! You told el mago I gave you his number! Fuck you!!"

Joe had been expecting that. He had told Miguel he wouldn't share with El Mago how he had come to possess his number. It was not ideal, but he had no other bona fides to offer El Mago. He'd make it up to Miguel later. At the moment, as his taxi maneuvered through the heavy traffic to the airport, he had something else on his mind.

After probably a dozen messages and calls, he'd received no response from Veronica. She was supposed to have returned home yesterday. Too much had happened in recent days for Joe not to harbor a crackling fear that something very bad had happened to her. If it had, if he had put her in harm's way—he couldn't think about it. So he found himself hurrying to the customs office.

The taxi left him amid a scrum of tourists arriving for flights home, their bags hastily piled curbside. Joe moved quickly through the sliding glass doors into the cool interior of the building. The Puerto Vallarta airport is small. Were it not for the steady stream of planes lifting and landing you might not even notice it as you passed it on the highway. The arrivals area buzzed with activity. A flight had recently come in. Wide-eyed visitors pushing their towering carts, the resort touts grinning and reaching out their hands. Joe thought about what it must have looked like the first time his father landed here. He'd talked about the grass runway, the same one that John Huston had landed on to scout for *Night of the Iguana*. The same one Liz Taylor had famously landed on to keep an eye on her wandering husband, Richard Burton, and his costar, Ava Gardner.

Reaching Veronica's office, Joe found her desk empty. Numerous unreturned calls and texts, and now she did not seem to be at work. Joe felt a surge of fear as the events of the preceding days cascaded through his mind: Cesar's murder, Darrell's murder, his conversations with Miguel and El Mago. What had he mixed her up in? It was nearing the end of the workday. Perhaps she had gone home early. He would try her place next.

And then, just as he turned to leave, Veronica appeared from the hallway. It had been only a couple of days, but he had forgotten how striking she was. She wore her long dark hair back in a ponytail. She had her glasses on, which suited her even though she'd said she felt like her mother when she wore them.

"You *are* here!" he said. "Thank god. I was getting worried. With everything that's happened, I just—I'm so glad you're home and everything is fine. I was getting worried."

"What are you doing here?" she asked.

"You didn't answer my calls or texts and I started to think that … that something had happened. I had to make sure you're OK," he said. "Now that I'm here, and you're OK, I can take you out to dinner. How does that sound … after a long day of customsing?"

"I'm pretty busy."

The air of the small office crackled with a kind of static Joe could feel but not immediately identify.

"Oh," he said. "OK. No problem. How about later? Meet somewhere."

"I'm sorry. I'm very busy today," she said, moving past him to her desk.

"Yeah, you said that," Joe said. "Seems like you've been busy for the last couple of days. I've called and texted and you haven't responded."

She busied herself organizing papers on her desk and said nothing.

Joe watched her. "You received my messages, but just didn't respond?"

Veronica stopped. "Joe, I think you should probably just go."

"What's going on?"

"Nothing is going on," she said.

112

Still she didn't look at him and opened one of the manila folders before her.

"I'm confused," he said. "Did something happen?"

She shook her head. "Please just go."

"Can you at least tell me what I did? Where is this coming from? If memory serves, the last time we saw each other we had a good time. Am I crazy?"

She dropped her gaze to the floor.

"Don't I deserve some explanation for why you're kicking me out of your office?"

After a moment, she said, "There is an expression about Americans that move to Puerto Vallarta. We say that those people are either wanted or unwanted."

She took up one of the pieces of paper on her desk and showed it to him. "I just didn't know that you were both kinds."

In her hands she held a copy of a *New York Times* story. "Wall Street Wunderkind Questioned by Authorities."

She held up another: "Ward and Williams Rising Star Fingered in Subprime Fallout."

And then another: "Subprime Collapse Shakes Wall Street, Indictments Expected."

All of the air went out of Joe. Veronica thrust more printouts at him.

"You lied to people. Even your own family!" Veronica said. The blood had come up in her cheeks and her eyes had transformed from soft brown to dark beads of black.

Joe said nothing.

"You ruined people's lives. These people who trusted you, they lost everything. Older people." She lifted one of the copies as a lawyer might a piece of damning evidence. "Retirements — gone. Homes gone. Even your father-in-law? It's so … ugly."

Joe carried this disaster with him every day. It hung on him, dragged on him, tried to take him to the ground. And it had. For a long time, he'd been buried under it, not sure he would ever get up again. No light had penetrated those days. People did not care that he'd tried to stop it, that he'd told his bosses it was a ticking time bomb. Once the world latches onto a story, it can be impossible to turn them to the truth. Joe could not fix what had been broken, but he was trying to put it behind him. And then out of the blue, when he needed him most, his father had died, and before Joe could explain to him what had happened, that he'd never intended to hurt anyone, that all of Wall Street had sunk its teeth into subprime. Joe never had a chance to tell him that his son's appearance on the front page was because it had turned out that he was very good at something that he didn't realize was very bad until it was too late.

"It is horrible," she said, dropping the pages to her desk. "And for what? Money? So sad. And you fooled me too."

Words came into Joe's mind, but he let them pass. He'd offered so many words on this subject for so long. They tasted stale on his tongue now. It didn't matter. You just could not escape some things. Some things left their mark on you.

"I liked you," she said. "And you know the funny part. I was in D.F., at my hotel, and I missed you. I missed you. Can you believe that? I didn't even know you. But now I know you. I cried when I saw these stories. I cried for how stupid I'd been."

All Joe could do was let her say her piece. It had become clear that at the same time he was trying to move his life forward, this other Joe Lily still lived and breathed too. That grotesque caricature of him would endure forever in newspaper stories, in the memories of those who'd decided or been told that he was the next Bernie Madoff. That Joe Lily still creeped behind him like a malevolent shadow.

"You told me that you got divorced because you 'grew apart.' You are a good liar. I will say that. I believed you. Ruining the lives of your wife's family, that …" She stopped and shook her head.

"I should have told you."

"It's … pathetic."

The statement buzzed in the air like a wasp.

"You know the really crazy part, the crazy part is I didn't believe it at first. When I saw the first story, I thought, this is wrong. Even though there was a picture of you right there. I couldn't believe it. I wanted to call you and ask if you'd seen these crazy stories?"

"So you called my ex-wife," Joe said. Now her call made sense.

"I had to know if it was true. She was very nice."

Joe nodded. "She is."

Veronica raised a hand to her mouth and began to cry.

Joe stood for a long moment just inside the doorway. He felt made of shards of glass, each movement cutting some different part of himself. There was so much to say, so much to clarify and explain. But it all seemed suddenly too deep a well to draw from.

114

"I'm sorry. I never meant to hurt you. I hope you can believe that. And maybe someday I can explain how it all happened." And then he turned and walked back down the hall and out of the airport.

What better sign did Joe need that it was time to go. Time to collect his stuff from the hotel and take the first plane back to Portland. The whole incredible idea looked absolutely delusional now. Crazy. Embarrassing, if he were being honest. One collection of antiques was really going to save the store? A few tables and chairs, some ironwork and picture frames, were they going to be sufficient? Who was he kidding?

And to make it possible, he was going to solve a murder, two murders really? To call this whole fucking sordid mess a quixotic disaster was to malign quixotic disasters. The truth was, he was hiding. From his mother, the business, his accountant. Everything at home. He *was* the wanted and the unwanted, just as Veronica had said.

The sun had set with deep reds and oranges decorating the horizon. Soon, that too was gone, leaving the sky washed in murky blue-black, turning the outlines of the distant boats into charcoal sketches. In the morning, he would pack up and head home. He would have the hard conversation with his mother. Her support of him had never flagged. He owed it to her.

He had the taxi drop him at the beginning of the Malecón. The cobbled street glowed from the street lights, which had just come on, and the light issuing from the clubs and restaurants. The promenade bubbled with activity. People exhausting the last moments of their day while others were just getting their evening started. Joe took up a spot on a bench and watched the proceedings.

A vendor in white pants and matching white shirt stopped before Joe with his mobile display of rings and earrings. Joe suspected the man had been working all day, walking the streets, the beach. On impulse, Joe bought two sets of earrings. He would send one to his daughter. No, she didn't wear earrings yet, at least as far as Joe knew, but he would send them anyway. And a pair for his mom.

Joe joined the stream of evening strollers, stopping to admire the wild sculptures scattered along the path. Farther on, a man sold watercolors, and another scooped ice cream from his rolling cart. On the other side of the small pedestrian bridge, Joe stepped off the walkway and joined the sand. He dug in his backpack and found a Leon joint. He walked and smoked, restored by the feeling of the cool sand on his naked feet, the silver burnish the moon brought the wave crests and the contours of the beach. It felt good to step off of the path and into the dark.

When he eventually reached the Mecurio, the hotel buzzed with activity.

"Buenas noches," Javier said. "¿Cómo estás?"

"You know, I don't really know."

"Did your friends find you?"

"My friends?" Joe asked.

"Sí, they stopped by earlier. To go fishing. But you weren't here," he said.

"No. I never heard from them. Man? Woman?"

"Two men," he said.

"I'll call them. Gracias."

Joe walked to his room, past the busy pool and pool bar. Small groups of men, looking freshly showered, shirt collars open, laughed and talked and drank. Opening his door, Joe saw that his "friends" had indeed been there. The mattress had been tipped over, his suitcase dumped, the drawers of the desk pulled open. The items that had been on the desk were now littered about the floor. Joe could not tell if the visit had been a search mission or merely a message.

Chapter 7

J oe woke as the morning sun spread across the floor of the room. He saw again how thorough the visitors had been. Last night, he'd started to reassemble things and had lost momentum and gone to bed. Items from the dresser and table were still on the floor. The mattress remained out of kilter with the box spring. He was just glad he'd had his laptop with him.

The disaster of the room mirrored that of his life. There was his business, his marriage, his relationship with his daughter, his father's death, things with Veronica. It was a fucking four-car collision of failure. And each day seemed to bring a fresh wreck. But he couldn't deny that something in the honeyed light of the morning reignited his engines. This had been his M.O. his whole life. It just wasn't in him to give up.

So Joe rose, showered, and threw his daypack on the bed. He had a trip to take, but it wasn't to Portland. He threw a few things in the bag and zipped it up. When the voice in his head asked what he really hoped to gain from this next gambit, he ignored it. Action. That was the thing. Do something. Be the chin, as Leon had said.

Outside, the street had only just begun to stir. Birds gossiped in the creeping bougainvillea. Looking straight down Calle Rodolfo Gómez the ocean was a hazy watercolor. Joe had seen a trip to Talpa listed among the excursions offered at the stand on the corner. He found the spot staffed by a woman this morning and not the man he'd seen there before. She quickly booked his trip.

"The plane leaves in two hours," she said. "You must be there 30 minutes before the flight." She handed him his receipt. "Have fun!" She smiled, revealing a chipped front tooth.

He had time for a quick breakfast. The restaurants on Olas Altas remained mostly empty. He took a table outside at the railing in front of Burro's and ordered a coffee and a plate of chilaquiles. A truck stood parked along the curb across the street unloading supplies into Kaiser Maximilian's. A shop owner a bit farther down emptied a bucket of water on the sidewalk before his store. A truck with "Bimbo" emblazoned on the side rumbled slowly down the cobbled street.

If Joe could find Vega coffee—how big could the Talpa be?—maybe he could find Rafa Vega as well. He ignored the nagging reality that chasing a killer, and one who uses a blowtorch, might be a sign that he needed psychiatric help. He thought he'd better alert someone where he was going, just in case. He sent Molly a quick text. "Heading to Talpa this morning. I'll report back. Talk to you later."

Arriving at the airport, he was directed to a neighboring building and not the main arrivals and departures hall. He was sorry to learn that he would not likely run into Veronica. He handed his receipt to a disinterested clerk who directed him to a few chairs sitting outside in the shade of the building. He called his mom but it rang through to voicemail.

Joe had not seen another passenger or any other staff when a short time later the clerk appeared from the office and pointed him to a small prop plane sitting on the tarmac. It reminded him of the plane his old boss at Ward and Williams had flown Joe and Alison on during the occasional weekend trip to his place in Cape Cod.

When Joe climbed the rolling stairs and into the plane, he found that he was not, in fact, the only passenger on board.

"I was beginning to wonder," Molly said.

Joe stood in the middle of the aisle, his hands on the seatbacks.

"Surprised?" she said.

"Just a little."

"Figured that we might learn something about what happened to Cesar."

Molly had a tirelessness, an energy that seemed to radiate off her like heat off a highway. He had known women of this sort in his old life. His ex could be classified in the same category. Stumble or flag and you risked being run over.

"OK," Joe said, still trying to put the pieces together. He took the seat next to her.

"Camila, who you talked to on Rodolfo Gómez, I see all her bookings because we offer free trips for anyone dumb enough to sit through one of our time-share pitches." Her face, tanned and angular and pretty, leaned in toward him conspiratorially. "Visit one of our properties and I can get you a free breakfast and a booze cruise."

Just then a van pulled up onto the tarmac and at least half a dozen tourists piled out, straightening skirts, dropping sunglasses to their eyes.

"And here are the rest of them," Molly said. "I guess we shouldn't talk about the fact that a killer might just be roaming around the little town they're going to."

She leaned into him and laughed.

118

The small plane stayed low in the sky, offering stunning views as they put the Bay of Banderas behind them and climbed toward the Sierra Madre. The plane took them over browned and withered country split here and there by dusty arroyos. Hawks floated below circling over the same waste in wide looping arcs. The hills rolled in shrub and cactus and stunted trees across miles. This was the Mexico of the movies—beautiful, quiet, a romantic desolation.

"Someone turned my room upside down yesterday," Joe said. He turned to find Molly arch-backed, eyes wide, her hands gripping the armrests. A small bump and she grabbed Joe's knee. "Sorry," she managed.

"Not a flyer?" he said.

"I hate it. Hate it. When I saw how small this—" another shake and she gasped. "Damn it. When I saw how small this plane was, I almost turned around."

In profile, he could see in her something of his ex, the long, slender neck, the sharp jawline and somewhat flattened angle of her nose.

"And you can't even get a drink," he said.

"That's what you think." From the purse at her feet she produced two small bottles of tequila.

"One for me," she said, handing him one of the bottles, "and one for you."

They clinked bottles and emptied them, Molly making a face like she had a hair in her mouth.

The plane flew low over the foothills, in radiant blue skies until they bounced their way down the grass landing strip at the Talpa Airport, little more than a couple of squat buildings sitting incongruously on a flat patch of high desert.

Joe thought it nice to exchange the sticky salt air of the coast for the mountain variety for a while. He breathed it in deeply, noting a hint of pine at the edges.

"So, what's the plan?" Molly asked.

"You're standing in it," Joe sad. "I just figured it would become clear once we got here."

"So, what, we just … walk around town asking if anyone knows this murderer named Rafa Vega? Sounds good."

They found a taxi and drove toward the old silver town. Today Talpa de Allende is known more for its guava candy, guayaba, the sugary sweet

119

smell of which seemed suspended above the town, and its famed church. The Basilica de Nuestra Señora del Rosario Talpa dominated the town. It drew scores of pilgrims each year, some traveling hundreds of miles, some crawling its steps on bloodied knees to petition the Virgen del Rosario who is said to perform miracles.

But it's mostly a country town. Quiet and quaint, its heartbeat the slow clip clop of men on horseback traveling the cobbled streets. They listened to the birds in the nearby trees. A child cried in the distance.

"How does someone go from this ..." Molly gestured to include the church, the sleepy town, the shady, pine-covered hillsides, "to become a cartel hitman?"

Joe shook his head. From the video, it was clear that this man was not like others, that he measured himself against different standards. If the world could create a Virgen who dispensed miracles, could there not be those whose role it was to deliver pain? Such a person might very well believe that such acts are necessary and, by virtue of being necessary, ordained by God.

"Let's get a cup of coffee," Joe said.

They walked Talpa's small center, discovering a small coffee shop, Café Casa Rosa. Joe admired the old country table in the front window. Old-growth wood. Beautiful metal work. Who had built it? How did it get here? What he did know was that it would sell in a second back home.

Molly was charged after the flight and fretted and fidgeted, glancing after every person she saw. "Vega has probably come for coffee here. Maybe they sold their beans here."

They ordered and took up seats at the large window overlooking the street. A truck loaded with bags of cement rattled past, two men placidly sitting atop the load. Three women in matching uniforms walked by in conversation.

"Let me ask you this," Joe said. "What do you know about what Cesar did at work all day?" He blew gently on the steaming coffee.

"What do you mean? He ran the shop. He rented computers, opened Cokes for people. Nothing special. He was tired of it."

"Did he ever tell you about Los Fantasmas?"

"Los Fantasmas. No. Never heard that before."

Joe was surprised that Cesar had kept this part of his life hidden from her. "It's an online ... organization. Others might call them hackers."

"Hackers? Like people who steal other people's identities online?"

"Sort of," Joe said. "Los Fantasmas is more activist. From what I can tell, they're an anti-cartel, anti-corruption group. Started by Cesar."

Her face went dark. Joe had learned it had a way of clouding over when she was not happy. "Cesar? No way. A hacker organization? How do you know that?" Her voice took on a chilly tone, like Joe was trying to trick her.

"Miguel. I finally tracked him down. He's part of the group as well. Spoke with him yesterday."

"You spoke with him yesterday?" she asked. "What did he say?"

"He said Cesar was a proud guy. He wanted to make a difference. Stop the violence. I'm guessing you already knew that though."

"Was that it?" she said. "That's *all* he had to offer?"

Joe noticed a keen insistence in her voice now. "More or less," he said. "He wasn't really that interested in talking to me. Seemed a little scared, if I'm being honest."

"Scared? Why?"

Joe shook his head. "Don't know. Just a sense I got. I mean, he doesn't know me. This stranger enters his workplace and starts asking questions about his best friend who got murdered. Might put me off too."

Molly blinked. Joe saw the muscles in her jaw flex.

The young woman who had served them their coffee started to reposition the chairs at a nearby table, wiping the top clean.

"Perdóname," Joe said.

The woman stopped and looked up. "¿Sí?"

"Um, su cafe? ¿Quien es su …" He turned to Molly. "How do you say 'grower'?"

She shrugged. "Rancho maybe?"

Joe turned back to the woman. "¿Conoces rancho de Vega?"

The young woman smoothed her ponytail and then shook her head. "No sé," she said, made another swipe with the towel and departed.

Joe thought he'd seen a hint of something in her face when she heard the name, but he couldn't be sure.

"Let's go *do* something," Molly said.

The two left the shop and rejoined the street. Children had just been released from school and bumped into each other in little clusters down the sidewalk, each dressed smartly in their school uniforms and carrying backpacks.

Joe had a name: Rafa Vega. He hadn't thought much beyond looking for and introducing that name and seeing where it led. He could be pretty sure what someone looking in from the outside might say about him asking after a known cartel killer. But it was clear in Joe's mind that you can't expect to find the answer to a question you never ask.

They walked the streets of Talpa like normal tourists, soon finding themselves where every visitor to Talpa de Allende eventually did, in the plaza before the Nuestra Señora del Rosario church. Joe was struck by its rough-hewn beauty. It offered an austere sanctuary that looked to have sprouted from the very ground on which it sat. With its two bell towers, a clock in the middle, it looked for all its plainness like a church out of an old Western film. And behind it, watching over the town, loomed the Sierra Cacoma.

"Should we check it out?" Joe said, gesturing toward the church.

Molly pinched up her face. "No thanks. I'll pass. Churches kind of give me the creeps."

Joe walked the stone steps up to the church. At its heavy gate, in a heap of rags, sat an old woman, hair white as chalk. As she turned to him, he saw that her eyes had been removed from her head. In their place sat rough puckered holes. She offered a toothless smile, and Joe put a 50 peso note in her extended hand.

Entering the church, Joe felt the cool air expressed by the old walls. The narrow interior was flanked by long benches dotted with people, the men hooking their cowboy hats on their knees. A line of people inched toward the far altar on their hands and knees. A child cried, and the sound filled the vaulted ceiling like birds released inside.

As he stood there staring at the altar, Joe tried to imagine a young boy, the son of coffee farmers, standing there, watching his family, his neighbors, bow their heads and appeal to the Virgen for aid. For some, it would be a source of hope, of calm, of meaning. For others, when the rains did not come, when loved ones still perished from disease or want, when the rich remained rich and the poor still went hungry, they might have grown angry. They might have decided that there is no law, no order, no ears to hear. Or maybe they would have turned to another savior, one who believed that the meek, far from inheriting the earth, were grist for the strong. That strength was its own brand of worship.

Joe purchased three white candles. He lit each in turn, one for his dad, Cesar, and Darrell Haddock.

Returning to the glare of the outside, it took Joe a moment to reconcile the real world with the feeling of being inside the church. He spotted Molly sitting on a bench in the plaza, legs crossed, her thumbs working feverishly on her phone.

Coming up beside her, he asked, "Hungry?"

She put her phone away. "You were in there a long time," she said.

"Was I?"

"Seemed like it," she said.

They left the plaza just as a band began to set up on a small stage nearby. Joe bought a bag of nuts from a man at the edge of the park. He asked about Vega. The man whose thick white mustache matched his white hair shook his head and handed back their change.

Down a shady side street, they popped into a cobbler's shop and watched a father and son work strips of leather to make huarache sandals. Neither expressed any familiarity with the Vega name either. Still, it seemed to Joe that they answered too quickly.

"No one seems to know him," she said.

"Hard to tell."

For lunch, they found a place called El Patio, located a couple blocks off the plaza. Stepping inside the beautiful interior courtyard, it felt like entering the hidden bower in a children's story, with leafy trees in large earthenware pots and flowering plants climbing the walls. The wrought-iron tables sat on Talavera tilework. Because he had been asking everyone, Joe asked the waitress if she happened to know the Vegas or Vega coffee. The woman shook her head and left the menus.

"I like how you just go around asking about a known murderer."

"Wasn't that the whole point of coming up here?" Joe asked.

"I guess," she said. "It just seems, I don't know. What would we even do if someone said *yes*?"

"Ask the next question."

"What's the next question?"

"Good question," he said.

The restaurant slowly filled up. A guitarist began to play in one corner, the notes of the music lifting skyward like bubbles.

They ordered margaritas and food.

Joe was going to tell her that sometimes you just need to push on things. See what happens. See what moves. But instead he asked about her father. How he and Cesar had got along. Molly took a long time to answer and then only said not very well. He hadn't been in favor of the wedding, thought it a mistake that Molly would regret. But she said that if Joe were wondering if her dad might have had a hand in what happened, that was impossible. He could be an asshole, but there was no way he could do that.

They drank and ate. They talked about Joe's business, which was really his father's business, he said. He'd only moved back to Portland to help out his mom with it when his dad had died unexpectedly. Heart attack. Molly's eyes welled up. It had been hard, but they were making it work. And no, he wasn't married, not anymore. Maybe they'd married too young. But he had no regrets because it gave him his daughter.

"Oh, I love this song! Don't you love this song?" Molly said as the guitar player launched into a Spanish version of the Beatles' "Blackbird."

Molly lit up the small courtyard. She had this person in her as well. Spirited, enthusiastic, a smile that made her blue eyes shine. After what she'd gone through, the murder of her fiancé and then her colleague, she was due a little distraction.

The waitress set another pair of margaritas down on the table and departed.

Molly reached and took Joe's hand in hers. "Thank you," she said.

"Thank you? For what?"

"For caring about Cesar. For being the only one really trying to help. It means a lot."

"Oh, I haven't done anything," Joe said.

"That's not true. I felt, well, I felt like I was going through all of this alone. Like no one cared. He was just another Mexican killed by the cartel. But he *wasn't* just another Mexican. I know you have your own reasons for trying to figure things out. But it doesn't matter. You've been wonderful. So thank you. I won't ever forget it."

Joe raised his glass to meet hers.

"When you were in the church, I was thinking about it. And I think I figured it out."

"Figured what out?"

She paused and then said, "Cesar is gone and he's not coming back. That's all that matters. I guess it took getting out of Vallarta to really show me that. I have to start thinking about what's next in my life."

When the bill came, Molly snatched it from the table. "I insist," she said. She set the cash down.

Joe was eager to get back out and make the most of their time in town. The scheduled return trip to Puerto Vallarta gave them a few more hours and Joe wanted to put the time to good use. The guidebooks had mentioned a public market. Perhaps they could turn up something there.

When they exited the restaurant, Molly took Joe's arm and leaned into him. Joe wondered if that second margarita was such a good idea. He had his answer when only a few feet farther on, she stopped them.

"I've been trying to figure out how to say this without making myself look, well, horrible. But I think we should stay here tonight, fly back tomorrow."

"Stay here, in Talpa?" Joe asked.

"Yeah. We could do a bit more looking around this afternoon, and then later—I know we just had lunch—but we could find a good place for dinner. Maybe there's something happening in town. We wouldn't have to hurry. I just, I just don't want to be alone. Is that crazy?"

"No, it's not crazy. I—"

And then without preamble Molly put her arms around Joe's neck and pressed her lips to his. Joe felt the warmth of her body, her hands on his skin.

It didn't feel right for all kinds of reasons. He felt stupid that he hadn't seen it coming.

"Molly, I—"

"It would be fun," she whispered.

"Hey, you've been through a lot, more than you should ever have to. And I think—" He gently separated himself from her.

Molly's face hardened. She crossed her arms as if at a passing chill. "Oh, blah blah. Seriously? That's the line you're going with? Fuck you." She turned and started walking back toward the city center.

When Joe caught up to her, her face was flushed.

"Molly, look," he said.

"Forget it," she said. "It doesn't matter. I don't want to talk about it. Let's just go check out the market and then get the hell out of here."

Joe figured this was about the best outcome he could hope for, so he just walked and kept his mouth shut.

They found the public market. It wasn't difficult in the small town. It spread for blocks in a warren of sellers' stalls, people peddling everything from clothes and toys to kitchen utensils and religious ephemera. The rows and people went off in every direction. Joe thought that one of the produce farmers, especially the coffee sellers, must surely know the Vegas.

But first he needed to offer an olive branch to Molly. He could use her help if she could be persuaded to focus on why they had come to Talpa. "I think we need some dessert," Joe said. "And I see just the thing." He led the way through the tide of bodies to a wheeled paleta cart operated by an ageless man in a weather-beaten New York Mets hat.

Joe peered inside the cart, the cool air feeling good on his arms and face. The seller boasted every flavor imaginable, the collection stacked in an array of pastel colors inside clear plastic wrapping. He was reminded of Veronica who had introduced him to the treats, but he put her out of his mind.

"Now, I'm particular to the lemon ones," he offered. "But that's just me. I know that chocolate and coconut have their fans. Although, you know, I'm thinking maybe today feels like a watermelon day to me. What do you think?" When he turned to ask Molly, she was nowhere to be seen.

Joe scanned the area. Clusters of Mexican shoppers moved everywhere, a slow-moving river of bodies filling the narrow paths between the rows of stalls. He looked back in the direction from which they had come. Nothing.

Perhaps she'd been drawn by some shiny artisanal trinket, a blanket, a piece of jewelry. But given what had happened in recent days, Joe's imagination wanted to jump to the darkest possibilities. His inquiries about Rafa Vega had found the right ear, and they hadn't liked it. Joe moved briskly down the row, slicing through the bodies, keeping his head on a swivel. She should have stood out like a dandelion in the grass, but she was nowhere to be seen. Reaching a crossroads in the rows, he stopped and surveyed again. Still nothing. And Molly was no wallflower. If she'd been grabbed, she surely would have put up a fight, made a noise, wouldn't she? Joe hurried left, taking himself deeper into the market.

He cupped his hands before his mouth. "Molly!" But his voice disappeared in the general hubbub of other voices and music and barkers.

He turned down another row. They all looked the same and he was getting himself turned around. Why hadn't he been paying better attention? He'd been asking about a cartel killer, for Christ's sake—and in his hometown. What had he thought would happen?

Joe pushed through more shoppers and was about to shout again when all of sudden he spotted her, standing about halfway up the row talking animatedly to a stall vendor. He took a deep breath, closed his eyes.

"Goddamn it," Joe said as he reached her. "You can't just walk off like that."

She looked at him squarely. "I was talking to someone. Isn't that why we're here, to ask questions?" Her eyes flashed, her expression hard.

Joe read the stall's sign: "Paraiso Coffee Co."

"I asked about coffee and they sent me here. So I asked this couple if they knew the Vegas, the Vega farm. They sell coffee, they should know them. He said yes, didn't you? You said yes. But then *she* said no. She's not being honest."

The couple, a pair of small, dark-skinned farmers, looked dumbstruck by the interaction and not a little unnerved. The woman glanced at the other booths. She shook her head and waved her hand at Molly. She clearly wanted no part of being the subject of stares.

"Usted los conoce!" Molly. "Dijo que los conoce!" She gestured at the man, whose implacable face did not change expression, even his eyes ceased to blink.

Joe put his hand on her elbow. "Molly."

"I need to find out," she told them in English. "Necesito … what the fuck is 'find'! A donde rancho de Vegas? Por favor! You know!"

"Molly. Molly," Joe said. He put his hand on her arm. "They don't want to talk. Let's leave them alone. Come on."

"They should be ashamed! You should be ashamed!" she said, pointing a finger at the woman.

Joe managed to lead her away. He had to remember that her fiancé, the man she loved and had endured no small amount of family strife to be with, had had his head separated from his body. Her world had collapsed. And even though she denied that there was any possibility, in Joe's mind there still existed the outstanding question of her father's possible involvement. Given everything, she was entitled to some misplaced anger—or ardor.

They wandered the market for the next hour largely in silence, Joe casually asking after the Vega name when Molly was out of earshot. But he got the same response each time, a blank shake of the head, but always with, Joe thought, this cloud passing before their eyes, a pause, a worried recognition. Or perhaps Joe was simply putting it there, wanting so much to turn up something, anything.

But in the end, it was just a public market, in the mountains. Eventually, it was time to head to the airstrip for their flight back to Puerto Vallarta. The trip had been a long shot—everything was a long shot these days. And it seemed only to have muddied the waters while putting a new obstacle between Joe and Molly.

They grabbed a cab near the plaza. The battered yellow taxi clattered its ways out of town. Joe watched the towers of the church in the review until they were gone. The sun made its slow descent to the west sending long shadows across the landscape.

Molly's mood remained sour, distracted. She looked at her phone, banged out a quick text and then threw it back in her purse and stared out the window.

"I'm sorry this trip was such a bust," Joe said. "I hoped, I don't know, I hoped it would turn up whatever the next step is."

"There are no next steps," she said with a kind of exhausted finality. "Cesar is gone. Nothing I do is going to change that. I just have to live with it."

A truck rumbled by in the opposite direction, men sitting atop white bales of something in the rear. They passed simple concrete block homes with corrugated metal roofs. Rangy horses idled in the heat in a dried-out paddock. And then at a small turnout, the cab driver unexpectedly slowed and pulled over.

"Un momentito," he said, and without another word exited the car and disappeared down a side street.

"Wait, what's he doing?" Molly said. "Where's he going?"

"I don't know. Señor."

"Hey!" Molly leaned across Joe to yell out the window. "We have a plane!"

Just then, without announcement, another man appeared from the opposite side of the car. He jumped into the driver's seat and threw the vehicle into gear and sped back on to the road, kicking up dirt.

"What the hell?" Molly demanded.

"Hey!" Joe shouted.

The man accelerated down the bumpy road. He said nothing and soon turned left, taking them bouncing down a rutted dirt track flanked by jacaranda trees. Joe braced himself with a hand on the roof of the car. Molly held tight on the back of the driver's seat. They bounded past small, squat houses, scruffy dogs barking from the dirt yards.

Joe's mind raced. Every response scenario seemed like a recipe for a wreck. Though that was very likely a better conclusion than whatever this driver had planned for them. They had no choice but to jump out. Joe turned to Molly and then, without warning, the driver turned sharply down another dirt road before coming to a skidding stop in front of a small little home built of gray concrete blocks and corrugated metal. An old woman stepped from the dark doorway, a rifle leveled confidently at the car.

No one moved. A curtain blew through the house's glassless window. The driver climbed out. "¡Ven!" he said. Come!

Joe and Molly slowly exited the vehicle. Joe led with his hands out, Molly clutching his elbow. The driver said something to the woman that Joe didn't catch.

He wanted to appear unfazed, calm. Startle someone, make the wrong move, and things could go bad quickly.

"Señora Vega," the driver said.

The woman peered at them out of a face as inscrutable as the Sierra Cacoma behind her. Dark eyes sunk in a round face etched by sun and privation and suffering. Unlike most Mexican women of her age, she wore her hair down, its thin gray strands tucked behind her ears and lying limply over her shoulders. She wore a weathered shift, which may have once been blue or green but now just highlighted the dark brown of her arms and legs. She spoke incoherently, as if her mouth were full.

"She wants to know why you are asking about her," the driver said.

She spoke again, once more in a garbled, indecipherable tongue.

"She doesn't know why you are asking about her," the man said.

Joe exhaled slowly. "Please tell her we are sorry to have worried her. We don't mean her any harm."

Molly started to speak, and Joe laid his hand softly on her forearm.

The man relayed Joe's message in what now was clearly a dialect other than Spanish. The woman looked long at the two of them. She waved her rifle in their direction as she responded.

The man turned from the woman back to Joe and Molly. "If you want her son then you must be criminals or police, who are just criminals with badges."

"We promise her we are neither of those," Joe said. "I run an antique business. And Molly, she sells real estate in Puerto Vallarta. Her son is Rafa Vega?"

At the sound of the name she screamed something and moved the gun to her shoulder.

"Whoa!" Molly said. "Tell her we don't want anything!"

The man conveyed the message in the strange tongue, and she answered in an agitated, urgent voice.

"Why do you ask about her son?" the driver asked.

Her breathing came fast and ragged, her body all wired tension, wound tightly from her feet through her arms into the stock of her weapon.

"She doesn't talk about her son. She does not speak his name," he said.

She rambled off another string of words, her old, weathered hands trembling now.

"Tell her not to shoot," Joe said. "Please. We just want to ask her a couple of questions."

The man said, "She asks me again why have you come here? Is it about Ruben? She already answered the questions from the police."

Joe glanced at Molly. He collected himself and spoke to the driver. "We don't know anything about Ruben," Joe said, though it was a name Joe recognized. "Tell her that this woman," Joe laid his hand on Molly's shoulder, "her fiancé was murdered. A Mexican man named Cesar Castillo. He was killed. And then her colleague, Darrell Haddock, an American, he was also killed. The police believe her son might know something. We're just trying to learn anything we can. We mean no disrespect."

The driver listened and then paused for a long moment. He looked at Molly. He seemed to be deciding if and how to share this information with the woman. And then slowly and methodically he relayed the message to her. Her face showed no signs of understanding until the tears ran down her cheeks.

The woman spoke softly.

"She said she is very sorry for your loss."

Molly nodded. "Gracias."

"Does she know where her son is?" Joe asked.

This time the man answered for her. "He is gone a long time. He broke the family. They had a farm, but he destroyed it. And then he leave and never come back."

The driver addressed Joe. "The man you are looking for, he is bad. A black heart. We know him. Many years ago, he fight with Señor Vega. They always fight. So one day he get very mad and so he block the door, and he burn the house. Señor Vega and the two girls, they die. Only Señora Vega live. But she is blind from then."

The first man opened up the broad patio doors and the sound of the ocean rushed in. "This is nice," he said. He wore a track suit one size too small for his ample frame. As he surveyed the large condo, he sipped from the straw of the drink he carried.

"Look at that view," he said.

A.J. glanced at the two other men who had taken up seats at the kitchen bar. "What can I do for you gentlemen?"

The Mexican's neck was ringed in darkened rolls, his black hair thinning at the crown. "You can see all the way to Punta de Mita. You see?" He drew on the straw and pointed north.

A.J. said, "This building was our second property. It was a good lesson for me. I was reluctant to take it on. The seller was a banker from Guadalajara. He was asking way too much. The place had been damaged in a hurricane, I don't remember which one, and it had been sitting empty for months. But the guy refused to come down. He wouldn't even admit it had been hit by the hurricane. It was crazy."

"So what was the lesson?" the Mexican said.

"What?"

"You said it was a good lesson for you? What was the lesson?"

Something about the question put A.J. off. "I guess just that you have to be patient with these things. I'm proud that we managed to save this building and bring it back to life."

A cell phone rang, and one of the two other men answered in Spanish.

The man handed the phone over to the one in the tracksuit who fired off a few words to the person on the other end, and then handed the phone back.

"Well, I have another lesson for you. You want to hear it?" the man said.

A.J. didn't know what to say. He was trying to stay calm.

"No?" the man said.

"Yes, of course," A.J. said.

"OK, bueno," the man said. He looked at his men and half whispered so all could hear, "I was going to tell him anyway." They smiled. "The lesson is that sometimes things will actually continue to live *after* death. Increíble, ¿sí?"

A.J.'s heart began to beat a little faster. "Please, señor, what can I do for you? I'm afraid I'm not feeling very well today."

"Yes, we heard about your partner. Terrible, terrible."

The man casually checked his watch. He gestured to one of his men who nodded and left the room.

"Very sad," he continued. "We have a saying: Ahogado el niño, tapando el pozo. It means basically after the child drowns, they close the, what do you call it? Where you get water."

A.J. shook his head.

"You drop the bucket … to get the water."

"A well?" A.J. offered.

"Yes, yes. A well. English has too many words that are the same but have a different meaning. Fucking confusing. Yes, a well. They close the well. The lesson is that it's better to plan before tragedy happens." He shook his drink, assessing what remained.

"Darrell and I shared this business. But we kept our private lives separate. I never knew what sort of … arrangements he had outside the company. That was his business."

The man smiled. "You didn't listen to my Mexican proverb. If you ignore things," he shrugged, lifting his track jacket to reveal a sliver of his stomach, "you can fall through the floor and end up in the well."

"I'm sorry, señor, I don't want to seem rude. But if you could tell me what you need, maybe I could help you. Who do you work for?"

The man laughed. "Para quién trabajamos," he said to the other man who stood off to the side. "Señor Brandt, you know why I am here. I am here because Señor Haddock, he entered into a contract, an agreement. Sadly, he has not fulfilled that agreement. So, as you are his partner, I have come to you."

A.J. could feel a prickling heat spread across his neck and chest. "I'm afraid that Mr. Haddock has died. Unexpectedly. We're all just devastated. We're just trying to deal with all of that right now. I'm afraid I don't know anything about any agreement. Darrell had his own ... interests."

"I'm very sorry for your loss," the man said. "But I'm afraid that him being dead does not make the agreement go away. As a businessman, I'm sure you agree that an agreement made must be fulfilled. And you, you are his partner. So, it falls to you. ¿Claro?"

A.J. took a breath and as calmly and evenly as he could said, "Señor, I mean no disrespect, really, but if I was not involved, if I don't know anything about it, why would it be my responsibility?"

The man shrugged disinterestedly. "I don't care about your questions." He gestured to his colleague who placed a file on the coffee bar. "You're going to read that and then you're going to text the number and tell me. And you're going to do it in two days. Or maybe with my friends we go visit your property down at Mismaloya, the one you're getting ready to announce? I'm sure you wouldn't want anything to happen to that."

A.J. said nothing and then nodded. "OK," he said.

"Good. Good meeting." He tugged at the bottom of his jacket, which had ridden up.

As they made their way to the door, the man stopped and turned. He pointed at A.J. with his drink. "Now I want to be clear for you. Because maybe you are not as smart as you think. If you get ideas, go to the police, try to fuck with me, know that I will come back and I will remove your skin from your body, strip by in strip, and dress you in salt like a fish. You understand?"

He took a sip from his straw before spraying the remainder of the cup's bright green contents across the living room. "I feel lighter already."

Joe left another message for Veronica. He understood that this was part of his recompense, part of the righting of the scales. Doors had closed to him. People had turned away. The truth about what had really happened remained, but some didn't care to consider it, and he had to be OK with that. All he could do was accept and endure, and in time, maybe new bridges could be built. He put the match to the end of the joint.

He sat on the beach in a shady spot next to the rocks that marked the southern end of Playa los Muertos. To his right it was condos and hotels crowding the broad curve of Banderas Bay. People decorated the sand and bobbed in the shifting sea.

Today was Friday, which meant that he had been in Puerto Vallarta for nearly two weeks, and he didn't feel any closer to liberating the items he'd purchased from Porfirio than when this whole thing had started. And now he'd even lost his ally in the customs office. Plus, every question just led to five more.

Still, he did know more now than when he'd started. Wasn't that progress? His father used to say your chances of achieving something go way up when you actually start *trying*. He'd learned the name of the potential killer of Darrel Haddock. He'd learned further that the possible killer was not much liked in his former hometown. Kill your father and sisters and blind your mother, and you forfeit that legacy.

But the most interesting recent item to Joe had been one small thing Señora Vega had said. "Is it about Ruben?" On a hunch, Joe did a quick Google search. It turned out that Ruben Bermúdez, the attorney, and former owner of the beautiful Moorish trunk Joe had purchased, had also grown up in Talpa. At some point, together or separate, Bermúdez and Vega had found their way out of Talpa and into some dangerous circles.

Then it came to him. He *had* heard Vega's name before. When he'd gone to San Sebastián to see the Bermúdez hacienda, the caretaker had asked Joe if he'd bought the antiques from a Señor Vega. And hadn't he said that Señor Vega had *just* been there? The realization sent a current of electricity shooting through him, almost like Vega had been hiding inside his own head the whole time.

Joe kept moving the pieces around like the squares of a Rubik's cube. But he couldn't get the colors to align. He kept coming back to Miguel. Something told Joe that Cesar's friend and fellow Los Fantasmas member knew more than he was letting on. Perhaps he feared for his own safety. Lives did seem to be precarious things these days. Maybe they had stumbled onto some information that they shouldn't have. There was only one way to find out.

When Joe arrived at Panadería Esperanza he spotted Miguel getting off his motorcycle with grocery bags.

Joe held the door for him. "Buenos días," he said.

134

"Buenas …" Miguel started until he saw Joe. "… tardes." The young man's face dropped.

"Buenas *tardes*, right," Joe said. "I'm always getting that wrong."

A woman's voice called from the rear of the shop. The lone customer exited with a coffee and a bag.

Miguel took up a spot behind the counter. "What do you want?" he asked.

"Well, right now, I'd love one of your banana muffins and … a sugared donut." He pointed at the glass front of the display.

Miguel slowly retrieved the two items and placed them in a bag.

"Oh, and a coffee please," Joe said.

Miguel set an empty to-go cup on the counter.

Joe took the cup to the coffee station and filled it. "And thank you for your kind texts. Sorry. I was so moved I just didn't know how to respond."

"Come on, man," the young man said, scratching at his couple days' growth of beard, "can't you just leave me alone?"

Joe tore off a piece of the doughnut. "I don't understand. He was your best friend."

Banging pans could be heard in the back of the shop.

"Sí. He was my best friend," Miguel said. "So what?"

Joe shook his head, raised his hands. "I'm just trying to figure out what happened."

"Why?" Miguel asked.

"Why?"

"You didn't even know Cesar."

Joe nodded. "True. That's true."

"So why are you involved?"

Joe thought about the question, and how to answer it. "Look," he said. "I freely admit that my involvement began because I have personal reasons to be interested."

Miguel idly wiped down the counter.

"But it's also true that things have changed since then. I met Molly. I met you. I feel as if I know Cesar. And you might think this is crazy, but I think I would have liked him. That we could have been friends. I mean, I like you, Miguel. I know you don't necessarily care about that or even share it, but I figure if I like you, I would like him. What I'm trying to say is I think he deserves justice. I don't want his murder to become just another forgotten cartel killing."

Joe's testimony was interrupted by shouting from the rear of the bakery. It was a woman's voice, sharp and emphatic. Joe waited for Miguel to respond, but the young baker kept his attention on cleaning the counter and didn't flinch. Joe continued. "Because of how I came to be involved, I can't stop thinking about him and what happened. And I—"

Another slightly louder and more agitated monologue issued from the back, the voice rich with frustration. Again, Joe paused for Miguel to investigate or reply in some way to the disruption. When he didn't move, Joe asked, "Is that your mother? Do you need to … answer her?"

Miguel shook his head, and then a moment later there came more yelling, the woman's voice high and accusative now.

"What did you do to make her so mad?" Joe asked.

"She's not talking to me," Miguel said. "She's talking to my abuela, who doesn't listen to anyone."

"Ah," Joe said.

"Plus, she's a bitch, you know?"

The surprise of this remark pitched Joe into a real laugh. A grin crept onto Miguel's face.

"She opened the bakery, but it's not even her place anymore. But she still calls all the time, telling us what we are doing wrong."

He laughed and both men relaxed into the moment as they listened to Miguel's mother shout into the phone.

Joe took a long drink from his coffee. And then Miguel said, "So why do you think it was Los Primeros that killed Cesar?"

Joe wasn't sure he had heard this correctly. "What?" he asked.

"You said Cesar was killed by the cartel. Why do you say that?"

Joe was not a block from Panadería Esperanza when his phone dinged. It was a text from Molly. "My dad just texted me. Said he needs to see me right now. Will you come with me?"

Joe dropped into a spot of shade made by a shop awning. He looked at the message. Go with her? He'd just learned that Miguel doesn't think the cartel killed Cesar's. Now A.J. Brandt had something he needed to talk about with his daughter? He had to go with her.

"Where should I meet you?"

She responded immediately. "His place. Pelicanos."

In for a penny, in for a pound. "Meet you there in 15."

The Pelicanos condos were only a few blocks away, occupying a stunning stretch of beachfront not far from the Banderas Properties offices. Just about a block away from the building, Joe saw Molly striding swiftly up the street. She did high strung well. It suited her somehow. The long limbs, the wide, urgent eyes. They had talked little since Talpa.

"Thank you," she said when she was still 15 feet away. "But then how are you supposed to respond to a text like that, right?"

"I've wanted to see the places in this building anyway. Who knows, maybe I'll buy myself a time share while I'm here," Joe said.

"Funny, aren't you?" she said.

The two fell into step as they headed into the building.

"Do you know what this is about?" Joe asked.

"I don't even want to speculate."

As they entered Pelicanos' airy lobby, Molly's shoes clacked on the sparkling marble floor. They passed uniformed employees wearing practiced smiles.

When they reached the bank of elevators, Molly stopped and turned to him. "So, I really don't know what this is about, but I have a feeling that it's ... that's it's not going to be good. I know my dad."

"OK," Joe said. "So what is—"

"What do I want you to do? Just—" She shook her head. "Just be there. And then later, when I wonder if I remember it right, you can tell me that I'm not crazy."

"Not crazy, got it."

"As hard as that will be for you."

The elevator opened onto the floor of A.J. Brandt's penthouse condo. The landing had been decorated in a faux Asian style. Large framed landscape prints. Bamboo in heavy red earthenware pots. A black lacquered table beneath a large mirror.

Molly rang the doorbell. "He's going to be mad you're here," she said.

"Ah, good to know."

A.J. opened the door and his face immediately clouded upon seeing Joe.

"OK, I'm here," Molly said.

"I see that, but who the hell is this?"

"Daddy, rude," she said, pushing her way past him into the large, airy interior.

"Seriously. Molly."

Joe smiled and nodded, acknowledging to his host that he too found himself someplace he hadn't expected to be. He extended his hand.

"Lily. Joe Lily," Joe said, finally retracting his hand when the offer was not reciprocated.

"I don't care who you are," A.J. said.

Joe smiled again and placed his hands in his pockets.

"Molly, what in the hell is going on?" her father asked.

"Daddy, he's a friend. I asked him to come with me."

"I'm sorry, but you're going to have to go," A.J. said.

"Can I talk to you?" she asked. "Joe, will you excuse us for a minute?"

"Of course," Joe said. Molly and her father retreated to one of the bedrooms, leaving Joe to admire the beautiful space. Gleaming marble floors, high box-beam ceilings, fabric wallpaper in blue and gold. From the foyer he could see into the broad living area, which was bright and open.

After a few minutes they returned.

"OK," Molly said. "I need a drink." She smiled and led the way into the living room before heading to the kitchen.

"Sorry about that welcome," A.J. said. "It's been a day." Sweat made dark half-moons in the pits of his blue silk shirt.

"No problem," Joe said. "We've all been there."

A.J. looked hard at Joe as if deciphering a language he only partly understood.

Joe said, "I was so very sorry to hear about your partner. Molly told me."

A.J. exhaled and nodded. "It's, it's just fucking horrible. He was a great guy. I wouldn't have taken a chance on this business if it hadn't been for him."

The spacious living room opened out onto a large veranda. Floor-to-ceiling articulated doors had been retracted to open up the entire room to the breeze off the Pacific.

Molly returned from the kitchen, three opened beers in her hands. "What happened to the couch and wall there? Jackson Pollock stop by?" Green stains decorated the furniture, curtains, and wall.

"Not exactly," he said.

"OK, so what is it that I needed to drop everything and run over here? Is it about Cesar?"

"Look, I'm going to say this one more time," A.J. said. "I don't know anything about what happened to Cesar. Did I want you to get married? No. I've admitted that. But I would never do anything like that. Never."

"It was pretty obvious you didn't like him," she said.

"Didn't like him? Honey, I didn't know him. All I knew is that you two getting married was a bad idea. It would have … held you back."

"Held me back?" Her voice rose an octave.

"For once will you just admit that you don't know everything? I've been on this earth a lot longer than you. I've been in Mexico for 10 years. I've seen it happen time and time again. It just doesn't work. I'm very sorry Cesar is gone. I am. Believe me or not. Because I know you're hurting. But I'm *not* sorry that you won't be making a mistake that you would have regretted. Do we really need to do this in front of our guest?"

An image of Veronica passed across Joe's mind. He took a long pull off the beer. The cold of it felt good.

When Molly didn't respond it became clear she was crying. She had turned away and wept into her hands.

"I'm sorry," A.J. said. "I'm sorry you're having to go through this."

After a moment, Molly collected herself. "Joe thinks all I do is cry."

Joe smiled and shook his head. It seemed to him that her relationship with her father had probably always been this way. A pitched battle. Piqued conversation, raised voices, crying. He could see a well-rehearsed reenactment of lines they had been delivering since she was a little girl.

"And I believe you," she said. "I just, I don't know." She stepped to the patio and stared into the distance. At length, the spell having passed, she said, "OK, so if it's not about Cesar, what's going on?"

"Let's sit down," A.J. said.

They all took a seat. The wide porch and tall windows made one feel like you were sitting outside, perched in the upper branches of some impossibly lofty tree.

Once comfortable, A.J. turned to Joe.

"You mentioned my partner. I said he was a great guy, and he was. But we all have our challenges, let's call them. I think those are what got him killed. And unfortunately," he leaned back and, his hands on his head, "they've now got me into a … situation."

"A situation," Molly said.

A.J. spoke again directly to Joe. "You seem like a nice guy, but I don't know you. So I hope you don't take it wrong when I say I'm only sharing this in front of you because my daughter insisted on it for some reason. Please don't make me regret it."

Part of Joe wanted to remove himself from the scene. The last thing he needed was more drama. But another part, the what-if part, the part that some might say had too often taken the wheel in his life, wondered if this might somehow advance his own interests as well.

"I respect that. I'm just here because Molly asked me to be. That's it," Joe said.

A.J. looked hard at Joe for a beat and then resumed. "OK," he said, almost to himself. "About six months ago, I don't remember exactly when, Darrell came to me and said he'd found this incredible piece of property, up the coast. We had to snap it up. He wanted to put a resort on it. Now he didn't do that very often, come to me with a place. Usually it was me who did the scouting around. But this time he did. And he was excited about it. Unfortunately, the timing really couldn't have been worse. I tried to explain that to him. But he wouldn't let it go.

For weeks he kept hounding me about it. Telling me what a goldmine it was. We had to get it. I kept trying to explain to him that the business wasn't in a good spot to take on something like that right now. He didn't see what he didn't want to see. And he wouldn't let up. So then we're on the golf course and he started up again about it. I'd just had fucking enough. I told him it wasn't happening, we weren't going to goddamn do it, and I didn't want to hear another word about it. He launched into this tirade about how it was him who'd started the business and how I thought I ran things now. Thought I was smarter than him. Blah blah blah. We'd had fights. Work with someone long enough and you're bound to. But this, this was a big one. I actually thought it was going to come to blows right there on the fucking first tee." A.J. paused and shook his head.

Molly opened her mouth to speak and A.J. held up his hand. "Just let me get through this," he said. "A little time passed, and we managed to get over it. I mean, you have to. I didn't hear anything more about it. And so I thought we were past it."

"He doesn't bring it up again?" Molly asked.

"He doesn't bring it up. Work gets back to normal. Which is good, because we're really busy at the moment. One of the reasons why this idea of his just wasn't going to work. And then he comes to me one day, says he has something to tell me. He's all excited about something.

140

Actually, he tells me he wants to take me somewhere new for lunch. But like I said, I'm busy, I got shit to do. Still, I'm thinking we had this fight, we're still mending fences. I should do it. Smooth things over. So we get in the car and he starts driving. We head north out of town. I'm thinking it's a restaurant or something. He's just smiling and driving. We pass Bucerias and I'm thinking, where are we going? After Punta de Mita, he pulls off onto this dirt road that winds around and then he finally stops. But there's no restaurant, there's nothing. Dirt. Nothing. So I say, 'Dude, what in the hell are we doing?' And he says, 'We did it!' And I say, 'Did what?' He spreads his arms out and says, 'You're standing on the newest addition to Banderas Properties!'" A.J. stopped and exhaled like he'd been holding his breath.

Joe wanted to ask a question. He wanted to ask many questions. But he kept his mouth shut. It was better that A.J. forget that Joe was even there.

"I don't understand," Molly said.

A.J. shook his head. "The bastard went ahead and did it. He bought the whole goddamned parcel. A huge plot. A little up, with spectacular views. I mean, it's beautiful, but there's just no way, one, we had the capital to finance it, or two, that I wouldn't have known if Darrell had used Banderas Properties to buy it."

"So what are you saying?" Molly asked.

"I'm saying he got help. And not from me. He kept telling me that we were going to establish this new tourist beachhead. He called it Playa Toscana. Said it would all be Italian themed. Thousands of rooms, shops, beachfront. People love Italy but they want it closer. We were going to give them that. He had it all worked out in his head."

"He borrowed the money," Molly said.

"I let him talk, not that I could've stopped him. And maybe it is true that I'd been rolling over him lately. Sometimes certain projects require a ... delicacy that Darrell didn't always possess. Don't get me wrong, he was great with other stuff. The nuts and bolts. Keeping on contractors. He was a genius at that. The money part, that just wasn't his strong suit. That's how he ended up in Mexico in the first place. And here's the thing. I know his intentions were good. I know he cared about the business. But I knew right away this was bad. Really bad. I asked him where the money came from. Investments, he told me. He kept saying, 'We'll make it back hundredfold.'"

The words hung in the air like the smell of the ocean from the open patio door.

"OK, so, so, do you know who—"

A.J. cleared his throat. "I do. They just visited me."

Chapter 8

S leep had been fitful. And now there was a loud knock on the door of his room. The front desk? The cleaning staff?

"No necesito limpio," he said hoarsely.

But this was followed by another knock. Joe dragged himself from bed, the stray threads of a bad dream slowly disappearing back into the darkness of his imagination.

"No necesito limpio," he said again, opening the door just as a man launched himself at Joe, knocking Joe to the ground. They hit the corner of the bed and rolled onto the floor. The man struck Joe in the ribs and stomach, taking the air out of him. Joe managed a blow to the guy's face with his elbow. Joe was larger and stronger than his attacker, but he was moving too slow and the man was wiry and fast and never stopped moving. They rolled into the small table, knocking it and the toaster to the floor. They torqued away from and against each other, crashing into the chair and sending it to the ground as well. Twisting and arching, they grappled on the cool tile like battling crocodiles. One would take control and then the other. Now fully awake, Joe used his superior strength and size to get himself into a position with some leverage, the man's back to him. The man tried to get to his feet as he attempted to strip Joe's arm from the position it now took around the man's neck. He tried wrenching himself free, throwing his head back into Joe but Joe had begun to tighten his grip, feeling the give of the man's throat, the cutting off his air. The man struggled, all limbs working now, scratching at Joe's arm until no sound came from him.

"Relax," Joe said. "If you don't relax, it's lights out. ¿Comprende?"

The man tried again to stand.

"Stop. Stop."

The man relented. His coiled body relaxed. He stopped fighting.

"OK?" Joe asked.

The man nodded.

Joe quickly patted him down for any signs of a weapon. Finding none, he said, "I'm going to let you go. But make a move and I'll fucking take you out. I promise you."

The man nodded again.

Slowly, Joe relinquished his hold, getting to his feet and backing away. The other remained on the floor rubbing his neck and coughing and trying to catch his breath.

"Who are you and what the fuck do you want?" Joe demanded.

The man, after another moment, got to his knees and then turned to Joe.

"Miguel? What the fuck? I could have killed you!"

The young Mexican remained short of breath. "They smashed ... our shop ... because of you!"

"Who smashed your shop? And what in the hell did I have to do with it?"

"You went ... and threatened El Mago. They came ... and told my mother they would ... kill her and me. Everything is broken there. Everything."

Joe wanted to defend himself, but at least part of the accusation was true: he had gone and seen El Mago on Miguel's information and, Joe knew, against his wishes.

"Is everyone OK?" Joe asked. He reached down to help the young man stand, but Miguel batted away his hand.

"Why do you care? You don't care about us. My mother, she is crying all the time now. The shop is ruined."

"But they didn't hurt her," Joe said.

"No! But maybe they will, they could. They know where we are. Why? Why did you have to go there? I told you. I told you."

"You think it's El Mago?" Joe asked.

Miguel shrugged and shook his head. "He lives in Culiacán. Los Primeros are in Culiacán. You go there, then our shop is broken."

His best friend had been decapitated, his ears sliced off and stuffed into his mouth. In the universe in which that can happen anything can happen and none of it made any sense in the end.

Joe said, "Did they ... say anything? What did they want?"

Miguel continued to rub his throat. "They told her I should mind my own business. Or they would burn the bakery."

He put his head in his hands. "I can't help you. I miss Cesar. But with my family, I can't."

Joe poured Miguel a cup of water and handed it to him. "I understand. I do. And I promise I will leave you out of all this. But I need you to do one last thing for me."

144

"No! No more. Don't you listen?" Miguel shook his head, his long bangs sticking to his sweaty forehead. "Just leave me alone."

"Give me Cesar's computer," Joe said.

"What?" Miguel exclaimed.

"Let me have Cesar's computer. That way, you'll really be free of all of this. It will be safer."

"I don't have Cesar's computer, I told you that."

"Miguel, come on. I know you have it. And if I know, they know. Give it to me and you and your family will be safer. Right? And I promise I'll do everything I can to protect your mom and the bakery."

"What in the hell can *you* do? You sell fucking furniture. You don't know these people. They do whatever the fuck they want. You get in the way and you get what Cesar got."

Joe had no plan for making good on his part of that bargain, but he needed that laptop.

"True. I don't know these people. But we both know that they want that laptop. They took every other system out of the shop before anyone could get to them. I'll take it, and you can concentrate on putting this behind you, protecting your family."

Miguel stared into his water glass for a long moment. "I'll think about it."

Joe could live with that.

Joe exited the taxi. The day was hot, hotter it seemed than it had been. Stepping from the cool of the car felt like he was battling a physical presence. The heat could be a force that lay on top of you. It tried to take you to the ground. Once inside the airport, he stood for a second and breathed in the air-conditioned air. His skin tingled and the little hairs rose along his forearms. Travelers pulled their suitcases and pushed their carts full of luggage, kids swimming alongside in the way of small, tropical fish.

Joe thought about when he had arrived in Puerto Vallarta more than a couple of weeks ago now. He saw himself leaving customs and dragging his bag along, unsure what to expect but hoping that it would go smoothly so he could return home and report that the business would live to sell another day. Instead, things had veered sharply in another direction, taking him down a very dark road.

The idea had struck him like a long shot: Veronica didn't want to see him, but perhaps she could be persuaded to do something on Miguel's behalf. Joe had no one else to turn to. He walked purposefully to her office. He had just joined the hallway when he saw her traveling toward him from the opposite direction with her boss. Joe smiled as sincerely as he knew how.

"Well, hello," he said.

"Señor Lily," said Señor Quiñones. "¿Cómo estás? Nice to see you."

Veronica remained quiet, staring at him blankly as if at a stranger.

"You are just the people I was coming to see," Joe said. "How are you, Señor Quiñones?"

"Tired. I just returned from Houston. Too many meetings."

Joe laughed. "We've got to keep the makers of bad coffee and conference tables in business."

The man, his black hair graying at the temples, smiled. "Great barbacoa though. And we saw a chamber orchestra perform Bach's Brandenburg Concerto No. 3. Outside under the stars. Beautiful. But I see you have no bags, so must I conclude that your presence is not because you are leaving? I was also sorry to hear from Veronica that your items remain in quarantine. I hope that is resolved soon."

"Yes, I do too. It's actually on a sort of related matter that I was coming to see you both today." He looked at Veronica. "Buenas tardes. I remembered this time. Past noon, Buenas *tardes*."

"Buenas tardes," she said.

If Señor Quiñones felt the hammer weight of that brief exchange, he didn't let on.

"Well, let's go back to the office," he said. "If we can help, it will be a good day."

Joe realized the man had a small limp, and that Veronica had trimmed her hair.

Once in the office, Señor Quiñones took up a spot behind his desk. Veronica sat at her desk and proceeded to ignore the two men.

"So how can we help you?" he asked.

"Well, it involves a young man who I think I spoke to Veronica about earlier. His name is Miguel Peñaherrera. His family owns a bakery in Old Town."

"He is a Mexican national?"

"Yes," Joe said. "Veronica, do you remember him?" Joe was going to ignore the cold shoulder and soldier on. He had learned something during his days on Wall Street.

She reluctantly raised her head. "I do, yes." She moved a strand of dark hair from her eyes and looked directly at Joe. "He is a friend—*was* a friend—of the young man who was killed."

"Exactly," Joe said. "I won't bore you with the background, but Miguel has been trying to help me, a little reluctantly, but he's been trying to help. And I'm afraid his help seems to have drawn some attention. Yesterday some men came into his family's shop and, well, sent a message. Not good. So I'm trying to determine if there's anything I can do to help him. I thought maybe you might have some ideas."

Señor Quiñones exhaled slowly, leaning back in his creaking chair. He stared at some spot above Joe's head and crossed his arms at his chest. "Well, we are customs, right?" he said. "I don't know what we could do, but let me think about it. Let me see what I can find out."

Joe nodded. "Thank you. I appreciate it. I'm starting to run out of ideas, and time. I really need to get back to the States. But thank you. I just want to do whatever I can for him. I think he's a good guy. His friend was murdered. The last thing I want is to put him at risk."

"Yes, of course," Señor Quiñones said. "I'm afraid that is the world we live in. Bullies and thieves. Tell him to be safe. I know how young men can be." He nodded.

Joe took a last drink from his coffee, stood, and extended his hand. "OK, thank you," he said. "I really appreciate the time you both have already spent on trying to help."

"Nice to see you, Joe," Señor Quiñones said. "I'm sorry we haven't been able to do much."

The two men shook hands and Joe turned and exited the office. He held little hope that anything would come of it, either for Miguel or for himself. And as for Veronica, she remained steadfastly aloof. It was just as well. Having just said it out loud, he knew it was true: It was time to head home. He thought himself a bit mad for even trying. Maybe Alan, his long-suffering accountant, could think of some genius way to keep the business running. If not, well, he would figure that out too.

He was nearly out of the airport when he heard his name being called. Turning, he found Veronica hurrying toward him. The elegance and composure she carried with her made everything else around her seem awkward and tawdry and tired.

"Hey," he said.

"I caught you," she said.

They stood for a moment in silence, the world moving around them on squeaky luggage carts and flip flops.

"I was thinking about your friend. Is it Porfirio?"

"Porfirio, yes," Joe said.

"Yes, didn't you say he has an uncle that works for the police?"

Joe was still surprised to find her standing there. He wasn't listening.

"Maybe he could help Miguel," she added. She stood straight and serious. "You've probably already thought of that."

"No," Joe said, "I hadn't. That's a good idea."

Veronica nodded.

"I'll check with him. I need to talk with him anyway. Thank you for running all the way out here."

"I didn't think I'd catch you."

"You are fast in those heels," he said. "I pity the person looking to dodge customs in this airport."

She let a small smile creep across her face.

"Well, thank you again, for everything," Joe said. "And please thank Señor Quiñones for me."

She nodded, her hands clasped in front of her.

Even in the manufactured light of the airport departures hall Veronica stood out. A few days ago, Joe would have pulled her to him and kissed her, but today he only smiled, gave a small nod, and took himself into the extravagant Mexican sunshine.

Porfirio gave Joe a hard time when he entered the store.

"Carmen is mad at me, so I'm mad at you," he said.

"What? Why?" Joe demanded. "What did I do?"

"You have not been to dinner at the house," he said.

"You Mexicans," Joe joked. "I don't come to your house for dinner and it's my fault. Will you finally quit blaming the Americans for *everything*?"

Porfirio, always quick to smile, broke into his squeak of a laugh. The act managed to highlight the indigene qualities of his face, the widely spaced eyes, the dark, high cheekbones.

"Your father used to say that," Porfirio said.

"Dad said everything first," Joe said.

"Where have you been?" Porfirio said. "I called you."

"I know, I know. I'm sorry," Joe said. "I've done a bit of traveling. Visited Talpa."

Porfirio furrowed his brow thoughtfully.

"Just checking on a few things," Joe said.

"Joe," his friend said.

"I know. I'm always careful," he said. "That's actually one of the reasons I'm here. Do you remember Miguel, Cesar's friend?"

Porfirio shrugged his shoulders. "I don't think so," he said. "Why?"

"Well, some guys came into his family's bakery and busted up the place. Threatened his mother."

The bell on the shop door jangled. They turned to see a man enter the store. He did not acknowledge them and began to browse the jumbled collection of old iron candlesticks, ornamental mirrors, weathered wooden frames.

Joe lowered his voice. "They scared her, and Miguel too. He thinks I'm to blame because I've asked some questions of the wrong people, I guess. This morning, he visited to let me know that he's not very happy about it. It's true that I probably haven't helped. So I was thinking, 'I wonder if Porfirio's brother-in-law might be able to help.' You know, just keep an eye on the shop, his family. Possible?"

"Do you think they will come back? The ones who broke into his store?"

Joe shrugged. "I don't know. But maybe he could arrange to have one of his guys, I don't know, keep an eye on the place? Just for a little while?"

"Let's go ask him," Porfirio said. He raised a finger and then disappeared into the back. Joe checked his phone and saw that he had received a call from Veronica. Things were looking up. Joe could hear his friend communicating with his staff. He watched the place's lone customer mill among the bric-a-brac, bowls of Milagro charms, old sun-bitten tools from the rancho, wrought-iron hooks, and dusty paintings with sagging canvas. The man, a Mexican, looked directly at Joe and seemed to smile. From a small box he picked up a tarnished sword, testing its weight in his hand, inspecting the blade.

"Spectacular, no?" he said to Joe. Spec-toc-oo-lar.

"¿Listo?" It was Porfirio.

The two men exited the store, exercising the bell as they dived out into the bleached afternoon.

Paz, Porfirio's brother-in-law, sat at a table under an umbrella with a plate heaped with tacos. He drank from a bottle of Coke. The clerk at the station had informed them where to find him. Paz bore none of the indigene in him. His were Spanish features. Long face, aquiline nose, crisp mustache. Joe remembered that they were related by marriage, not blood. His big hands worked nimbly on the tacos.

"¡Buenas, hermano!" he said.

"Buenas," Porfirio said.

Joe and the man shook hands. It had been some time since they'd last spoken, and the police department had, as far as Joe could determine, made little progress on Cesar's case.

"I'm very sorry about your friend," Paz said right away between mouthfuls.

"My friend?" Joe asked.

"The American. On the video." He shook his head. "Very bad."

The Darrell video. "Yes. I didn't really know him. But you're right. Truly horrible."

Paz nodded, his mouth full. "Los Primeros. They are, how do you say, bárbaros."

"Barbarians."

"Barbarians, sí."

"Any news on that?"

The deputy sheriff shook his head as he washed down his taco with a long drink. "Shadows and ghosts," he said. Joe wondered if Porfirio had broken a confidence with his brother-in-law by sharing Rafa Vega's name. He asked nothing more on that score.

They sat beneath the umbrella, and its pattern made strange blocks of colored light on the ground and Joe's leg. Trucks and cars and buses clattered by behind them in a haze of exhaust. Straight ahead stood the marina where the cruise ships docked, empty this morning but for the crisp blue of the Pacific. Drive the other direction and you found yourself after a few miles in the small satellite city of Pitillal, home to many of the Mexicans working in Vallarta's hotels and resorts.

Porfirio and the man exchanged a few words in the truncated language of family.

"So how can I help you?" the man said.

"Well," Joe said. "There is a young man. Miguel Peñaherrera. I'm hoping to get some help for him."

"Miguel Peñaherrera," the deputy sheriff said.

"He is the best friend of Cesar Castillo, the one who was killed a couple weeks ago."

"Yes," he said. "The one whose head—" he tapped his head with a knuckle. He sighed. "There are so many cartel killings now. It is a problem." He tilted his head to launch into another taco.

Joe said, "Right. Well, this friend, Miguel, he's having a rough time. You know, first his friend is killed. And then yesterday a couple of men smashed up his family's bakery. Threatened his mother. And so I was wondering if it might be possible for you or one of your men to keep an eye on their bakery for a few days. Give them some peace."

Paz took another drink from his soda even as he was shaking his head. "Not possible," he said. He dispatched the reminder of the taco in one bite and wiped his hands.

"I was just thinking that one of your officers looking after the place, it might help calm things down. After all they've gone through."

Paz removed a toothpick from his breast pocket. "I have no men," he said. "Sheriff Garza has assigned most of us to the show down the coast. I'm very sorry."

Joe nodded. "Show down the coast?"

"You haven't read the papers?" Porfirio asked.

"There was a big protest. In Old Town, in the plaza," Paz said as he handed the woman at the large grill-top a handful of coins.

"An American company," Porfirio added. "They're working with local government here. It will bring jobs, they say. Lots of money for people here. But government always says that, and nothing changes."

The demonstration. He could forgive himself for not immediately remembering, as he'd been floating along in the dumbstruck afterglow of his first night with Veronica.

"Yes," Joe said. "Now I remember. Oil."

"Sí. Drilling south of Mismaloya. Lots of people are angry and making some problems, you know. Most of my men will be there."

151

"I understand," Joe said. "That demonstration was the last time I saw Darrell Haddock." He wanted to ask about Rafa Vega, share what had happened in Talpa to him and Molly. But he also wanted to know if the police knew what A.J. had just told him and Molly, that Darrell had borrowed a large sum of money from someone. "There are just so many questions."

The brother-in-law worked the toothpick, staring at Joe. "You don't want to get involved with this, my friend." He set his napkin on his plate.

"Well, so sorry to interrupt your lunch, Señor Ibarra. Thanks a lot for your time." The men shook hands.

Walking back to the car beneath cloudless skies, Joe said, "It was worth a shot."

"Joe," Porfirio said, "He's right. You should stay away from it."

Joe laid his hand on his friend's shoulder. "Stay away from what?"

Joe dropped Porfirio off and headed directly for Banderas Properties. He wanted to talk to A.J. and Molly about his conversation with Porfirio's brother-in-law, maybe even learn something more about Darrell. If Vega was indeed behind both, it was hard not to conclude that the two murders weren't linked in other ways. But how?

The two young female receptionists at Banderas Properties greeted Joe with a synchronized "Can we help you?" One wore a top with the word "Baby" stretched in sequins across the front. The other pulled at the two strands of dark hair that she'd curled to frame her face.

"Buenos días," Joe said. "I'm here to see Mr. Brandt."

"Oh, he's not here," the first one said.

Not there. "Hmm, I'm supposed to have a meeting with him."

The second one, who assumed an air of authority, said, "He's in Mismaloya."

"Mismaloya?"

"For the party," the first one said.

"The groundbreaking," proudly corrected the second, using a word it was clear was new to her.

"I see." Could it be the same "show" that Paz had referred to? "Is Ms. Brandt available?"

"No, she's not here."

Joe thanked them and exited back into the bright sun.

As everyone else seemed to be taking in this event in Mismaloya, he figured he might as well too. He was about to hail a taxi when he received a call from Miguel.

"Señor Lily? It's Miguel."

"¿Cómo estás, Miguel?"

"I came by your hotel. You weren't there. I need to see you."

"OK," Joe said. This was a far cry from the young man who had burst into his hotel room and tried to break his neck. "How about Daiquiri Dick's?"

"OK, when?"

"Let's say 20 minutes."

"See you then," Miguel said.

What was that in Miguel's voice? Anger? Fear? Joe couldn't tell.

Daiquiri Dick's is a Puerto Vallarta landmark. It was Joe's dad's favorite spot, and he insisted on at least one visit on every trip to town. "Tacos at Carmen's, a cold Pacifico at Cuates y Cuetes, and a meal at Daiquiri Dick's. I'm not in Vallarta until I check those off the list," he'd say.

The waiter led Joe to a spot outside with a wide-open view of the bay. Home seemed a long way away and a long time ago. He'd slipped into a pleasant tropical reverie when the hostess arrived. "Sir, there is a man who says he is meeting you?"

Joe looked past her to the entrance of the restaurant where Miguel waited, his backpack slung over a shoulder.

Joe waved Miguel over. As the young man passed the hostess going in the other direction Joe could see Miguel say something at which the hostess frowned but made no reply.

Miguel took up a seat opposite Joe.

"What did you say to her?" Joe asked.

"I said 'Tú también eres mexicana,'" Miguel said. "You're Mexican too."

"'You are Mexican too'?" Joe said.

"Sometimes I don't like the people that work in these places," he said. "They get confused. They see tourists up here." He held his hand above his head. "It's embarrassing. And then they act like they are better than the rest of us. I told her I was here to see you. I pointed to you. But she said to wait. You think she would do that to a gringo? It's bullshit."

"Would a beer help?" Joe asked.

"No, thank you," he said. "I'm not staying."

153

"OK," Joe said. "You sounded sort of urgent on the phone."

Miguel glanced quickly around. "Another man showed up at the bakery. He didn't do anything. But everyone is scared now. My aunt is always crying. I am done with this. So I'm doing what I told Cesar I would never do."

Joe felt the backpack pushed against his feet.

"Cesar is gone. I don't want my family hurt too. So take it. Now you can leave me out of it." Lowering his voice, he said, "The password is omarbravoisking1919."

"Omar Bravo?" Joe said.

"One of Cesar's favorite players," Miguel said. "And 1919 is the year Zapata was killed by the government. Cesar used that one a lot."

"But you're the expert here. I need your help figuring out what's on here."

Miguel stood. "Buena suerte." He'd only taken a step when he turned. "Cuidado, Joe," he said.

Joe remembered that Veronica had called and tried her number. It went straight to voicemail. He adopted a voice of easy-going charm. "Bummed I missed your call. Hope all's well."

A cold beer and then Joe would dig into Cesar's computer and see what he could make of it. He entered the foyer of the Hotel Mercurio. He greeted Javier at the front desk, and he'd proceeded through the archway to the pool area when Javier caught up with him.

"I'm sorry," Javier said. "Señor Lily, you have a package."

"A package?"

Javier handed him a box. It was wrapped in plain brown paper and bore no return address. His friend Leon, Joe thought, shaking his head. If only he knew Leon's address, he would love the chance to thank him with a surprise of his own. But Leon kept on the move, his whereabouts hard to pin down.

In his room, Joe immediately removed his sweat-soaked shirt and turned on the ceiling fan. He knew it probably wasn't incredibly wise to bring the computer here after the redecorating he'd received a couple of days earlier, but he needed a shower and change of clothes. Then he'd find a safe place to investigate Miguel's gift. If he were lucky, the contents would lift the veil on why someone wanted Cesar dead, which might then break up the logjam that had trapped his items in the police evidence room along with the future of the business.

Still, just to be safe, Joe brought the backpack into the bathroom with him, setting it atop the towels while he showered.

When done, Joe dressed and checked his phone. Nothing from Veronica. He wondered for a moment where he should go to dig into Cesar's laptop. He had an idea. Then he remembered the package Javier had given him. He grabbed the box and took up a spot on the bed. He casually weighed it in his hands. It had some heft and, Joe thought, gave off the scent of, was it coffee? What was Leon up to this time?

Joe removed the wrapping and opened the box to find, just as expected, a loose mass of dark, oily coffee beans. The beans gave off a rich funk of earth and smoke. It took Joe back to his neighborhood coffee shop and in that moment Portland came rushing back to him. His apartment, his mother, his dog Maximus, who he missed like crazy. He hoped his mom was managing OK. A feeling of regret and self-pity snuck in behind the reverie.

But amidst the coffee beans there did not appear to be a note. There must be a note. So Joe began to empty the beans onto the bed. Very quickly a different smell found his nose. Rotting cabbage. Sharp, vaguely sweet. And then he saw it. It sat at the bottom of the box like a misplaced prop. A simple ring still adorned one finger. The hand had been severed cleanly at the wrist. Joe's stomach lurched. The room stretched away from him and a cool, prickly sensation ran up his neck. He stumbled to the bathroom and emptied his stomach into the toilet.

Joe's head swam. He felt unsteady. He splashed water on his face, and in the mirror his reflection looked to him strange and unfamiliar. He returned to the bedroom and sat down in the chair and stared at the opened box. First, he would inspect the rest of the box. Then, he would find another place to stay.

Covering his nose and mouth, Joe returned to the bed. The hand was small, but weathered, sun-darkened, dirt still clearly visible beneath the nails. It looked to be that of a man, one who worked with his hands. And then Joe spotted the piece of paper partially hidden beneath the loathsome gift.

"Dear Señor Lily,

"I hope you enjoy your first pound of Vega Family coffee. You were so interested in getting your hands on it. As you can see, someone got theirs on it first. But I wanted to make sure you had an opportunity to try it. I recommend a French press. Let steep for four minutes for the best cup.

"The beans cost you nothing. They are my gift to you. I am sorry to report that your questions did, however, cost Señor José Luis Rivera his right hand. He's the coffee farmer you met at the Talpa market. Perhaps it is too early to know if he will remain a farmer. But these rural people are stubborn. He will learn to be half as productive. His wife and children thank you for your interest.

"RV"

Something gave way inside Joe. Gone were concerns about his items moldering in a police impound warehouse somewhere. Gone were worries about the solvency of the business. They would figure something out. They would survive. As long as he could move nimbly enough to turn over rocks, he would pursue this, whatever *this* was. Joe had made some mistakes in his life. But he knew just as confidently about himself that he could find a way in when others said there were none. He had to do that now.

He placed the note in his pocket and reclosed the box. At the desk, he asked Javier if he had been present when the box was delivered. Javier said the man did not leave his name, but that he was Mexican.

Joe grabbed the backpack with the laptop and the box and took a taxi directly to Porfirio's shop.

Upon seeing Joe's special delivery, Porfirio bowed his head. "I am sorry, amigo mío," he said. "My country ..." He shook his head with a real and weary sadness.

The two men immediately drove to the brother-in-law's office, setting the box on his desk. Paz used his pen to dig about through the contents.

Paz said, "OK, we will look into it. But I think maybe you should not stay at that hotel."

"You must stay with us," Porfirio said.

"Thank you, my friend," Joe said. "But I think I have the lodging thing worked out. At least for right now."

Porfirio laid his hand on Joe's shoulder. "You have been through a lot. It is not good to be alone."

"I'll be fine."

Back outside, Joe hailed a taxi. This one took him back to the airport. He walked directly to Veronica's office. She looked up from her computer. Joe wanted to beat her to the punch.

"I'm sorry I didn't tell you about my … past. I should have. There were plenty of opportunities to tell you. I kept telling myself next time. Because I thought if you knew, that'd be it. I hate what happened. But it happened. I got into something I didn't know how to get out of. I followed other people when I should've asked questions. I should've tried harder to put a stop to it. And people got hurt, people I care about. I don't expect anyone's forgiveness, so I'm just trying to do better, be better. It's a work in progress."

Veronica removed her glasses, which softened her face. The two of them remained still, connected in the quiet by Joe's words. She looked at him intently.

"People can change, Joe," she said. "What is life for if not that, to learn to do better? That is the lesson of my faith. But I didn't grant that forgiveness to you. So I am sorry too. That is why I called you. That is what I wanted to tell you."

Joe bowed his head. "I appreciate that. It means a lot."

"You must have wondered why I called?"

"Interested in a subprime mortgage?"

She gave him a stern look and then smiled.

"OK," she said. "Now that that's taken care of, what brings you here for the second time in two days? I'm afraid we don't have any job openings."

"Two-drink minimum in the customs office. I need to tell Señor Quiñones you deserve a raise. Not looking for a job, but I am looking for a place to work. There have been some developments since I last saw you."

"What do you mean 'developments'?"

He laid out everything, from his trip up to Culiacán and meeting El Mago, to Darrell's murder and the video, to learning about the Goat, to his visit to Talpa. Joe unzipped the bag and removed the laptop.

"And then there's this," he said.

"A laptop?"

"It's Cesar's. Before he died, he gave it to his friend, Miguel, who just passed it on to me after some guys smashed up his family's bakery the other day."

"That's horrible," she said.

"I know. Thankfully, no one was hurt."

"So what are you going to do with it, the laptop?"

"Good question. I'm not really sure. The first thing is I just need to see what's on it."

"But you don't want to do that at your place?"

"Well, that's another little update actually. Someone paid my room a visit when I was out. Turned the place upside down."

"Joe, seriously?" she said.

"Yeah. They chose early mob design. Not exactly my aesthetic." He decided she didn't need to know quite yet about the special delivery he'd just received that day.

"Don't joke. This is serious! What would have happened if you were there?" she demanded. "OK, so you need a safe place to work. You were thinking the airport?"

Joe shrugged. "I figured it's got food, A/C, decent Wi-Fi. As you know, I do prefer places that cater to gay men, but I'll manage."

"No, I don't think it's safe." She grabbed her purse and retrieved a set of keys. "Go to my place. That's better. Work there."

"Veronica, really, the airport will be fine."

She waved away the defense. "No," she said. "Here." She handed him the keys. "It's safer. I don't know about the airport. You have to be careful. Go. Help yourself to whatever's in the refrigerator. And then when I get home, you can take me to dinner. To thank me for my hospitality."

Joe couldn't say no to that offer.

Chapter 9

The house welcomed Joe with Veronica's unmistakable fragrance. He stood for a moment in the foyer and took it in, acknowledging how entirely crazy it was that he was back in the house at all. Not even a former Wall Street guy would have taken those odds.

He lay the backpack on the tiled kitchen counter, the one that just a week earlier he had sat at and watched her cook chilaquiles. Stepping onto the patio, he lit up a Leon joint and looked out over the Pacific. The breeze found his sweat-dampened neck. He let the smoke tickle through him and find those deeper cogs he was sure he would need for what was coming next.

After helping himself to a beer, he set himself up under the fan in the sunken living room. He had to concede it beat the hell out of working at the airport. He turned on the computer and was encouraged to find that the password Miguel had given him worked. It took him to a wallpaper picture of Molly. She was sitting at a table beneath an umbrella, shoulders naked and tanned in a spaghetti-strap dress, raising a glass to her photographer.

Once in, navigation proved a lot more challenging. There were a dizzying number of files, some in English, some in Spanish. File names rarely matched the actual contents. The result of haste, misdirection, or a woeful lack of organization, Joe couldn't tell. Other files were themselves password protected and unreachable.

After a couple of hours of investigation, he'd only managed to uncover a heated correspondence between Cesar and the new owner of the building in which Cesar's shop sat. An online translation tool returned the increasingly nasty results. Molly had said that the landlord had been trying to get Cesar out for some time, despite his uncle's requirement upon selling the building that his nephew be allowed to remain at the existing rent for as long as he liked. The landlord, a Señor Abrantes, had tried cajoling at first and then descended into taunts and threats over months of back and forth. Cesar had not been innocent either. In one particularly salty exchange Cesar said if the guy was going to fuck him he should at least have the courtesy to buy him dinner. Joe did the math and realized that Cesar's death had followed the last communication in the string by just two days. And then two weeks after that Joe himself had received the rental pitch from a guy in front of the shop. Remembering that the man had given him a business card, Joe was pleased to find it still in his wallet: Sr. Gael Abrantes.

"Hello!" Joe heard the door open and close, shoes kicked off, bare feet on the tile floor.

"Just in time," he said as Veronica appeared in the living room.

"Just in time for what?" she asked.

"Too many questions. Take a seat on the patio."

Veronica followed Joe's direction as he grabbed two cold beers from the refrigerator and followed her to the small patio overlooking the city and the glittering bay.

"The beers have just this moment reached their ideal drinking temperature." He opened the bottles and handed one to her. "It's science."

"How lucky for me," she said, "to have a scientist here."

"Es verdad," he said.

They clinked bottles and drank.

"I could get used to this. What does a scientist charge by the hour?" she asked.

"Conveniently, one beer."

Veronica smiled. Joe knew there must be a part of her that still saw in him the person she had read about, the one the papers had chosen as the poster boy for the market crash. He couldn't help that. All he could do was prove what he'd said, that he'd found himself playing with forces beyond his control, that inexperience mixed with a young man's hunger for pushing limits had put him on the wrong side of the worst financial catastrophe since the Great Depression. It still made him feel sick to think of those who had undeservedly paid the price.

"So how did the computer work go?" she asked.

"Frustrating. Too many of his files are password protected. Turns out it's hard to hack a hacker."

"So what are you going to do?"

"Right now, I'm going to drink this beer and ogle you."

"Ogle. That's a word I don't know."

"It means to honor and show respect for," Joe said.

"Somehow I don't believe that," she said.

Joe leaned over and gave her a long, unhurried kiss. A start-over kiss. When he pulled back, her eyes remained closed. So he kissed her again.

"I'm glad you're here," she said.

"I am too," he said.

They remained that way, frozen in the spell of having refound each other. A bird darted amidst the purple bougainvillea that climbed up the patio wall. Ranchera music drifted up from below as Joe slowly lifted off the straps of the light shift Veronica wore. In the open air of the patio, they discovered each other again, emboldened by the sheer unlikeliness of it all and energized in their movements and breathing by a humming urgency that did not have time for talking or planning. It crashed them into each other as if there were no time left for anything but this.

When they had finally collapsed together, now in the full red and orange of a Vallarta sunset, Veronica began to giggle.

"Well, not exactly the review I was looking for," Joe said.

"No, no," she assured him. "It's just that we're outside. Like teenagers. We couldn't even take the time to go inside. And quite a show for everyone."

"Too late for a tip jar?"

By the time Veronica headed to bed, it was late, and the moon hung in a smear of coastal clouds, embossing the Pacific in streaks of silver. The street below had gone dark, shops closed, people home. But Joe's mind refused to call it a night. It busied itself trying to connect the assorted dots he had collected since this adventure had begun. He ran them down one by one. A murdered internet cafe owner and devoted hacktivist with a fervent hatred of cartels. A time-share tycoon who sought to scotch his daughter's wedding plans. A well-heeled Mexican attorney who had a taste for fine furniture but who apparently lacked the same discrimination when it came to his clientele and friends. A second murder victim, this one the increasingly disgruntled partner of the aforementioned time-share boss, who had gotten himself mixed up with the wrong money lenders. A mysterious member of the secret hacker organization who called himself the magician, hailed from the capital of cartel country, and who battled with Cesar about the mission of the group and perhaps more. A shadowy monster nicknamed the Goat and known in his hometown for killing his father and blinding his mother, and now sending Joe a special delivery hidden in a box of coffee beans. There was even, Joe had just learned, a greedy landlord who wanted desperately to rid himself and his building of the young internet cafe operator, a man whose head would end up spilling from a trunk originally owned by the attorney and purchased by Joe.

It all made Joe's own head spin. He revisited the motley dramatic personae again and again, trying to map out connections, only to run aground each time. Someone had decided Cesar needed to die. One thing seemed clear to Joe: the death represented much more than the early departure of a talented, smart young man about to start his married life. He kept coming back to the same thing: the answers must be on Cesar's computer. But after hours of searching that computer, he'd only been able access a portion of the files and folders and those he had managed to open returned very little. Joe went to bed thinking he may have finally run out of avenues to pursue.

The next morning, after breakfast, Joe realized he had no choice. "Care to join me on a suicide mission?"

"How can a girl say no to that?"

Veronica drove. They dodged the downtown, taking the libramiento, the ring road that skirted along the base of the hills that marked the perimeter of the city. The route took them past mechanics' garages, tire shops, sellers of lumber and concrete, a small cemetery, and a scattering of homes dotting the hillside. After traveling through a pair of successive tunnels, they found themselves at the far end of the Zona Romantica, Old Town.

"OK, go right at the next street," Joe said.

They passed tiendas and small restaurants. A woman emptied a bucket of water on the sidewalk before her papelería. At the corner, a line of Mexicans patiently mounted the steps into a shuddering blue bus.

"OK, now left there," Joe said.

"We are close to the suicide?" she asked.

"Almost there."

In another couple of blocks, Joe directed her to pull over.

"Damn," Joe said. The windows of Panadería Esperanza were boarded up.

They sat in silence, the engine running. He had explained Miguel's recent run-in to Veronica the night before.

"It's not your fault."

Joe stared at the darkened shop.

"We make our own choices," Veronica said.

They sat for a beat. A truck passed, the oompah oompah of the Mexican banda music blaring from an open window. "How about one more stop?" she asked.

"Where did you have in mind?"

"Come on, don't you love a good mystery?"

Joe couldn't help but laugh.

They drove with the windows down. The Pacific raced south with them, interrupted only by the big vacation homes and condo complexes that decorated the hillside leading to the ocean below.

Without thinking about the consequences, Joe impulsively tapped out a text: "I have Cesar's computer. Leave Miguel and his family alone and it's yours. Mess with them again and you'll wish you hadn't."

Maybe that would be enough to draw attention away from Miguel and his family. It also reminded Joe that after he'd apologized to Veronica last night, she had offered a mea culpa of her own. She had not, she confessed, learned about his Wall Street past through an idle internet search. She had received an anonymous email. It had included a link to a *New York Times* story. But who possibly could have sent it? And why? It made no sense.

"Look at all the traffic," she said. "It's crazy."

"Fitting. I feel like I've been driving toward crazy since I got here."

The normally quiet coastal highway buzzed with cars, all of them headed south. Progress was slow, bumper to bumper. But eventually the vehicles began, one by one, to pull off onto the narrow shoulder and park. Veronica followed suit, squeezing in behind a truck, its bed full of people. And then Joe saw their signs.

"The event I mentioned last night," Joe said.

"I figured let's see where all the police were headed."

It didn't take long to spot them. Officers in dark helmets and matching uniforms and flak jackets stood at intervals along the road, rifles gripped in front of them.

Joe and Veronica joined the others walking on the hot road. A loudspeaker blared in the distance. Raised voices chanted and yelled in Spanish. In another few hundred yards they followed the others off the highway onto a dirt road and then some distance farther on they joined dozens of others, all gathered tightly together behind a rope line and a wall of police. They held signs and banners with messages Joe had seen

163

before: "¡No al fracking!" "¡Prohibición a la fractura hidráulica en Jalisco!" "¡Salva nuestra costa!"

Beyond the officers, in rows of folding chairs, sat a small audience of a couple dozen people facing a stage decorated in bunting and US and Mexican flags. On the stage a dozen men and women in crisp business attire shielded their eyes from the sun and dabbed their foreheads. TV cameras lined the sides. Over the stage an arch of balloons had been erected and vibrated in the coastal breeze. A balding Mexican man in dark-rimmed glasses and a gray suit clutched the podium.

"Este es un día muy emocionante para Puerto Vallarta y para México!" he declared.

The speaker clapped and the others clapped with him.

"What do their T-shirts say?" Joe asked into Veronica's ear. He gestured at the protesters with whom they stood.

She leaned in. "It's a play on words. 'Ours. Not *Mine*.' Like for mining."

A large billboard had been planted just to the side of the dais that read: "Pemex/Summit Energy Partnership. Bringing jobs and opportunity to the south coast of Jalisco. Groundbreaking May 2017."

Joe surveyed the area. It was a stunning stretch of open coastline. Located at a turn in the road, there were no properties in view to either side. It was not immediately clear where the development was to be located, but it boasted lots of open land and plenty of virgin hillside. Returning his attention to the audience, he spotted something else and a jolt of electricity shot through him.

"Well, now isn't that interesting," he said.

"What?" Veronica had to lean in to hear as the crowd had launched into another chant.

Joe pointed to the seated audience. "I wonder what A.J. Brandt is doing here."

payaso: I'm telling you he's a fucking spy
gorrión: a spy??
gorrión: I don't know
payaso: I DO know
payaso: he's fucking cartel
payaso: the guy just showed up out of nowhere?
payaso: and then c-dope gets killed and our shop gets trashed?!!
XXX99: that's a big thing to say
gorrión: your place got smashed up?
payaso: yeah
payaso: threatened my family
gorrión: you think it's el mago?
gorrión: what do we do?
XXX99: wwcdd
gorrión: ?????
XXX99: what would c-dope do?
gorrión: hahahaha
payaso: we have to change it up
payaso: go back to the shadows
gorrión: we don't need a spokesman
payaso: shampoos and car companies have spokesmen
payaso: that shit made C-dope so pissed
XXX99: el mago is smart though you have to admit that
XXX99: he got us attention
payaso: exactly!
gorrión: you said that before, why do we want attention?!!
XXX99: it helps our case
payaso: it gets people killed
payaso: c-dope used to say the most powerful enemy is the one you don't
see
XXX99: strike and disappear that was it
gorrión: ninjas!!!
XXX99: I don't think el mago is coming back
gorrión: he hasn't been on in days
payaso: if there's one el mago there will be others
gorrión: c-dope is dead and now theyre on payaso

XXX99: maybe el mago did what he needed to
XXX99: completed his job
XXX99: and now were all fucked up and don't know what to do
gorrión: he could just be sick
payaso: it doesn't matter we just need to decide
XXX99: for c-dope!!!!!!
gorrión: for c-dope!!
payaso: for c-dope

"A.J. Brandt at a groundbreaking for an oil development project. I guess he's diversifying his portfolio." It immediately took Joe back to the conversation in A.J.'s condo about Darrell and Los Primeros. What was his connection to the project and why hadn't A.J. mentioned it?

Joe and Veronica had stuck around for a couple of the presentations, including one by an American oil executive from a company called Summit Oil and Gas. The man towered over the podium like a golem, sweating in the tropical heat and insisting that the partnership represented a new era for Mexican-US economic cooperation.

"Maybe Señor Brandt was just invited by someone," Veronica said. "Free champagne."

"Maybe," Joe said.

"But you don't think so."

"I don't know." Joe shook his head. "Something seems like it's trying to reveal itself and I just can't seem to bring it into focus."

Then he realized there *had* been a recent development that he'd not shared with Veronica. "There is actually one thing that I haven't told you about yet," he said.

"OK." She looked wary.

"I got a package in the mail yesterday."

"A package," she said.

"I told you that Molly and I went up to Talpa. I just thought if I was there maybe we could learn something about this guy whose name keeps coming up. They call him the Goat."

"La Cabra."

"Your Spanish is really coming along."

"Gracias."

"Have you heard that name before?"

She shook her head.

"So yesterday I got this package. No return address. I figured it was from my friend Leon. It's the kind of thing he'd do. It was nothing special. A small box. When I opened it, there was a bunch of coffee, loose coffee beans, you know, like they'd been poured in there, and— why in the hell am I telling you this? You don't need to hear this."

"No, you have to tell me!"

He knew he did have to tell her. "OK. Well. Well, I didn't see a note or anything, so I started to dig around. Look for some clue as to who it was from. But I found something else first."

"Something else? ¿Qué?"

Joe took a breath. "Underneath all the beans, there was, I found a … hand, human, a human hand."

She covered her mouth.

"That is … That … Someone sent …" She couldn't finish.

Joe didn't try to downplay it. It had been a horrific message.

"There was a note. From La Cabra. Rafa Vega is his name. I'd learned that he was from Talpa. Part of a coffee-growing family. So I decided to go up there. Ask around. I guess it must have gotten back to him. So he cut off the hand of one of the people I spoke to."

Neither of them spoke, Joe certain Veronica harbored the same thought that he did: If he hadn't gone up there, if he hadn't inquired after Vega… He put the thought out of his head.

After collecting herself, Veronica said, "So these people, they know where you are staying."

"Looks that way. They already visited my place once. And now this. So yeah, I guess the secret's out."

"You can't go back there," she said. "You have to stay with me."

Joe tried to convince her that he'd already found a different hotel— the city was full of them. It would be easier that way, not to mention safer for her. She wouldn't hear of it and he caved without too much persuading. But he just couldn't shake the idea that he might be putting her in harm's way.

En route back to town they stopped for lunch at a place Veronica knew. It sat on the beach in Boca de Tomatlán, the next town on the way north to Puerto Vallarta. They sat at a table on the sand of the small picturesque bay. Veronica knew the glum matronly owner, who served them fresh-grilled fish with pico de gallo and rice and beans.

And then Joe's phone dinged.

"Meet me at La Página en el Sol at 2:30. Or I know where you stay."

He showed Veronica the phone.

She read it and looked at Joe, her eyes wide.

"He goes by El Mago. He's a member of the same group that Cesar and Miguel belong to, Los Fantasmas."

"The guy in Culiacán?"

"Good memory."

Her face had gone very serious.

"I'm pretty sure it has something to do with the text I sent him earlier today. I told him I have Cesar's laptop. I was hoping that might take the heat off of Miguel and his family. I wasn't sure El Mago cared, but I guess we answered that. Now I just have to figure out why."

"I don't understand. If he and Cesar were friends, why the secrecy and drama?"

"Well, I don't think they were friends exactly. Cesar started this organization, this hacker group, with, as far as I can tell, the main goal of inflicting damage on the Los Primeros cartel."

"And you said Cesar was a smart guy?"

"I know. Brave. Or stupid, depending on who you ask. He starts the group and the anticartel thing is going on for a while and then this guy calling himself El Mago starts showing up on their forum. They did get new members, but he's different. Pretty quickly he's challenging things, challenging Cesar. He wants to change direction and become spokesman for the group. Start engaging the press. That wasn't how they operated. And then once they learned he's from Culiacán—"

"Home of Los Primeros."

"Exactly. Once they learned that, well, some, including Cesar, started to express their reservations about him. What's his real story? I couldn't tell you, but I will say that what I saw when I went up there didn't help his case."

Veronica stared hard at Joe for a long moment, and then said, "So what are you going to do?"

"Well, right now I'm going to finish this delicious snapper and beer, maybe find us a couple of paletas, and then I'm going to go meet the Magician."

On the drive back to town Joe managed to convince Veronica not to join him for the rendezvous with the would-be mouthpiece for Los Fantasmas. She dropped him a couple of blocks from La Página en el Sol, a popular coffee shop and used book store just off the Zócalo in Old Town.

He wanted to approach the place slowly, cautiously, see if anything caught his eye or looked out of place. He didn't admit it to Veronica, but after Culiacán and what had happened at Miguel's family's bakery this whole thing set his nerves on edge. It was public, yes, but Los Primeros had proven that they were not above public killings and they were certainly no strangers to kidnapping.

It was the in-between hour and the sleepy square stood mostly empty. One man napped in the small bandstand. Kids' voices drifted over from the nearby elementary school. No one else looked about as the afternoon sun baked the stones and pavement. Joe kept to the margins and the shade. Nothing presented itself to him as cause for concern. No conspicuous vehicles. No men milling about. It was siesta time. Then Los Primeros probably didn't care about siesta time. They were ex-military. Strike fast and get out.

Joining Calle Lazaro Cardenas, Joe sent Veronica a quick text as promised. "Almost there. Everything looks normal. I'll call you when I'm done."

Open to the street, the coffee shop bore the same post-lunch somnolence as the plaza. Joe could see a few patrons. They sipped iced drinks, picked at muffins, or scrolled through their phones. Surrounded by books, Joe thought, and all but one person remained fixed on the little screen of their phone.

Joe entered without fanfare, picked up a dog-eared copy of Jack Kerouac's *On the Road* from an empty table, and took up a spot inside, out of view from the street and as close to an overhead fan as possible.

He'd been there barely long enough to place the backpack at his feet when the waitress, a young woman wearing pigtails and an ornate tattoo encircling one wrist, drowsily shuffled over to his table.

"Your friend left this," she said.

"My what?"

The waitress handed Joe a piece of paper and then slowly returned to the front counter and her phone.

Joe took another good look at the others in the place and then unfolded the slip. Inside he found a short note scrawled in an erratic hand: "Meet me at 506 Cardenas. I am waiting."

The message sent an electric charge through him. Why the change? Was it meant to put him off balance? Maybe there had been something about the coffee shop El Mago hadn't liked? So why had he chosen it in the first place? Perhaps a switch had always been the plan, was standard practice for the cartel. Despite the voice that told him to stop now, to abandon this almost certainly stupid decision, and despite the fear that came with it, Joe knew he had to see how this played out.

The new address was not far, still on Cardenas, but he doubted it would permit him to come at it unseen. After a short walk, moving out of the principal tourist center in Old Town, he discovered that 506 Cardenas sat in the middle of a long block of quiet businesses. With a fading yellow façade, its sign read: Cenaduría Celia. A traditional-style restaurant, it looked closed and dark inside. His phone buzzed in his pocket. "Please be careful," Veronica messaged. What in the hell was he doing? Joe wondered. He set his phone to record and stuck it in his pocket.

Once inside, it took his eyes a moment to adjust. The place was empty, not a soul around save a woman wiping a nearby table. She pointed Joe to the rear of the room. As he proceeded into the dark interior, he could make out a large figure at a back table. Joe heard the woman lock the front of the place behind him. Well, he was in it now, whichever way this was going to go, he was in it.

"Hungry?" El Mago said. He looked younger than Joe remembered, smooth, round face. His jet-black hair added to the sense of youth, cut and combed like a schoolboy's. His robust frame filled his side of the table, his big hands resting before him like two blocks of dark wood.

"No, thanks," Joe said. "But I'd take a beer. I seem to recall I bought the last one."

El Mago gestured to the woman.

"This is my auntie's place," he said.

"Why change the meeting location?" Joe said. "You trying to work some magic, El Mago?"

Joe pulled out a chair and sat, placing the backpack between his feet.

El Mago shook his head. "Don't call me that. My name is Archivaldo."

170

Joe leaned in. "I don't care what the fuck your name is. What I *do* care about is Miguel and his family. Tell your people to leave them alone. I have the laptop. And for the right price, you can have it."

The woman set a beer down in front of Joe and a Coke in front of the other, and then disappeared back into the kitchen.

"I don't know anything about any of that," Archivaldo said. "I texted you for something else. I didn't know who to call. I need help. They're going to kill us, me and my family."

"They come one day, and they tell me they have a job for me," Archivaldo said. "I am not with them. Never. Never. I just keep to myself. But someone tell them that I know computers. That I can do computers. So they come and say that I am going to help them with something. They say this guy, he hacked some people, stole information."

"Cesar," Joe said.

"They don't know who he is. They say to me I find him. I don't know. So I start looking on the internet. I find Los Fantasmas, but I don't know what to do. And the men, they always come to me, to my house, and tell me if I don't—they tell me bad things will happen." And then the big man stopped. He shook his head, wrung his hands.

Joe had not seen this coming. He remained taut and on guard.

"I join the group. I say to C-dope to stop the fight with Los Primeros. Stop with Los Primeros. No more. But he did not listen. And they ask all the time, what's his name, what's his name, who he is, and I say I don't know. I couldn't do nothing."

Here Archivaldo paused again. They sat in the dark of the quiet restaurant. "And then, one day, I'm on the computer and they tell me C-dope is dead. Killed. But I could not do anything. I feel … I feel … " Tears ran down his cheeks.

"Wait. So did you know his name? Did you tell your boss?"

"No! Never I didn't," he said. "I never know his name until the newspaper."

"So how did Los Primeros know his name?"

"I don't know." He made the sign of the cross. "I don't know his name. Never. I don't want to do any of it!"

"You learned about it in the newspaper?" Joe asked.

"Sí."

Joe sat back in his seat. It didn't add up. He kept the backpack tightly held between his feet.

"So why are you telling me all of this?" Joe asked. "Why call me?"

Archivaldo wiped his face, gathered himself. "They think I do it. I kill him. Why? How can I? It is impossible. They say now *I* have his information and I must give them. But I don't have nothing!" He shook his head and for the first time looked directly at Joe. "They are bad people. Muy peligroso. They don't care about people or life. I must protect my family. I don't know anyone to help."

Joe took a long drink from his beer. He understood that he had a choice to make. He could choose to disbelieve this story and quickly devise a stratagem to get himself out of this locked restaurant and free from whatever might be coming next. The guy had, after all, been the same one who had threatened Joe in Culiacán with a few thug friends. Or, Joe could choose to believe him. If he took this line, despite the risks, Archivaldo brought valuable information about the cartel and Los Fantasmas. He also offered an expertise with computers, something that Joe desperately needed.

"Why in the hell should I believe you?" Joe asked. "Only a few days ago you and your friends wanted to rearrange my face."

"Yes. Entiendo. I know. I am very sorry, Joe. They tell me what to do. I must do it. I say no, they kill me. What can I do?" Archivaldo dropped his face in his hands.

The young man seemed genuinely distraught. He collapsed his large frame in an effort, it seemed to Joe, to disappear.

"Do you understand?" he asked. "We must go. My mother and my brother. But I don't know how. I need help. You help Cesar. So I think maybe you can help me too. Please, Joe."

If the young man was lying, he was good. It all made Joe think of the missed opportunities in New York. And the grisly message he'd just received in the mail. If this man needed help, and Joe could provide it, which he wasn't sure he could, perhaps it would provide some countervailing weight to the scales.

"If I help you, you have to do a couple of things for me first."

"Sí! Anything," Archivaldo said.

Joe texted Veronica. Parked nearby, she promised to be there in minutes.

172

The two men stood. Archivaldo no longer seemed the physical presence he had in Culiacán. A woman appeared and he spoke to her in low tones. They hugged. At the door, the woman took Joe's hand in hers. "Muchísimas gracias."

Back out in the glare of the afternoon, Veronica pulled up and they got in.

"This is Archivaldo," Joe said, taking up a spot in the back seat. "Formerly El Mago. That character has been retired. This is Veronica. You can thank her now."

"Muchas gracias," Archivaldo said as he began to join Joe in the backseat.

"No, go ahead and take the front," Joe said.

"Mucho gusto," Veronica said as Archivaldo got in and closed the door. Joe loved how calm she remained. Their eyes met in the rearview to confirm he hadn't lost his mind.

"Archivaldo here is in a bind. It seems the people he was working for are not very happy that he wants to retire. I'm going to try and help him, but first there's something we have to do first."

"Claro que sí," Veronica said.

Joe provided directions that took them out through the small tunnel to the libramiento. They passed beyond the outskirts of Old Town, leaving the cluttered blocks of businesses behind for a more wide-open expanse of hillside and simple homes. Hawks or vultures circled high in the bleached sky.

A mile or so out of town Joe directed Veronica to a nondescript road that veered off the highway. A stray dog roused from its dirty bed to watch them as they passed. The side road was paved, but it had seen better days. Ruined by sun and rain and neglect, the concrete had disappeared, leaving only the crude cobblestone beneath. It made for slow going. The Cuale River followed them on the right.

"Paso Ancho," Veronica said. "A girlfriend of mine used to live out here."

In a mile, they turned away from the river, heading up the hillside, the road narrow and rough. The road passed simple homes, small shops selling tacos or sundries. This soon gave way to dirt and the houses grew sparser, separated by fields of tall grasses.

Archivaldo had not spoken, asked no questions, and simply stared out the window until he could hold off no longer. "Where are we going?" he asked.

"To apologize," Joe said.

In a dirt yard, a man working on a motorcycle lifted his head to watch them pass.

"OK, it's that one there," Joe said.

Veronica pulled up before a crude, one-story home. It had been constructed of cinderblocks, with a flat corrugated metal roof. A curtain stirred in an open window. Joe took notice of the car parked in front.

"I don't understand," Archivaldo said. He suddenly seemed nervous.

Joe got out of the car. "I can tell you that it will be less painful than what Los Primeros has planned for you."

A stout Mexican woman of indeterminate middle age opened the front door.

"Tell her we're here to talk to her about her son," Joe said.

Archivaldo, head bowed and hands clasped before him, translated the message for the older woman.

At first, it was not clear she had heard him. She didn't move or speak for a long moment.

Finally, she said, "Mi hijo está muerto." My son is dead.

Archivaldo looked back at Joe. "Go ahead," Joe said.

The woman wore a simple dress that had once been blue and white, but over time had been worn to different shades of gray. Her hair, also gray and white, she wore pulled back, setting off her round face.

Archivaldo said something to her that Joe didn't catch. He spoke deferentially, quietly. Once again, there followed a long pause before the woman stepped back and opened the door so that they might enter.

The lintel was so low Joe had to duck as he passed through the doorway. The dirt floor deadened their footsteps and gave the room a subterranean feel. The air was hot and close and smelled of earth and cooking oil and a floral cleaning astringent. She invited them into the main room and directed them to the small couch and a pair of simple wooden chairs. She disappeared into the kitchen.

Veronica leaned over to Joe. "Where are we?" But before he could answer the woman had returned with a clay pot and matching clay cups. These she placed these on the room's one table and proceeded to pour out small cups of café de olla, a spiced Mexican coffee.

When all had their drink, she said, "¿Cómo conociste a Cesar?" Joe admired her hands, dark and timeworn, but still managing to retain a stubborn, indelible femininity.

174

Joe looked to Veronica. "She asked how did we know Cesar," Veronica said.

Joe spoke first. "I'm afraid I never actually met Cesar," he said. "But this young man did and has something he would like to say to you."

Veronica quickly translated.

Archivaldo, his large hands wrapped about the cup, cleared his throat and spoke slowly and softly. The woman's expression transformed as she listened. Archivaldo talked about how he was a few years younger than Cesar, how they shared a love of computers. How computers had really saved him, shielding him for many years from the fate of so many of those he knew, who by circumstance, inheritance, or simple survival had fallen into a life that they didn't want but couldn't avoid.

Like Cesar, computers had brought him some income as he had started fixing systems first for friends and then for local businesses in town. He worked from home, where he spent most days, preferring to be with his family. He had a mother and a younger brother. He told Mrs. Castillo that they were happy, even if they didn't have much. They are a tight little unit. His hope had been that he could work and save his money and that one day he could get them a bigger house away from Culiacán.

But life is not easy, and one afternoon two men came to his home. Archivaldo knew who they were. They said they wanted to talk to him about a job. They needed someone who knew computers and the internet. Everyone knew that no one knew more than he did. At first, he tried to tell them that he didn't have time for another job. He was busy. This had only made the men laugh. They gave him an address and a time. They said if he didn't show up, they would have to come back, which they didn't want to do. The address was the home of El Martillo, the Hammer. Though the man needed no introduction.

The spell broke at the sound of tires on the dirt drive outside.

Señora Castillo sat up.

Suddenly, Joe feared he'd made a terrible mistake. Had this man played them? With his sad story about being forced to work for Los Primeros. And now they had been followed. He leaned over and whispered into Archivaldo's ear. "If those are your guys, you're going down with me," Joe said. Archivaldo said nothing as Joe quietly moved to the window. The others sat frozen. Peeking out the curtain Joe could just see the back end of an SUV. He had no weapon. If things went sideways, he was just going to have to make do. But why had he involved Veronica in all this? If she got hurt, he would never be able to forgive himself.

Joe grabbed a candlestick from the table and positioned himself behind the door. If he could lay out the first one, perhaps he could retrieve his weapon, give them a fighting chance.

"Joe," Veronica said.

Joe put his finger to his slips, even as Señora Castillo urgently asked Veronica what was happening. His heart raced. A drop of sweat dripped into his eye. Here we go, he thought.

The visitor knocked and then without waiting for a reply pushed open the door. Señora Castillo stood. Joe raised the candlestick, kicked the door closed, and launched to strike, only to be stopped in his tracks. There, standing before him, was not an AK-47-toting sicario but Molly Brandt. She shrieked and threw up her hands, jumping sideways like a startled cat.

"Molly!" Joe said.

"What the hell? Why? What are you doing here?" She glanced quickly at Archivaldo and Veronica.

"I'm sorry. I thought you were—never mind." He put the candlestick down. Señora Castillo stared dumbstruck at the proceedings.

"You thought I was who?" She took in the room again and shook her head. "What's going on?"

Señora Castillo disappeared into the kitchen.

"You got here just in time to find out." He turned to the others. Water could be heard in the kitchen. "This is Molly Brandt, Cesar's fiancée."

Veronica and Archivaldo stood.

"This is my friend Veronica."

"Mucho gusto," Veronica said.

"And this is Archivaldo Ríos. You might know him as El Mago."

Molly wore a look of confusion mixed with something else, as if it were they who had just barged into her home.

"El Mago," she said.

Señora Castillo appeared from the kitchen with another cup and a plate of cookies, but just then Molly, without warning or preamble, threw herself at Archivaldo, swinging her arms wildly like she had just stumbled into a swarm of bees. Unprepared and wearing a look of abject

176

terror, Archivaldo recoiled, tripping over one of the chairs and taking them both to the ground. Señora Castillo began shouting and waving as Joe and Veronica tried to intervene. The two rolled about the dirt floor, Archivaldo trying desperately to scramble away from his attacker. Finally, Joe managed to pull a screaming Molly free, her arms and legs still in motion.

"Murderer! Murderer! Why did you bring him here? Why?" Her face had gone red and wild.

"Hold on! Hold on! Stop!" Joe demanded. Molly's body buzzed like a downed power line. Joe held her tightly, having got his arms around hers. She struggled, pushing against him.

"Molly!" Joe's voice cut through the noise.

This seemed to break the spell and she finally relented, even as she still breathed hard and leaned toward Archivaldo.

"It's OK. Everything is OK," Joe said.

Archivaldo got himself to his feet. He wiped the dirt from his pants, his face having taken on an even more boyish aspect with his eyes wide, his cheeks flushed.

"Lo siento, Señora Castillo," Joe said. "Todos bien ahora." He apologized and assured her everything was fine.

Veronica added something in soft tones to the woman and she nodded gravely. She began cleaning up the fallen items.

Joe turned to Molly. "The truth is, you got here just in time to hear Archivaldo's story. It's not what you think."

"I don't care about his story!"

Now Archivaldo spoke up. "I did not kill Cesar," he declared. "Never." He made the sign of the cross.

Señora Castillo stared intently at the young man.

Archivaldo continued. "They tell me I must find him. Find his name. His home. All the information. But I never. I did not. I did not want any of it. Nada." This he followed with an earnest, rapid-fire Spanish directed to Señora Castillo that Joe couldn't follow.

"They forced you, sure." Molly scoffed. "I can't believe you brought him here. To Cesar's *house*. To his *mother*."

"Just let him tell you," Joe said. He gestured for Archivaldo to continue.

Archivaldo took a breath and pressed on. "Two men, Los Primeros, they come to my house. In Culiacán. They come because I know computers. ¿Verdad? I don't know Cesar. Only he hates Los Primeros.

He writes bad things on them. Many bad things. They are killers and they destroy Mexico. Every day. He says everyone must stop them. And then he hacks them. They say to me he steals things. I don't know. Files and passwords. Email. Bank information. They don't tell me. They only say to find out who he is. They say to me if I don't, El Martillo come to my house and take my mother and my brother."

Archivaldo's voice cracked and quavered now. His large shoulders slumped like he was trying to escape into his large frame. He looked first to Señora Castillo and then to Molly. "I am sorry. I wanted to run. I wanted to. En mi corazón. But I could not."

"So you told them who Cesar was and then they killed him," Molly said.

"No!" Archivaldo said. "Never! I did not want to know. I join Los Fantasmas. Sí. I find them. I join. Then I try to get C-dope to stop attack Los Primeros. I tell the group it is not good. We must change. ¿Verdad? It is dangerous for everyone. But I never know C-dope's name." He shook his big head.

"I don't believe you!" Molly tensed and coiled up like a cat readying to attack.

"It is true! Please. That is why I call Señor Lily. He come to Culiacán. To ask me about Cesar. That is when I know I cannot do it anymore. I am finish. For my family."

"How did they learn Cesar's name, how did they find him?" Joe asked.

"I don't know," Archivaldo said, placing his hand on his chest. "They never tell me. I do not know what happen to him. It is horrible. Now the men, they say Los Fantasmas has the information about them. They say I must get it. But I won't do it. I won't!" Tears fell from Archivaldo's eyes and his chin wrinkled as he tried to keep it together.

Veronica had continued to translate for Señora Castillo, who now slowly rose from her seat and came to stand next to Archivaldo. She put her hands out and he stood and she pulled him to her and wrapped her arms around him. He towered over her and shook and she whispered to him things only meant for him.

The room remained quiet and still, except for Molly who seemed to vibrate with electric energy.

"Lo siento. Lo siento," Archivaldo said as he cried.

Veronica spoke for the first time. "I might be able to help you."

Archivaldo sat with Señora Castillo on the couch and listened. She spoke to him softly and held his hand.

Veronica took the dishes into the kitchen.

Joe and Molly stood.

"I don't believe him," Molly said.

"Come on," Joe said.

She shook her head. "He admits working for the cartel. He admits joining Cesar's online group. And then Cesar ends up killed? But he had no hand in it? Bullshit."

Joe changed the subject. "Oh, hey, I saw your father."

"That's more than I can say. He's never around these days," she said.

"He was at the ribbon cutting for the new mining operation down the coast."

"Mining operation?" Molly shook her head. "No, that couldn't have been him."

"OK," Joe said. "Ask him."

She shrugged. "Why? Who cares if he was there. I've been trying to get him out of the goddamn timeshare business anyway. Ah, here comes your little friend."

Veronica appeared from the kitchen, wiping her hands on a dish towel. She gestured to Joe that maybe it was time to go.

Molly promptly turned away and took up her phone.

"So what now?" Joe asked.

"I will take Archivaldo to my office," Veronica said. "Maybe I can help him and his family somehow."

"That forgotten purse of yours is just full of amazing things."

She smiled. "How do you know it was forgotten?"

Joe had Veronica drop him at the Banderas Properties offices. Even if Molly wasn't curious about her father's role down the coast, he was. So was the small crowd of people that had collected in front of the building. They chanted, carried signs in English: "Ours. Not **Mine**!" and "Jalisco Sold Out to Toxic Mining!"

Inside the building, the place buzzed with activity. There hung in the office a palpable feeling of tension and urgency, of parts moving against each other. The two receptionists each had a phone to her ear and took no notice of Joe. The waiting area stood full.

Joe took himself up the stairs, reaching A.J.'s office just as the door opened.

"Alright, I'm counting on you, Oscar. Don't let me down," A.J. told the man who had just left his office and moved past Joe.

"Quite a crowd you have down there," Joe said.

"They are being paid by the opposition," A.J. said. "Remind me, you are?"

"Lily. Joe Lily."

"Well, Mr. Lily. As you can see, I'm a little busy today. Whatever it is you need, you'll have to come back at another time."

Joe took a seat. "I actually just wanted to offer congratulations on the deal with Summit."

"Thanks," A.J. said, returning to his desk, which was covered with papers and files and coffee cups.

"How long have you owned the parcel?" Joe asked.

A.J. messed with the papers on his desk. "We've had it for a little while," he said.

Well, Joe thought, that answered the question regarding A.J.'s connection to the project. It was Banderas Properties' land.

"Quite a different use than your usual business model."

"You work in time share and you can't pay people to fucking talk to you, but make a deal with an oil company and suddenly everyone wants to chat."

"Yeah, I just walked through a crowd of people who look eager to chat with you," Joe said.

"Those people will end up getting jobs out there. Mark my words. Good pay. Benefits. Then they can spend their time taking care of their families rather than making signs. Last time I checked, shouting about shit you know nothing about doesn't pay much."

"And I'm guessing Banderas is looking at a pretty good upside here too, yeah? More than a bunch of condos."

"If you're not growing, you're dying."

"So did Darrell know?"

"Did Darrell know what?"

"About the deal with Summit?"

A.J. didn't answer right away, continuing to organize the documents in front of him. "Not your concern," he said after a beat.

"I was just asking because the other day, at your condo, you mentioned that he'd come to you about an idea for a big development. You shot him down, but you didn't mention the Summit thing."

A.J. stopped and looked hard at Joe. "Who are you?"

"Nobody," Joe said. "Just a guy trying to understand. I don't know anything about timeshare, but I've dabbled in finance, and it just struck me as odd that your partner felt like he had to go borrow money, maybe not from the best people, when his business was on the verge of this huge, game-changing deal."

A.J. looked up from his papers. "I'm going to give you three seconds to get the fuck out of my office."

"OK," Joe said. "But tell me: Why didn't you want your partner to be part of the Summit deal?"

A.J. stood, leaned on his fists on his desk. "I'm not going to say it again, asshole, get the fuck out of my office. Oh, and just a little advice, because you don't seem to have learned it. Down here, you stick your nose where it doesn't belong, sometimes you can lose your whole head."

Joe smiled. "And sometimes you get torched for it, right?"

Joe left the building, his adrenaline pumping. He pushed his way through the protesters in the parking lot. A.J.'s parting line rang like a bell: "Stick your nose where it doesn't belong, sometimes you can lose your whole head." Lose your whole head. He could feel himself getting closer to understanding. The pieces were shifting and moving. Joe texted Veronica.

"Buenas tardes, señorita. Just left Molly's dad's. I'll tell you when I see you. How about I bring dinner? Want to hear what you learned about Archivaldo's options."

Joe stopped for a beer on the beach to think. It was between the lunch and dinner hours and the only customers were a few random stragglers like himself. "Puerto Vallarta is full of the wanted and the unwanted." That's how Veronica had put it. This gave Joe an idea, and he texted Veronica again. "Hey, if Archivaldo is with you, do me a favor. Give him Cesar's laptop. I need to know what's on it. Looking for anything about Summit Oil. Maybe he can crack the code. See you in a bit."

He sat on the open-air second floor and looked out over the blue-green bay. Gulls wheeled in the shore breeze. The beer was cold and perfect. Things had begun to move very fast. They seemed to be colliding into each other, mixing up, changing shape. What it all meant, if it meant

181

anything, remained as out of focus as the few fishing boats he could just see at the horizon line.

Joe had the taxi wait while the young woman packed up the chicken. She scooped in the potatoes and peppers and then closed the styrofoam boxes and placed them in a plastic bag. On top of this she set a smaller bag of salsa wound tight with a rubber band and a bag of hot tortillas.

The taxi driver worked the traffic like a pro, moving to the lateral road to avoid the worst spots. They pulled into Veronica's driveway with the food still too hot for Joe's lap. He paid and was not even out of the car when Veronica appeared in the doorway. She wore an urgent look.

"Hurry!" she said.

"I didn't realize you were that hungry," he said.

She shook her head and waved him in.

"Is Archivaldo here?" Joe said, as he set the food down on the kitchen counter.

"He found something."

Joe walked into the living room and saw Archivaldo hunched over Cesar's laptop.

"Buenas tardes," Joe said. "¿Cómo estás?"

Archivaldo paused and looked up.

"Tell him," Veronica said.

Joe took a seat across from Archivaldo. On the table sat an open potato chip bag and a large bottle of soda.

"What do you got?" Joe asked.

The young man wore a look Joe hadn't seen on him before, one of astonishment and excitement mixed with fear. "Miss Veronica said you wanted me to get into Cesar's laptop. It wasn't easy. Cesar was smart."

"OK," Joe said.

"It looks like Cesar found some things," he said.

Joe glanced at Veronica. "Found some things. What do you mean? About Los Primeros?"

"Sí. We knew he posted about them all the time. But I found something else."

Veronica came to sit next to Joe on the couch.

182

"Cesar, he also hacked the computer of this lawyer, Ruben Bermúdez."

"Ruben Bermúdez?"

"You know him?" asked Archivaldo.

"No, not personally. But our lives have already intersected once. He owned the antiques I came to Puerto Vallarta to buy. It was in his trunk that we found, well, that started this whole thing."

"What?" Veronica said. "Those things were *this* guy's?"

"I've even been to his house in San Sebastián, if you can believe that. A beautiful place. He was a wealthy guy. Came from money and then made a lot as a high-profile attorney. From what I could learn, he mixed with the rich and famous too. A playboy. And then somewhere along the way he got mixed up with some not-nice people. He represented some pretty nasty guys. And then a couple months ago he turned up dead. The paper said heart attack."

"That was *his* trunk," Veronica repeated. "I am so confused."

"Cesar hacked his computer? How? Why?"

"Sí," Archivaldo said. "Once I got into Cesar's computer—he was very smart the way he set it up. But once I got in, I saw the files. He had all of Bermúdez's emails, bank statements, all that stuff."

Joe shook his head. "But why? Why did he care about this dead lawyer?"

"That's the other part," Veronica said, her eyes lighting up.

"Señor Bermúdez was working with Summit Energy," Archivaldo said.

"The same Summit that just broke ground down the coast?" Joe asked.

"Exactamente," Veronica said.

"And so the same one that A.J. Brandt is now working with," added Joe. His head was spinning.

Archivaldo then walked Joe through the trove of emails Cesar had plundered from Bermúdez's computer.

Mon 4/30/2016 9:42 AM

Dear Mr. Bermúdez,

Thank you for your phone call. I hope my assistant proved helpful. As it happens, I was in Mexico City. Hated the smog but loved the Tamayo museum. I have a couple Tamayos in my collection, so that was damn exciting.

To the matter at hand, urgency is paramount. We do not have time to dither. When can we meet with your person and talk details? I have alerted my team to be ready to move quickly. And I'm assured by leadership that every possible support will be provided. Please advise.

Sincerely,

David Rudolph
Summit Energy Corporation, Inc.
Senior VP of Global Operations – Latam
D: 281-734-1877

Mon 4/30/2016 1:54 PM

Hello Mr. Rudolph,

Good morning. All necessary steps are under way on my side. As I always say, speed is the reward of having the right people in the room. So that's what I am doing. The arrangement will come together very quickly. That is my expertise. I know everyone in Mexico, or they know me. And want to work with me. Trust me, this is going to be very good for Summit.

I am communicating with both parties. Do not worry. I will have more information and a date for you very soon.

Thank you.

Ruben Bermúdez
Attorney at Law
+52 322 266 3839

It turned out that Cesar had stolen and catalogued hundreds of emails. There were dozens of exchanges between Bermúdez and Summit staff, mostly a vice president named David Rudolph. Communications addressed land rights, law enforcement, government support and oversight, environmental regulation, and how Bermúdez could help them navigate each step on the Mexico side.

Joe wrote down the names and dates. Something about the task reminded him of his work at Ward and Williams. The answer lay hidden somewhere in the data. Some pattern. Some overlooked detail. Some seam no one had investigated. Joe had made his name, and his money, because he pressed on when others gave up. But that same doggedness had undoubtedly contributed to his downfall as well. He needed to watch his step.

"And then, just before you got here," Archivaldo said, "I found this." He turned the laptop around so Joe could read.

Tues 2/21/2017 8:38 AM

Dear Mr. Bermúdez,

We have a situation unfolding that I am hoping you can help us with. In the last week, we have learned that our computer systems have been hacked. The perpetrators exploited a vulnerability we were not aware of and have installed what I'm told is an unusually sophisticated piece of ransomware. They have threatened that unless we cease and desist, they will release plan details as well as personal emails and other sensitive information to the news media.

As you can imagine, this puts us in a very delicate position. Much has already been done and invested in Jalisco. But as a company, we cannot risk what would likely result if the specifics of this arrangement were to be made public. Our experts tell us that the breach originated in Mexico. I have to believe the hackers reside somewhere in the region around the site.

This morning, Mr. Haney personally asked me to consult with you to see if you or your many contacts may be able to draft a solution. I'm afraid we have little time. We will continue to work on our end, but we would very much appreciate you engaging your network to investigate as well. Mr. Haney and I look forward to your report. If you would prefer to speak, please use the secure number.

Sincerely,

David Rudolph

Summit Energy Corporation, Inc.
Senior VP of Global Operations – Latam
D: 281-734-1877

Joe paused. He looked at Archivaldo and then at Veronica and then scrolled down and resumed reading.

Tues 2/21/2017 12:54 PM

Mr. Rudolph,

This is very distressing news! These hackers must be stopped. They are creating havoc around the world and must be dealt with firmly. Of course, I will help. I know people who manage such things. I will contact them immediately. Such illegality cannot be permitted. I am confident that we can find the people who are doing this and resolve it quickly. The project must and will continue. I will write you with an update.

Most sincerely,

Ruben Bermúdez
Attorney at Law
+52 322 266 3839

There didn't appear to be a follow-up from Bermúdez. At least not in the emails. Perhaps he'd used the secure phone line David Randolph had mentioned. The next communication was about a week later.

Tues 2/27/2017 11:21 PM

Dear Mr. Bermúdez,

Mr. Haney has asked me to thank you for your help in resolving the situation. He had planned to make the trip to Puerto Vallarta for the groundbreaking to do so in person, but now he is to be in Washington D.C. during that time. He sends his apologies.

I can report that Summit's portion of our agreement is being executed presently and will be deposited by the end of this week in the manner and location you requested. You will find a modest bonus included as special thanks from Mr. Haney. We both sincerely appreciate you managing the resolution completely on your end.

We are enthusiastic about the great possibilities this project will mean for Summit and for the people of Mexico. Change is a difficult prospect for many, but those of us employed in the commanding heights understand that progress and prosperity all too often require change, often profound change. It falls to men of our vision and station to ensure that complacency and inertia do not win the day. We can count this as one more victory in that battle. Thank you for your help.

Sincerely,

David Rudolph
Summit Energy Corporation, Inc.
Senior VP of Global Operations – Latam
D: 281-734-1877

Joe stood and stared outside for a long moment without saying a word. He then walked to the kitchen and retrieved three beers from the refrigerator, removed the caps, and brought them back to the living room. He sat down and then just as quickly stood again.

"I fell for it," he said.

"Fell for what? What do you mean?" Veronica said.

"So many people are killed by the cartels all the time; who would pay much attention to one more?" Joe said. "Hide Cesar's body amidst all of the other bodies. What did the newspaper headline say? 'Cartels add another casualty in grisly war,' or something like that?" And then Joe remembered something from his trip to Talpa, something Señora Vega had asked, "Is it about Ruben?"

"Archivaldo, you ever heard of Rafa Vega?"

The young man stiffened. "La Cabra."

Rafa Vega stopped and bought a couple of packs of cigarettes, a bouquet of flowers, and a six-pack of beer. He also purchased a black candle. The shop owner had remained fixed on the small TV in the rear of the room. But when he saw Rafa, he moved with purpose to the counter and quickly bagged the items and returned his change.

"Muchas gracias, señor," the man said, looking at Vega's crisp tie rather than his eyes.

On the street, Vega turned left. The sun was descending and a sheer, glassy light suffused the street, reflecting off car and shop windows in soft golds and reds. The day was winding down. People had gone home for dinner. A woman on the far side of the street carried a shopping bag in one hand and pulled a child along with the other. Vega recognized her as the woman who worked in the salon a few blocks on.

At the alley, Vega turned left again. Strings of papel picado hung across the cobbled alley. He had intended to come earlier, but it just hadn't been possible, and he felt as one might who, used to a particular medication at a particular time, is prevented from taking it on schedule. He walked with intention, the heels of his shoes reporting like gunshots off the closed doors and narrow brick walls.

A pair of young men stood at the entry of a house calling itself Casa López. They dropped their eyes as he passed. At another home, an old woman in an apron swept the sidewalk, sending the debris into the gutter. She slowed her sweeping but did not raise her head as he moved by, resuming her busy stroke once he was beyond her.

Vega knew this place well. He had lived here for many years. Until his life had changed. It retained a dull, persistent pull for him, like a place where a bone had been broken and never healed properly. He was a different man now, occupying a different life. What he had known as home was not a reality for him anymore. Certain undeniable forces now made movement his home. Transit. Motion.

He took a final left. And now he could hear the voices, smell the incense. A kind of release mixed with sadness came over him. With each step he felt a greater lightness, a freeness that he did not permit elsewhere. An ache of openness and vulnerability that was only evidenced by his increased heart rate and his eyes, which had left the narrow alley, the laundry hanging, the skulking street dog.

A serenity entered him as he stepped through the large wooden doors. The voices rumbled indecipherably, each seeking its own path to the skeletal ear of Santa Muerte, La Dama Poderosa. Men and women stood in loose rows, arms crossed at their chests, eyes closed, bobbing in veneration before the altar. Looking down through its dark and hollow eyes, surrounded by offerings of food, fruit, liquor, cigarettes, and flowers, stood señora de las Sombras, the Lady of the Sorrows. Patroness of the dispossessed, the forgotten, the children of the dark. Mouth agape in the rictus of a scream, she welcomed to her bony breast all of the left behind.

Vega removed his suit coat, folding it neatly. He took up a spot amongst the small congregation. These altars had to be set up out of view, in private homes. Prevailing Catholic mores did not look favorably on what they considered a cult of death, even though to Vega's mind the Catholic church was the real cult of death. So they had to invoke her aid in back alleys. Luckily, the grandmother of a local cacique worshiped here, so they were left alone.

Stepping to the altar, Vega set among the other offerings the cigarettes, beer, and flowers he had brought. He then lit his candle and placed it with the others at the feet of the figure. As the wick took flame, he felt the same in himself. Some cold corner inside him illuminated. It suffused with light and warmth. He closed his eyes and undertook his benediction.

"Santisima Muerte, you play no favorites and reap all of us to you, young and old, rich and poor, beautiful and ugly. You take us in without payment, without judgment. In whatever condition, by whatever means. You ask no questions. You make no demands. You are open and forgiving. You are the mother of all. Because in death, through you, there is life.

"I am your child. I am your loving son. I am your devoted agent. I harvest what is finished, what has come to its end. I raise your scythe and draw it across the tilting stalks and drop them into piles. In your name, and by your grace, I turn over the earth. I administer the truth with dutiful intent. My work is your work. My heart, your heart. My hands, your hands."

His words lifted out of the fire in the center of him. Sparks released into the dark, drifting like embers to set down on some fertile tinder, he imagined. All of it escaped with those sparks, departing from him into the benighted world. He pinched his eyes tighter as the tears began to move down his cheeks.

This adoration of Santa Muerte was the only thing he still possessed from his family. The rest he had destroyed. When he left the rancho, he vowed to never return, and he had not. But the church reminded him of the days at his abuela's knee learning about la huesuda. The stories she

189

told. The signs she read for him. She remained a vital light, even though the old woman had been dead now 20 years. Santa Muerte was his conduit to her.

"From this low place, I petition you for your guidance, your mercy. Deliver into my hand the weapon of your will. Pour into my mind the knowledge to turn this into artful worship. Guide me to pierce the world like an arrow. With my eyes open, open wide enough to see beyond appearances into the truth that lies behind the veil. Direct my feet so that I might walk with you. Channel my violence for your purpose. Free me from the confines of common men so that I might return to you those who have forsaken you. Put into my hands all of the power to separate men from their confidence in this world, leaving them in the lap of fear and frailty. Reward me, oh Santa Muerte, with all that can be gathered in this world of riches and comfort and freedom. I will earn it, but I beg you to put vast distance between me and the dirty desperation of other times. Never again.

"And for my enemies, take them from this world in pain. Peel their skin from them in strips. Radiate them in agony that crushes their bones and vaporizes their blood. Choke them. See them torn apart by dogs. Fill their insides with burning ants. Those who say they are better than me, who think of me only as an instrument, let them be squeezed until everything is broken against itself and they are only pieces that I can spray into the gutter. Fill me with courage so that I can raise my sword higher than my enemy and drop it faster.

"So this I ask of you, beloved señora de las Sombras. I appeal to you as your servant, as your son, to answer my prayers. I lay my hands on my heart, which is your heart, and ask with all that I am that you hear my pleas. Each day I devote to you. Each breath I take bears your name."

When Rafa opened his eyes, he saw a world returned once again to his control. He felt a dose of quicksilver charge him. When his abuela spoke of Santa Muerte, her wrinkled face took on a dark and serious air. After prayer, her face would open up, relaxed and happy, and there would be that crooked smile. Vega left his hands at his heart for a moment longer in her memory.

The room remained full, mostly of the rough and ragged of the community. The poor. The forgotten. He knew them because he had come from them. But he was of them no longer. If they were lucky, la huesuda would liberate them as she had him. They just had to want it badly enough. Vega grabbed his suit coat and delicately shook it out as if it were vestments of his own. He stepped out of the dark room and incense into the afternoon light, the fresh air, and felt strong. He breathed deeply. He put on his coat and took his measure in a shop window selling baked goods, smoothing the front and doing the two buttons and tightening the knot of his tie. He traced the part in his hair with his fingertips, not wanting to upset the set of the pomade.

Vega's shoes sounded sharply on the alley cobblestone.

"Buenas tardes, señora," he said as he passed the old woman, who having finished her sweeping was now sitting quietly in a chair before her door.

Chapter 10

The next morning, Veronica and Joe took Archivaldo to the airport. Veronica had managed to arrange for the small family to fly to Los Angeles. They met Archivaldo's mother and younger brother in the Departures lounge for a tearful reunion. The mother, Angie, appeared younger than Joe had expected, somewhere in her early 40s. She did not speak English, but she expressed herself to Joe with such feeling that her message was clear.

"Le doy las gracias," she said over and over as she held Veronica's hands in her own. "Le doy las gracias." I thank you.

Archivaldo's brother, Roberto, a wide-eyed 12-year-old in a LeBron James T-shirt, affected the youthful slouch of his age but could not hide the worry in his eyes. As Veronica and Angie spoke, Joe pulled Archivaldo to the side. He put his hand on the young man's shoulder.

"I want to thank you," he said. "Without your help, we'd still be chasing our tails."

Archivaldo nodded but didn't speak. He looked nervous, distracted.

"You should also be proud of yourself for what you're doing for your family," Joe said. "It takes a lot of courage. Your family is lucky to have you."

Archivaldo looked at his feet.

Joe reached into his pocket. "If I can ever help, call me." He handed Archivaldo his business card along with a few US bills. "And a little something for the trip."

"Gracias," Archivaldo said. "I am happy I called you."

"I am too."

"We should get going," Veronica said. "Joe, I'll get them checked in for the flight."

"OK," Joe said. "Buena suerte, Familia Ríos." He hugged Angie and shook Roberto's hand.

Archivaldo extended his hand. "Gracias por todo, Señor Lily."

"Igualmente," Joe said.

Joe watched Veronica lead the small family toward the exit of their old life and into a new one.

He wondered about the future waiting for them. Sometimes circumstances of your own making force you to abandon your life, to give it up for good and start over. Joe understood that better than most. He knew what it felt like to barely escape. He knew that when you have lost everything, when you lift your head to find that it is all gone or broken at your feet and you are alone, that you are not really alone. You revert to the fundamentals that make up a life and you embrace them with all of the strength you have.

Archivaldo and his family would be OK. Or, he had to admit, there was the chance they wouldn't. But they would face it together. It was the same for him. Maybe these last few weeks would amount to nothing. Maybe this would mark the final stop on the long life of this business his father had built year by year, item by item. But he could say that he had tried. And if it failed, then he would try to honor his father in some other way, and he and his mother would find a different way through.

But right now, he had to make some noise. He had to beat the bushes, flush the beasts that hid there into the light for a proper accounting. Joe texted Porfirio that he was on his way and he needed his help.

"Buenos días, Joe!" Porfirio said as Joe entered the store. "¿Cómo estás?"

"Bien, bien, amigo mio," Joe said. "But I need your help. I need you to take me to your brother- in-law. I believe I know who killed Cesar."

Porfirio stopped. "¿Cómo?"

Joe half nodded, half shrugged. "But I need to talk to your brother-in-law."

Porfirio held up a finger and then disappeared into the warehouse where this whole incredible ride had begun. When he reappeared, his hair was combed and he jingled his car keys.

They pulled into a spot in the parking lot of the Puerto Vallarta police station. Porfirio turned off the engine.

"I have to ask you a question," Joe said. "I don't mean it to sound, well, the way it's going to sound."

"Why do you ask me after I turn off the AC?" said Porfirio. "All sitting in the car should be with AC."

"Can we trust your brother-in-law?"

"What do you mean?" Porfirio said, his expression serious.

"You know what I mean," Joe said. "I love Mexico. You know that. But you know Mexico. Things are not … always as they seem, let's say."

"You can trust him," Porfirio said.

"That's all I needed to hear," Joe said. He remained uncertain and unconvinced, but he needed Porfirio, and he had to take the chance.

"You know the killer of Señor Cesar Castillo," Paz said. "How is this possible?"

"Let me explain," Joe said. "La Cabra, Rafa Vega, the same man you think is in the video with Darrell Haddock. I believe he's the one who killed Cesar too. Vega's friend, an attorney by the name of Ruben Bermúdez—they'd been friends since childhood—he was working a deal with an American oil company. You may have heard of them. Summit Energy."

"From down the coast," said Paz.

"Exactly," Joe said. "They just had the groundbreaking. So Bermúdez is the go-between for this deal. He's connected and is helping clear the way for the project. Well, Cesar, he has been fighting the cartel forever, right? Writing about them. He even hacked them. With his group Los Fantasmas."

Paz puts on his hat to leave. "I'm sorry, hermano, I don't have time for this Hollywood story. I am busy."

"Please, just give me a minute. So Cesar hates the cartels. Thinks they're destroying the country. Somehow he manages to hack members of Los Primeros, where he finds info about Bermúdez, who has represented some high-level guys. I'm just giving you context here. So in the stuff they find from the cartel breach there's info about Bermúdez. Cesar hacks him next. Inside he finds all this information, including emails between Bermúdez and Summit about this fracking deal planned down the coast. Who's involved, who's OKing it, everything. Cesar is very angry, angry that some US oil company is now going to come into Mexico, his home, and destroy a piece of the Jalisco coastline he loves. He vows he's going to do whatever he can to stop it. So he and Los Fantasmas hack the Summit website, take it over for two days. You might've seen that in the news. And then Cesar tells them that he has all of these emails between them and an attorney for members of a Mexican cartel. He has plans, spreadsheets, financial data. Stuff they don't want out. So he tells them that unless they kill the project, he's going to release it all."

Porfirio, holding his cap in his rough hands, animatedly embroiders Joe's account with a string of Spanish that seemed to cool his brother-in-law's impatience. It's not lost on Joe that in this world, in this thicket of

194

connections and opportunistic alliances, Porfirio's brother-in-law cop might very well find himself in a spot with not much room to turn around.

"OK," Paz said. "And so?"

Joe took a breath. "So the oil company, Summit, they can't have these emails getting out, right? It will ruin this huge project of theirs. They have to do something, and they have to do it fast. The groundbreaking is right around the corner. But the only info they have is that the leader of the hack is someone called C-dope. That's Cesar's name online. So they go back to their friend Ruben Bermúdez for help, which he is happy to provide, for the right price. And who does he go to but his old friend, La Cabra. Rafa Vega. The plan is created to make it look like a cartel killing. Which is easy for Vega. He invented the cartel killing. Cesar disappears. No one knows what's happened to him. Days go by until his severed head falls out of an antique trunk, his ears stuffed into his mouth."

Paz exhaled slowly. He ran his hand over his head of thinning hair.

"The only thing I don't know," Joe added, "is how they identified Cesar. We figure that out and I think we will have a good picture of what happened to Cesar Castillo."

Paz cleared his throat, looked at Porfirio and then back at Joe. "I will check it. Bring me the emails. Now I must go." His bootfalls made distinct knocks on the tile floor.

"What does 'check it' mean?" Joe asked. He couldn't hide his frustration. Paz had asked no questions and seemed only passingly interested in the explosive new information Joe had just delivered to him.

Porfirio wore a worried look and fingered his car keys like prayer beads.

Carmen, Porfirio's wife, insisted Joe stay for a lunch. She made tortas heaped with meat and lettuce and fresh avocado. They sat on the building's covered rooftop patio. They looked out over the Old Town and listened to the birds in the trees and the trucks rattle by below. Joe said nothing about their meeting with Paz. He didn't need to. They talked about other things, Porfirio and Carmen's children, the weather.

And then Joe's phone rang. He answered without looking.

"Joe?"

Joe stepped away from the table.

"Alan," he said. "Buenos días."

"Buenos días my ass. What the fuck is going on down there? Your mother has been trying to reach you."

195

"I know," he said. "I didn't want to talk to her until I had things more figured out with this stuff."

"'This stuff?' Is that what you call it?"

Joe didn't have the energy for an Alan encounter. "What's up?"

"What's up? Good question. Let's start with time. Time is what's up, with the bank. I can't do anymore dancing. What the hell is going on down there? You know there's a business up here to run, right?"

"I've hit a bit of a snag," Joe said.

"Well, that's the other thing, I'm sorry to tell you that you've hit one up here too. You're being sued."

"Sued? By whom?"

"George T. Lansdowne."

The news took the air out of Joe. He'd been working so hard trying to look forward that the past had sneaked up on him.

"Did you hear what I said?"

"Yeah, I heard," Joe said.

"It's a shame. It's a fucking shame."

Joe wondered for a passing moment about staying where he was, about not returning home. He could start a small business, buy a small house. See where things with Veronica went. But even as the idea passed through his mind with the same aimless floating as the seagulls, he knew that it was crazy.

"What's wrong with you, Joe?" Alan asked.

"I don't know—you tell me. You seem to have a pretty good handle on that subject."

"I tell you you're getting sued—and forget for the moment that the business is already tanking—but I tell you that you're getting sued—by your father-in-law—and you don't even seem to really give a shit. Well, I can tell you that I'm almost out of shits to give myself."

"I sort of can't believe he didn't do it sooner. They want to eviscerate me. That's how that world works."

"The fucking shame is you brought this all on yourself. Do you ever think about that? And now, now, I don't know, now you seem to have just thrown up your hands and said 'Well, fuck it. I'm just taking what's coming to me.' Jesus Christ, grow a pair. Have a little self-respect."

"I'm doing my best."

"No, you're not. This is not your best. Not by a fucking long shot. I watched you grow up, son. You're a five-tool player. It was *your* fucking decision to put those tools to work for Wall Street." He spat out the words

196

like bitter seeds. "That's what set you on this course. None of us saw that coming. I will never understand it. Blows my mind. That place is where the worst of our species go. Rapacious, selfish, small-minded, bloodsucking assholes. They don't do anything or make anything. They add nothing to the world. Going there was your first mistake. Because, as you found out, that place corrupts your talents. It weaponizes them for one purpose: making fucking money. It's fucking ugly. And you did it. Lucky for you it didn't totally ruin you. But I'll tell you this, lay down for those people and they will annihilate you. They will grind you into a gummy paste on their fucking overpriced loafers. Humanity is a weakness to them. You have to fight back."

Joe looked down on the street below. A man pushed a cart over the cobblestones. Joe didn't have the energy to take all of this on right now.

"Alan, at the moment, I just need to wrap stuff up down here, and then one way or another I should be home soon. We can talk about it all then. Now I've got to go. Say hi to Mom."

"Don't hang up on me, Joe," Alan said.

"I've got to go. But give that spleen of yours a rest. That dark bile will kill you. And give Maximus a squeeze for me. Talk to you soon."

And Joe hung up before any more could be said. A breeze made its way down from the mountains above Old Town, rustling the laundry hanging on a line on the building across the street. Joe closed his eyes and the clothing still hung in his mind.

Joe had one more stop to make before reconnecting with Veronica. She didn't know it, but he planned to treat her to a night out. Life was such a twisted, convoluted, absurd thing. Bad luck could turn into good without you quite noticing. No grisly discovery in that trunk, no commandeered antiques, and there is no Veronica. There was some consolation in knowing that even the worst turn of events, even what had unfolded over the last year, that even that might one day be transmuted into a positive. Perhaps it already had.

In the meantime, there were questions. Among them, Joe wanted to know when and why A.J. Brandt entered the Summit development plan. Where on the road from those emails between Summit and Bermúdez had he entered the picture? What did he bring? And how did Cesar figure in any of that?

Joe thanked Porfirio and Carmen for lunch.

"Next time, it's on me," he told them, thinking again of the overlap of ill fortune and good. "I'm almost happy that all of this has happened. I've been able to see you both more."

"You are loco," Porfirio said, laughing.

"If I had a peso for every time someone told me that," Joe said. "I'll stay in touch. And let me know if you hear anything from your brother-in-law. Hasta la vista!"

Carmen hugged him. "Cuidado, Joe, cuidado, Joe." Be careful.

Joe felt a strange buoyancy, like this wasn't his life but just a riddle he was working out. An exercise, a game. He took himself down the street, stopping only briefly for an iced coffee at A Page in the Sun before carrying on toward Banderas Properties.

When he reached the time-share offices, he found the building still besieged by protesters, but there were fewer than before. Joe realized why when he got closer. The office appeared to be closed. The reception was empty and dark. He tried the door only to find it locked.

"They are scared of the people knowing what they do!" a woman said. She carried a sign that read "Get the frack out!"

"But they *were* here?" Joe asked.

"Sí," said the women. "But they run away!"

Joe tried A.J.'s phone. He got an automated response in Spanish that he could not understand, and then the phone went immediately to a dial tone. He rang Molly. She picked up before the first ring had finished.

"Joe!"

"Hey. Is everything OK?"

"Yeah, why?" Molly asked.

Joe stopped. "I'm at the Banderas office and no one is here. It's closed and dark. I tried calling your dad and got some automated answer in Spanish."

"Weird. No, everything's fine. Why are you trying to contact my dad?"

"Just wanted to talk to him about a couple of things."

"What things?"

"Well, mostly just wondering why he was at this oil development groundbreaking."

"Oh, I actually asked him about that. After you mentioned it. Some friend invited him. I don't remember who."

Joe watched the protesters. "Do you know there are dozens of people down here shouting at your building about that mining project?"

"There are *what*?" she said.

"Yeah. They have signs like you guys are involved."

"The Mexican people, they do love a good protest," Molly said.

"Do they know something we don't?"

"Why don't you come over? Maybe we can figure it out. Figure out these protester hallucinations you're having."

"Damn. I'm afraid I can't tonight." He watched two women fold up a larger banner as if it were freshly laundered linens.

"Come on. One drink. I can tell you could use it."

"I can't tonight. But soon. One more question. Does the name Ruben Bermúdez ring a bell? Your dad ever mention him?"

"You're way too interested in my dad. Boring. Never mind." And she hung up.

Joe's listened for a moment to the silence Molly left behind and then put his phone away.

"Well, we got Archivaldo and his family off without any problems," Veronica said. They stood in the kitchen of her house, the windows thrown open to admit the late afternoon breeze.

"They owe you big," Joe said. "And so do I."

"Oh, believe me, I'm keeping track," she said, smiling.

"Well, I was actually thinking, why don't I make a small contribution to my debt by taking you out tonight? A proper date."

Veronica crossed her arms and leaned back against the kitchen counter. "I like this idea," she said.

"Qué bueno. I've been wanting to try this Café Des Artistes everyone is always going on about."

"Wow, you know you're not on Wall Street anymore, right?"

He stepped to her, placing his hands on either side of her hips on the counter and leaned in. He kissed her lightly on her red lips and then slowly turned his attention to the curve of her chin, the sweep of her long neck. She closed her eyes and let escape a small, hushed gasp. Joe moved across her trembling geography to the shadowed divot of her throat. He undid the top button of her blouse and she wrapped her arms around him, and in one deft move he lifted and carried her down the tiled hall to the bedroom. The late-afternoon light spilled into the interior, with its poster bed and shimmering linens, turning everything a shade of translucent gold. In a moment, their bodies too, tanned and healthy, seemed to glow as they moved with each other. The fan whirred above them out of time and then in sync with them.

Later, after they lay together there, relishing the breeze and the birdsong that traveled in with it, Veronica kissed Joe lightly on the lips.

"Perfect appetizer," Joe said.

She smiled, kissed him again, and then headed to the shower.

Joe padded into the living room, the cool tile under his bare feet. He made reservations at the restaurant and then stepped out onto the balcony. He lit a Leon joint, and thought again he would have to thank him properly next time he spoke to him.

Joe looked out over the tumble of streets and houses, the gently waving papel picado. There was much to love about Mexico, he thought, but nothing quite so much as the turn from the insistent heat and glare of the day to the unhurried afternoon exhalation. It eased the mind and delighted the heart. Joe resisted the pull of the past and tried to simply enjoy the moment. There had been a lot of bad. The last year of his life had been almost unequivocally bad, top to bottom. He had learned that you can get in over your head. That despite your best intentions, things can still explode in your hands. But this moment, this view, this woman, these sounds of children playing soccer in the street below, they gave him hope that there was life left to make it better.

While he waited for Veronica to get ready, Joe thought he'd take another look at Cesar's computer. There had to be something in the files that he'd missed or at least misunderstood. He started with the dozens of email exchanges between Bermúdez and the guy at Summit Oil. The two men discussed the plan for the development down the coast. Bermúdez would tap his networks in government and beyond to smooth the way. "Remove any obstacles," as he put it. David Rudolph at Summit said that they expected Jalisco's to be the first in a series of fracking projects in Mexico in the years to come. If this first effort went well, there was no reason Bermúdez couldn't be their agent for those that followed, he'd said.

Joe's time on Wall Street had taught him that beneath the thin veneer of principled honesty, the world moved by opportunism, greed, and a destructive zeal to win. In one of the emails, Bermúdez admits as much, defending the arrangement as "a source of national pride." He asserted that it takes courage to be the first. You had to have vision. "Some will be angered by the project," he wrote, "but only because they did not think of it first. Just watch, their names will appear at the top of the *next* project. We have learned a lot from the Americans."

Joe read email after email. The problem was he didn't know what he was looking for. Something they'd missed. Something that would help him understand this mix of people and intentions and maybe any lies and misdirection.

He'd been at it for a while when Veronica appeared in the living room. "How about this?" she asked. She wore a gossamer-light white dress. Sleeveless, with a plunging neckline, hair pulled back, her eyes dark and lips red. It struck him dumb and he could only stare and shake his head.

"No?" she said.

"Yes, that's a yes," he said. "The sunset should be looking at *you*."

"You already got laid," she joked.

"Yeah, well you know us greedy Wall Street types."

She joined him on the couch. "You're back on the computer."

"I was just hoping some detail might jump out at me from all of Cesar's files."

"Are those the emails from the oil company?"

"Yeah, and from this attorney, Bermúdez." Joe sighed and shook his head. "But I'm not getting any revelations."

She peered at the screen. "What are you looking for exactly?" she asked.

"That's the problem. I haven't got a fucking clue. Some connection to Rafa Vega or Cesar. I don't know, something that helps me connect the dots." Joe sat back and clasped his hands behind his head. "Alright, well, it doesn't matter. Let's get out of here."

"You said Bermúdez. Who's Rudolph?" She peered at the screen.

"He's the guy from Summit Oil," Joe said.

Veronica nodded. "And what about KM?"

"KM?"

"KM." She pointed to the screen.

Joe looked again. And sure enough there in the email cc: line was another recipient, KM@mtrpa.com.

"KM. I have no idea," Joe said. "I hadn't noticed that." He scrolled through a few of the emails. "It's on a lot of these."

"Mtrpa," Veronica said. "Does that mean anything to you?"

"Not a thing," Joe said. "Mtpra. Let's see."

Joe did a quick search. The very first link in the results returned: "MTRPA | Public Affairs | Strategic Communications."

"Well, there's a PR company with those same letters," he said.

Joe clicked through to the company's homepage. It looked like a million other websites. The shot of a downtown skyline with the headline "Elevating Business Potential." After a second the image changed to a shot of the Capitol Building in DC under the words "Your Mission Is Built on Communication." In another moment, it changed again, this time to an image of what looked to be a recent industry event, people dressed in suits and dresses smiling for the camera. The headline read "MTRPA Takes Home Gold at American Marketing Federation Awards." And then the carousel returned to the first screen.

"If it's the same MTRPA, it looks like a public affairs agency. Based in DC."

Joe scanned the details on the page for something to connect this MTRPA to the one in the email. The carousel continued to rotate through the three images.

"It's a pretty unusual name," Veronica said.

"Wait." Joe felt a charge of electricity race through him.

"What?"

"How do I go back? I need to go back." He found the spot where he could reverse the carousel, stopping at the picture of the group of people in evening dress, arms around each other, smiling.

Joe sat up straight. He looked at Veronica, his eyes wide.

"Look," he said. He pointed to the screen. There on the left, adorned in a sleeveless black dress and heels, hair pulled back off of her face, smiling broadly, stood Molly Brandt.

"Isn't that your friend?" asked Veronica.

"What the fuck?" Joe said.

He quickly clicked on a tab marked "Our Team." The tiled page showed a collection of headshots with the person's name and title underneath. Second row, second in, and there she was, in a smart blue blouse and pendant necklace: Kathleen McNally, Vice President, Crisis Communications.

They talked about the bomb of the Molly/Kathleen revelation all the way to the restaurant. What in the hell was she doing in Puerto Vallarta? How was she involved in all of this? Who was she working for? So many questions. But once at Café des Artistes Joe agreed to put the whole thing aside for the night. He would deal with this cataclysmic revelation tomorrow. Now he would concentrate on Veronica and the evening. Certainly, after weeks of turning over rocks one night was not going to matter.

The restaurant delivered as advertised. Incredible, expertly executed food, solicitous service, all in a setting that managed to be elegant without seeming at all pretentious or fussy. As they dined on adobada broiled octopus and lobster tail in coconut, they took each other down the backstreets of their childhoods, from school to parents to old romances. They sketched out their origin stories for each other and finished with espresso and soufflé à l'orange.

As they rejoined the warm night, both sighed. She took his arm on the cobblestone street.

"That was sublime," Joe said.

"Perfectamente," Veronica said. "That octopus. That is some kind of, what do you call it, hocus focus?"

Joe laughed. "Hocus pocus."

"Hocus pocus. I can never remember that."

The night air refreshed them. Smells of sea and cooling cobblestone. The evening breeze stirred the upper branches of the jacarandas.

"OK, now we're fueled. Time for stop number two," Joe said.

"Stop number two?" she asked. She lit up at the surprise. "Where are we going?"

"Just come along," he said.

They walked the quiet streets, under a spray of stars. The ocean blinked and sparkled in the moonlight at the end of Calle Guadalupe Sánchez. When they reached the lights and bustle of the Malecón, Joe led them up the busy promenade to a spectacle of a bar front. Arcing colored lights, booming music, and an enormous, high-ceiling interior open to the street.

"No! Really?" she exclaimed.

"Let's work off that dessert."

"I just told my coworker that I really wanted to go dancing!"

The two entered the club, joining an assault of sound and light and movement. Bodies, shadows, flashes of skin and color. Faces were caught by the roving spotlights and then disappeared back into the dark. People wound around people, bare shoulders, smiling teeth, everything in a fluid, shifting flux. Joe and Veronica worked their way to the bar and got a cocktail and watched the throbbing legion on the dance floor. After taking in the scene for a time, Joe gestured to the mass of bodies, and they finished their drinks and joined the tumult. It was loud, so you spoke in gesture, touch, and expression. Joe just admired the honest joy of her movements, the way her body inhabited the beat. A head in a trunk and then this. What a collision of irregularities.

The throng carried them through a few songs, Veronica joyously giving herself to the music. They smiled, laughed, moving close and then apart and then back together. At a break between songs, sweaty and hot, they escaped to the bar.

"Incredible!" Veronica said. "It feels so good to move!"

Joe smiled. "You're a machine out there."

She kissed him.

After another drink and taking in the spectacle from the periphery for a few songs, they joined the joyous jumble of bodies again. The insistent music boomed and crashed and worked its way into them. After a couple more songs, Joe gestured that he had to take a break. "Baño," he mouthed. Did she want a drink? She gave a thumbs up.

Joe navigated the crush of bodies, undertaking a different kind of dance as he moved through the color and motion and bounce of the busy place. In the time since they'd arrived it had filled with people. It was a big club and it took some doing to get to the far side where the bathrooms were. Joe finally managed to exit the main floor, passed the bar, and threaded his way through those milling at the margins.

The bathroom stood at the end of a long, neon-lit hallway. The design relied on black lacquer and a spectral blue glow. Joe stood at the sinks next to two Mexican men joking with each other in the mirror. Joe splashed a bit of cool water on his face and dried it with a paper towel. A sense of hope and optimism washed over him as he stepped to the urinal. And then in the next second a hand covered his mouth, followed by darkness.

It started as a hum. Distant, but resonant. It came from everywhere, all around him. Or was it in his head? Maybe it was in his head. He couldn't be sure. What he did know was that he felt it in his chest. Like being too close to the speaker at a concert. Then it grew to more than just a hum. Louder, insistent. It surrounded him, a rising roar coming from all sides. And his back hurt, his legs. Everything felt in the wrong place, twisted. Upon opening his eyes, he spied little explosions of light, tracers in a black void. They jerked and darted out of view and then returned.

He thought he also smelled gas, gasoline, very close to him and very strong. The odor woke him further, and he realized that the noise was an engine, and it was just feet from him. He lay on the floor of a boat. When he tried to move, he found that his hands and feet were bound. Attempting to lift his head, some force from beyond him drove his own tied hands hard into his face, knocking his head against the rough, wooden bottom of the boat and into the skim of salty water collected there.

Based on what he could see and feel on his back and legs, he concluded that the boat was one of the simple pangas that plied the waters of the Bay of Banderas. Water taxis, many of them. But Joe could not see past the gunwales and could only really discern the spray of stars overhead in the blue-black Mexican night. Just then the engine grew louder, the roar filling his ears and drowning out all other sound save the pounding of the boat's hull into the waves as it thundered forward.

Veronica! The realization rushed in with all the urgency of a heart attack. Was Veronica here? Had she been taken too? "Veronica," he said. "Veronica!" This was followed by a sharp kick to his head.

"Cállate!" a man yelled, striking him a second time.

Joe tried to see if Veronica also lay in the boat. But the darkness only permitted him to identify the dark shapes of two men sitting at the prow, facing into the wind. If something had happened to her, if she had been hurt, he would do whatever it took to make them pay.

The boat banged hard into the waves for a long time. Joe couldn't be sure how long. An hour maybe. He was groggy and ill and disoriented. And then without warning the boat turned out of the wind. It slowed, the engine quieted and Joe could hear the men in front talking to each other. In another few hundred feet, the boat slowed further, and then came to an abrasive halt. The two men disappeared and then Joe felt the boat tugged onto what sounded like sand. Someone pulled Joe to his feet. That's when he realized his bound hands were connected to a long wooden pole. The man cut Joe's feet free as someone else pulled him hard with the pole, sending him over the gunwale and into the shallow water. The man dragged Joe forward off balance as he struggled to get his feet under him.

Joe could now see that they stood in a small dark and deserted bay. Two murky outlines were visible up the beach, waiting. Darkened behind them were the outlines of several empty beach restaurants. Palapa roofs, tables with stacked chairs. The man at the end of the pole dragged Joe forward over sand silvered by the moon and stars.

"What have you done with the woman?" Joe said.

None of the men answered.

"What have you done with her?"

"Cállate!" one of the men said.

The boat's driver and a second man stayed behind with the boat. Joe labored up the beach in deep sand, trying to keep up with the one at the other end of the pole. They passed the restaurants, moving farther into the dark, until they came after a few hundred yards to a broad estuary that disappeared into the black of the inland jungle. The man pulled Joe into the knee-deep water of the still river. The water was warm and everywhere hung the smell of rich, tropical vegetation. The river level rose to his chest and Joe wondered how he'd swim with his hands tied should that become necessary, but the water quickly dropped again. Once across and back on solid ground, they joined a narrow trail. They followed this for the next half hour down dark, palm-leafed paths that required the men in front to light the way with flashlights.

As Joe walked, the movement and the cool air gradually woke him from whatever had been used to knock him out. His eyes adjusted to the darkness. He had to conclude that this hike was intended to end with his death. But why hadn't they already killed him? Removed his head and tossed it to the sharks. He considered his options for escape. None looked good.

They walked in the frog-colored light of a moonlit jungle. The man in front of Joe, the one who held the long pole, laughed with the others when Joe would fall. As they moved through the lush landscape, the jungle talked to them. It chittered and chirped and murmured. It made strange trilling noises and disturbed the brush at the trail's edge.

206

In time, they departed the dirt path to start up a flight of broken concrete steps that took them steeply up the hillside. The stairs proceeded in jagged turns and uneven intervals up and through the trees. In some spots the stairs had been washed out, leaving just rubble and dirt. At one point, Joe thought he could hear music. The man yanked on the pole. "Más rápido," he insisted.

"Untie my hands and I could move faster," Joe said.

The man continued to pull Joe up the hill. The two others followed close behind. Yes, it was music. Piano. Trumpet. In another hundred feet or so the steps reached a plateau and stopped. Now he could see light as well. To the left, a short distance off the path, sat a lone house, the source of the light and music. It was tucked into the hillside and surrounded by thick bush. The man pulled Joe into the small yard fronting the place. The house appeared to be entirely open air. Not a solid door or a pane of glass anywhere.

A single bulb hung in the small kitchen. A second illuminated an open living area, hanging on a long chord from the high palapa roof. The bulb, hidden in its rattan shade, cast strange shapes on the walls and tiled floor. On the far side of the long common room was a heavy wooden dining table with matching chairs. On the opposing side, a sitting area with a couch and a pair of rustic lounges and a table. At the far side, adjoining the main room, stood a darkened bedroom. Joe could see a bed enshrouded by a mosquito net. Everything open to the outside.

Joe recognized the music but couldn't place it. He stood in the yard taking in the strange sight until the man yanked him up the two stairs to the tiled floor of the main room. Chairs sat facing out to the small yard encircled by dark jungle. Beyond the thick trees, down the hill they had just climbed, Joe could make out the estuary they had crossed and then the beach. Out in the bay, the frail lights of a few fishing boats sparkled in the night like distant campfires.

The two other men disappeared, leaving Joe with just his keeper, who pushed him onto a chair at the end of the long, wooden dining table. The man disengaged the pole, but left Joe's hands tied. Now in the light, Joe could get a good look at him. A young Mexican man with pocked skin and an incipient mustache. No one he recognized.

"¿Dónde está la mujer?" Joe asked. Where is the woman?

The man said nothing and departed, leaving Joe alone. The music circled above his head with the jungle bugs bouncing into the lightbulb, some falling to the table where they feverishly worked their legs in their air. Around him, the walls of the place doubled as shelves, every inch filled with books and bric-a-brac.

In the kitchen, another man, not one from the boat, stood at the sink, a towel over one shoulder, washing his hands. Their eyes met briefly before the man turned the water off, casually wiped his hands on the towel, and then draped the towel over the long neck of the faucet and disappeared.

Joe sat and waited. For what, he didn't know. He wondered if this was his chance to run. But where? The ceiling fan turned slowly, and he tried to evaluate his options. As he sat there, out of the dark, from the deep night, jumped an enormous toad. It landed with the size and sickening heaviness of a human organ being tossed onto the floor. A moment later a second landed, this one from the small yard, soon followed by a third. Where in the hell am I? Joe wondered. They seemed bad omens—dark, oily messengers from whatever miserable fate awaited him.

And then without warning, a crashing clap, sending a jolt through Joe as he jumped and turned to find a man slamming down onto the table what looked to be a woman's handbag—Veronica's handbag. The man, a Mexican, early 40s, pushed the purse in front of Joe and then sat himself at the opposite end of the wood table.

"What have you done with her!" Joe demanded.

The man smoothed his suit coat and then said, his head slightly canted, "You never thanked me for the coffee I sent you. That's not very polite. So," he gestured at the purse, "I am trying another gift."

"Where is she?"

"Open it," he said. He wore a crisp linen suit with a dark blue tie and matching pocket square. He was framed by the shelves of books and dusty ephemera behind him on top of which sat a pair of large black earthenware pots in the Oaxacan style that drew Joe's curator's eye.

Joe squirmed in his seat, his breathing coming in quick, shallow beats.

"Go ahead," the man said.

Joe couldn't move. He'd drawn Veronica into this mess and now—what had he done to her? He wouldn't let his mind go there.

"Open it!"

With his hands bound, he inched the purse closer. Her familiar rosewater-tinged fragrance lifted from the bag and reached his nose. He'd been through this before and feared what might lurk inside.

"You are the Goat," Joe said.

The man let a cool smile drift onto his face. "Some call me that, sí," he said. "Please." He motioned again toward the handbag. From his look and comportment, this man could've easily been one of the men with whom Joe had worked at Ward and Williams. He exuded the same air of confident provocation.

Slowly, Joe worked the leather strap and snap.

"I hope it fits," the Goat said.

His heart raced. With trembling hands, he drew open the top of the bag. The stark light of the room's single bulb landed on strange, indecipherable shapes. He opened it further and like an explosion the grisly contents suddenly came into view, punching the air out him.

Joe thrust the purse away, spilling out its horrific gift. Before him lay a loop of twine onto which had been threaded 10 human fingers. A woman's. Brown skin. Long and slender.

"No!" Joe howled. He felt everything hollowing out of him and then into that empty space rushing horror and an incandescent rage. "You motherfucker."

"But you must try it on," the Goat said.

Just then a set of hands grabbed the gruesome artifact while another yanked Joe at the hair and pinned his shoulders as the necklace was placed over his head. Joe shook and recoiled but there it hung. He could feel the fingernails on his skin and smell the raw ends where the flesh had been cauterized.

Vega sat, legs crossed, as comfortable as if the two men were discussing what they might have for dinner. "I told you," he offered. "I said if you continued to put your nose where it doesn't belong, there would be an answer. Did I not say that? Can you blame the stove for burning the hand of the stupid child? How are we to learn?"

Joe didn't care anymore about what happened next. There were no rules, no limits now. It was only Veronica. She had done nothing, guilty only of being associated with him, of trying to help him. The thought of her pain, her fear, it made him want to detonate. Only hours ago he'd felt those fingers on his body, and now. And now.

"Why? Why hurt *her*? She did nothing to you! She was not a part of this."

"The bigger the heart, the bigger the target," Vega said. He offered a hoarse chuckle.

The first moment he felt the men relax their restraint, Joe tore the string from his neck and onto the table. He wanted to gag, to vomit. "You'll pay for this," he hissed.

Vega nodded. "Yes, of course. But it will not be by you, and it will not be how you think. If we conduct ourselves with right vision, then we can only deliver right action. We rise above the level of common conduct into a different realm."

Joe was shaking, electrified. "Predators always become prey, eventually."

"Excellent," Vega said. He smiled. "I hoped you might be this person. Due to my work, do you think I can speak to most men? They are like these—" he waved at the toads, which now numbered nearly 10 on the patio floor. "They jump and shit. And when they die—" Vega in one fluid motion produced a long knife from his pant leg, speared a nearby toad through the back and flung it into the dark, "no one cares. Because they are just replaced by another."

"You kill, for money. You torture. You destroy families. Is there anything lower than that?" Joe's mind accelerated. He had to do something, or he too would be lost to this man's black heart.

"Now we are getting somewhere," Vega said. "You believe that the universe follows a moral code: Love is the answer. Do unto others. Man is basically good. That is your first belief. But just because you believe it, just because someone taught it to you, that does not make it so. Think for a moment. Think what if the universe does not care about your behavior? What if, in fact, just as on the plains of Africa when the lion kills the antelope, nature is satisfied. It is ... honored when the order of things is expressed. Isn't that beautiful?"

"You want to know what I believe?" Joe said. "I believe your father was a tyrant, your mother a silent witness, and all you saw in their life, in that place, was misery and failure. You felt trapped, ignored. But you didn't have the courage to do anything to free yourself. So you took the coward's way and tried to destroy it. You thought burning down your house would solve your problem. But it didn't, did it? Yes, it killed your father, and you thought it killed your mother as well, only she didn't die, because she's tough, tougher than you."

The smile wilted on Vega's face. "You know nothing of my life."

210

"No?" Joe said. "Isn't that why you and Ruben Bermúdez became friends growing up? You both hated that place and that life. You were too big, too smart to be stupid, poor farmers. Right? You talked about how pathetic it all was and how pathetic they were to submit to it. You *deserved* something bigger, something better. And if your parents couldn't give it to you, then you would take it. Do I have that about right?"

The loose, easy confidence cooled on Vega's face. His jaw flexed.

"Well," Vega said. "You visit this small town in the mountains, you go there for one afternoon, for one day, and you talk to a few dirty peasants and suddenly," he spread out his arms, "suddenly you understand everything." Vega nodded. "You must be a very smart man. You can really see into my soul, is that right?"

The indolent ceiling fan did nothing to combat the heavy heat that seemed to breathe out of the jungle. Sweat dripped down Joe's spine. It pooled at the back of his legs.

"I see enough," Joe said. "I see a man who, in cold blood, took the life of a young man whose life was just getting started. You destroyed him and in destroying him destroyed the lives of his family, his friends. It was pointless."

"Because you cannot see nature's point is not the same as pointless," Vega said. "His head got him into trouble, and so it would be his head that he would pay with. Do you see? Because he was clever, I had to be clever. I told myself there could be no blade. I was very pleased with the solution. It had a simplicity, an elegance."

"You are nothing more than a murderer for hire," Joe said.

The Goat produced a long stick from beneath the table. At the end of the stick had been affixed a nail bent at 90 degrees. Joe's flesh pricked, his heart rate jumped.

"No," Vega offered, "you are not quite right. Killing, when it is thoughtfully conceived and mindfully executed, it is more than murder; it is art. It is prayer."

He idly rolled the stick over and over on the floor near Joe's feet, the nail making a scratching sound on the tile.

"Why do humans continue to make the same mistakes over and over? Can you explain this to me, Mr. Lily?"

"And then when you killed Darrell Haddock, you videoed it. That is inhuman."

Vega looked up at Joe, his expression one of confusion. He shook his head "Video? No, you are mistaken. I know nothing about this."

"Why lie?" Joe said. "You did it. You killed him with a blowtorch."

"No," Vega. "You are wrong. I don't know what you are talking about."

Joe didn't know what to say. For some reason, Vega was lying. Vega must have been behind Darrell's death as well. Right? They were too connected to be separate. Weren't they? Plus, the torch had seemed precisely the sort of demented flourish Vega might incorporate into his awful act.

"It may be that this man deserved to die. I cannot say," Vega added. "But I had no part in it."

"You didn't kill him?"

"I did not." It seemed to set Vega on edge to have someone else's murder ascribed to him. His face darkened. "Video. That is … not right for such proceedings. It is ugly. I serve beauty!"

"Perhaps you are not so different than every other one," Vega said. "You trust your mind. But your mind is an abscess that must be cleaned by right thinking. A man is killed. I am a killer. Therefore, it must be me. Your truth is untrue. I give you this gift. It is the fingers of a woman. That woman must be your friend. Again, your truth is untrue. Clearly, your mind is not to be trusted."

It took Joe a moment to decipher what Vega was saying. He looked more closely at the fingers that lay in a loose bundle on the table. A woman's yes, but on closer inspection they were shorter than Veronica's. The chipped fingernail polish a different color. Joe put his bound hands to his mouth. Tears rolled from his eyes.

"These belonged to—un momentito." He removed his phone from a pocket. "Señorita Alma Gutierrez. Do you remember her? She served you coffee in Talpa when you came asking about me. I don't know what she's able to do now for work. You see, nature decrees that no action is made without a reaction. Payment can be slow, or it can be swift."

Joe had never encountered anyone like this man. Wall Street was full of sociopaths and predators, but Rafa Vega stood apart. Perhaps there never had been anyone like him. He gave off a vital energy, not unlike that of the darkened jungle itself. Deep, unknowable, inexorable.

Joe knew that every minute he stayed in this house he put himself one step closer to death, so he tried quickly to outline his options. There were no doors, so that was good. And once beyond the light of the house, the

212

darkness was complete. That might work in his favor. If he could get out there, into the thick bush, he might have a chance. But he didn't know where he was and then there was the little matter of his having been boated in. He also didn't know where the other men had gone. So he kept talking.

"Was trying to burn your own mother alive, was that payment decreed by nature?" Joe shook his head. This line seemed to have an effect. "You took her husband, her home, and her eyesight, but she survived. She survives still. And despite being blind, she sees you very clearly."

Vega twisted the stick on the floor. "Well, I can see too," he said. "Don't you know that I have the X-ray vision? What I see is another arrogant American. You judge, but it was you who bankrupted people and should be in prison. Didn't you even ruin your own father-in-law? And now you go digging into other people's business and tell them what's wrong with *them*?" He shook his head. "No. Your opinion means nothing. You mean nothing."

The chittering in the dark mixed with the music. A ballad, the singer singing, "Dueño de ti, dueño de que, dueño de nada." Another of the black toads landed with a wet clap on the tiled floor.

Vega stood, the stick in his hand.

"You are just another hijo de puta only out for himself. You don't even care about your wife or your child. The world, it is full of men like you," Vega said. He held the stick in his hand. "And you're not even good at it. You failed. Because you don't understand that there is no redemption in greed."

He got up and began to slowly walk the room, leading with the stick like a sightless man. He came to stand near the rear of the room, beside one of the place's woven rugs.

"The truth is," he said, "the world is made of an X axis that represents beauty and a Y axis that—" In one deft motion, Vega flipped over the rug, exposing a scorpion, which arched its tail angrily and tried to back up only to be pierced through with the nail. "A Y axis that represents suffering." He raised the stick to inspect the impaled scorpion as it writhed. "You're just a common thief," he said. "For me, I seek to live at that intersection of those two lines, beauty and suffering." He took up his seat at the end of the table. "That is the province of God."

Joe felt the hair on the back of his neck stand up. The man curdled the night air. Joe needed to act, and he needed to do so quickly.

Vega began slowly to move the scorpion over the table as its tail wildly stung at the air. "They love the dark and are very angry when you remove them from it. They become a single thought and that thought is to kill." He inched the stick toward Joe.

"And all this because I owed an old friend a favor. What is the saying, 'No good deed goes unpunished'?"

"A favor?" Joe said.

"You are right that Ruben Bermúdez was my friend. We grew up together. He needed assistance. I told him no. I explained to him that because I have left Los Primeros, they would come for him if he worked with me. But he persisted. And now he is gone." As he spoke, he continued to slowly move the scorpion closer to Joe.

"You helped him get rid of Cesar for the US oil company."

"I helped *him*, not an oil company. And you, Señor Lily, you are just an unexpected demand. I guess this is more personal, you can say. Yes? You will have to forgive me that your exit lacks some elegance. I admit. But then there is a certain pleasure in improvisation too."

The scorpion approached Joe's shoulder. It was now or never. Joe planted his feet and with all the force he could muster he drove the long table into Vega, punching him hard in the gut and driving him into the bookshelf behind him. The impact doubled Vega over, eliciting from him a deep, guttural gasp. The impact rocked the bookshelf, sending the large Oaxacan jug down from its perch and onto Vega's head with a sickening thud. Joe bolted for the yard. In two steps he was at the short wall separating the patio from the grass, which he used to launch himself into the yard and from there into the dense jungle beyond.

His hands still tied, Joe's balance suffered, and he immediately fell hard onto his side not far into the bush. Scrambling to his feet, he raced forward through the broad fronds and tree limbs and vines. He couldn't see well and took a pathless route downhill like a ski racer cutting this way and that, shouldering into gates, bouncing from one obstruction to the next. Behind him he heard shouts, but his own breathing huffed loudly in his ear and he couldn't be sure. He threw himself down the hill with one thought: move. Move as fast as you can. Something caught his shirt, tearing it open at the chest. He slipped but stayed on his feet. Now he was sure he could hear others, footfalls, branches breaking. It seemed to be coming from everywhere. Faster! Keep moving downhill. He tore through, around, or over whatever came into his path.

As he ran, he tried to work his hands free, but the rope was too tight. He veered left over a small mound of earth. The trees were thick and reached for him as he tore through their large leaves. Visibility was a few feet at best, but he couldn't slow. His breathing, his heart, his feet pounding the ground swirled into one insistent, syncopated rhythm. Were those flashlights?

And then Joe's foot caught on a root or a rock and all of sudden the ground was gone and so was Joe. Nothing under him. He flew, legs flailing, crashing hard into a cluster of thick bushes. The impact took the air out of him and he felt a sharp pain in his side. He lay there, uncertain which was up. But he had to keep moving. If they caught him—they couldn't catch him. He struggled to all fours, finding that the fall had loosened the rope binding his hands. He quickly extricated himself and rubbed his raw wrists. That's when he saw that he lay mere feet from a deep cleft in the hill. On the other side waited a drop of 30 feet down a rocky slope.

That's when he heard footfalls in the dense underbrush. Someone was close—too close—and moving fast in his direction. They must have heard his fall. He didn't have much time. Running would tip the person off and he was clearheaded enough after his tumble to know that he couldn't outrun a bullet. He had an idea, but he had to work fast. He quickly found two small trees about five feet apart. Their position wasn't perfect, but it might work. To the lower trunk of each he tied one end of the rope that had bound his hands.

Next, Joe took himself a few feet away into denser cover. He could now hear his pursuer's breathing but how far away he couldn't be sure. He could also see in the distance what seemed to be flashlights burst here and there out of the darkness. They were getting close. He needed to act. Joe retrieved his cell phone. It was a crazy gambit, but he had few options—and no time.

But before he could execute the rest of his plan he was yanked back by his collar. His shirt raked against his throat as the man dragged him from his hiding spot and shouted to the others. "¡Aquí! ¡Aquí!" Joe scrambled to his knees just as he took a blow to the side of the head that sent him to the ground again. The scene whirled. Indistinct shapes jumped in his vision, tree and bush and movement. He tried to get to his feet, but the loose detritus of the jungle floor made it hard to get purchase and he kept slipping. The man kicked him hard in the side, sending a bolt of pain shooting across his back. His attacker reeled back for another strike but this time Joe saw it coming and caught the man's foot, pushing it and the leg upwards with as much force as he could muster. This sent the man into the air and into the bushes. Both men quickly clambered back to their feet and launched into each other, sliding about on the ground as they grappled for advantage. His attacker was strong, but smaller than Joe, who worked his way into a position in which he had the man from behind, his arm pinned around the man's neck. Then a gunshot tore through the tree limbs. The man slipped Joe's grip and scuttled back a few feet. Another gunshot, closer this time. And then all of sudden the man had a pistol fixed on Joe. He spat into the dirt. "Saludar a dios," he said, smiling, breathing heavily. He raised the gun just as his foot caught the rope Joe had earlier tied between the trees and in one graceful motion like someone falling into a bed the man tipped back and disappeared over the edge and down the rocky hillside.

Joe wasted no time and found the broken stairs they had taken on their trip up. He bounded down them as fast as he dared. Another gunshot rang out and Joe hustled back into the cover of the trees, stopping to get his bearings. That's when he heard someone, someone very close, say his name.

"Joe. Oh my god, are you OK?"

He froze.

"I can't believe I found you," the voice whispered. "Come on. We've got to get you out of here."

Nearby, Joe could hear people thrashing down the hillside. Voices. He saw spots of light through the thick leafy foliage.

"We've got to go now!" the person demanded. A warm hand grasped his arm.

Turning to the voice, Joe stood dumbstruck. Standing before him, urgent face now visible in the frail light of the moon, hair pulled back in a ponytail, stood Molly Brandt.

Without thinking, Joe said, "Kathleen."

At this, Molly instantly released his arm. Her expression went flat. Gone the look of pleading concern. She wiped her hands on her pants.

"Well," she said to herself as much as him. "I guess that changes things, doesn't it?"

"It does." Joe quickly tried to orient himself, determine the best line to the beach.

She seemed ready to offer a retort, but instead checked her watch.

"I don't imagine you'd agree to let me go," Joe said. "For old times."

She shook her head. "No, sorry. Can't do that," she said, producing a pistol from her waistband.

Joe thought he could see the estuary they had crossed earlier in the night. If he could get there, maybe he could get to one of the boats. If they weren't being guarded. He had no idea if there might be a road nearby, but he knew he had to work fast.

"You really work with that monster up there? Have you seen his handiwork?"

"I bet you're pretty proud of yourself. Yeah? Making this little discovery. Aren't you smart?" Her voice dripped with sarcasm in the humid air.

Joe said nothing.

"Probably makes you feel a lot better about yourself. Right? I'm this despicable person. This horrible person. How could I work with these people? But you got to get the job done. Do what you have to do. You can't always choose, right? You know all about that. We're actually a lot alike. Don't tell me you didn't see it, feel it. We're both focused. We can push everything out of our minds except the job at hand. That's our gift. It's how we're wired. You can lie to yourself all you want, but it's the truth."

Joe calculated that he could launch himself from his position and reach her before she knew what hit her. "I've made mistakes," he said. "They're out there. I can't take them back. But the difference is I know they were mistakes. I tried to stop them. But no matter how bad it was? No one got killed because of my mistake. You can stop this. You can. You can make that choice, start over."

She stared at him without a word and he wondered if maybe he'd gotten through to her.

"You don't have to do this," Joe said. "We can get out of here. Right now. Come with me."

Joe could hear other voices now, not far off. He was running out of time.

"'Come with me'? That work with your Mexican girlfriend? And how coincidental that she's a customs agent who can help with your stuff. But I'm sure that's not why you're fucking her. The real truth is, you're just a liar." She hissed this. "We both know that. Everyone knows that. And now you're lying to yourself. Subprime Joe is gone? You crash and burn and suddenly you see the light? That's some pretty coincidental timing. But here's the thing, I don't even blame you. I'd use that strategy too. Do whatever it takes. When others will use every tool available, and you don't, you're going to lose every time."

With that she produced a flashlight, snapped it on, and shone the bright light on Joe who had to cover his eyes. Molly whistled loudly and the men could be heard changing direction, shouting, and now thrashing toward them.

Just then, some distance to Joe's left, someone shouted his name. "Joe!" He recognized the voice but couldn't place it. Turning back to Molly, he found only darkness. She was gone, disappeared back into the jungle. Joe immediately raced to the other voice, punching through the last bunch of trees.

"Paz!" Joe said.

"Joe!" Paz stood with another officer.

"They're right behind us," Joe said.

The men tore through a final cluster of trees, entering an open grassy field painted in dabs of moon wash. Suddenly, shots peppered the ground around them as they sprinted toward the beach. Shouting voices echoed. Gunshot reports reverberated up the hillside. Joe, Paz, and the other officer scrambled down the last hill leading to the estuary, plunging into the shallows and high stepping through the slow-moving waters as quickly as the slippery bottom would allow. Everything rushed in Joe. His heart, his breath, his thoughts. Reaching the sand of the beach on the far side, they put their heads down and sprinted toward Paz's waiting boat. The beach stood dangerously open and Joe expected at any minute that one of the bullets would find his back or leg. But somehow they reached the boat without injury and swiftly jumped in and pushed off. As the engine coughed to life, they saw their pursuers, three men, reach the river. The three ran, shooting wildly at the boat. The officers returned fire until the boat had banked toward the mouth of the bay and accelerated.

Paz shouted over the din of the engine, "Are you OK?"

Joe gave a thumbs up. He turned his face into the wind. He relished the air, the smell of the sea, the night sky that arched above. His body tingled. He was alive.

They were just around the corner when they heard the other boat.

The other panga followed at high speed, the whine of its engine reaching them even through their own roaring outboard.

"Hold on!" Paz yelled. He shouted to the man at the rudder and the boat pressed its speed, racing full tilt into the waves.

Joe, Paz, and the two other officers sat holding tight to the gunwale. Paz checked over his shoulder and unholstered his gun.

The boat pounded its way north up the coastline, the land just shades of charcoal representing beach, forest, sky. Ocean spray wetted Joe's face. He turned and could see the thumb smudge that was the other boat behind them. They were getting closer.

Paz leaned in close to Joe. "This is an old boat! We must get to Quimixto. If we get to Quimixto, I don't think they can catch us."

All he could think about was Molly, Kathleen, whatever her name was, that this woman, this woman he had gotten to know, become friends with, felt sympathy for—that she had assigned this madman to kill him. To end his life in some jungle keep. He thought of the kiss in Talpa and that fleeting moment when things might have gone a different way.

The boat gained on them, thundering north on their port side. Joe could almost make out shapes now. Was she in the boat? Was she pushing the driver to go faster? He wanted to ask how far to Quimixto. And then their pursuers began to shoot.

Paz and the other officer returned fire, everyone now coiled tighter, leaning forward like a rider over the neck of a galloping horse, demanding it to accelerate.

Paz grabbed Joe and shook his head. "We don't have enough time!"

"Give me a gun!" Joe shouted.

"No gun!" Paz yelled. He waved for Joe to sit down.

"Give me a goddamn gun!"

The other boat had now come to within a hundred yards of them. Paz took a long look at Joe and then had a quick back and forth with his officer. The man handed Joe a pistol.

The boats exchanged gunfire, but the darkness, the motion, it all made it very hard to do so with anything like accuracy.

And all the while the other boat gained on them. They boasted a far superior boat. No wonder the cartels operated with impunity. They had better equipment. Their panga had come to within about 50 yards now. When a bullet struck something metal right in front of Joe, Paz barked instructions to the pilot and, without warning, the boat bolted sharply shoreward. A passing cloud obscured the moon and they passed into darker darkness. They heard the other boat throttle down as it too changed course. Now the pursuers had Joe and the others, and they knew it.

"What the hell are we doing?" Joe yelled.

"¿Aquí?" the pilot shouted.

"No! Go!" Paz yelled. He waved his pistol insistently toward land.

"They'll gun us down before we get out of the boat!" Not for the first time Joe wondered about this man's motives. What in the world could his objective be here? Was he hoping to ditch the boat and escape by foot? It seemed a foolish strategy. And, very likely, a deadly one.

The boat, prow up, hurtled toward the beach, cutting the distance quickly.

"¿Aquí?" the pilot yelled again.

Paz said nothing. The engine roared. The dark shore rose up.

Everyone waited. Joe tried to prepare for the mad scramble off the boat when they hit sand and had to dodge the fire of Vega's men. Or maybe it was more appropriate to call them Kathleen's men. Either way, things were about to get crazy. He gripped the pistol tighter.

And then all of sudden Paz bellowed, "¡Aquí! ¡Aquí!" And the boat, having come within 30 feet of the beach, abruptly turned hard left, throttling up, and raced north again. The boat tore up the coast, now out of the wind of the open ocean. It seemed to fly on the water, jumping into an entirely different gear as the shoreline sped in the opposite direction.

The two officers gave a shout, and everyone craned their necks to see the distance that had so quickly been put between their boat and the other.

"I thought you said this was an old boat!"

"Old boat. New engine," Paz offered matter-of-factly.

The boat now launched itself from wave crest to wave crest, a spray of lights twinkling on the distant horizon. Everyone held on tight. Little by little they increased the distance between themselves and the others. Joe saw one young officer make the sign of the cross.

The pilot beat the boat toward the city, pushing it, and they slowly pulled away from their pursuers. The coastline followed in charcoal blue, except where the water turned to ghostly froth crashing against the rocks. The pop of the guns sounded smaller. And then, some distance in front of them, out of the dark and empty sea, a searchlight blinked on. And then off. On. Off.

Paz and Joe turned to see the pursuing boat turn sharply out to sea, taking the sound of their engine with them until they were gone from view.

The welcoming police boat led Joe and the others to the pier at Playa los Muertos in Old Town. The bars and restaurants were dark. Joe figured it must have been three or four in the morning. Streetlights shone down on three police cruisers, headlights on. Among them, Joe spotted Porfirio—and there was Veronica. She was safe.

As the men climbed the ladder to the dock, Veronica hurried to him, wrapping her arms around him.

"I'm OK," he said. "I'm OK."

She held him tight, pressing her face into his neck. They remained that way for a long moment, suspended together out of time, as the waves tumbled up the beach.

After a moment, Joe said, "It was Molly."

"What was Molly?"

"All of it," he said.

Molly's words rang in his head. "We're actually a lot alike." He would not believe it. His mistakes were his, yes, but they had been errors of ignorance, trust, youth. Forces that he had not intended to trigger had, once in motion, resisted all attempts at control until they finally ran him over. But what she had done, and sought to do to him, everything she had orchestrated—for money—it remained hard to fathom.

Porfirio grabbed Joe at the elbows. He looked up into his face, this son of an old friend. Joe saw real fear in the man's eyes and real relief. "Carmen, she wanted to call your mother. I said you are fine. We shouldn't worry her. You will be fine. I prayed you are fine."

"I am. I'm fine," Joe said. "You didn't have to come all the way down here. In the middle of the night."

"You are loco," Porfirio said, his face breaking into that wide smile of his.

One of the officers approached. "Señor Lily, you can go with us?"

Joe nodded. "Sí."

"We will meet you there," Porfirio said.

At the police station, they led Joe into a plain room with no windows. A garrafón of water stood on a stand in the corner. Joe helped himself to a drink and sat at the metal table that with the four chairs was the room's only furniture. He told Paz and another cop, this one in street clothes, everything that had happened, from the hand over his mouth in the bathroom at the club until Paz found him.

"OK, now say again who is the woman?" Paz checked his notes.

"I knew her as Molly Brandt. That's how she introduced herself to me. But her real name is Kathleen McNally," Joe said.

"Two names?" Paz said.

"It looks that way."

Paz had him write both names on a piece of paper.

"She works for a public relations company in the US. They represent Summit Oil and Gas. The company doing that big project down the coast."

"How do you know her?" the man in the suit asked.

"Well, I met her because of Cesar Castillo. The man who was killed a couple of weeks ago. She was his fiancée. She also worked with Darrell Haddock."

"Who is Darrell Haddock?" the man said.

This question surprised Joe. "The American. Who was recently killed."

Paz and the man glanced at each other. It was clear neither knew the name. How could an American, and one of some standing in town, be so brutally murdered and the local police couldn't place his name?

"He was killed?" Paz asked.

"You don't know about that?"

The other officer said, "About Señora Brandt, we will check her apartment and her office. Anywhere else she might go?"

One other address came to mind. A little nothing storefront on Calle Insurgentes.

Joe shared every detail he had collected. Los Fantasmas. Cesar's campaign against Los Primeros and the role of El Mago. The hacking of Ruben Bermúdez's email and the trove of communications he discovered related to the mining enterprise that had just broken ground down the coast.

By the end, after more than an hour of this, Joe was beat, bone tired. All he wanted was a shower and sleep.

But that was not to be.

As the men stood to leave, the door opened and in strode a man Joe had never seen before. He wore a white cowboy hat and a dark handlebar mustache that immediately reminded Joe of pictures of Pancho Villa or Emiliano Zapata. The man, who carried an undeniable authority, took no notice of the other two officers before removing his hat and extending his hand to Joe.

"Señor Lily," he said.

Joe offered his hand. The man's grip was strong.

Paz said, "This is Sheriff Garza."

"Mucho gusto," Joe said.

"I have heard about your adventure. Is there anything you need? Anything we can do for you?"

"Thank you, Sheriff. No, I'm good. I can't thank Officer Ibarra and his men enough. I hate to think what would've happened if they hadn't arrived. Now, all I need is a hot shower and some sleep."

"Muy bien. One question. Did you see Señor Brandt?"

"Señor Brandt? No. I haven't seen him. I actually visited his office yesterday, but he wasn't there. The place was dark."

"Any idea where he could be?" the Sheriff pressed.

Joe was confused. He'd just nearly been killed by Molly Brandt (aka Kathleen McNally) and the sheriff seemed more interested in determining the whereabouts of her father. It didn't make any sense.

"No, I'm sorry."

Just then a breathless young officer appeared in the doorway, delivering a rapid-fire Spanish that Joe couldn't catch. The officer glanced at Joe and then quickly departed.

The sheriff returned his hat to his head. "We found Señora Brandt." He turned to Paz, offered a few clipped words before turning back to Joe. "If you see or hear from Señor Brandt, you call me," he said. He tipped his hat and exited the room.

"Vamanos," Paz said. "We go see Señora Brandt."

They hustled to a pair of waiting cruisers. In moments, they were speeding through the streets of early-morning Puerto Vallarta. They tried the Banderas Property offices but found it dark. Joe next took them to A.J.'s building. No one was home. She likely knew that those would be the first places they would look for her. He realized that he didn't actually

223

know where Molly lived. She'd always come to him or they'd met at the office. But it seemed unlikely that she'd head home to hide from the police.

And then he had an idea. There was one other place she might be.

Joe directed Paz to the libramiento, the highway marking the northern edge of the city. Traffic on the road was busy and the cruisers turned on their lights to make room through the morning trucks piled high with watermelons or bags of concrete or chickens in cages. Passing through the large tunnel, Joe directed them off the highway toward the hills outside Puerto Vallarta. They crossed the Río Cuale and then through a small community of homes that stretched up the hillside. "Here in Colonia Buenos Aires?" Paz asked. "No, not here," Joe said.

Joe directed them to continue to follow the river, until the river turned and they crossed over the river a second time and started to climb. The progress was slow as they bounced along on the rough, poorly cobbled road. Paz asked again if Joe was sure. It was just an idea, Joe said. They passed homes butted right up against the roadside. Here and there people sat outside and blankly watched them go. After some distance they turned again, leaving the rough-hewn cobbles for dirt. The houses were fewer now and cruder in construction. They'd put the river behind them and entered into a field of tall grass baked yellow in the sun when Joe said "OK, turn right there." Cesar's mother's house had just come into view when a black SUV skidded past them going the opposite direction.

"That's her car!" Joe said.

There was no easy place for the cruisers to turn around and they had to continue forward into the place's dirt yard, jostling awkwardly for room. Señora Castillo stood confused in her doorway, shielding her eyes as the cars hurriedly changed direction, kicking up dirt and rocks and sending a large cloud of dust billowing into the air.

They fishtailed down the dirt track and then back on to the broken cobbled road. The black SUV managed to keep a good distance, finally reaching the highway, where it bolted into the traffic, darting and dodging through the cars and trucks. The cruisers, their lights pulsing, attempted to keep up. Joe's heart battered in his chest, and it occurred to him that in the matter of just a few hours he had gone from being the chased to the chaser.

The police cars maneuvered between vehicles and at one point even opted for the shoulder, nearly shaking the doors off as they sped over potholed asphalt and the inconvenient speed bumps built at regular intervals into the roadway. The SUV would disappear from view and then reappear. Joe thought of what she had said in the jungle—was that just this morning? "We can push everything out of our minds except the job at hand."

A truck piled high with mattresses blocked their way. The man sitting atop the load looked down on them as police car tried one way and then the other to get around, honking its horn, the lights sending red and blue against the side of the truck. Paz yelled and waved his arm, but there was no place for the truck to go.

Once around the obstruction, Joe thought he saw the SUV enter the mouth of the tunnel. But it was hard to tell. Too many SUVs were on the road, and too many black ones. As the cars and trucks tried to get out of the way of the urgent cruisers, it seemed to only make the situation worse. Finally, it became clear that they were unlikely to catch her now. Paz slammed his hands on the steering wheel. She'd simply put too much distance between them.

Joe dropped back in his seat. The adrenaline that had been coursing through him, tightening his every muscle, began to recede. First, the man who'd admitted killing Cesar Castillo, and was prepared to do the same to him, had escaped from a place only reachable by boat. And now the woman at the center of the scheme also appeared to have escaped, outrunning two police cars during the morning commute. How is that possible, he wondered.

The police cars had just pulled into the parking lot of the station and Joe had just said goodbye to Paz when Joe felt his phone buzz. It was a number he didn't recognize.

"Hello?" queried a Mexican man's voice.

"Hello? Who's this?" Joe said.

The person cleared his throat. "It's Archivaldo Ríos. Is this you, Joe?"

"Archivaldo. Sorry, I've had quite a morning. Didn't recognize your voice. How are you?"

"I am very good. Thank you."

"And the family?" Joe asked.

"Everyone is good. We owe you so much. That's why I am calling you."

"You don't owe me anything."

"Are you still in Puerto Vallarta?" Archivaldo asked.

"I am. Why?"

"Well, I learned something. You might want to know," he said. "I did some research. I was curious. And I found out that your friend, Miss Brandt? That's not her real name."

Joe smiled to himself. Archivaldo now seemed the age that his circumstances in Mexico hadn't permitted him to be.

"Yeah, Veronica actually figured that out. Smart, isn't she? Molly had been lying to us the whole time. Incredible." He thought a moment about sharing what had happened since learning that information but decided against it.

"Oh," Archivaldo said. He seemed mildly disappointed to have been beaten to the punch. "OK. So you know that she's leaving today, leaving Puerto Vallarta?"

"She's leaving? How do you know?"

"Sí, she's leaving. She's going on a boat. From the marina."

"From the marina? Do I want to know how you learned this?"

"Probably not," Archivaldo said.

"Did this info, did it say *when* she was planning to leave?"

"They didn't say a time. Just that it is today."

"Thank you for this, Archivaldo. One of these days, I'll tell you everything that's happened. And you'll realize how important this call is."

Archivaldo remained silent. Joe heard muffled voices in the background. "My mother says to say hello," Archivaldo added. "And to say hello to Ms. Espinosa."

"I will. Archivaldo, you're still a magician."

They hung up and Joe immediately called Veronica. He didn't want her to worry, so he told her he was at the police station, which he was, but only long enough to step back into the building to tell Paz what he'd just learned. Paz grabbed his hat and told Joe to go home.

226

Chapter 11

Marina Vallarta sits between the Malecón and the airport. The boats glinted in the late morning sun, their hulls white as the clouds passing unhurriedly overhead. Joe joined the small esplanade that split the rows of boats on one side and the bars and fishing outfitters on the other. Paz had told him to let them handle it. But Joe had seen how that had gone so far. Paz and his men had saved Joe's life, that was undeniable. But bringing in the perpetrators had proven another matter altogether. And where were they now, Paz and his men? Joe didn't see any sign of them.

As he walked, Joe surveyed all the boats that seemed to him sufficiently large to undertake a trip to the US. Beautifully sleek sailboats, masts tipping lazily from side to side. Big, muscular, ocean-going craft that seemed designed for escape. Molly could already be aboard and hidden from view. For all Joe knew, the boat had already exited the marina and was on its way. And this was all assuming, of course, that Archivaldo's information was accurate.

Joe needed a spot from which to survey the bulk of the marina, so he took up a position in the El Faro Lighthouse Bar. It provided a good vantage point from which to observe the boats come and go and follow the activity on the docks. Joe also wanted to keep an eye out for Paz and his men. Up in the bar, hopefully they wouldn't see him and realize he hadn't, in fact, done as instructed and gone home.

Joe ordered a beer and watched the esplanade below. The scene could've been anywhere, San Diego, Fort Lauderdale. Tanned, well-heeled gringos strolled by in linen shirts and creased shorts. He knew this breed, the wealthy American whose money had so distanced him from the common class of concerns that he fixated instead on things like the brand of his watch or the size of his hotel suite. Money, Joe had learned, had a way of distorting things, bending and stretching what one saw until you became utterly convinced that the funhouse mirror view was real. It might even lead you to believe it reasonable or even a mark of distinction to — how had Molly put it? — do whatever it takes to get what you want.

It all made Joe feel suddenly very tired. The events of the last 24 hours, which had been constantly stirred up in him like the flakes in a snow globe, had finally begun to settle, and it brought a weight and a weariness Joe could feel spreading from his feet upward. What was he doing anyway? Did he think he was going to apprehend her? And what if he did? What if all the dominoes fell in the right order and he managed to stop her, solve this crazy puzzle, and in so doing free his pile of Spanish-era antiques, was that really going to save the store? Alan, his long-suffering accountant, would've laughed had he known.

The cold beer helped. And he was about to order another when all of sudden he felt a hand on his shoulder.

"I would think you'd want something a bit stiffer at this point," the voice said.

A.J. Brandt dropped into the seat next to Joe. He looked beat. Bags under his eyes. Pallid beneath a couple days' growth of beard.

Brandt always seemed to appear when least expected. The last time was when Joe had spotted him at the groundbreaking down the coast. "Oil tycoons' brunch at the El Faro, is it?" Joe asked.

"That's right. Beer's on me," A.J. said.

"As it doesn't look like you're surprised to find me here, I'm assuming you're keeping tabs on me for some reason."

"Let's just say I've heard things."

A waiter set down a napkin and a drink in front of A.J.

"The truth is, I'm here because I need your help," A.J. said.

Joe laughed, sat back, and crossed his legs. "You need my help? You might be mistaking me for someone else."

"Maybe. But I know you know someone in customs. And I know that that someone helped another person get out of the country quietly."

Joe tipped the bottle back, taking a long drink. He tried to keep an eye on the marina. So far, there was still no sign of Molly or Paz and his men.

A.J. went on. "As you may know, things have gotten … complicated for me here."

"What about your business chums? Your Summit Oil colleagues? You're a well-connected sort. Surely the guys in the local Rotary can help you more than I can."

"Yeah, well, they can't really be seen helping someone who owes money to a Mexican cartel, even if my partner was the one who borrowed it."

Joe took another pull on his beer. "Well, what about your daughter?"

A.J. smiled and shook his head. "You're not as smart as I thought you were," he said. "I don't know what I'd do if she was actually my daughter."

228

Joe tried not to look surprised. And then the pieces fell into place and he indeed felt foolish.

"Kathleen McNally," Joe said.

Now it was A.J.'s turn to laugh. "So you did figure *that* out. I'm impressed. The whole father-daughter thing, that was her idea. She said it would be a great cover. I thought it was stupid, but I guess it worked on some people."

Joe said nothing and took a drink.

"The truth is, she's the fucking well-connected one. She even put Ruben on notice. Do you know who *he* was friends with? That's when I knew to tread lightly."

"Ruben Bermúdez?"

"He called me—I knew him from a deal years ago in Nuevo Vallarta—and he said he had this opportunity of a lifetime. An American oil company. They wanted this parcel of mine down the coast. I told him that wasn't really my thing. Oil? I develop vacation properties. Condos. Ruben told me, in that way he could, that it might *seem* like there were two choices, but there was really only one."

"Who was Ruben working for?"

"Ruben was always working for Ruben. That's what finally got him killed. But I'd rather not go into that."

Joe asked, "Was it the same thing that got Darrell killed?" He scanned the marina.

A.J. stared for a beat into his whiskey and soda. "Darrell. Poor fucking Darrell," he said. "That son of a bitch just couldn't tell the difference between land and landmine. I tried to explain it to him. I told him we've got to do this deal. We don't have a choice here. But he kept pushing and pushing. He had a different plan for that land. Thought I was just being an asshole, didn't trust him. So somewhere he gets this idea that if he buys another piece of land and starts his own company he could, I don't know, show me how he was the smart one? I don't know. The problem was, he didn't have that kind of money. It wasn't his strong suit. Never was. So he fucking borrowed it. I don't even know if he knew exactly whose money it was he was taking."

"And now, as his partner, they expect you to pay."

A.J. touched a finger to his nose. "They told me I was in on it with him. I tried to convince them I wasn't. So they kill him to send a message. Pay up or it's lights out. You heard about that when you came to my place. I didn't know what to do. These are bad guys, so to buy some time

229

I gave them a small chunk. Wired it to some HSBC account in the Caymans. Said I was working on the rest. But I'm not going to let them ruin me, everything I've built. You know, I even asked Kathleen for help. I said that it was her project that'd turned everything upside down. You know what she said? She said that her statement of work had nothing in it about paying off a cartel loan. Isn't that fucking amazing? Her statement of work!"

A.J. ran his hand over his thinning hair. He exhaled and seemed to wander into that busy intersection where *what is* meets *what could've been*. He turned his glass a few times on the table and then brought it to his lips.

Joe broke the spell. "Do you happen to know that she tried to have me killed last night?"

A.J.'s bleary eyes fixed intently on Joe. "I only just learned this morning. I swear."

"You trying to tell me that you didn't know? Bullshit."

"I swear. I know you have no reason to believe me, but it's true. Do you think she tells me anything? You've met her. She's not the sharing type. I didn't know. I heard about it this morning. Don't ask me how." He gave Joe a searching look. "I was surprised. I thought she really liked you."

For a long moment, Joe stared out the large window of the El Faro. He raised his beer and finished it in one slow draw and then set the empty bottle back on the table. "So why would I help you? After everything. You've been lying to me since the moment we met."

A.J. set his own glass down and tilted his head slightly. "Because," he said, "I know which slip Kathleen is docked in."

Joe joined the busy esplanade. As he looked for a map of the docks and slips, he remembered something his old friend Leon had said to him. "Look, Cubby, you've got instinct to spare. And that's good. Surviving in the jungle demands keen instincts. But goddamn it, you've got to know how to channel it. Otherwise, your next job will be as a lion's fucking breakfast burrito."

That had been early in Joe's evangelism about the wonders of subprime mortgages or, more to the point, his enthusiasm about how bundling groups of mortgages of different grades together effectively, or so he'd been assured, inoculated those investing in those mortgages from risk. Risk had finally been solved. Ward and Williams had cracked the code, and its lucky clients were poised to cash in. Leon had tried to get Joe to an offramp, but he hadn't listened.

And now, as Joe quickly searched for slip E-22 and a boat called Seas the Day, he wondered what Leon might say about this particular gambit: blundering into an unknown situation, unarmed, on the word of a man he didn't trust, to find and intercept a woman who had pretended to be someone else so as to more effectively plot the eventual murder of a young man she professed to love. A woman, by the way, who had sought to take out Joe as well. All that and he was going in without support or backup as there was still no sign of Paz or his men. On second thought, Joe was pretty sure what Leon would say.

Joe eventually located dock E, but it and its boats sat behind a locked metal gate. He took a moment to quickly text Veronica, telling her, in as cool and calm a way as he could, where he was and why. "I guess I just can't get enough of boats these days." He would tell her about A.J. later. He also texted Porfirio, asking him to get a message to Paz to hurry or they risked losing her again.

Now he had to find a way to get past the gate and do it fast. Unfortunately, the thick metal barrier was too tall to scale, and anyway doing so would undoubtedly draw attention that he didn't need. He looked for boaters on the other side that he could sweet talk into letting him through—my keys are in my other shorts!—but he could see no one. It looked like his only option was to get wet. He would have to quietly slip into the water and then maneuver himself around the gate that way.

He'd just picked a good spot to enter the water when he spied a small group of people turn from the esplanade onto the long dock leading to where he stood. They were carrying grocery bags. This gave him an idea. Spotting an untended cooler nearby, he picked it up and then pretended to be balancing it as he searched his pockets. They took little notice as one of the men produced a key that opened the gate. And then there it was, a woman in the group held it open for Joe. "Thanks so much," he said. "They'd kill me if I forgot the beer." She smiled. "Well, we can't have that."

He was in. Now to find E-22 and Seas the Day. The group ahead of him turned off at the first set of slips, their flip-flops slapping out a syncopated rhythm as they went. Still lugging the cooler, Joe carried on past a lineup of shiny, silent vessels. E-11, E-12. The docks stood quiet, save for one man who busied himself with a length of rope on the deck of a shiny catamaran. Joe figured most must have been ashore shopping.

E-13, E-14. A.J. had only been able to tell him where her boat was located and nothing more. By the time he located the slip, the boat might be gone, already lit out for the horizon. Or she might not be there. Then another thought hit him. It landed sharply like a slap on a sunburned back. Might the Goat be aboard? It shook him to think about it. The man brought a darkness that seemed wholly incompatible with the sunny afternoon and blue sky. Perhaps the blow Joe had dealt him with the unforgiving edge of that long wooden dining table will have kept him from seafaring anytime soon. Or maybe getting crowned by the heavy Oaxacan pottery that had fallen from the top shelf had the done trick. E-15. It was impossible to know.

E-16. A burst of echoing laughter reached him from the bars on shore. Joe was glad it remained light out. Doing this in the dark would have posed different challenges. The realization that he had not slept in more than 24 hours passed briskly through his mind. But where he'd felt like he was crashing a short bit ago, he now felt the adrenaline buzzing through him. Game time. Joe passed F-17 and a smaller fishing boat called the Reel Life. E-17, E-18. E-19 was empty.

And then he saw it. Seas the Day sat tucked into the last occupied slip on the long dock. Below the calligraphic name in red script it read "Newport Beach, CA." The boat sat solidly in the water, maybe 50 feet in length, her bridge reaching a good five feet higher than any other boat around it. Its muscled, arrowhead shape shouted speed and power. Had it been the one chasing his panga last night, it would've been all over.

As Joe considered how best to approach, the decision was made for him. A man appeared from the boat's interior. White, with graying hair and mustache, dressed in pleated shorts and a logoed navy-blue Polo shirt out of which sprouted hair that matched the color of that on his head.

"This Seas the Day?" Joe asked.

"What do you need, partner?"

"Good name. The boat. Seas the Day. I like it. But what I *need* is to drop off this food order."

"Wrong boat," the man said, absently shaking his arm to return to his wrist the gold bracelet caught in his thick forearm hair.

Joe balanced the cooler on his thigh and reached into his pocket. Retrieving and checking his phone, he said, "Slip E-22. Seas the Day." He waved the phone at the man before depositing it back in his pocket.

"What's the name?"

"Come on, man. I'm just trying to do my job. I got a bunch of deliveries today," Joe said, casually scanning the boat for other crew or passengers.

The man sought to position his too-tight shorts higher on his hips. "Goddamn it. Hold on."

The moment the man disappeared down the short flight of stairs to the boat's interior Joe quickly climbed aboard. He set the cooler down and positioned himself out of view. From below, he heard muffled voices, one of which sounded like a woman's. Could it be Molly's? He thought he could discern at least two speakers. But how many in total, it was impossible to tell. And what about the Goat, Rafa Vega?

The floorboards creaked below as the man made his way back to the stairs. As he arrived up top again, he said, "Like I said, wrong boat, partner."

Just then Joe stepped from behind the door and hooked the man around the neck in a chokehold. His surprised captive struggled, twisting and grabbing at Joe's arm, his speech reduced to a kind of rasped clucking. Joe cinched his grip tighter. "Shh," Joe hissed. "Or it's lights out. Got me?"

But the man continued to squirm, trying to reach over his head to get at Joe. So Joe cinched his grip still tighter, feeling the voice box compress. It took only a few seconds of airlessness for the man to tap Joe's arm and nod his assent.

"Here's the situation," Joe whispered to the boat captain. "That woman you're transporting? She's a murderer. They found her fiancé's head in a trunk. His ears had been cut off and stuffed in his mouth. And because I knew, she tried to have me killed too. She's traveling by boat because the police are waiting for her at the airport. She's not—"

"I'm impressed." Molly stood at the top of the stairs, a gun pointed at the two men. Joe felt the man stiffen. "I told you. Didn't I? When we get fixed on a project, we're dogged. Nothing stops us. You just keep coming. I can't believe you thought to check Cesar's mom's place. Not bad for a fuck-up import/export guy."

"So did I describe things pretty well?" Joe asked. "About your role down here? I don't know if you also had a hand in Darrell's murder or Bermúdez's. Maybe those are yours too?"

She waved the gun—no. "None of my business. Or my concern. Though Darrell *was* an annoyance. But you know, there are always costs to messing with the plan. As you're learning, change orders can be pricey."

"So now what?"

"Well, I guess that depends on you. If you let Barry there go, so we can get the hell out of here, I think it'll just be saying adios, vaya con Dios. But if not, I fear things are going to get ugly."

"But you're not a killer yourself," Joe said. "You leave that to others. Pulling the trigger is for staff, not management, right? Plus, on a boat, where holes are a problem, not the greatest idea. Just a thought."

Joe saw a look of uncertainty pass over Molly's face.

"Barry, it looks like we should've left earlier. Stupid. But we didn't. Looks like we may need to leave without the others. Because I'm guessing Joe is not the only one who is heading our way."

The man no longer fought Joe's grip, but he remained tense, alert.

"I don't want to, you know, be pessimistic, but even if you get out of here, don't you think you're going to be chased all the way up the coast? I'd expect there'll be police boats waiting for you all along the way. Certainly not part of your project brief."

"Maybe, maybe," she said. "But this is the fun part, isn't it? When things don't exactly go how you expect? You adapt. You get creative. So here's what we're going to do. You're going to let Barry go. That's first. And we're just going to go on an outing together. I hope you have your passport."

"Which one are *you* using, Molly or Kathleen?"

Her expression changed but only slightly and only for a moment. "Is that what all this is about? Were your little feelings hurt because you were fibbed to?"

"A little, I won't lie," Joe said.

She laughed. "What do you mean you won't lie. Come on, we all know about you, Joe Lily. Lying seems like it comes pretty naturally to you. Bankrupt your wife's family? That's low. Even for a Wall Street creep."

Joe wanted to keep her talking for as long as he could. "I got in over my head. That's true. Maybe that's what we actually have in common. Thinking we're smarter than we are. Thinking that we can fix anything. I never intended for things to turn out the way they did. I don't know how much you know about these fancy new financial instruments, but they're damn confusing. The people selling them don't even understand them. I certainly didn't. I made the mistake of believing what I was told, and when I eventually realized it was all a sham, I tried to turn the tide. You know how that went."

"Sure, sure," she said. "I understand. That's the kind of thing we say when we get caught. I'm sure it's why I had to be the one to tell your Mexican girlfriend about your heady days as a Wall Street tycoon. I was pretty sure you hadn't told her yourself."

On the man's back, hidden from Molly, Joe tapped out a message. He figured any skipper worth his salt would have Morse code at his command: -- --- .-. ... . (Morse). Joe had learned it as a Boy Scout, but he couldn't remember the designation for a question mark. It didn't matter; the man answered on Joe's arm: -.--- (Y).

"Ah, so that was you? I should've guessed. Jealousy makes us do some crazy things. I know I hurt your feelings when I rejected your attempt there in Talpa. I would say I'm sorry, but I'm not." This struck a nerve, Joe could see. His mind unspooled a film of that visit to Talpa. The crude need she gave off. It was the only time she'd seemed truly open, vulnerable. And all of it somehow suffused in a palpable sadness and loneliness.

"Jealous?" She laughed. "You've got to be fucking kidding me. You think I really wanted to fuck you? Some washed-up Wall Street asshole? You're dreaming. I needed to know what you knew. That's it. Whatever it takes, right? It's all about the project. It's the only reason I went up there with you in the first place."

"If you want my perspective—"

"I couldn't give two shits for your perspective."

"You're smart, there's no disputing that. I'm sure the good people at, what is it, MTRPA? Sort of a mouthful, that one. I'm sure they value your intelligence. But you're too tightly wound, you know? Too … severe. I guess some guys like that, but it's just not my taste. No offense.

I prefer a woman who is more confident in her own skin. Natural. You know what I mean?"

She started to say something but then stopped and forced a cold smile. "Yeah, well, I'm beginning to think I might just *naturally* shoot you both, right here. Dump you overboard and be on my way. Is that your taste?"

"Good plan," Joe said. "Because I'm sure you're also an expert at navigating in open ocean and eluding federal agents from two countries. Who knows, maybe this was all part of the crisis communications plan you sold Summit: Engage a known cartel attorney, find out who's bad-mouthing the client online, pretend to fall in love with that person, and then have him killed. Then escape by yourself, captaining a boat a thousand nautical miles up the coast. Reads more mob than PR to me, but then I'm just a washed-up Wall Street asshole."

Joe kept an eye over Molly's shoulder looking for any sign of Paz and his men. But the docks remained empty. Joe tapped the man again: ..... .-.. .--. (help). The man's response: -.--- (Y).

Molly moved a strand of stray hair behind one ear. You could see her strategy revising itself again. "It's just business. You can't steal a company's information and expect to get away with it. My client was just operating its business—legally, by the way. Why should some know-nothing troll in an internet café get to decide which projects move forward and which don't? Because he doesn't like oil? Who cares if he doesn't like oil? Who the fuck is he?"

"Well, I hope you were paid well," Joe said.

"Joe, you should know. When unsolvable problems get solved, clients are happy to pay." She waved the gun for emphasis, causing the man to tense.

"Molly—Kathleen—just put the gun down. Come on. No one needs to get hurt. The police are already on their way. It's over."

"How'd you find me anyway?"

"You don't want to know."

"No, I do."

"Well, here's the thing about living the way you do. You make enemies. Enemies want to see you crash and burn. Like your *father*."

She smiled. "Surprise," she said. "He was the weak link from the start. Made everything so much harder. The only reason he was even involved was for his goddamn land. But he kept wanting to be part of things. 'I know Mexico!' Nothing fucks things up like a rookie."

"But you won, sort of. The obstacle was removed. The hacking stopped. And the Summit project went forward despite it all. Even though you'll be going to jail."

"Exactly. Except the last part. People like you and me, we don't go to jail."

"Quit saying 'people like you and me,'" Joe said. He tapped out a final message on the man's arm: -.-- . .-.. .-.. -.-. --- .--. ... (yell cops).

Molly put on a simpering look. "You don't like me saying—"

"Police!" the man shouted.

Molly quickly turned toward the dock and in that instant Joe was on her, knocking the gun from her hand and sending her to the ground. But she proved nimbler and stronger than he expected. Quickly getting back on her feet, she came at him swinging her arms, kicking, throwing everything she could at him as she dashed for the weapon. Joe intercepted her, crashing the two of them to the deck. Her long limbs made her hard to subdue as she scraped and scratched and twisted, their two bodies banging violently against each other. She got loose and made another go for the gun but now the captain kicked it away. Joe tackled her from behind. She dragged her nails across his back. The two tussled and tumbled over a chair, breaking a small table. Scrambling to their feet, she sought to take Joe down with a well-placed kick, but Joe managed to catch her foot and then, using it like a lever, lifted and launched her hard into the gunwale and then, unexpectedly, over the side into the bay.

Molly landed with a splash and immediately began to thrash about in the water, her eyes gone wide, mouth agape.

"I can't—" Her face dipped below the surface and then popped back up, coughing. "I can't swim!"

Joe grabbed a nearby life ring hanging on the wall and tossed it to her. "This won't help with the sharks though."

Just then sirens pierced the marina followed moments later by the hammering footfalls of Puerto Vallarta police officers as they raced up the dock, through the gate, and to slip 22.

One of the officers immediately recognized Joe.

"Todo bien," Joe said. Everything's good. He gestured toward the water.

Two of the officers quickly climbed aboard the Seas the Day and proceeded to pull Molly into the boat and cuff her.

Paz was nowhere to be seen. "¿A dónde es Paz Ibarra?" Joe couldn't understand why Paz wasn't with them.

"Trabajando," the officer said.

"Working?" Joe repeated.

Molly's wet hair clung to her head. She rattled off a litany of complaints and threats between coughs, baring her teeth and giving off a crackling feral energy.

"You have no idea who you're dealing with here! But you will. Trust me, you will. In about an hour I'm going to be released, I'm going to fly home—first class of course—and then I'm going to bring down such a fucking shitstorm on all of you. Payback is a fucking bitch. And you, Joe Lily, we're going to sue you into the ground. You'll wish you'd just slunk out of here like the loser you are!"

Joe nodded. "Yeah, well, you can't win them all, can you?"

More police arrived. They swarmed the dock and the marina parking lot. But where were they an hour ago? Joe wanted to know. And where was Paz? An officer put Molly in the back seat of one of the cruisers. He could see that she was still talking, leaning forward, gesturing with her head. But he could no longer hear what she said.

Joe filled in the one officer on what had transpired. "Have Paz call me if he wants to go over it." As another officer took information from the boat's captain, Joe reached in and extended his hand to the man.

"Thank you," Joe said.

"No," he said. "Thank you, partner. The Morse was some quick thinking. I owe you big time. What's your name?" His face was flushed. Sweat glistened on his forehead and hung in beads under his eyes.

Joe took a business card from his wallet. "Joe Lily. Come by if you're ever in Portland. It's 20% off for anyone I nearly got shot with."

Joe slipped out of the marina in the commotion. A part of him feared that Molly might be right. That the people she knew and the people they knew would intervene. But he couldn't think about that right now. She was in custody. It was over. Rather than get a taxi, he decided to walk for a while even though he could feel the adrenaline rush begin to give way to bone-weary fatigue. But there were a couple of things he still needed to do.

238

Two police cars, lights flashing, sped by him toward what looked like the marina. Joe walked for a while. Past the new mall, past the public running track and the Sheraton complex. He finally hopped one of the blue buses for Zona Romantica. It felt good to do nothing, to simply stare out the window and watch everything pass by. He texted Veronica. "It's all over. Molly arrested at the marina. I'm fine. I'll explain everything when I see you. Have a couple of things to do first." He would call Paz too, but not right now.

Once in Old Town, Joe got off on Calle Insurgentes. Without quite planning to, he found himself a few feet from Cesar's shop. At some point, the door had been painted or replaced, Joe couldn't tell. The windows were covered in butcher paper with the message "Sunglass City Coming Soon!" written in Sharpie across it.

Life cares so little for death, Joe thought. You are murdered, and in the span of a couple of weeks your existence is replaced by a peddler of sunglasses. And poor Señora Castillo. Her son was still gone. He would never be coming back. Joe couldn't imagine, didn't want to imagine, what it would feel like to lose your child. The thought brought Elinor, his daughter, so far away, a little closer for a moment and he let it seep into him.

When Joe reached Panadería Esperanza, he was glad to find it open. The window had been repaired and the debris cleaned up. Joe could see Miguel inside. He jangled the bell as he entered. Miguel saw him but went back to sweeping. "We're closed," he said.

"My Spanish is not great, but I happen to know 'Abierto' means open."

"Why can't you leave me alone? You show up and things go bad for me."

Joe said nothing and smiled.

"What do you want?" Miguel asked.

"I want you to be happy, Miguel. The new window looks great."

"Man, seriously, I told you, I'm done. I got my family." He gestured emphatically with his broom handle at the bakery.

"I'm here because I have news. Good news. I wanted to tell you that you were right about Molly Brandt."

Miguel stopped and fixed Joe with a serious look.

Joe leaned back against the counter and crossed his arms. "Turns out her real name is Kathleen McNally. She works for a US company that, surprise, surprise, represents Summit Oil. She came down here to … clear the way for their project down the coast."

Miguel's face dropped. The very air in the room seemed to stop. "Cesar."

Joe exhaled slowly. "Yeah. Looks that way."

"She did it." He swallowed hard. "Dios mío."

Joe let the information slowly fall and settle. "I'm sorry, Miguel."

"How did you figure it out?"

"It was all on Cesar's laptop. Sadly, he never spotted the connection to Molly. As for her, the police just arrested her. In the marina. She was trying to escape Vallarta by boat. I just wanted to come by, let you know. And to thank you for your help."

Miguel stared at the floor for a long moment. When he finally lifted his head, his eyes were wet. He nodded at Joe but said no more. He didn't need to.

Joe jangled the bell again on the way out. When he looked back, Miguel had changed the sign to "Cerrado."

Barely a block away Joe's phone pinged. Pulling it from his pocket he was stunned to see not Veronica's or even Porfirio's name on the screen but one he'd not seen there in nearly a year: Allie. Allison Lily nee Lansdowne, his ex-wife. His first thought was of his daughter.

"Hello, Allie?" he said.

There was a long pause on the other end, so long that Joe wondered if they'd been disconnected.

"Hi, Joseph," Allison said.

A voice he knew so well.

"Allie," he said. "Is everything OK? Is Elinor OK?"

"She's fine. Elinor is good."

Joe waited. At first, she said no more, as if they no longer spoke the same language and she was trying to put the words together to be understood. "Mom told me not to call."

"Funny, because she's been calling me things for months now."

"Not funny," she said.

"OK, sorry. I'm just glad Elinor is fine. You had my heart racing," he said. "What is it, Allie? You haven't answered my texts or calls in months. Why now?"

Another long pause followed. "I just wanted you to know that I wasn't, that I'm not in support of the suit my father is bringing against you. I tried to talk him out of it. I wanted you to know that."

Now it was Joe's turn to take a moment. He didn't want to tell her that the suit had been the least of his concerns of late.

"Thank you," Joe said. "I appreciate that."

Allison cleared her throat. There was more. Joe waited. "And you should see Elinor. She misses you."

A collapsing feeling rushed into Joe, like some bulwark inside of him, something that he had pushed against and pushed against, had now suddenly given way.

"I would love that," he said.

Allison remained silent for a long moment. Then she said, "Pick a day and let me know. I've got to go." A second later there was a click and the line went quiet.

Joe looked at the name until the phone's screen went dark. The sounds of the street returned. The buses. The banda music from passing cars. And then there were those three words: "She misses you." She misses you. They echoed off the walls of his mind.

On the beach, a volleyball game was under way and Joe stopped to watch. He'd been a decent player himself at one time. Tall and strong, coordinated and quick, he was built for the game. On a different trip, at a different time, he might have joined in.

Instead, Joe kept walking, past the sunbathers, beyond the umbrellas and loungers, past the famous blue chairs, and carried on down to just before the rocky outcropping that marked the southernmost end of the Playa los Muertos. There he found a quiet spot in a block of shade and dialed his mom.

"Well, this is a surprise," his mother said.

"How's everything up there? How are things at the shop?"

"Oh, good. You got my heart going. Everything here is fine, good. I played cards with Pam last night, but I think I ate too much Chex mix."

Joe chuckled as he figured that was her way of saying she'd had too much wine. "Did you win at least?"

"I did!" she said. "I'm up $7."

"Excellent. Take no prisoners."

"She gets so mad when she loses. It's fun." His mom laughed lightly. "Now, you're weren't calling to just say hello. There's something."

"There is," Joe said. "I think I'm finally just about wrapped up down here. Hopefully, now we'll be able to get our stuff out of customs and head back to Portland."

"Oh, that's wonderful! Did you hear that, Maxi, Joe is coming home! Maxi's very excited."

"I'm sure. Maybe now he'll stop texting me all the time now."

His mother chuckled. "Maxi, you can't interrupt Joseph when he's working."

"It's been a long one down here. Once I hang up with you, I'll confirm with customs and then, fingers crossed, get my ticket for home tomorrow."

"I'm so pleased," his mother said. "It does seem like you've been gone a long time. And I know Alan will be eager to see you too. He's been checking in a lot. Though he's been in a foul mood lately."

"Yeah, well, that's sort of the other reason I'm calling. Allison just called me."

"Allison? Is everything OK? Is Elinor OK?"

"Everything's fine. Elinor is fine. In fact, Allison said she wants me to come out and see Elinor. Isn't that great?"

"Oh!"

There followed a loud clattering crash followed by muffled noises Joe couldn't identify.

"Mom?"

"Sorry, honey, I was so shocked—so happy!—I dropped the phone! That is the best news I could ever hear. I'm so glad she, so glad Allison decided that no matter what has happened that Elinor shouldn't have to pay the price. But why now?"

"That's the other piece, and probably why Alan is not so happy these days. Mr. Lansdowne is suing me."

"What? Suing you? Why?" Joe forgot his mom's voice had this higher register to it. "Why didn't you tell me?"

"I'm telling you. I don't really know the details. Alan informed me. I'll figure it out when I get home. But Allison also said she tried to talk her dad out of it. That's something."

"Honey, that's more than something. You see, it just takes time. Things will work out. They will."

Joe loved his mother's endurance. She could withstand the forces of nature like no one he knew. Patience and a kind of understated grit. He hoped he was developing the same.

"I believe you. OK, I should go. Just wanted to give you an update. Give Max a squeeze. I'll email you the flight details when I have them. Can't wait to see you."

"Us too. Travel safe."

Joe hopped a taxi to Veronica's. Before he could talk himself out of it, he bought himself a ticket for the following day's afternoon flight from Puerto Vallarta to L.A. to Portland. He knew he was supposed to feel excited about it—it had been a few weeks now and more than once he'd wished he were home. And part of him *was* excited. He was eager to see his mom, his dog, even his accountant, Alan. Another part of him, a deeper part, a part that he'd only begun to reach told him that this experience had changed him and that leaving too soon could undermine what he'd gained, what he'd learned. But he knew that going was the only way to find out.

Veronica opened the door just as the taxi pulled up.

"I've been trying to call you," she said, wearing a worried expression.

"I know. I'm sorry. You'll understand when I explain."

She ushered him inside.

"But everything is OK?" she asked.

"Everything's great."

Veronica got them drinks and hurried him to the patio. "OK, tell me!"

Over cold beers, Joe walked her through everything, the entire sordid mess. How the work of one young Mexican man in a forgotten little internet café had set in motion a chain of events that he could not have imagined. And how the woman who had claimed to love him, who had played his wife-to-be for months, was now in police custody for his murder. When Joe was done, they sat in silence as if waiting for all the words, all the facts, to lock into place. And then Veronica raised her bottle.

"You did it, Joe. You told me that first day that you would resolve this, and you did."

"No, it's you, Veronica Espinosa," he said. "Never has a misplaced purse been quite so full of treasures."

She smiled her brilliant smile, ruby lips framing white teeth.

"Seriously. I could not have done this without you."

They clinked bottles.

A lovely breeze came in off Banderas Bay, stirring the tablecloth and the leaves of the potted plants. The bell of the cathedral rang out from the plaza.

"Speaking of treasures, I'm confident that we'll be able to free your items from their prison now. Oscar—Señor Quiñones—told me they don't want them—there are too many things!—and they just needed a reason to release them."

"You didn't tell me that."

She smiled again and shrugged.

After the update, all that remained was the two of them and the inescapable truth that his time here was fast rushing toward its end, that very soon Joe would leave for home, back to his world and his work and everything he'd left behind unfinished. He'd not been looking forward to this conversation.

"Veronica, tomorrow I—"

"I know," she interrupted, her voice soft, resigned. "I know. Can we not talk about it right now? Let's just … enjoy tonight."

So they spoke no more about plans or departures or antique Mexican trunks. Instead, they sat together under a blanket on the patio, measuring time by the imperceptibly slow movement of the moon and stars, listening to far-off voices drifting up to them from the Malecón.

And it was absolutely true that he couldn't have done it without her. It was true as well that she had also helped repair some scorched chamber of his heart in the process. He exhaled and let himself tumble into the soft, bright beauty of her.

In the morning, Joe awoke to an empty bed. Wandering into the kitchen, he found Veronica just returning through the front door.

"Coffee," she said, holding up a tray with two cups, "and donuts!" shaking a bag in the other hand.

"Beautiful," he said. "But shouldn't you be at work?"

"I'm sick. Can't you tell?"

"Yes, yes, you do look hot," he said.

She gave him a playful smirk. "I just wanted to be here today."

"I'm glad. And with donuts."

"You've earned your donuts," she joked, but Joe's face was serious. They looked at each other for a long moment without a word, acknowledging what they had not quite acknowledged the night before.

She put the coffee and bag down on the counter and came to him, took his hands in hers. "My father is fond of this Spanish proverb. It translates to something like 'Fortune is like a wall that falls on those who lean on it.' We should rejoice at what we have and what we are given. I'm happy we found ourselves at the same restaurant that day. It's been … fun."

They both laughed.

"But I expect you to call me," she said. "Tell me how things are going, how the business is doing. How your Mexican antiques are selling! How Elinor is doing. ¿Si?"

"Sí."

She put her arms around him.

They spent the morning at the kitchen bar like they had that first morning. Drank their coffees, ate their donuts, Veronica pulling one piece free at a time. The time departed moment by moment with each arrival and departure of the tide on Banderas Bay. They avoided promises or predictions. And then it was Veronica who, checking her phone, said, "You should get going. One flight a day. You miss it and you'll be *stuck* here."

Joe could only muster a partial smile. "Yeah," he said. She walked him to the door.

"I wish you'd let me take you."

"They'll see you and want to celebrate your amazing recovery from your horrible illness."

"You are a funny one," she said.

Joe hoisted his backpack onto his shoulders and put his arms around her.

"Do one more thing for me, OK?" she asked. "Remember, no matter what anyone says, you are not your past."

Joe leaned in, kissed her a final time, and then stepped once more into the glorious Mexican sunshine.

The taxi driver sang along softly to the radio. Joe stared out the window, recalling the incredible string of events that this coastline had been witness to over the last couple of weeks. Despite it all, he could see why his father had so loved Puerto Vallarta. The city reclaimed you anew each day. It was always welcoming you, around every corner, down every

245

cobbled backstreet. He knew he would be back. And who knew what might happen?

Before he left, there were two things Joe needed to do. His first stop was the liquor store on Basilio Badillo. He bought the best bottle of tequila on offer. Next, he visited the bank and took out cash. He split the bills, putting equal halves in two envelopes, along with the note Veronica had helped him write.

When the envelopes were sealed, he had the taxi take him up Calle Carranza. At the counter, Porfirio was speaking to the same young woman who had made the grisly discovery that had set all of the events into motion.

"Buenos días," Joe said.

"Joe!" Porfirio exclaimed. "¡Buenos días! How are you? I heard about the marina! I tried calling you."

"Everything is good," Joe said. "Yeah. I don't know what's going to happen, but I really hope Señora Castillo gets some justice after all of this. She deserves it. Now it's up to Paz. I also wanted to tell you, in person, the good news that it looks like all the Bermúdez antiques are finally free to go back to the states with me."

"¡Sí!" Porfirio said. "I am very happy for that. So you come to buy more things?" The little man thought this quite funny.

"Only if you have a different Mexican trunk laying around."

Porfirio laughed. "I'll make you a good deal."

"I thought it was strange I didn't see Paz at the marina yesterday when they grabbed Molly Brandt." The truth was, Joe had begun to harbor suspicions about potential divided loyalties with his friend's brother-in-law. It was an occupational hazard in Mexico. Everywhere really. The man *had* saved Joe's life in the jungle. There was no disputing that and he would be forever indebted to him. He just feared that Molly's assertion that she would walk free would prove true, and it troubled him further to think about the possibility that Paz could have some hand in it. But there was no good way to talk to Porfirio about that.

"Yes! I talked to him. He is in the hospital."

"Hospital? What? What happened?"

Porfirio pointed at his thigh. "He got shot. In his leg."

Joe stood dumbstruck. When had Paz been shot? It hadn't happened when Joe was with him.

"When?" Joe asked.

"When they go to get La Cabra."

Joe found himself surprised a second time. He'd heard nothing about Rafa Vega's fate after their escape the night before.

"What happened? I haven't heard anything!"

"Sí. They found him. Hiding in a house in Bucerias. He needed a doctor. He was bleeding inside. Not good. But there was much shooting. Paz he got one in his leg."

"And he's fine?"

"Sí. He's fine."

"What about La Cabra?"

"La Cabra is dead."

Joe wanted to shake Porfirio and ask why he hadn't called him the moment he'd learned.

"He's *dead*?"

"Sí. He shoot himself." Porfirio fired a fake gun under his chin.

A cold shiver passed through Joe.

"Paz said no one cries for him." Porfirio shook his head. "His mother does not cry too."

The two men remained quiet, each acknowledging the passing from the Earth of a dark shadow, a malevolence that had seemed to Joe strangely beyond death.

"Wow." It took a few beats for the news to really sink in. And then Joe put the man and all he'd done out of his mind. There was no forgetting him. He would forever occupy a dark corner of Joe's memory like a kind of malignancy. But he didn't have to think about him now. He'd had a separate reason for stopping at Porfirio's. He retrieved the bottle of tequila from his bag and set it on the counter. "I actually came to say adios—I'm flying out in a few hours. And I wanted to thank you. For everything. I couldn't have gotten through this without you."

Porfirio extended his hand and they shook. With the other, he waved off the thanks. "No, no," he said. Then he playfully glanced about and pretended to secret the bottle behind the desk.

"Share it with Carmen," Joe playfully chided.

"Better for my girlfriend," Porfirio said, his face breaking into a broad grin.

Joe smiled and shook his head.

"Oh, and I wanted to ask you one last favor." Joe pulled the envelopes from his bag. On the front of the first he'd written "José Luis Rivera, Paraiso Coffee Co., Talpa." On the second, "Alma Gutierrez, Café Casa Rosa, Talpa."

"Can you make sure that these letters get delivered? I know it's asking a lot. And I'm sorry I don't have proper addresses. But it's very important." Joe could not undo the savagery visited on those two by the Goat, the woman from the coffee shop beside the church in Talpa and the man from the coffee stand in the market. Each one had had their life irreparably changed simply because they'd crossed Joe's path. Perhaps he could make some small difference.

Porfirio, his face taking on a solemn look, received the envelopes.

"Please tell them I want to help them. They can contact me through the information in the letter. And you can also tell them about La Cabra, that they don't have to be scared anymore."

"Sí, sí. Por supuesto. I do it. No problem." He laid the envelopes on the counter and set his hands on them.

Then the two men hugged. "Come back soon," Porfirio said. "We always welcome you. And your mom. You are family, Joe. Always family."

"Muchas gracias, amigo mio. And please say goodbye to your lovely wife for me. I'll be back. Until then, take care and be well."

His tasks done, Joe had about an hour to kill before he had to be at the airport. Over the previous couple of weeks, he'd spotted a particularly enticing little beach bar tucked well off the road between a pair of hotels just before one got to the marina. With the help of the first female taxi driver he'd had, Joe located the spot, aptly named Bar Escondido, and took a table facing the water. He ordered a last Pacifico and final parting plate of tacos al pastor from the sleepy waiter.

Bob Marley played on the stereo. Not another customer was about. A dog slept under one of the empty tables in the cool sand. The surf crashed. The bright blue of the sky shone. A light shore breeze stirred one's hair and calmed one's soul. Joe dug in his backpack, located what he was searching for, and then wandered out into the sun and down to the waterline. The beach stood empty for a couple of hundred yards on either side. A shiver of comfort and calm passed through him. Putting the breeze to his back, Joe cupped his hands and lit the last of Leon's joints, admiring for a final time the glorious sweep of the beautiful horseshoe bay. In the near distance, a boat sped north, pulling a pale parasailer through the bright blue sky, his feet dangling like a baby's in a high chair. The coast seemed to grin with color—reds and oranges and yellows offered in splashes from the hotels, the umbrellas, the beachgoers.

As the water lapped at his feet, Joe let the view and the tropical air and the heady smoke push everything from his cluttered mind. Out tumbled the horrors he'd seen over the last couple of weeks, as well as the uncertainty about what waited for him at home. The breeze picked it all up like playing cards lifted from a table and sent it tumbling down the beach. It felt good. The release, the letting go. Joe had learned over the past year that there is no escaping misfortune and sadness in this life. But he was also discovering that, amidst it all, hope can always find a way in. That was something. Perhaps, in truth, that was everything.

Joe stubbed out the joint and walked back up, noting that this would likely be the last time for a while that he'd get to sink his bare feet in warm sand. It felt good. At the table, his beer awaited and he took a long drink, the contents so cold that it almost hurt to swallow. As he set the bottle down, Joe saw that another table now looked to be occupied. A single margarita and order of chips and salsa sat waiting. And then their owner returned from the bathroom, freezing Joe in his seat.

"Shit. I knew stopping for a drink was a bad idea."

Joe sat absolutely dumbstruck. Paralyzed. His mind could not square what he was seeing as the world seemed to tilt off its base. Joe didn't know what to say or how to say it as he stared, mouth agape, at the person inexplicably, unbelievably, miraculously standing before him.

Joe shook his head. "I don't … understand."

Darrell Haddock couldn't keep the smirk from creeping into the corner of his mouth. "Looking good for a dead man, huh?"

Joe had seen video of this man, this one now standing right in front of him in shorts, flip-flops, and a faded Hawaiian shirt. He'd seen him bound to a chair, tortured with a blow torch, crying for his life. He'd witnessed his tears, heard his screams and his appeals for mercy. He'd learned that his killers, agents of Los Primeros, had then boiled him in a barrel, liquefying him into an unspeakable stew. But somehow, despite all of that, here he stood, in one piece, healthy, and sipping from a margarita.

"I saw the video. The whole—I was, it was horrific." Joe just stared at this man, the lines of the past and the present refusing to meet.

"You saw the video? Damn. That thing got around. It looked OK to you? I wasn't happy with the lighting. You know, add a blowtorch and the levels kind of get fucked up."

And then the reality of it took shape for Joe, the pieces clicking together. He shook his head. "Why?"

"Why? Seriously? He tried to cut me out. The fucking asshole tried to cheat me. I'm his partner, but he starts this whole thing, creates this whole project with Ruben and the oil company all behind my back? The cocksucker. He figured he'd keep it for himself, leave old Darrell here standing with his dick in his hand while he positioned himself to make, I don't even know, millions?"

"He didn't tell you? You didn't know?"

Darrell scooped up some guacamole with a chip. "Those are two different questions," he said, depositing the chip in his mouth. "He didn't tell me. But I knew. I'm not a fucking idiot. He forgets that I worked down here long before he showed up. Let's just say I have friends."

"Someone tipped you off?"

He stuffed another chip in his mouth, shaking his head. "I'm not going to get into that. But I found out what was going on. I mean, fuck, I taught him this business! I introduced him to Ruben. Ask him, ask A.J., he'll tell you, I fucking saved his life. I'm why he has his condo on Los Muertos. It's because of me that he drives that Land Rover he loves so goddamn much, why he has his place in Sayulita and now this other place over in Merida. Me. He didn't know his ass from a fucking burrito when I met him. He had nothing. Except two ex-wives and a house in foreclosure. And this is how he repays me?" Darrell shook his head. "No. Not going to happen."

"It's quite a set-up."

Darrell shrugged, tipped his glass to his lips, wiping his mouth with his hand. "I made a video. I had a few friends visit him. That's it. I never hurt him. No one would've ever hurt him. I could've." He shrugged. "I could've." He let this hang out there for a beat. "Down here things can happen to a guy. But I just wanted to make sure that he paid me what he owed me."

Perhaps due to the cool shade or something it now sniffed in the air, the sleeping dog roused itself, shook, and ambled out of the restaurant.

"So he paid up? A.J. paid?" Joe didn't share that he'd seen and spoken to A.J. the day before and learned that he'd delivered a portion of the sum he was told he owed. He also didn't share that that was all he planned to hand over.

"Of course he did." A simpering, self-satisfied look came over Darrell's face. "He always thought he was smarter than me. My ideas were always 'it's not a good time, Darrell. That won't work, Darrell.' He was the brains of the business. If it was his plan, like to, say, move our offices from Old Town or buy that big property in Bucerias, then it must be a great idea. Right? Even though both of those moves were stupid and ended up costing us thousands and thousands of dollars. But do you know what he did when that became clear, that they were mistakes? He said it was me, that *I* was the one who wanted to do them. Can you believe that shit? After a while, he just got it in his head that every success was his and every mistake was mine. Money can do that."

"So you had one more lesson to teach him."

The straw of his drink in his mouth, Darrell, eyes wide, pointed at Joe in affirmation. "Exactly," he said. "Do you know jiu jitsu?"

"Do I what?"

"Jiu jitsu. Did you ever study it? The martial art?"

"No, I never did. Why?"

"Well I have. I guess I'm pretty much a black belt at this point. Anyway, the whole idea behind it is you use the momentum of your opponent *against* them." He stood and took up a fighting position, feet wide apart, hands in front. "They come at you, right? Doesn't matter how tough they think they are, how big. But with the right positioning, the right technique." He shifted his hip and then made a motion that looked altogether to Joe like emptying a garbage can. "You just take their attack, their movement, right? And you use it to throw them. It's pretty simple actually." He sat again, patting down the few strands of hair that the movement had disrupted on his mostly bald head. "So you know, that's what I did. I used him against himself. I used him thinking I was stupid enough to borrow money from the cartel against him. I guess we know who the smart one is now." Darrell casually raised his glass in salute. "Borrow money from the *cartel*?" He chuckled. "Sure."

There remained a part of Joe that still couldn't align this turn of events. Darrell, poor murdered Darrell. Converted into a stew. And now here he was eating guacamole and discussing jiu-jitsu. He seemed to be enjoying it all, sharing the story, gloating, strutting a bit.

"Oh, and I'm glad you nailed that bitch too. She deserved it maybe even more than he did."

251

"You knew about her?"

Darrell made an inconclusive gesture. "I never trusted her. It just seemed off. I even told him that and it made him so mad. Worked for the oil company, huh?"

Joe nodded. "Looks that way." He thought about sharing all the details, the escape from Yelapa, her capture yesterday in the marina, but it all seemed too much to go into. He did mention one additional fact.

"And you knew she wasn't A.J.'s daughter."

"Not at first, but later, yeah. That's some crazy shit right there, isn't it? I mean, I know I did it too, but, man, so many lies. Sometimes I think they're what the world runs on, you know? Well, she better hope she gets jail up there rather than down here. Prison's no joke in Mexico."

The comment hung in the air asking for follow-up. But Joe's beer had lost its crisp coldness and it was time to go. He emptied the bottle in one final draw. "So what now? What are you doing here? Isn't it dangerous to be in town now?"

"I just stopped in to have a last drink on the beach before heading to the airport," Darrell said.

The man smiled and one could see in the expression what he must have looked like as a boy. "I met a woman. Online. Hiroko. She's Japanese. So I'm going to Japan. Crazy, right? Never been. We'll see. Can't stand the food, but she's incredible."

Joe stood, put a few bills down for his beer, and grabbed his bag. "Speaking of planes, I've got one to catch myself. When they ask me if I have anything to declare, I can declare I've seen a dead man drinking a margarita."

Darrell laughed. "I like it. You do that."

"Good luck, Darrell."

"Alright, man. See you in the funny papers."

Joe left the shade of the bar's palapa and rejoined the bright, hot Mexican afternoon. He hailed a taxi for the short ride to Puerto Vallarta International Airport. Warm air blew in through the open window. It was time to go home.

ACKNOWLEDGEMENTS

Writing may be a solitary exercise, but its publication is not. Sincere and abiding thanks go out to a team of contributors. Thank you to Joe Vine for printing and distributing readers' copies from his business, the Copy Center, in Red Bluff, California. Ethan Coyle, Leyna Coyle, Stacy Griffin, Sharon Huber, Lily Jones, Chet Malinow, Jody Reeves, Kevin Richardson, Gabe Rosenberg, and Ingrid Rosenberg all deserve my deep gratitude for reading and offering guidance on an early draft of the book. Sincere appreciation must be extended to Savannah Villaseñor, who played the critical role of helping sharpen and validate the use of Spanish in the book. With readers asked to choose from among so many titles today, big thanks to Heather Vine for the development and design of the book's striking cover art. See more of Heather's work, including her designs for musical icon Santana, at heathervine.com.

Finally, special thanks are reserved for Shawn Jones, my wife and creative partner, for her dogged editorship over numerous drafts as well as her loving encouragement from the first capital to the final period. Honey, I couldn't have done it without you.

PLEASE LEAVE A REVIEW

If you enjoyed *Muerto Vallarta*, please write a review on Amazon. Every review is read, and each one helps new readers discover this book and others by Greg Coyle. Thank you!

ABOUT THE AUTHOR

Greg Coyle was born in Cairo, Egypt, and has been lured by new and distant places ever since. He began his writing career as a journalist and newspaper editor in the Seattle area. For the last 25 years, Greg has worked as an advertising copywriter in Portland, Oregon.

ALSO BY GREG COYLE

Alas, Poor Country

Five strangers find themselves desperately scrambling for the same dangerous payoff in the red-rock canyons of the American Southwest. Like the gold seekers before them, these hopefuls join the thousands pouring into the Four Corners during the Uranium Boom of the 1950s and 1960s in search of another lucrative quarry—uranium. Along the way, one rogue miner turns up dead, and as each of the five seeks cover, their lives are irrevocably changed by the land, by uranium, and by their heedless pursuit of fortune.

Made in the USA
Columbia, SC
26 September 2023

23232859R00141